The Ghost Toucher

By
Gerald Rice

Copyright © 2010 by Gerald Rice
Copyright © 2010 by Severed Press
www.severedpress.com
Cover art Copyright © 2010 by David Lange
http://davelange.carbonmade.com/
All rights reserved. No part of this book may be reproduced or transmitted in any form or by any electronic or mechanical means, including photocopying, recording or by any information and retrieval system, without the written permission of the publisher and author, except where permitted by law.
This novel is a work of fiction. Names, characters, places and incidents are the product of the author's imagination, or are used fictitiously. Any resemblance to actual events, locales or persons, living or dead, is purely coincidental.

ISBN: 978-0-9807996-2-0
All rights reserved.

Forward

Who am I? Why am I here?
Relax; I am not the existential type. I have been known to question everything from "Why is the sky blue?" to, "Is it contagious, Doc?" It's about being well informed and ensuring the well-being of others.
Having written only one novel and an episodic web comedy series I was a bit shocked when asked to pen the foreword to a novel written by a friend of mine. It is no easy task, of that I am certain.
How does one put aside his natural penchant for sarcasm so that he may lay praise to the author whose book you now hold in your hands? How do I stop talking about myself long enough to put into words how incredibly entertaining his novel is?
How does one humble himself enough to point out that the very journey on which you are about to embark is both terrifying, humorous and unlike anything you have read before and much more entertaining than anything I have ever come up with?
The fact is the journey is just as much for the author as it is for you. As you enter a strange world full of the unknown, so begins an author's journey into a world just as mystifying.
When a person decides to take up the mantle of 'writer' they take up all the hardships that come with it. Coming up with the story, putting it to paper, submitting queries, getting rejected, starting all over.
That is just the beginning. Countless rewrites abound, watching your work become unrecognizable in the hands of an editor, yelling

about how your artistic vision has been compromised and swearing that you are going to become the next Hemingway, forgetting that his life ended with a self-inflicted shotgun wound to the head.

But, to quote Abraham Lincoln: "With great power comes great responsibility!" I am pretty sure it was Lincoln that said that. Alas, I am too lazy to Google it. It is the responsibility of a writer to entertain you and take you to places and worlds that you might not otherwise visit and maybe you just might take something from your voyage. Just make sure it is something you really want like money or food; you don't want to be stuck with a demon or a ghost. Or gruel—whatever the hell that is.

Two people were born on the day this novel went to press: a novelist and a fan. I am sure that most anyone reading this story will fall into the latter category and like a Wal-Mart greeter, I welcome your company.

It's who I am and why I'm here.

Anthony Harrington
Author of "Frayed" and "Genrefinity: The Series"
www.genrefinity.net

To my old creative writing teacher at Cranbrook and my wife.
The one who started the fire and the one who stokes the flame.

What's a stout roost?

"It is a shame that the dead could be treated so disrespectfully like that. You people should be shamed that you could put a show on like that. I've never seen something so shameful in all my life."

These kinds of phone calls were typical. Old men and old women who complained because they needed to talk to someone to somehow still be viable to society. Kelly Greene took these calls everyday and logged them in the AS400 system along with the caller's demographic information. No promises were made that the show would reflect their complaints, no policies were changed and no callers received a call back. He was simply a professional apologist.

"I understand you have a complaint with our programming, Ms. Moore," he said. "The Network strives to provide quality programming for all our viewers and we're sorry to hear we're not meeting your needs. Ms. Moore, may I ask what your date of birth is?"

"Birthdate? Why do you need my birthdate?"

"To be able to better track our viewing audience."

"I don't need you tracking me. Just get that terrible show off the air!"

She hung up. The complaints rolled off him. He'd been taking them long enough to recognize the same voices. Bertha Hodges today would be Edna Hopkins tomorrow. Edward Coolidge had the same slurry cadence as Donald Bloom. Emma Titwidge's lisp was just like Carey Coor's lisp. George Bauman liked to yell and not let Kelly get a word in edgewise just like Bill Love. Every single one of them was a closeted fan. Couldn't keep their eyes off the show and couldn't admit to themselves they liked it so they called and made complaints as a means of penance.

Kelly let the next call ring until it went to his voicemail. He sat back in his chair with his fingers laced behind his head. His eyes wandered of their own accord to the bottom drawer beneath the desk of his tiny cubicle. He wasn't brave enough to look in there. No. That drawer only came open once or twice a year and he didn't have the heart. Kelly was glad to have gotten them out of the house; he had no idea what he would have done if he'd had to look at them every single day.

His phone rang again. He glanced at the caller ID and saw it was an internal number. Kelly picked up.

"Hello?"

"Kelly Greene?"

"Yes."

"Artie Brimmer needs to see you upstairs." Kelly only knew the name. Brimmer worked in marketing or something like that. "It's the thirty-third floor. Do you know how to get to his office?"

"I'll find it. Be right up."

"You'll need to type in pass code forty ninety-eight when you get off the elevator."

"Okay. Thanks."

Kelly logged out of his phone and made his way through the maze of gray cubicles to the elevator. There were a bunch of new faces around here lately. It was fall again. Must be intern season. He thumbed the 'Up' button and the doors popped open.

The thirty-third floor was completely different than his. Everything above thirty was executive level. He stepped off the elevator into an ovular-shaped waiting area. There was a glass wall with a fish tank built into it separating him from the floor proper. Kelly slid his fingers across a small black leather couch in the middle of the room as he walked to the big oak door in the middle of the wall. There was a security access panel with a phone next to it.

Kelly fingered the pass code and the access panel beeped, the little light at the side changing to Greene from red. He pulled the handle and stepped inside a hallway that ran the length of the waiting area. He turned to the right and walked into a wide open area filled with much larger cubicles. There was a man in one of them, in a suit, reclining in a chair much nicer than Kelly's, wearing a headset that was much fancier as well. He passed through this area and another that was just like it before wandering through a kitchenette area and realizing he was lost.

"Excuse me," he said to a brunette pouring creamer into a cup of coffee. She looked up. "I'm trying to find Artie Brimmer's office? Could you point me in the right direction?"

She dropped a stir-stick into her coffee and said, "I'd love to, but I don't speak any English," and walked out of the kitchenette. He wandered out after her and became lost again. He wound up at another set of elevators, but was unsure if this was the same place he'd come from.

Kelly turned to his left and spotted an office down from a long row of cubicles. He walked over to it and found a column of closed offices. He followed them until he came to an open one with 'Arthur Brimmer' on the nametag on the door.

"Can I help you?" a middle aged woman with her back to him said.

"Uh, I'm here to see Artie Brimmer?"

"Kelly Greene?" she said without turning around.

"Yes."

"Oh. You don't look like you sound. Go on in. They're waiting."

Kelly stepped inside the office. The first thing he noticed were the open windows with a view of a wooded area with some moderately-sized houses mixed in. Brimmer's office was bare save for a dozen or so pictures on his desk and the wooden shelf built into the wall behind him.

Artie Brimmer was a balding, late thirties man with a gut, love handles and a hearing-aide in one ear. They shook hands and Kelly had to suppress the urge to wipe his palm on his pants leg. A tall, pale man sat in one of the two chairs in front of his desk by the window. He hard dark blond hair and the kind of face that could be mistaken for anything between thirty and sixty. Brimmer didn't introduce him.

"Please have a seat so we can begin."

Kelly sat down in the open chair, wondering exactly what they were supposed to be starting. Brimmer took a remote out of his desk and turned around, aiming it at the television in the corner. The television came on and he fingered another button that tinted the windows.

Stout put the camera up to eye level. He pushed the front door open and stepped in. It was cold. Much colder than outside. He pulled the flashlight out of his coat pocket, wishing his helmet cam hadn't been broken the last time out.

It had taken a while to find the pendant, but he'd found it down at an auction in Orlando. He wore it on a necklace and if everything ran smoothly tonight it would serve him well. Old Man Turner had been an nth degree bastard in life and had kept on in death. He'd driven four wives to their graves, each one inheriting a diamond pendant from the wife before. Turner had given it to his fifth, a pretty young thing from Boise, and right after giving birth to their daughter she ran away to Florida. Regardless of all his money and influence, by the time he'd found her he was on his deathbed. When he kicked they said he'd been clutching a picture of her in his craggy old hands.

Over the last eight decades the house had changed owners at least two dozen times until white flight and urban decay had left it empty and beat up. There were a couple of local legends about kids going in to vandalize the house who had been somehow 'violated', but Stout figured those tales were either fake or some dumb kid had been lured there by somebody with a head full of bad ideas and a lot of lube. Still, there were plenty of documented cases reporting a variety of disturbances ranging from someone in the house throwing furniture around to screaming and even an old man sitting on the front steps just staring at passers-by.

He might have dismissed the old man on the porch bit if it hadn't been for how they described his appearance. 'Gussied up' was the phrase a lot of them used, weird when you thought about how people normally spoke. But he'd found in many cases that places with true hauntings tended to influence people's speech or behavior in the neighboring area in some way.

A set of rickety stairs were directly ahead. Stout went over to the railing and stomped on the first one. It didn't collapse.

"As always, it's a good idea to check the steps," he said in a loud whisper. "The amateurs like to walk up either side, but that gives you a false sense of security if you're being chased out because you're just going to run for it. I'd rather break my leg going in than coming out. You don't want to get munged by a ghost."

It had happened to him on his first time. He'd gotten the skinny woman going until she was in a murderous rage. Of course ghosts couldn't kill, but piss one off and that won't stop them from trying. The skinny woman had charged him and he had turned to run, not realizing she'd leaked sploot all over the floor and fell flat on his face. Ghosts tended to leak in highly charged emotional states. The skinny woman had wrapped those long fingers around his neck and shook him. That part wasn't so bad, but then her hands had passed through his flesh, touching something inside of him. The effect immediately made him evacuate from every hole in his body. He even had ear wax running out of his ears and the gunk that comes out of your eyes while you sleep. Stout would have loved to have captured the experience on camera, but he'd broken his when the skinny woman attacked him. He had no intention of it happening again and had a doodle of her tattooed on his arm to mark the experience.

Stout stomped his way up the stairs and found all but one to be sturdy. When he reached the landing he swung the flashlight around to the other half of the stairs. He saw the top half of a bedroom door from where he stood and cast his light left and right, checking the walls. He took a heavy step up the second flight and saw something from the corner of his eye.

Old Man Turner looked up at him from the foot of the stairs. Stout turned, stepping back to get a better view when the apparition appeared about a foot away from him. He jumped into the wall, the flashlight and camera dancing in his hands. He wasn't afraid of ghosts anymore, but they surprised him from time to time.

"Why did you think you could leave me?" the dead man said. Stout aimed the flashlight at the ghost staring up at him. He was at least six inches taller, but to be fair about a third Old Man Turner's legs was in the landing.

The light passed through him, giving him an ethereal light blue glow around the edges. The camera would only catch it as bright points of light reflecting off nothing so it took a little more to catch the experience on film. That's where the piss-spray came in.

He'd come up with it himself. Part holy water, part animal urine, part garlic. It had some other stuff in it too; he didn't make it the same every time, but it always worked. Maybe they were offended by holy water, maybe it was the pee smell or maybe they were allergic to garlic. But whatever it was almost always got some kind of a rise out of them. Stout put the flashlight between his teeth and fished out the spray bottle. He gave the air a few spritzes.

Scattered pieces of furniture and wood levitated off the floor. An immediate reaction. That was bad. Old Man Turner's face twisted into a ball of rage and became an empty hole as he screamed. Stout threw himself up the stairs seconds before something crashed into the window behind him.

He rammed his shoulder into a door, the flashlight left somewhere in the hall. He crouched by a wall, flicking on the camera's night vision and turning it on himself.

"That noise you're hearing is Old Man Turner approaching and he's pissed because of this." He held the pendant in front of the camera and dropped it. "I'll be lucky to get out of here alive." He always liked to say things like that. It was a one-in-one-hundred chance for a ghost to kill anyone and he'd been doing it long enough to be smarter than most.

The floorboards groaned. Despite being dead ghosts didn't have much on the side of preternatural senses and you could surprise them. He wished there was a camera that could capture the surprised look on their faces when he sprang out of nowhere on them. Classic.

Stout peaked out into the hall and stared at a giant eye that filled the narrow doorway, staring back at him. He tried to leap out of the way, but the door flew open and a giant cold hand wrapped around his head. His arms and legs were free but something was holding his torso in place. The hand turned his head to the left, then the right, then slowly to the left again. Turner was a lot stronger than most.

But Stout had a plan. Even the strongest ghosts had weaknesses. He snatched the necklace off and tossed it onto the floor. The hand and whatever else that was holding him went slack and he felt Old Man Turner pass him.

"Alice. Alice. My sweet, sweet Alice," he heard the old man say.

Stout snatched away the pendant, on a string of fishing line tied to his belt loop and jumped out of the room, running back the way he'd come. Old Man Turner roared, the house vibrating as furniture danced and banged and scraped across the floor. He took the stairs by threes as something big hammered its way down behind him. The rail fell over onto the stairs, scraping his back as he ran off. Stout made a beeline for the front door when it slammed in his face.

But that's where proper preparation came in hand. Before he'd turned the camera on he'd gone into the house and loosened the hinges. It was a big oak door and took some tugging, but the door was already loose from disrepair and he stepped back as it fell.

The radiator on the wall in front of him rattled before ripping free and hurling itself at his head. Stout ducked and it exploded into the wall by the stairs. He turned the camera on himself and turned around.

"I should be dead after that." The face on the screen looked nervous. The image blurred a moment as the view spun from the man to the hole where a wall used to be. The camera showed a wider view of the porch as he backed out of the house. The front door creaked and pushed itself off the floor to shut in front of the camera's view and then he went down the stairs.

The camera view swiveled back on him and he swiped his hand down his face bathed in orangish street light before glancing left and right. A roar came from inside the house and the view spun on the house again as *something* knocked heavy sounding objects around in the abandoned residence. An armoire rocketed through the front door and smashed into an old red Beetle parked at the curb. The picture blurred presumably as the man began running, laughing all the way before the screen turned to snow.

"And that is the last anyone has heard from Stout Roost." Artie Brimmer thumbed the off button on the remote and the screen went black. He paced in a circle before settling down in his plush leather captain's chair, his expensive gray suit stayed immaculate on his chubby body as if it were a second skin.

Kelly Greene glanced over for the dozenth time at the man seated next to him. Kelly couldn't look into his wild eyes when he had held his hand out for a shake. The man didn't take his hand but stared at him.

Kelly didn't like being kept in the dark. It made him uncomfortable to be semi-involved. That's why he never gambled. Too much chance involved for him to feel he had any real sense of control.

Why was he even here? He was in customer service. He rarely watched television and had only the briefest awareness of *The Ghost Toucher* show other than the irate callers who yelled at him about it. The name of it alone told him it wasn't a show for him. Watching the unedited tape a moment ago had solidified his assumption as a good one. A book correctly judged by its cover. And what a bad idea to antagonize a *ghost*.

"Kelly, I'm sure you'd like to know why you're here. It won't make sense, but it should be enough that it's what the Board wants. Stout Roost, as you know, has single-handedly reinvigorated the Network. He's captured thirty-nine percent of the male sixteen to thirty-four audience and his numbers in all other demographics are better than average."

Kelly began clenching his jaw, still wondering what this had to do with him. *ChiChé* had fifty percent of the same demographic and that was a show he could watch.

"Now, it's true, his numbers have begun to slide but in a pitch-meeting Stout came up with an idea. Revolutionary, bold, Emmy-getting—*his* words, not mine. But he wouldn't tell anyone what the idea was. We hadn't heard from him for two months before this tape showed up on my desk last week. I mean literally showed up. I turned my back a moment and there it was when I turned back around. It had his signature on a patch of duct tape—well here it is, you see it—just like always, but it hadn't come in a package and when I called the mailroom Paul said it hadn't come through him. And I believe him; Paul's a big fan of the show and he makes a special trip to put this in my hands when the courier comes.

"I'm sorry; I think I got a little side-tracked. Just thought that was a little amazing, was all. The Board decided to hire a detective a month ago, but after a week our deposit was returned and he stopped answering his phone." He looked at Kelly. "Mr. Israel here—"

"Just Israel."

"—uh, right. Israel is a 'special' detective." Brimmer wiggled both his indexes and middle fingers with the word 'special'. "Considering the kind of work Stout was doing the Board thought perhaps a different kind of detective work needed to be conducted."

"I can pull the recorded calls for—"

"No-no," Brimmer interrupted. "Nothing like that, Kelly. But that's not bad thinking. But what we *do* need..." He turned left and right in his chair, chewing his lower lip a moment. "There is a second issue to be considered and we need a bottom line guy to kind of... steer things along. The Board was forced to consider the possibility Stout met with some sort of mis...adventure. While his on camera work has been a windfall for the network his personal life has fallen more into a category that could best be described as a... 'liability'."

With that last word Brimmer wiggled both indexes and middle fingers again. Kelly's interest was piqued. He hadn't been in accounts receivable in almost three years. Why wouldn't they want Liz Hooper? She was still there. He glanced at the folder on the desk that no doubt held information they would need in finding Roost. Who named themselves after a male chicken?

"Roost." Israel locked eyes with him a moment before facing forward.

What? He hadn't spoken anything aloud, had he? Kelly shook his head.

"In all the various locations Stout has shot in across the country and abroad he has also... become familiar... with many of the local women."

"How many and what do you want us to do about it?" Israel said.

"We suspect as many as fourteen, maybe even more."

Kelly knew he was slow in catching on.

"I'm sorry? Fourteen what?"

"Children." Brimmer turned to Israel. "And there really isn't anything for you to 'do' about it. The Board has come up with an acceptable figure for the cost and duration of this investigation, balanced against what the Network would have to pay each of these children out of what we would owe Stout. Now if he's declared dead there is an indemnity clause, but of course we don't want to rely on that. The amount we would owe these children would be… considerable. It would be much better for us long term if he were found alive."

"So find him, but only if it costs less than a certain amount?"

Brimmer stared at him, but didn't answer.

"I don't know much about detective work, but it can't be all that expensive." Kelly looked away to Israel. "No offense, but not even a 'special' detective can be that expensive."

"Oh, I don't take my payment in cash."

"Okay, so what are we talking about, expenses? Do we need to grease some palms here?"

"Well Israel here is the expert. The Board has its figure." Brimmer pulled out a pen, scribbled something on a post-it and slid it over. Kelly gave a mental whistle. "Don't go over that."

"And how do we pay for all this?"

Brimmer slid open a drawer in his desk and pulled out a white envelope the size of a credit card and handed it over. There was a credit card inside.

"Use it where you have to, the PIN number's in there too in case you need it. All expenses will be reviewed, of course, and you know the standard meal and hotel amounts."

Brimmer pushed over the file to Israel who immediately handed it over to Kelly. Kelly began leafing through the pictures and documents, committing the faces to memory from the former and skimming the latter. Friends and family, people who were opposed to the show, including descendants of some of the 'ghosts' had some sort of file in here. Pictures of the women he had allegedly fathered children with were in here.

"There's a Parke Car waiting for you outside," Brimmer said.

"Now? You mean go now? I haven't had time—"

"I think I've explained how important this is to the Board and the Network. Right now I need to know if you're in or go back to the Board and explain how I need more time because we have to pick someone else."

Kelly got the picture.

"I'm in."

On their way to the elevator Kelly had trouble keeping up with Israel. He wasn't walking very fast, but he was much taller and took long strides, easily putting distance between them as Kelly struggled to not drop the thick folder.

He bumped into someone and the whole thing fell from his hands, papers fanning out across the floor.

"Sorry," he said without looking up. Kelly knelt and began scooping the papers into a sloppy pile. He grabbed a thick rubber band on the floor and after he had all the papers in he stretched it over the folder to keep the papers secure. He was about to stand when he spotted an errant sheet that had gone in a different direction than the others.

The heel of a black pump ground into the paper. Kelly looked at the shoe and the foot that was in it, then up a slender calf. A woman stood before him in a white blouse and knee-length dark grey skirt pulled taut by her parted feet. She had her hands on her ample hips, glowering down at him with large brown eyes. Her olive face was framed by long dark, curly hair, her red lips fixed into a grim line.

"I'm LaGina," she said.

Kelly stammered something unintelligible and tore the paper from underneath her heel. He felt like he'd just seen a ghost. He crammed the paper into the folder, afraid to make eye contact with the woman, but not being able to take his eyes off her.

Give her a different nose and slightly shorter hair and she looked just like Martha.

Kelly stumbled his way around and into cubicles catching up with Israel just as he got to the elevator. The taller man looked down at him, making a face as if he were about to say something and forgot. The elevator dinged and the doors slid open. They got on.

LaGina's work had only begun. So far the Network's attorneys had blocked her paternity suit against Stout. She wouldn't be able to join the class action until she had proven paternity and she couldn't prove paternity because Stout had dropped off the face of the planet. They were hiding him, but where?

She looked at the set of keys she'd swiped off the schmuck she'd bumped into. Mel had pointed him out after they'd gone into Artie Brimmer's office. If this guy was going to find Stout she'd keep tabs on him and be there when he did. In the meantime she had to find out as much as possible about him.

Crazy old lady, pt 1

Artie opened the drawer and took out his talking cloth and planchette. He unrolled the cloth, revealing faded letters and numbers stenciled across it. The planchette was new, with a track wheel beneath it like a computer mouse would have. He placed his fingers upon it and thought of her.

Artie couldn't help himself, he'd fallen in love. When the SVPs had asked him to summon someone from the other side he'd given them Israel, but she'd caught his eye while he was diddling around.

She was an angel, a *goddess*. She couldn't come through the same way Israel had or he would have brought her through a week ago when he'd called the dead man. Artie only needed a corpse to channel his spirit into, which was difficult enough, but bringing her through was proving to be much more difficult.

First, she already had a body. Artie thought everyone over there was a dead person from over here. Apparently, that was very wrong. They had cities, cultures, history. *While she told him about them he busied himself with falling even more in love with her.*

He realized this had become an obsession for him. Artie only communicated with her at work so he always was finding excuses to work late or go in early. *Most people surfed internet porn, instead he hunched over his talking cloth.* Even when he was home with Carol and the kids he was thinking about her.

"F-O-N-D-A-W-A-Y-T-H-R-U," she spelled out through the cloth. "N-E-E-D-U."

"Where?" he said. "I'll be there."

She was royalty where she was from. She must have wanted him too for her to cross over. She spelled out a set of numbers and after he thought about it, he realized they were GPS coordinates. He plugged them into his phone.

It was in Downeck.

Of all the places for her to come through, why did it have to be there? He shook his head, he would be there. Artie had to have her.

"When?" he asked.

"N-O-W", she replied. He let go of the planchette and it flew off the desk and bounced off the wall. She must have been trying to tell him something else. *He got up and quickly grabbed it.*

"What is it, baby?"

"B-R-I-N-G-G-O-A-T-S."

Artie didn't have a problem with animal sacrifice. He'd done that before too. But the trouble was where to find a goat in the city.

* * *

"So I figured our first stop should be to find someone named 'Primer'," Kelly began. "I was reading the file, and he's an oxycontin addict. I heard excessive usage causes a person to lack empathy for others, but I have a couple ideas on how to reach him."

"No," Israel said.

"No what?"

"We're not going there." Israel sat straight in the backseat of the car, just like he had in Brimmer's office.

"Then where are we going?"

"To see Roost's mother. She lives on the East side."

He gave the driver the address even though Kelly hadn't seen it in the file. Israel must have already known it.

"Ooookay." Kelly put the papers back in the file and looked at the man. "So what's your story?" The driver drove out of the lot and onto Evergreen, presumably headed to 696. *Israel turned to face him with same wild look in his eye.*

"I'm a specialist in the unknown. Most might mistakenly take my expertise to be in the Occult, but I assure you there is no such thing."

"The Occult or your expertise?" Kelly joked. Israel looked at him as if he hadn't understood. Kelly cleared his throat. "So you're telling me something I pretty much already knew."

"No. There is something out there. Ugly and evil and old. But you won't find it in any book. At least, not entirely. Imagine if you were thousands of years old and could have destroyed the world several times over at one point. Would you allow some insignificant life form to catalog everything about you?"

"I suppose not."

Israel nodded. "It's good you don't believe. It's best you don't. Once you've seen is when you become the Heard. They typically die soon after."

"Okay."

"I suppose 'die' is being a little disingenuous. *Usually they are killed in a very rude, gruesome and brutal fashion.*"

They rode in silence on the freeway a few minutes.

"So why his mother? The file on her showed Roost wasn't close to her at all. He hasn't spoken to her in years. If not this guy Primer, why not the original detective?"

"Emotion. We aren't going to find Roost by any *ordinary* means. But I can get on his trail if I follow the right clues."

Israel faced forward and said nothing else.

They pulled off the freeway shortly after and weaved through streets Kelly was unfamiliar with. There were small, single story homes with sparse trees in the neighborhood where they stopped.

"You should probably stay here."

"Nah. I think I'll come," Kelly said.

"Your choice. Just keep in mind you're walking down the path of the Heard. Given time they *will* hear you."

Okay, he didn't believe any of the crap Israel was saying, but it *was* creepy. He followed Israel across the lawn and up a walkway to the porch. Even though there was a doorbell, he knocked.

After a moment a little white-haired woman opened the door. She looked at the two of them, her red rimmed eyes darting back and forth.

"Y-yes?"

"Mrs. Messler?" Kelly thought he should do the talking, but he didn't really know what they were doing here. "I'm Mr. Greene and this is Mr. Israel. We'd like to ask you a few questions about your son if possible."

"You found my Leslie?" The waver in her voice was hard to listen to. This was a woman who definitely loved her son.

"Leslie?" Kelly said. "I thought his name was—"

Israel elbowed him.

"Angus Israel, Ma'am." Israel's tone had suddenly become human. He was upbeat, rushed, as if he had a million dollar check in his pocket that could fly out at any moment. "We may well have a lead, Mrs. Messler. We just need to ask you a few more questions to help clarify some things about your son."

"Oh, really?" She blinked tears out of her eyes, which were suddenly larger than they should have been through her bifocal lenses. "Yes-yes, certainly." She swung the screen door open and Kelly had to jump back as if she hadn't seen him standing there. Israel shook her hand and flashed that smile at her again.

"Come in."

The shorter one followed the taller one into the living room. What was the taller one's name again? Angus Israel, she'd have to remember that. She plodded across the thick brown carpet, past the large leather couch by the far wall, painted a comfy coffee color. She'd left the kitchen light on, but it could wait until the two young men were done. She wondered if they had come alone, but remembered there was a driver in the car they had climbed out of.

"Would you like tea? Water?"

"No-no. We won't need to take up that much of your time, Ma'am." The tall one gestured toward the couch and she nodded before he sat. The short one accompanied him on the couch and she wondered how many strikes against the wall it would take to split his skull open.

"Like I was saying, Ma'am," Angus Israel began. "We're looking to get information on your son that maybe prior investigators hadn't gotten around to." He was strange-looking.

Like he should be castrated and his balls stuffed in his mouth. The more she thought about it, the more she was certain she was right.

"What kind of information?"

The little one put a hand to the bigger one's shoulder, which he nudged away with a smile. The little one had a worried look on his face, but said nothing.

"Well, we're working on what we call an 'external' profile. I'm sure you've heard of profiling where we're able to piece together aspects of someone's personality based on the things they've left behind?" She nodded. She didn't know what he was talking about. "Well this works much the same way except we build a profile based on what people had to say about the person in question."

"Oh, that sounds promising." Mrs. Messler wanted to offer them tea again. If they'd take it, she was certain there was rat poison or something in the cabinet. She could hide one of the kitchen knives in her brassier. "What do you need to know about my sweet boy?"

"How do you feel about your Stout—I mean—Leslie?" Angus Israel pulled a paper and pen out of his inside coat pocket. He leaned forward on the edge of the couch and was poised to jot down whatever she had to say.

"My Leslie," she began. "He was... the light of my life. I literally would die for him. I really would."

"Mmhmm," the little one said, rubbing his chin. He didn't seem to really know what was going on. He was a cocksucker.

"Was he spanked as a child?"

"Not my Leslie," she lied. "I spoiled him after my Henry died. Every day was a whole new joy."

"Whole... new... joy." The tall one was writing down everything she said.

"The sun rose and set on him. He was my heart."

"Sun... rose and set... was... heart."

She felt her gorge rising but resisted the urge to vomit in their faces. There would be time for that after she had torn out their fingers and stuffed them into their empty eye sockets.

"He was—"

"Thank you, Mrs. Messler," Israel cut in. "I think we have all we need."

"You do? But I haven't gotten you any tea. Wouldn't you like tea?" She walked toward the kitchen.

"No, but maybe you should check on your bird. I didn't hear it at all."

"My bird?" She almost screeched. Nothing could happen to Tolot. She dashed into the kitchen and doffed the sheet covering the cage. He was still there and lifting the sheet had awakened him. He cocked his head and hopped closer to her on his bar.

Had they tricked her?

Mrs. Messler went on all fours, scurrying back to the living room. The door was wide open and the screen door was shutting. By the time she got to it they were getting in the car that had brought them here.

She stood on her hind legs, pressing her chubby wrinkly body against the screen door. She raked her fingers down the window and howled.

"What the hell was that?" Kelly asked.

"Mrs. Messler. Don't look. Just get in."

They shut their doors and Kelly tapped the driver's seat. They pulled off.

"Take us to a liquor store that sells porn." He looked at Kelly. "Mrs. Messler is possessed. More than likely by a Tolot."

"What's a tolot? And why do we need porn?"

"It's a *machín* that typically possesses a small bird and can gradually switch with a human if they're in close enough proximity for a significant amount of time."

"A ma-*what*?"

"Never mind. You'll understand it later."

***

It hadn't stopped nagging LaGina as to why Brimmer had picked someone not in the Controller's office to keep tabs on the purse strings behind the Stout Roost investigation. Kelly Greene hadn't been in the department in three years. Maybe they were trying to be low-key, maybe they suspected what she was up to.

No, they couldn't. Otherwise, they could have just fired her. There was something else going on. Maybe there was a special reason they'd picked Greene. She looked him up on the company directory and made her way down to his floor. All the floors the Network used in this building had mostly the same format so you'd have to be an idiot not to figure out your way around once you read the cubicle numbers.

She found his in a nest of empty cubicles on the west side of the building. The directory listed him as being in customer service, but so far as she could tell he was the only one here. Very odd.

Greene had no pictures on his desk and she couldn't recall if he'd worn a wedding band. Maybe he wasn't married. There were a few papers neatly stacked to one side, a phone and a PC. She pushed the mouse and a blue screen popped up showing his desktop had been locked. LaGina checked his top drawer, unlocked, and found pens, blank index cards, a stapler, paper clips... nothing she needed.

The second drawer only had a bag of Made-Goode hot chips. She tried the bottom drawer and it was completely empty. He had a second cabinet on the other side of the desk.

Why two? she wondered. He barely used one. There had to be something in there. LaGina tried the top drawer and it was locked. The other one was vanilla, why lock these drawers? She rooted through the other top drawer until she found a letter opener. It was always the ones who appeared normal who had something to hide. Maybe it wouldn't help her find Stout, but it could give her leverage over Greene. If she could twist him to her purposes she could get what she and her children deserved.

LaGina rammed the letter opener into the lock and twisted. The lock turned and she slid the drawer open. Locks were only license for a false sense of security, much like so many other things in life, like love. There was nothing in the first drawer. Nothing in the second. She hesitated before opening the third. There could be what she needed in here, but it could be dangerous. Maybe he had porn in there, maybe even the kiddie kind. Maybe he had important corporate documents or maybe this one was empty too. She was expecting anything.

LaGina opened it. There were some yellowed papers on top of something. She picked up the papers and turned them over. They were children's drawings and from the likes of them by a girl or girls a few years younger than her twins. Beneath the drawings were pictures in nice wooden and metal frames. It was Greene with a woman and two girls who looked close in age.

Why would he keep them in here? And the frames were much too nice to keep at work—had he taken them from home?

She checked beneath the pictures for anything else; anything that might be damaging. This was so normal it was just... weird.

Suddenly, LaGina felt as if she had gone too far, like she had peaked in on him as he was going to the bathroom. She began stacking the pictures back in the drawer, hopefully the same way she'd picked them up. Before putting the last one back, LaGina looked at it. It was all four of them on a summer day. They must have been at an amusement park because there was a rollercoaster in the background and he had on a hat that reminded her of a cartoon character whose name she couldn't remember. The youngest girl had an orange bear that was as big as her. Everyone was smiling.

But there was someone else in the picture too. It was strange because she hadn't seen this new man the first time she looked at the picture. Something was wrong with the picture because the man was half-faded, translucent, but he had his arm around Greene's shoulder.

She realized she knew that face.

It was the man Greene had left with a little while ago.

Greatest of all time

It took a little while, but Artie found a goat. He hoped one would do the trick. He'd called a couple restaurants in Mexicantown until he found a guy willing to part with his for the right price. Artie had changed into his exercise clothes but the bastard had raked him over the coals for the thing. She'd better be worth it.

Artie had to pick up his wife's dog from doggie daycare. A seven pound beast that pissed all around the house and humped anyone with at least one leg. Another thing she was too busy to take care of.

His mind drifted back to Kelly Greene. Poor sap. His wife and kids. Nobody deserved that. He remembered seeing the story on the news and realizing he worked for the Network too in the Controller's office. He'd had a breakdown, took six months off, and when he finally came back they moved him to a 'special' department until he was ready to come back. But he'd stayed there three years. This whole Stout thing was going to also work to push him out. Greene's special position was being eliminated whether he failed or succeeded in finding Stout; it was just a matter of how they had to spin it. Artie felt bad, but to hell with him. People went through tragedy every day.

The dog jumped in his lap as he said a silent prayer heading to Downeck. It wasn't an ideal place to drive and he'd vowed never to go back. Ever since the Gary twins in ninety-six the world hadn't been the same and it had all started there. People thought Stout Roost had started it all, but they'd just forgotten. Or their memories had been erased after the Garys. He'd almost died with those two lunatics and the world didn't have a clue.

They were supposed to know about the black arts and all their lives they had been trying to prove the existence of another realm. Until then they had been clowns in the magic industry; real low grade stuff, but what they had planned was supposed to put them on the map.

They were much better salesmen than magicians. Their tricks never lived up to their hype, one or both of them usually got injured during their stunts, but somehow they always found a way back onto television. Maybe people watched them because they were a joke.

It was a live special on Friday night. Artie was a camerman back then. One of the two the network sent. They'd found the place of 'perfect balance'—no one knew what that meant—a hundred year old house in Downeck and began a long and boring ceremony with ancient, cookware-looking items and chanting gobbledygook. It was nice filler, nobody watched TV on Fridays. Everyone was at the bar or a movie.

But then Glenn or Garver, Artie couldn't tell which one was which, started lighting up. Kind of like a flame flickering in and out all over his body. He'd seen what they'd caught on tape much later and nothing that looked supernatural had been caught. But Artie had seen with his own eyes as the brothers stood toe-to-toe and that flame began leaping between both of them until they were bathed in blue fire.

Instead of running around and beating off the flames they stood there. Instead of burning to death they linked hands and kind of *melted* together. They didn't seem to be in any pain and the longer it went on the more he realized they weren't melting—they were being sucked into something.

A weird wind picked up out of nowhere. Not a wind, actually. Random items in the room kind of floated into the air and gravitated toward the Garys. They were only heads and two pairs of feet when Bill, the other cameraman, lifted into the air. The last of Garver and Glenn sucked down into the nothing and it began dragging other things in behind them.

"Help me, Art!" Artie remembered Bill saying, but it was already too late. His foot had already vanished into it. Artie turned to run and something large smacked off his head. He went down, but got right back up, running for the stairs.

Pieces of the wall ripped off and flew past him. A high-pitched whining sound started and he had to put his hands to either side of his head. A moment later it stopped, but as he ran for the door he realized he couldn't hear anything. Artie broke through the front door and the porch steps were yanked from under him as he ran down.

Artie looked back and the house was gone. He stood and looked around. A second later something hit him in the chest, knocking him to the ground. He staggered back to his feet and looked down at a ragged section of Bill's bloody naked torso with a piece of arm and leg attached. He heard the high-pitched whine inside his head and the earth beneath him felt like it shifted. Sometime later he thought that must have been when the Garys point of perfect balance became imbalanced, when the dead backfilled into the world of the living.

Artie wore the hearing-aide as evidence of the occurrence, but people seemed to not remember things being different than they were now. He knew there was a world once that didn't have ghosts, but no one else did. Ghosts were as accepted as cockroaches. You didn't see them everyday, but you knew they were around somewhere.

His phone told him he'd arrived. Artie parked at the curb, slipped a small duffle bag over his shoulder, tossed the dog onto the passenger seat and got out. He shut the door and it immediately popped up in the window and watched him, whining.

The air here was still different than air anywhere else. The sky was the same shade of blue, but still wrong somehow. He felt twitchy as he walked to the back of his Jeep and popped the hatch.

The old goat stared at him. He grabbed the animal by the collar and it pulled back.

"Smart boy, aren't you Wilmer?"

Artie yanked and Wilmer came, but he struggled. Wilmer fell out of the hatch and scuttled back upright. Artie shut the hatch. God forbid that dog jump out the back. He dragged the goat up the curb. Wilmer must have realized he wasn't going to overpower him and went limp, forcing Artie to drag him all the way to the middle of the open field.

The one benefit to doing this in Downeck was no one would see. The few residents who remained in this ghost town only left their homes to go to work or shop. Nobody went for a stroll here. There was no city government, no police, no fire, no homeless, no guy in a Santa suit ringing a bell for Salvation Army. No Knights of Columbus walking through traffic asking for donations. And nobody looked out of windows. Any city services that had to be provided were done by Detroit and they got in and out (if they ever came at all). The streets had fallen into disrepair. If you lived here you'd be lucky if the cable guy ever came.

Holding Wilmer by the collar so he wouldn't try to get away, Artie reached into his duffle and pulled out a chain and a spike. He put the chain around Wilmer's neck and the spike through two links, cinching the chain close to the goat's neck and drove it into the ground. Wilmer stood up, yanked the chain, and almost toppled the spike. Artie grabbed the goat by his scruff and drove the spike back into the ground. He held it as he fished out a mallet from his duffle and gave the spike about a dozen swats, driving it deep into the ground.

He let go of Wilmer and dug out the talking cloth. It was unnecessary to unroll it as they had already established a link through it. Artie held it out in front of him.

"Are you here?"

The talking cloth bent in the middle, folding over to his left. She was pushing it. He took the big knife out of his duffle and unsheathed it. Wilmer pitched back and tugged, but the spike held. Artie stood to the side of it and straddled it. He didn't need to lift the goat's chin to slit his throat as it was already held high on the loop of chain around its neck.

Artie slid the knife from one side of Wilmer's neck to the other. The goat pulled even harder and actually pulled free of the chain. The back of his head slammed into Artie's stomach and groin and he fell down to both knees in agony. He stayed on all fours for a long time, praying nothing was broken or ruptured.

When he was finally able to stand he checked himself over. His pant leg was torn, but there was only a red line where the goat's horn had scratched him. He scanned around for Wilmer, his eyes following the spurts of blood on the soft ground. He'd made it all the way back to the Jeep, his body underneath Artie's SUV except for his hind legs sticking out. It didn't matter where he died, just where the killing blow had been struck and the first drops spilled.

Artie turned back and saw a giant black chrysalis, pulsating about five yards away. It was about twenty feet tall, forty feet wide, and covered in cilia. It had three tapered ends and the one closest to him terminated in a yellowish flagellum that was slurping up some of Wilmer's blood. Once it had finished the appendage shuddered, turned a dark brown, shriveled, and hardened. The chrysalis shriveled and hardened as well, shrinking down to about ten feet tall by fifteen feet wide.

He approached it, the talking cloth still in his hand. No response. Where ever she was, she was gone now. This had to be her! Artie tried to touch the hard shell, but the cilia had frozen into spikes and pricked his palm. He brushed at them with the talking cloth and they broke and fell away until he had cleared a six foot radius.

He knocked on it and heard a faint knock back. Artie pounded his fist on it, trying to break the shell, but it was too thick. He looked around for a rock or something to smash it with, but couldn't find anything even close to the size of his fist.

"I'll be right back." Artie ran to the Jeep and the dog barely got out of the way before he hopped in. He started it up and made a big circle into the street, turning around to the lot. He bounced around inside as the SUV hopped the curb and he revved it up to twenty-five. The Jeep rammed the chrysalis and he flew forward, his nose banging into the steering wheel.

It was cracked, but still intact.

Artie reversed and pulled back to the curb. Blood streamed from his nose, it was broken and he had to breathe out of his mouth. He put on his seatbelt, took a deep breath and stomped on the gas, the Jeep lurching backwards again.

"Shit," he said, hearing Wilmer's body crunch beneath the tires as he bounced onto the street. He put it in drive and gunned it again. Something punched through the crack and Artie stomped on the brake and veered to the left, almost tipping his vehicle over.

He got out and ran over to the chrysalis. It was her hand. Artie tried peaking inside, but he was too short. She had some sort of goo on her arm, but he kissed her palm.

"I'll have you out in a moment, baby." He yanked on the jagged hole and the cracks spread some. He walked back to the Jeep and popped the hatch again. Artie lifted a panel in the bottom and took out his tire iron. He beat at the cracks until chunks began to fly off. She helped too, pushing out pieces as they loosened up.

She peaked her head out and looked at him.

"Arthur?"

She was *gorgeous*! High cheekbones, broad eyes, full lips, and that accent. She was covered in more of that goo, but first thing would be a shower at the motel. He'd already concocted the story he would tell his wife.

Artie ran over to his duffle bag and grabbed his towel. He handed it to her and she nodded. The crowbar made easy work of the cracked shell until there was a hole big enough for her to fit through.

He held her arm as she got out. She was tall. While inside the chrysalis he hadn't realized, but she was easily six-foot-five. That made more of her to love. Her legs were long and thin, narrow shoulders, and, well, he couldn't see beneath the towel, but Artie was certain the rest of her looked good too. He put his arms around her and felt her heart hammering. She leaned down to him and he kissed her. She seemed surprised but leaned into it.

"You're going to be a hero, Arthur."

"Well, I don't know about that." He wondered how she knew English.

"No. Because of you I will be able to save the universe."

What was she talking about? This was strictly a hook-up.

"Your name will be a remembered one throughout both our worlds."

"Hey, that's great," Artie started, not liking where this was heading. "But I was thinking we could head over to the motel first."

She looked at him and cocked her head.

"Oh, you mean the sex. Of course. We shall have sex innumerable times daily." She said it matter-of-factly.

Now that's what he was talking about. Well maybe two or three times a day for the first couple of weeks or so, then maybe they could peter it down some.

"Would you like to have sex right now?"

"What? Here? No. I have a place. A special place. It's got candles and roses and wine."

"Those things sound lovely. I'm sure it will be nice. A good place to conceive."

"Then let's get out of here." He took her hand. The joke would be on her. He'd had a vasectomy seven years ago.

They were almost to the Jeep when her towel slipped. His eyes bugged as he saw the line down the middle of her back and the twin dimples above her ass. She grabbed for the towel, but not before he caught a glimpse of breast with a brown nipple erect in the cool air. And a low-hanging, round gut.

"Hey, what is that?" Artie pointed to her pronounced belly and walked around. It wasn't that big and if it weren't for her dark nipples against her pale skin he might not have thought it was anything but a little beer gut.

He'd seen it on Carol three times before; she was pregnant.

"You mean my child?" She let the towel drop and rubbed her hand over her belly in a circular motion. "Do you adore it?"

"Child? You never said anything about a *child*."

"It never entered my mind. This is my perpetual state."

"Per*pet*ual? So you're always—are you kidding me?"

Her face changed. She stood with her feet apart and her hands on her hips.

"I am a Mother." At least she said it like the 'm' should be capitalized.

"So you already have kids? You didn't think to tell me *that*?"

"I have hundreds of children. *Thousands.* If anything I thought it would have made you love me more. I am known for my fertility."

"So... so what are you? Like a quarterback—you just throw it to anybody who'll catch it?"

"I am not a quarterback and I'm unsure of what you mean. If you mean lovers, I assure you I have only had two and both were some time ago. I can conceive my own children."

"You're one of those... *man/girls?*"

She looked offended.

"I am *not* a man."

"Ugh, I kissed him. I *kissed* him." Artie hunched over, his stomach doing flip-flops. "I think-I think I'm going to be sick."

"How *dare* you." She covered her breasts with one arm and stalked over to him.

"I can't believe what I was about to do. I gotta get home to my wife. My kids."

"You're married?" She gasped. The crowbar was right by her foot. She picked it up.

"Don't do anything crazy, buddy. Let's just figure a way out of this. Can we just put you back in there and send you back?"

Artie's stomach heaved and he fell to his knees for the last time. He felt her standing over him and realized he'd never asked her name. It was the last thing that went through his mind before she plunged the flat end of the crowbar through his head.

***

"So what do we need this stuff for?" Kelly was still a little embarrassed buying porn. Especially the gay stuff. There were only so many times you could say it wasn't for you. He wasn't certain how this would help anything or if it would be a legitimate expense. Israel took the half dozen greeting cards and threw the dirty magazines in the trunk.

"Where to, gentlemen?" the driver said from up front. He hoped she didn't see.

"Just a minute," Israel said. He took out all six greeting cards and placed them face down on the seat between him and Kelly in two rows of three.

"What do you think of these?"

"American Greetings, Hallmark, Green Mountain." Kelly shrugged. "Am I supposed to be seeing something?"

Israel just stared at him.

"What? What's a greeting card supposed to be telling me?"

"It's not just a greeting card. In each one of these cards you'll find something that Mrs. Messler said to us. Links... keylocks. From a polar bear sneezing in the Arctic circle to a teenaged boy taking his first shave."

"You're talking about the butterfly effect?"

"Yes, but no. Small variations most times result in imperceptible changes in outcomes. The point is everything is linked to everything else in at least infinitesimal ways." Israel laced his fingers together. "Think of my left hand as the past and my right hand as the future, the left, the time you jumped off the swing and flattened Andre Hill in second grade and the right, a... bolt of lightning that slices a tree in half and it falls on somebody's head. You can't do anything about the left hand—it's in the past, already happened. The right, if you were in the right place at the right time you could save that person's life."

"But how would I know where to look or when it would happen?"

Israel wiggled his fingers, making a water-wave motion with his hands.

"That's where the link comes in. We call them keylocks. You find the keylock you can anticipate anything. Prevent everything."

"Even cancer?"

"Disease is more difficult, but yes."

"Bull. You're saying turning left instead of right can prevent *genetics*. No way."

"Yes way. Why can you have three siblings pre-disposed to diabetes and only two get it? Or sole survivors of a plane crash? It's because all these things are keylocked. Most humans just don't know how to follow the bread crumbs. Even the ones who do are stumbling in the dark."

"What's that word you keep saying? Keylock."

"A key by itself is useless except in one particular door you may or may not find. A lock's only use is to keep things out. A keylock can work everywhere. It connects two or more things that would have otherwise have been kept separate."

"Like us from Stout."

"There you go. We find that keylock and we'll be led right to him. It'll be as clear to us as the sun on a cloudless day."

"Okay, so what do we do to find one of these keylocks?" Kelly didn't believe a word of what Israel was saying, but he was willing to play along for the time being.

"Coincidence. The first step is believing it's a myth. A man-made construction."

"So what—if I run into a buddy from high school at a party that's not a coincidence? There's some divine plan?"

"After you met that buddy, if you had had a finely tuned sense, it would have brought you somewhere. And then somewhere else. On and on like that until you had reached a logical conclusion extending from meeting up with your buddy again. Haven't you ever picked up your keys for no reason and turned to the door and stopped yourself? Or picked up a pen and thought, 'Why do I have this in my hand?' and realized you had no idea?"

"No."

"Sure you have. Everybody has. It's like having déjà vu about déjà vu."

"What?" Kelly said.

"You know—you remember remembering you've done a thing before, but you only remember remembering it when you're remembering it?"

"So when I'm not remembering it, I forget it?"

"You got it."

"No. No, I don't."

"Then try to fix in your mind the idea of what a keylock is. What it does. Try to keep your mind open to things that lead to things. It's not always going to be a straight line. Most times it isn't."

"All right." Kelly let out a small laugh. "I'll try."

"But keep in mind what else is implied by what I said. Keylocks connect everything. And that's how the bad guys will find you too."

"Right."

"I mean it. They'll use them to anticipate you. You'll think you left no tracks, that no one followed you, but somehow they'll still be there. You can't hide. As a matter of fact, hiding is the worst possible thing because that'll make you even easier to find."

Kelly was more interested in shutting him up. The Network had dug up a nut. He'd probably been paranoid all his life; aliens and the government all conspiring to get him. Kelly picked the card from the middle in the row closer to him.

"Here."

"Don't do that."

"Do what?"

"Dismiss this. It's real. Don't do that."

"I wasn't. I—"

Israel took the card. He turned it over several times, tore it in half and then began tearing one of the halves into pieces.

"Hey, you don't have to take it out on the card."

Israel looked at him.

"If you'd been everywhere in the world a billion times over, every place would feel familiar; every casual passer-by would be a mundane encounter, if you had already done everything, everything would be the same."

"That sounds pretty boring."

"And that's what it's like to be God. Imagine how crushing a crown that would be to a human being. There aren't any surprises. Your very first snowball was a thing of beauty, but the One who's made a bazillion of them already wouldn't find your particular snowball anywhere near as fascinating as you do. That's why God lives through us. Just my theory, anyway."

Israel set the pieces on his lap and began tearing up the other cards.

"Yeah, I was going to say I don't remember that in any Bible."

"Like I told you, They have no reason to give away their secrets in books."

"So God is one of Them?"

"No. They're mostly flesh-and-blood. Some of them have different color flesh and things other than blood flowing through their veins, but they don't exist on that level." Israel piled the pieces of the five cards together.

"Take a handful."

"You say it like you know for a fact." Kelly picked up a fistful and Israel swept the rest onto the floor.

"I suppose I don't," he said, taking the scraps from Kelly. "But I met a pretty powerful being who survived his own head exploding. It *allegedly* had a conversation with Him."

Israel placed pieces of the cards in what appeared to be random order. It looked to Kelly like he was making a ransom note except it began with a string of numbers from the UPC codes. He switched a couple pieces and added to it from the scraps of the first card. Apparently finished, Israel stared at what he'd done. Kelly looked at the pieces.

It was an address. Street number, name, city, and state.

Israel tapped the driver on the head and told her where to go.

***

Vince sat out on the porch in Sara's rocker. He hadn't come out here since she'd died twenty years ago and he'd lost his sight. He didn't want to be out here, it was cold, but he needed to be.

He could hear them coming when they were about a quarter mile away. In his mind he saw the black Lincoln Town Car coming up the unpaved road. He had long ago stopped growing corn and had leased the land to other farmers to grow wheat.

"So that's what Ford's building now," he said under his breath.

The Lincoln pulled into the dirt driveway and stopped. Vince saw the tall dead man and the short black man before they got out. The pretty young driver stayed in the car.

"Good afternoon, sir," the black one said. He was shifty. Looked around too much. Being away from the city must have made him uneasy. He must not have known the area; Flint was only a couple miles north.

"Good afternoon, gentlemen." Their footsteps sounded up the stairs. "How may I help you?"

"I'm Benton Israel," the tall one said, "this is Kelly Greene. We're looking for Stout Roost. Has he been through here?"

"That he has. Wanted to see my barn."

Vince wondered why the short one looked confused at the tall one. He wouldn't ask; the whole mysterious blind man thing didn't suit him.

"Did he say where he was going?" the black one asked.

"Nope. You can look in the barn if you'd like."

"Well, thank you, but why do you think we want to look in your barn?"

"Because it's haunted. Same reason Stout wanted to see it."

"Oh. Well. Do we just walk back there?"

"Aw, no. You don't wanna do that. I'll get Hernandez to take you." Vince cleared his throat. "Ay, Hernandez, you down there in the basement still?"

"Yeah," his friend said from deep inside the house. It was funny that he could 'see' how these two looked but he had no clue about Hernandez. He could have asked to feel his face, but that was too weird.

"Gotta couple fellahs here want to see the barn."

"Aw, hell." There was some banging from inside. "Here I come."

"Whoa," the black one said.

"You guys come with me," Hernandez said from the side of the house. His friend had a habit of being two places at once. He listened as his friend led the two men away. It wasn't meant for him to see what they were up to.

"Bear traps," Hernandez said, high-stepping through the high grass in the yard. He wore a sleeveless t-shirt and gray knee-length shorts. His left arm terminated before the wrist, a jagged scar running across the nub and up the underside of his forearm. Kelly looked at Israel. They followed in his footsteps like he'd told them. "We have to lay bear traps."

"What do you catch in them?" Israel asked.

"Ghosts."

Israel looked at Kelly this time.

"They come outta the barn at night. Roam around. We catch 'em, but..." Hernandez shrugged, "they're ghosts."

"You know they don't like that," Israel said. "To be called ghosts."

Hernandez turned and looked at Israel. He rolled his eyes and kept high-stepping. They made it to the barn and he turned to them with an odd smile on his face. The big doors were partially open.

"Not to sound like a cliché, but this is as far as I go." He folded his arms and stepped back, plucking at his handlebar mustache. "Take this." He fished a small flashlight out of his pocket and slapped it in Israel's hand. "Call me when you're ready and I'll come get you."

The heat inside was like a thick, moist blanket. The air was full with the smell of hay and old feces. Kelly felt sweat prickle his brow, but Israel seemed unbothered. He took off his coat and folded it over his arm as Israel flicked on the flashlight. Hernandez pulled the barn door closed.

"Okay, why'd he need to do that?" Kelly asked.

"I don't know, but look at that." Israel pointed ahead. It was dark in here but it looked like a doorway was far up ahead. "How big is this barn?" He turned the light left and right and everything in here looked like what Kelly imagined would be in a barn, but there was that doorway. It looked like it was floating in the air as nothing could be seen around it.

"Maybe we should get out of here." Kelly reached for the barn door that should have been right next to him, but his arm cut through naked air. Israel turned and the light shone on only more black. Kelly watched as he turned in a circle. The walls were gone.

Israel pointed the flashlight straight up. They could see the support beams of the barn and the ceiling, but when he went a few feet left or right it vanished.

"Is that door closer?" Israel said. Kelly looked. It was. At least by thirty yards and when he blinked he was sure it was moving.

"Should we move out the way?" Kelly said.

"I doubt that would make a difference. I think it's approaching us."

"Maybe it'll stop if we split up."

"I'm cool with that if you are." Israel gripped the flashlight tighter.

Kelly looked into the inky black. His mind conjured a dozen or so variations of the monsters he imagined in his room at night as a child. Except back then he knew they weren't really there.

As the door drew closer they could see something on the other side pushing at it, like it was made of rubber. Kelly steeled himself when it was about fifty feet away; he had no clue how to fight a door.

Forty feet. Thirty. Twenty.

At ten feet it slowed, coming to a stop about three feet away and two feet in the air. Kelly could see over the top. Must have been made for a little person. He could hear something like knives or claws carving down the other side.

"That what I think it is?" Israel said.

"I'm pretty sure."

The door swung in and both men pulled back. There was nothing there, but it wasn't the same darkness that surrounded them. At least Israel's flashlight could cut through the shadows, but when he shined the light in there it weakened and died.

"What are we supposed to do—go in?" Kelly asked.

"Maybe there's hooded midgets in there. Take a peak."

Kelly made a nervous laugh.

"Let me see your coat." Kelly handed it over without thinking. Israel threw it inside.

"What did you do that for?"

"I don't know. I thought it would fly back or something."

"Let's think about this. If Stout came in here he obviously made it out. He visited at least two other places before he made that tape."

"Unless he visited those two places, made that tape and *then* came here."

Kelly hadn't thought of that. If that were the case then there was a real chance they were about to find out exactly where he was.

There was a footstep in the hay. Kelly and Israel turned, the light dancing around where the sound had come from. Something was pacing in the hay, but there wasn't anything there they could see.

"What is it?" Kelly whispered. "Do you see anything?"

"No," Israel whispered too. "Nothing's there. I mean, *something* is, but I can't see it. And that's really weird because I can see invisible stuff."

Hay rustled from somewhere else in the barn, but before they could locate it the sound of shifting hay was coming from all over.

But the door just hovered there.

Something large bumped into Kelly's shoulder. He jumped and looked. There wasn't anything there, but it had left something warm and slimy on his fingers.

"There's something on my hand."

Israel held the flashlight on it but his hand looked clean. Kelly sniffed his fingers.

"Ugh, it smells like cow spit."

Then the mooing began.

Israel stumbled over a couple steps.

"Something pushed me!" he said.

"What, is this place haunted with cows?"

Something stepped out of the door. It looked like a shadow in the general shape of a human but the head was all wrong. It straightened, but something about the shape of its bulky body said it shouldn't have been able to. It faced Kelly and Israel, about Kelly's height, leaning, like it was about to charge them.

Kelly felt something nuzzling his hand. It had a giant head and he scratched behind its ear.

"Okay, so they are cows." He pointed to the door. "But what's that thing?"

The creature at the door didn't move.

"I don't know, but I think it's time for us to get."

"Agreed." Kelly slapped the side of the ghost cow he was scratching.

"Hey, Hernandez!" Israel began. "We're ready to get out of here!"

The shadow thing took a step towards them and stretched to be three feet taller.

"Mr. Hernandez, we want to go now," Kelly said.

They backed away from the floating door and it receded too. It was at least sixty feet away when the shadow thing started running in their direction. Even from this distance Kelly could see white jagged teeth when its wide head opened in the middle.

He felt the door at his back and turned to pound on it. Israel joined him. They both called to Hernandez as the creature closed on them, its mouth stretching wider and wider, displaying even more razor teeth.

A column of light appeared and an arm reached in and grabbed Kelly. He and Israel stumbled out into the light. A moment later something large knocked them over. Kelly fell onto his side and a moment later bear traps began springing in the yard.

"There he goes! There he goes!" Hernandez jumped and clapped his hand on his scarred forearm.

"You've seen that thing before?" Kelly said. He and Israel climbed off the ground.

"You could say that." Kelly tried not to look at his arm. "Mostly I just wait to hear the traps go off."

"How often is that?" Israel said.

"Every night."

"What the hell did Roost get out of coming here?"

Hernandez shrugged.

"Do you mind if we use your bathroom?" Kelly asked.

"Sure. This way."

Once they were inside Israel went to the bathroom and Hernandez disappeared back downstairs. The inside of the house looked better but not by much. Kelly walked around the large room. It wasn't a great room, as those were built in more modern homes and this one was easily a hundred years old, but it had a cathedral ceiling and a fireplace. There was no furniture, though, and Kelly's shoes echoed off the floor. He didn't want to go into the kitchen as that seemed intrusive, but he felt like he had walked into something that should have been kept secret. It almost would have been better if Vince hadn't allowed them to come inside. Maybe it wouldn't seem so awkward had the man come in too.

"All yours." Israel stepped out of the bathroom, wiping his mouth with a kerchief as the toilet finished flushing. Kelly went in and shut the door. This must have been an addition. The walls were a different shade of off-white, the toilet had a sleek, aerodynamic design and the floor was tiled. He wasn't sure, but Kelly thought powder rooms had come back into fashion in more recent years.

He lifted the toilet lid (funny, Israel hadn't gone since they'd met; did he put the lid down when he finished or just flush?) and started doing his business. As he went he spotted a beer can on an open White Pages.

He finished and flushed the toilet. As he washed his hands he looked at the can again. It was Guinness. Kelly had had it a couple times before. Pretty good stout.

Stout!

He turned off the water and dried his hands on his shirt. He knelt by the White Pages, looking for something. He wasn't sure what yet. A page had been torn out, but before whoever had done it they'd circled heavily enough to make an impression on the following page. Kelly traced his fingers over the name, Kenyon Murray. He tore that page out and closed the White Pages. It was for the current year. He folded the page and put it in his back pocket.

Kelly walked out of the powder room and saw Israel outside on the porch with Vince. He wanted to ask if he really thought Stout had been here. He wanted to tell him about the White Pages. But this was too crazy. Saying any of that aloud would lend credence to Israel's insanity. It was some kind of trick; Israel must have already known Stout had been here. Kelly joined them outside.

"Any idea of where he was going?" Israel asked.

"Didn't ask," the man said.

"We appreciate the time, Vince." Israel turned to Kelly. "C'mon, we have to get back."

"Good meeting you," Kelly said as he stepped off the porch.

"See you," Vince said.

"Drive," Israel said after they got back in the car.

"Do you want me to follow 'em?" Hernandez said.

"Nope." Vince put his hand up to the smaller man's chest. "Too many horses in this race. We'll get our chance later."

Hernandez disappeared again.

"Was that him then?" Syrah said. The porch door creaked open as she came out.

"Not yet, Syrah. Not yet."

"When." It was a statement, not a question.

Vince didn't know how to tell the girl to wait. She was destined to die and no matter how much he wanted to prevent it both of them knew there was nothing that could be done. But he still didn't want her to go.

His mind flashed back to that night. The fire that had killed Sara and taken his eyes. And the little girl he'd found in the still smoldering ashes who had no business there, let alone surviving. He'd made a vow to protect that baby and it felt completely wrong to now send her off to die. It was like he was murdering her himself.

"Tomorrow. Sometime tomorrow."

Saving the world is hard to do

It took Jemen a while to comprehend this conveyance. Not that it was difficult, but she gave birth shortly after killing Artie. She regretted having to do that, but he wasn't the broad-minded man she believed him to be. He would have been troublesome, perhaps to the point of hindering her mission.

But she had loved him even in the brief time they had known each other. She would honor that love, if not the man, and remember him. Jemen would speak his name when she had accomplished her divine task, for without that love she would never have been able to begin this journey.

Her son sat in the back, naked and gaunt. He stared at her with his giant eyes, shivering. No doubt he was hungry. She would have yet another hungry mouth to feed very shortly as her belly had already swelled. From what she had divined from the dead of this world was they used something called money to purchase food. It was a ridiculous notion, to barter for something essential to life, but the consequences for stealing would be detrimental to her cause.

Jemen had taken Artie's wallet and found green rectangular lint paper with the busts of men on them. She surmised the numbers in the corners must have been indicators of denomination, a twenty being the highest one she found. There were ones, fives, tens, but nothing between one and five, five and ten, and ten and twenty. She wondered how she would pay for something that cost sixteen dollars.

Jemen drove away, both her and her son jostling around in the SUV as she pulled into the street. The first step would be to find food for herself and her babies. The second would be to find the *machín*.

***

Israel was reading the paper. They'd grabbed sandwiches at a place called Oliver T's on Hill Road in Grand Blanc. Kelly had a grilled tuna on wheat with Swiss and Israel had a Georgia Reuben. The driver had insisted she wasn't hungry but Kelly got her corned beef on an onion roll.

They'd given them a side of that nasty slawse stuff. Kelly dropped his back into the bag, but Israel had blindly poured it all over his Reuben, blending it into the thousand island dressing. It was the juice from coleslaw except made into a milkier, thicker sauce and it was awful. Kelly had tried some once and had to throw away a whole cheeseburger. It was one of those polarizing things, like well water or city water. If you liked one you hated the other.

Israel shuffled the newspaper in his hands. Kelly read the headline; apparently Polk was being linked to some boat in dry dock. It described him as being "Slowski with Details" referencing the name of the boat and the Polk's already broken promise to be more transparent after the last mayoral election.

The page looked weird for a moment. Kelly blinked and it looked fine again, but he had a metallic taste in his mouth and his stomach queezed. He held a mouthful of tuna fish, saliva flooding over his tongue. Kelly grabbed the paper bag and spat the tuna into it. Better. He picked up his Coke and washed down the remnants. Much better.

His eyes returned to the page and whatever it was had returned. He blinked several times intentionally, but it didn't go away. It was the letters. Like they'd been italicized, but they were not. They stood out from the other letters, sparsed all throughout the page. A few of the letters were next to each other but his mind linked them together, making words, sentences.

The 'article' read:

> *Harper Hospital was the setting for what police are calling a gruesome terrorist attack and non-affected areas are currently being evacuated. Authorities are not releasing the attacker's name, but allegedly at 8:02 this evening a former employee released a deadly chemical in a hall down from Quiznos, the fumes overtaking and killing visitors and employees alike. Little is known about the chemical except that it seems to cause rapid decomposition of the flesh even before death as many people were seen fleeing the hospital with rotting limbs and exposed bones as skin sloughed off before expiring soon after the incident. The hospital was able to cordon off the affected area, but officials are unsure at this point if the measures will be enough. Police are asking those who have loved ones as either patients or employees of the hospital to please hold all phone calls to Harper or the Detroit Medical Center while they are resolving this situation.*

Kelly couldn't believe what he'd just read. He blinked again and could see the letters forming into words as plain as before. Could this be some kind of cosmic trick? Was it something in the sandwich? Was it just wicked wishful thinking on his part?

He checked the time on his cell phone. 5:38. If it were real, it was about to happen in a couple hours. Kelly felt silly saying something, but—

"Driver," he said, wishing he knew her name, "we need to go to Harper Hospital."

"What's going on?" Israel looked up from his paper. The driver pulled into the left lane and made a Michigan left. Kelly looked around but didn't recognize where they were. Israel's sandwich was gone, but he'd been hanging on to the edges of that newspaper since they got in the car.

"Something weird." Kelly pointed at the newspaper. Israel turned it around and looked.

"What, the shooting on Seven Mile?"

"No. The letters. Don't you see them?"

"Uh, I see a *lot* of letters."

"But some of them look different than the rest. They make their own words." Kelly fanned his fingers across the page. "You can't see it?"

Israel looked at Kelly then back at the page.

"No." He shook his head. "What's it say?"

"Some kind of attack at Harper Hospital. But the funny thing is it hasn't happened yet. It's supposed to happen at eight tonight."

"You want to check it out? What if we can't do anything about it?"

"I think we have to try. There's a lot of people who could die. Could this be that path you were talking about?"

"I don't know. You can never really be sure. It could be something totally unrelated. How about we just call the police? Leave an anonymous message?"

"No. This message was specifically for me. I have to do this."

Israel smiled. If Kelly had known him better he would have guessed Israel wanted him to say that. Israel sat back and looked out his window. Kelly did the same for a while until he felt Israel's eyes on him.

"It's what I expected," he said.

"What?"

"Stout is Obscured."

"What do you mean—like he's rare?"

"No, I mean even if we were standing right in front of him, we wouldn't see him."

Kelly stared at him.

"There's this... ear, constantly listening for things that don't belong. I know things I'm not supposed to know. Seen things that weren't supposed to be seen. Because of that its heard me and... things happen. People try to kill me sometimes. Sometimes they're not real people."

"What do you mean not real people?" Kelly wasn't buying any of this. Israel was another one of those people full of self-importance. "And what does any of this have to do with finding Stout Roost?"

"Let me finish. The company has given me a sort of *muffler* for lack of a better term that keeps that ear from hearing me. It knows

I'm still around, but it can't hear me well enough to pinpoint me. Makes it harder to find me."

"But not impossible."

One of the tires popped. Israel shook his head at Kelly.

***

She was heavy and he was tired. But he had to keep moving. He was just so hungry, though. His thoughts were foggy, but his daughter tugged on his shirt, tearing off his nipple and pointing at two men standing on the shoulder of the freeway. His mind sharpened somewhat and he said, "I see them... honey."

She giggled and clapped as the two crossed the grassy embankment, to the road, to the gas station. The man followed, shambling as the daughter grunted and kicked for him to move faster, pointing at the two men. He figured she was at least three years old, but she still couldn't speak. He grunted back when he tried to quicken his pace and his ankle snapped. He stepped off of the sidewalk and onto the lot of the gas station.

The man paused, feeling something rise from his stomach.

"Whoa. Down boy," he said, patting his belly. He pushed through the rear door and stood just behind the shorter one, confused.

She had gone quiet, clinging to him and staring into his face. Her eyes were wide and stinking breath fumed out of her mouth.

The man turned around and saw him.

"You okay, buddy?" Kelly asked the man. He looked terrible, like he would faint any moment. In the back of his mind Kelly worried about catching whatever he had, but when the little girl reached for him he took a step back. It sounded more superficial than he would ever admit, but she was really ugly. Stringy hair, wide eyes too close together, a malformed mouth that peeled back to reveal a gummy smile and a scattering of misshapen and crooked dark yellow teeth.

"That's a... nice haircut." The man belched and took an unsteady step forward.

The Ghost Toucher

"Step away." Israel was behind Kelly, pulling him by the shoulder.

"What?" Kelly let Israel pull him back just as the man's face turned dark green. He lunged at Kelly with surprising speed, but his fumbling hand pushed him into a Snickers display.

"Hey, hey, hey—what are you doing over there?" the associate screamed at them, but didn't come over to investigate. "You get out and pay. Right now!" Kelly panicked, kicking and punching at the air until he broke free of the display, stuck on his back like a cardboard turtle shell. The man took a noodly step toward him, the girl giggling and drooling and clapping. Israel slammed the last door of the refrigeration unit into him and he reeled back, cutting his windmilling arm on the shattering glass. He struggled to keep his feet, but more than that it seemed like he was trying to not drop the little girl, clutching onto him and screaming.

Israel pitched the can of soda pop he was holding into the man's good ankle and it gave out with a thin, snapping sound. He plummeted to the floor, landing on his tail bone before his head bounced off the linoleum tile. He was very still. The little girl stood, but it was obvious her legs were too weak and stumpy to walk. She leaned over and shook the man, rubbed her eyes and cried before reaching for Israel.

"Oh, no," he said and turned to yank Kelly to his feet. Israel hustled him up to the front of the store where the associate was still behind the counter.

"What's going on back there?" the associate said.

"Klutz here, tripped and fell into the Snickers display."

"I thought I heard a baby cryin'?"

"Oh yeah, my friend here stumbled into one of those refrigerator doors. Broke the thing—the glass."

"Yer gonna hafta pay fer that."

"How much do we owe?"

"Well I can't exactly ring up a broken door on this thing. Yer gonna hafta wait 'til Dale comes back."

"Hey no problem, but look; we're really in a hurry. Let's say there are two hundred, two fifty Snicker bars in that display." Kelly had passed by that display on the way in. At best there were only fifty. He looked at Israel and saw him leafing through a giant wad of bills. "Let's make it an even three hundred. What's a Snickers these days anyway, a dollar?"

"Th-that sounds right. To me." Kelly could see the man mentally licking his chops.

"Pay the man, Mr. Greene." Israel stuffed the cash back in his pocket and gestured to Kelly. He fished his wallet out of his pocket and pulled out the company card Brimmer had given him. The associate's face fell.

"Hope those don't go to waste." Israel winked. "We're both allergic to peanuts."

"Yeah—no," the associate said, a smile creeping into his face. "I'll make sure they get to a good home."

It took a few minutes to ring up all those Snickers, but as soon as Kelly signed Israel was hustling him out the front door.

"Oh and there's a mess back there we need you to clean up for us. We're really in a hurry."

Kelly looked over and saw a puddle of goo where the man was, but both he and the ugly little girl were gone.

"Hey, you think that little girl's okay?" Kelly asked.

"I'm sure she's fine. Let's get."

They crossed the street and climbed the embankment and got back in the car, flat fixed.

"To hell with this." Mel couldn't even begin to mop up this mess. He couldn't wring it out of the mop and he was just spreading it all over the floor. Some kind of acid—it had half eaten into the floor. Dale had been gone for two hours. If Dale didn't care, why should he? He stepped over the puddle and grabbed up the few Snicker bars that had spilled out of the display and dumped them back in. Mel thought a moment and ran to the back and grabbed an unopened box of Snickers, taking the change out of the take-a-penny-give-a-penny cup and dropped the box in the display too. He picked up the whole thing and went out the back door to his truck, but the bottom of the display fell out before he could put it in the passenger seat.

Mel knelt and began scooping them into the seat, wanting desperately to be long gone before Dale got back, if he was coming at all. He was still drawing unemployment; Mr. Bender had been paying him under the table. He could eat these Snickers himself or sell them.

Yeah. Go out with a Snickers stand and sell them to people driving down the street. Thanks, but no.

He felt someone behind him and spun around, panicked. It was a little girl, crying and crawling real slow in his direction. She was ass-ugly. What kind of baby had pimples? And her legs were really messed up too. Like they'd been broken and never healed right. No wonder she wasn't walking.

Mel could sympathize. He'd had to wear corrective shoes when he was young. He crouched and held his arms out to her.

"Are you lost, kiddo?" He wondered where her mother was. "Where's your home?" She looked old enough to talk, but after her she stopped crying she just said junk like, "Uh-uh-uhh," as she stood on her knees, holding her arms out.

"Oh, you want me to pick you up?" Mel scooped her up in his arms; she was way heavier than she looked. He slid her over onto his hip like his sister did when all her kids were little. Much better. "You wanna sit in my truck and have some candy?" He shivered at the thought of how creepy that seemed, but she nodded. At least she understood English. He sat her down in the passenger seat and she snatched up a Snickers, chomping right through the plastic, before he could get one for her.

"Oh, well, there you go." She tore the rest of the wrapper off and the whole thing in her mouth in two bites. "Hey, slow down. Don't choke on that, okay?"

She giggled.

She must be a brat, he thought. Way too heavy for a kid her age and the way she'd just stuffed that Snickers he could tell she was used to getting her way. He loaded up the rest of the Snickers on the floor of the passenger seat and by the time he was done she had another one unwrapped.

"Take your time on this one, okay?" She held it up to her mouth and he reached as if he were about to take it away. She screamed and swatted at his hand. Brat. Definitely. He'd unload her on the cops as soon as he could. Mel didn't have a child seat, but he fit the belt on her as snug as he could.

He huffed at her after he shut the door and she stuffed the other half of the Snickers bar in her mouth and by the time he slid into the driver's seat she had another unwrapped.

Mel was just about to say something about her unbuckling herself when she stood up and using the seat back to brace herself, walked to him. She gave him a big hug and kissed his cheek with her chocolate-smeared mouth.

He felt himself blush and looked back at her. She had a line of brownish drool on her chin and Mel wiped it off with his bare hand.

"Hey, I have an idea," he said to her, dabbing a tear from his eye. Where'd that come from? "Why don't I drive you to your mommy? Yeah, that sounds better. We can find her, right?" She smiled, clapping and nodding as a mass of chocolate pocked with peanuts came unglued from the roof of her mouth.

***

"Don't you think we should have called an ambulance or something?"

"For what?" Israel asked.

"For that guy. He was sick and he probably threw up that gunk all over the floor."

"That guy tried to attack you."

"He was sick. He was probably delirious."

"But. He was trying to kill you."

"You don't know that. You don't *know* that."

"Okay." Israel stared out the window.

"What?" Kelly asked.

"*What* what?" Israel repeated.

"What is it you're not telling me?"

"It's nothing. If I told you, you wouldn't believe me."

"That's going to stop you *now*?"

Israel shifted in his seat to face him. "It was the girl. She's the master, he was the puppet."

"What are you talking about?"

"You didn't step away from her because she was ugly. You stepped back because you sensed on an unconscious level there was something wrong. She feeds on her host and co-opts his mind. He believes the things he thinks are his ideas, but they're not. I've had run-ins with her before."

"You're absolutely right. I don't believe you." Kelly didn't want anymore of this conversation. "We're coming up on 94," Kelly said.

Israel nodded.

"How do we know it's not too late? What if that article had the time wrong?" He wondered why he couldn't accept what Israel had told him about the little girl, but he believed what he'd seen in the newspaper, despite it not really being there. Maybe he'd reached his saturation point for the impossible. Maybe because that guy at the gas station couldn't have known they were there. Maybe he just didn't trust Israel.

"Because we have our fingers crossed."

"And why is it we haven't called the police?"

"Even if we had his name and description, it's the same as with Stout. He's Obscured; they wouldn't be able to see him."

"Then why will I?"

"You're on the path. You will see him because you're becoming Obscured. Somewhat, anyway. The further you go, the more you'll see."

"Does that happen to everyone who gets on this path?"

"Probably. The nature of humankind is robust."

"I still don't see what any of this has to do with Stout."

"You can think of roaming spirits as lost. Or you can think of them as people who've become Obscured by death and are trying to return. Part of the reason they can't is because they're Obscured in their minds." Israel tapped an index to his temple. "The ones who have accepted death are gone. The rest..." He looked out the window and made an arching motion with his hand, feathering his fingers.

"That article didn't say a dead guy did it."

"I don't know. Living people who are Obscured is rare. That's why it's going to be difficult finding Stout."

"He could just be dead, couldn't he?"

"No. I checked." Kelly wondered how long Israel was going to play make-believe.

The driver pulled into the valet area in front of Harper Hospital. The car crawled up behind a column of other vehicles and Israel waved to her.

"We'll get out here," Israel said to the driver. "Stay close."

"Go get some dinner or something," Kelly said a moment before getting out after Israel.

They weaved between the idling cars as the sun finally set. Kelly wished he had his jacket. The temperature was dropping fast. He followed Israel through the revolving doors and came up behind him, standing in the lobby.

"All right, you're on," Israel said. "Which way do we go?"

"We have to go that way, but we'll need to get past the security guard." Kelly pointed to the middle-aged, dark-skinned man in a uniform at the mouth of a hallway to their right. He was sitting and leaned over on his elbows at a podium with a Christmas wreath by the wall.

"I.D.?" he said to them as they walked up.

"I'm here to see my Aunt Betty?" Israel's voice was suddenly filled with angst and worry. Kelly thought he'd make for a good actor.

"You gotta go to the information desk to get a visitor's pass." Israel nodded and turned to where he was pointing; a woman behind a low-sitting desk with a line of people in front of it. Israel made a drawn out huff and walked to the back.

"I'm with... I'm with him." Kelly said when the guard's tired eyes swirled on him. He scratched his salt-and-pepper head and said nothing.

Kelly stood next to Israel, who seemed to be concentrating on the back of the head of the man in front of them. He had on baggy jeans sagged down to his thighs, gray puffy coat and gray Lions hat over a nest of dreads, standing with one of his oversized Timberland boots propped up on the wheelchair in front of him.

The person at the front stepped out of line and walked down the wide hallway leading to Receiving. They all shuffled a few steps, including the guy in front of them who pushed the chair up, keeping his boot up at the same time.

Israel's eyes narrowed to slits and Kelly was about to say something when he belched. Israel began rubbing his stomach and chewing at the tip of his thumb.

After a moment or two the man in front of them made a sound like, "Hmmmp!" before ducking his head and pushing the chair out of the line.

"Whatchoo doin'!" the old woman yelled at him, throwing her arms up as if there was something she could catch onto. He picked up speed and Kelly saw Israel slide up into the empty space they'd left. There were only three people in front of them.

"What was that about?" Kelly asked. Israel shrugged and went back to worrying at his thumb, this time the other hand was tucked under his arm. The man in front of them was on his cell phone, talking a lot louder than was necessary.

"Yeah, I know," he said. "But if she doesn't listen, she doesn't listen." The man laughed. It was an obnoxious sound that was a cross between the bark of a dog and the hiss of a snake. "What was that?" He stuck his finger in his ear. "No-no. Not two-thirty. *Not* two-thirty. No, I said no. I said no. Wait a minute!" The man wandered around and eventually through the doors and outside where he continued yelling at the person on the other end.

Another person got out of line leaving only one more in front of Israel and Kelly.

"Uhhh, I completely forgot what I came here for," the old woman said. She had on a long winter coat with slippers and her frizzy grey hair clung to her head. Instead of moving, she held her spot as the beleaguered-looking heavyset woman watched with half-interested eyes. "Oh, my son... is here."

"And what's his name?"

"Oo. I can't remember."

She turned and looked at Israel, who was scratching his thighs furiously.

"Just a minute!" She turned back.

"Are you having a bad day, Ma'am?" The clerk's head tipped from one side to the other.

"Gee, I don't think so. This is so strange. *Robert!* No, that's not his *name*."

The Ghost Toucher

"Why don't we start with your name, Ma'am." The clerk's eyes flashed over to the security guard. As tired as he seemed he was alert. He was already halfway over.

"Gladys Trombley. No. That's not my name. I don't know a Gladys. At least, I don't think I do."

"Ma'am, is there something I can assist you with?" the security guard asked. Kelly took a subconscious step back. Tired he may well have been before, but the guy had a presence when he needed it. At least six-foot three and his deep voice came all the way up from his knees.

She swiveled her head around.

"Danny!"

"'Scuse me?"

"What took you so *long*? I have been down here so long just *waiting* on you."

Kelly thought if the man's eyebrows went any higher they'd crawl across his hairline.

"Mrs. Danvers!" Two men in scrubs light-jogged down the hallway to where they were. "There you are." They both had on badges. Dr. Miller and Dr. Dave. "You can't just wander away like that, Mrs. Danvers. We were worried about you."

"But I found my son."

The Indian-looking one looked up at the security guard and gave a nervous smile.

"We'll take care of her from here, Hank."

She mumbled in protest as they shuffled her into a wheelchair a third man was standing behind and a moment later they had disappeared into the shrinking dinnertime traffic.

Kelly tapped Israel's arm and stepped in front of him.

"Uh, hi. We're both former employees and we need to get our last paychecks from payroll down the hall."

The clerk nodded and plucked a sharpie out of a pen cup and wrote "Visitor" and the date on two day-glo green passes. Israel and Kelly took them and put them on.

"Okay, so we're looking for a man, preferably disgruntled," Israel began as they walked past the guard station. "I'll see if there's a paging system, you try to find that hall."

"What if I find him?" Kelly said.

Israel thought a moment. He grabbed Kelly's hand and roughly rubbed their palms together.

"Make a fist. Dig your nails into your palm and I'll come."

Kelly nodded and turned down a narrow hall.

"Wait a minute—why do we need to split up?" He looked around, but Israel was already gone. Kelly continued down the hall and was rounding a corner when he stepped on the heel of the man in front of him.

"Sorry, man I—" Kelly looked at the man in white who only turned and nodded at him, but the giant sunglasses rising above his eyebrows and shaved head told him he was looking at the terrorist.

Something on Kelly's face must have given him away as Brown, according to his nametag, turned to sprint away.

"Hey! Stop!" Kelly said and barreled his shoulder into the man's back, pulling him down to the floor. People walked around them, continuing their business as if the two men weren't there. Brown was thin, but wiry, and had easily flipped over and landed on his butt. He began punching Kelly in the back and hip and Kelly let go with one hand to try to ward off some of the shots. Brown slipped a hand under his armpit and flipped Kelly off, punching him in the solar plexus as he lay on his side.

He turned over onto his knees as Kelly wheezed in pain. He couldn't just lay there and watch while Brown walked away. Kelly climbed off the floor and hooked Brown's foot, sending him sprawling into a woman in a purple, ankle-length winter coat. The bag she was carrying from the Quiznos just down the hall flew up into the air and spilled its contents. Brown's sunglasses skittered across the floor right underneath the foot of a heavyset bearded man in scrubs. The bearded man looked down, made a face, and continued on.

Kelly was barely on his feet and about a yard away from Brown as he was drawing himself off the floor. The woman in the ankle-length winter coat shook her head, grabbed her bag and slapped the sub and chips back into it. She didn't seem to see Brown right next to her.

"You stop... whatever it is you're about to do." It hurt when he spoke. Kelly wondered if Brown had broken one of his ribs. The man on the floor spun his head around and snarled at Kelly.

His eyes were wrong.

For a second he forgot about his pain. What he was looking at couldn't be real. Brown's eyes had misshapen globs for irises. Like eggs that had just been dropped onto a plate except they were completely black and the edges wriggled.

Brown hopped onto the balls of his feet and pulled a tucked revolver from his waistband and pointed it. The strength left Kelly's legs; they were much too close for him to even think about diving for cover.

Kelly gritted his teeth, ready to go down fighting when a squawk came from overhead.

"*Oh I guess it would be nice!*" a raspy voice sang. "*If I could touch ya body! I know not everybody, has got a body like you-uu-uu!*"

Was that Israel?

Brown cocked his head to the side. Most of the people around them slowed, turning their heads to the PA speaker or looking around for it.

"*But I gotta think twice! Before I give my heart away! I know 'bout all the games you play! Because I play them too!*"

Kelly realized he wasn't shot and he looked back at Brown, who was looking off into space and mouthing the words. He leapt at him, batting the gun out of his loose fingers. It bounced off the wall and clattered across the floor, a woman in a white puffy coat kicking it unintentionally as she walked.

Kelly landed three good blows to Brown's midsection, tiny plosions escaping from the thin man's mouth with each punch. Brown brought his elbows down into Kelly's back, driving him to his knees. Kelly began to stand, looked up to see Brown looking around for his gun. They locked eyes.

His fists were balled tight, but when the man pulled a red vial from his pocket he charged, thrusting the heels of his palms into Brown's midsection. Brown windmilled his arms, backpedaling to keep his feet. Kelly's heart leapt in his chest as he saw the vial clenched in his hand. Brown caught his balance and punched him in the mouth, driving Kelly back a foot or two, then blasted him with a quick kick to the groin.

Kelly's vision went white and he doubled over. Israel's singing had stopped at some point but Kelly couldn't guess when. Long, skinny arms slipped around his head as he coughed and tried to get the wind back in his lungs. Kelly punched and gouged at whatever body part he could reach but Brown wouldn't let go. It felt like Brown's vise-like grip on his skull was tightening and then it went completely slack. Israel was stuffing something back in his pocket as Brown crumpled to the floor.

"Thanks," Kelly coughed.

"No problem."

They stood and watched the man a moment, motionless on the floor. People continued to walk around them like they weren't there.

"I don't think he's breathing," Kelly said.

"She's gotta gun!" Israel and Kelly looked behind them at a woman who stared at the revolver in the flats of her palms before two burly orderly types dive-tackled her.

"I think we better get out of here." Israel tapped him on the shoulder. There was a little girl tugging on her mother's jacket and pointing at them. The mother was pinning her child and herself against the wall, ignoring and protecting the little girl at the same time.

"Wait a sec."

Kelly fished through Brown's pockets and pulled out an ID. Suelo Brown had a medium sized afro in his picture and normal-looking irises. He slid the vial out of his clenched hand and spotted something scrawled on his palm. Kelly turned it over and saw the name "Bruce Strong" in an almost illegible scrawl.

"We gotta get out of here, quick," Israel said.

"Okay, this way." Kelly slapped the sub out of a man's hand who was in scrubs, standing at the front of a small crowd. He led Israel farther down the hall into a remodeled-looking lobby area. They turned right and went past a row of elevators and into another hall. Kelly pushed through a door and into a short hall with a view on a parking lot outside and they rounded onto some descending stairs.

"Oh my God!" a woman screamed behind them before the door closed. "Someone call security!"

They had to stop at the bottom of the stairs while a young, muscular man pushed a giant bin of dirty laundry past them and then turned around a corner, heading down another hallway to a pair of weather-worn double doors that opened up into the small lot they'd seen from the window upstairs.

"You know where we are?"

"Yeah," Kelly said, pointing ahead of them. "That's Mack right there. Call the driver and tell her to come around. We'll meet her at the corner."

Israel called and told her where to go. By the time security burst through the door they were in the car and speeding away to I-75.

Old friends

"You know we have to find this guy," Kelly said, touching his sore jaw. "He might be in on it."

"Already with you." Israel had his cell in his hands, plucking away with his thumbs. "I have one Bruce Strong on thirty-two twenty-three Roselawn on the East Side." He tapped on the driver's headrest. "You got that?"

She nodded and the engine roared as they swerved into the passing lane. The freeways were clear giving them a straight shot there.

It was dark by the time they reached Strong's neighborhood. It was in a quiet nest of blocks just removed from a busy and dilapidated Seven Mile Road. Very few of the houses were boarded up and the ones that were empty still were well kempt. They were all large homes even though they looked similar apart from their color schemes, with neatly trimmed lawns and hedges dividing one from the other.

"Hey, that's it up there," Israel said. Kelly wondered how he spotted the address in the dark, but looked and saw a heavyset man standing in his doorway, dressed up in a black suit with a white shirt and bright blue tie. The driver stopped in front of the house and Kelly and Israel climbed out.

"What do we say to him?"

"Not sure. I have no idea where this Suelo Brown thing is going, but it's something we can't just leave. Just back me up." Israel turned to the man on the doorstep. "Mr. Strong?"

The Ghost Toucher

The man turned and looked at them, his cheeks pink with exertion and a trickle of sweat at his forehead in the pale blue street light. He had a black trench coat over his arm. He was light-complected and freckled with large dark eyes. He was short and squat; a good hundred fifty pounds overweight.

"How can I help you, sir?" He seemed cautious at seeing two strangers on his walkway.

"Tom Israel." He extended his hand for a shake, beaming a smile and bright-eyed. "Did you have any business at the hospital today?"

Strong's already red face darkened even more.

"Oh, you gentlemen are from the hospital." His face relaxed and immediately tightened back up. "I just couldn't do it—you're not gonna tell my wife, are you?"

"Well, we don't *want* to," Kelly said, nodding at Israel. He had to clench his fists to keep from cupping his aching testicles. "But we have to ask why you didn't show up for your appointment."

"Look, I know I need the surgery, but I'm just not ready. Y'know, I gotta get my mind right for it."

"Bruce!" a woman called from inside the house. "I'm not goin'! This dress don't fit right!"

"C'mon, Earlie." Strong swiped at his sweaty forehead. "Take ya time, take ya time."

"Mr. Strong, I don't have to tell you the seriousness of *not* having the procedure done."

"I know, I know. And it's a same-day procedure—you do it all the time. The doctor told me all that. It's just... my daddy and my grandfather both died in the hospital." Strong shook his head. "I can't get my head over it."

"Mr. Strong, I understand your concerns. But you should be relieved to know we have made huge leaps in technology over the past few years and there's never been a safer time to have it done. As a matter-of-fact, Harper boasts the lowest mortality rate for this particular procedure out of the whole Midwest region. And that *includes* Cleveland. Why don't you speak to one of our counselors? Here, call this number." Israel handed him a card and Strong quickly shoved it into his shirt pocket.

"All right, Bruce, I'm comin' down!"

"Baby, don't forget your purse!"

"I'm goin' back up!"

"Look. Earlie don't even know I was supposed to have the surgery. I'll reschedule, I promise, but I need you guys to get up out of here right now before she comes down."

"Understood." Strong shook both their hands and they turned to head back to the car, but Israel turned back. "Do you know someone by the name of Suelo Brown, Mr. Strong?"

"No. Why?"

"He died at the hospital today. Had your name written on his hand."

"Anybody you can think of have anything against you?"

"I'd tell you no, but you should ask some of my tenants." Strong laughed.

"Where's your property?"

"Highland Park. A little place on the corner of Tennyson and Brush. I've been evicting them for three months now."

"Okay, call that number, Mr. Strong. Get rescheduled."

"Okay. You guys have a blessed night."

"Hey, you too." Israel winked. "And no strenuous activity, if you know what I'm saying." Bruce blushed again.

They sank back in the car.

"What card did you give him?" Kelly asked.

"I'm not sure. I swiped a stack of them back at the hospital. You wanna check out that house?"

"Not really, but we have nothing better to go on."

"Okay, first thing tomorrow morning."

Israel gave the driver the address to the hotel.

"You can't go back home," he said to Kelly. "At least not yet."

"Why not?"

"My gut. It could be nothing, but I want to play it as safe as possible."

"I didn't sign on for this. I almost got shot today—I'm not looking for a repeat of that."

"Look, I can only keep you as protected as you let me. Finding Roost isn't going to be easy and you had to have realized there could be danger involved. The guy is missing after all."

"Okay, but just for tonight."

"Right."

They made it to the hotel in less than a half hour and Israel told the driver to be waiting for them at seven in the morning. Israel only stopped by the front desk to pick up a keycard for Kelly. Apparently, he must have anticipated him staying here.

Their rooms were both on the second floor, but Israel's was a few doors down from his. They said goodnight and with a swipe Kelly was inside. As soon as he saw the bed he was exhausted. He crashed on the bed and was asleep in less than a minute.

Kelly dreamed of a distant figure. A man. Kelly couldn't see his face, just a silhouette. He was petting some kind of animal, also in silhouette, a dog maybe, except it had a really big head. It nipped the man's hand and in an instant he was holding it in the air by the scruff.

He held up a finger on his other hand. Either it was a really long finger or it had a really long nail. He poked that finger into the dog-thing's belly as it wriggled around in his grip. Its legs kicked even more feverishly and it whimpered right before it popped.

Kelly's phone rang. He popped up, the aftertaste of a dream still in his mind. Something about a man and a dog. He picked up the phone and hung up as the automated voice chimed that this was his morning wake-up call. The fog slowly cleared from his mind and the dream was forgotten. He met Israel down in the lobby twenty minutes later and saw he hadn't changed his clothes either.

"Take us to Highland Park," Israel said once they'd gotten in the car.

Sleeping on it didn't make Kelly want to go back there any more than he did yesterday. They took the road and within a few minutes were back on Woodward. They drove south, Israel thankfully silent as Kelly tried his best not to think of Martha and the last time he was on Tennyson.

"That's Albert's house," Kelly thought he'd said under his breath.

"'Scuse me?" Israel and Kelly climbed out the car.

"Oh. Nothing. It's a nice house is all."

Israel shrugged. Albert's house looked like he remembered it. He'd never been inside, but it was always the nicest looking house on the block. Mint green and white wouldn't have been his choice for a house's colors, but it had always had the feel like someone cared about how it looked.

Well, it almost looked the same. They walked up the cracked walkway, between a browning, weed-infested lawn and onto the little concrete porch. The white aluminum siding had dents and scratches here and there, not at all like Kelly remembered.

A skinny dark-skinned man appeared behind the screen door before Israel could knock.

"Yes-yes," he said with some sort of accent Kelly couldn't identify. "Please come in."

"Your home is owned by Strong Properties?" Kelly said as the man walked away.

"Yes. I must show you. Please come." They followed the man into the dark of the house, only seeing the white of his sleeveless t-shirt.

"I didn't see his eyes. Were his eyes okay?" Israel asked.

"I think so. He moved too quick."

"Please!" the man said from somewhere inside.

Kelly's eyes adjusted after a moment. The windows were covered by thick blankets nailed above them. To their left was a large television next to a wall with what looked like African art, paintings and statues in various shades of black and brown. There were stairs to the right with a black leather couch on the adjacent wall. A heavyset teenaged girl was sprawled across it, apparently sleeping.

"It smells like dog in here." Kelly looked around, but only saw clumps of animal hair in corners. His throat felt scratchy. They walked across the deep brown carpet, through the linoleum-tiled kitchen to where the man was standing by a door with a combination lock on it.

Everything in here was dirty. The stink of sour garbage wafted from the sink, half-filled with cloudy water and dishes with dark streaks on them. No wonder Strong wanted them out. Kelly looked at Israel, who either didn't mind or hadn't noticed from the look on his face.

"I cannot do like this," the man said, taking off the lock. He pointed downstairs and Kelly and Israel peaked down the stairs leading into a well of black. Israel flicked a switch inside that lit nothing.

"Why would I go down there?"

"Please. I cannot do. You must fix—you must fix." He kept pointing down the stairs.

"But it's dark down there," Kelly said. The man circled around the little island in the kitchen, snatched open a drawer, fished through it, and brought back a pen flashlight. He handed it to Israel.

"Do you know who we are?" Israel asked.

"You are from power company. Power is out."

"Riiiight! I apologize, Mr.—?"

"Jeremy." He didn't say 'Jeremy' but that's the closest Kelly could come to saying it.

"Well Mr. Greene, let's see if you can get that power back on, shall we?"

Israel flicked on the light and took the first step. It creaked, but held underneath him. The light danced around in his hand and he turned back to Kelly.

"Be careful. It looks like somebody took a bowling ball to some of these stairs."

Kelly nodded and followed with a hand on Israel's shoulder. Despite the cool of outside it was sweltering down here. Considering what he'd already seen yesterday his mind saw things in the dark he hoped weren't really there.

When they reached the bottom something skittered across the floor.

"That was me," Israel said. "Must have been a toy truck or something I stepped on." They stood there, looking around at whatever the little circle of light illuminated.

"Why isn't *he* down here?" Kelly whispered.

"The customer is allowed to be afraid of the dark. Well there's the power box."

The Ghost Toucher

Israel had stopped the light on a metal square with its cover open. They walked over to it and Kelly checked the breaker switches until he found the one in question. He flipped it back and forth.

"I don't think we'll need the home office."

"You can fix?" the man called from at the top of the stairs.

"Yeah, no, we're all over it," Israel said. "You just hold tight."

"Well, you're the one who said there's a point to all of this," Kelly said. "Why are we in the creepiest basement in the city?"

Israel flipped the main power switch back and forth.

"Wa-la." He turned, swinging the light to and fro, highlighting the basement. Surprisingly, it didn't stink down here. It actually smelled kind of fruity.

"Hello?" a female voice called. Israel and Kelly jumped. The light crawled over to a makeshift curtain that went from the ceiling to the floor. Kelly looked upstairs and saw the man was gone, but he'd left the door open.

"Who is that?" Israel said.

"Who are *you*?" the woman replied, agitation in her voice. "Hugo, did you leave the power men down here? Hugo? I swear that man is afraid of his own shadow."

Israel walked over to the curtain and pulled it back.

"Man, you are *fat*." Kelly came over to pull him away, but he got a peak of the woman's leg and it was pretty big. Israel stepped aside so he could see all of her. Most of her.

She was easily a quarter ton- Kelly had no idea how much more. Instead of clothes, she had a several blankets draped over her flank as no one blanket was enough. Her body was spread out over three mattresses pushed together with no bed sheets on them. She reached up a globby arm and flicked on a tiny bed light overhead. Atop the many chins was a face that may have been pretty once, but anything attractive about her was drowned in rolls upon rolls of excess flesh.

"Kelly Greene?"

He pulled his gaze away from the exposed calf draping off the edge of mattress and looked at her. The face didn't look familiar, but...

"It's me—Sendra Butler."

The Ghost Toucher

Kelly didn't remember that name at all, but he could fake it.

"Oh hey, Sendra. From Spanish 2?" He'd had Spanish 2 with everyone. Especially considering he'd had to take it twice.

"And Algebra, and Geometry, and Early American History, and Biology, and PhysEd." Whoa, she *really* remembered him. She giggled.

"Sendra, the power guys down there?"

"No, Hugo, just a couple guys I went to school with!"

"You want your tea now?"

"In a minute! I'm still working on my toenails!" To Kelly, "So, how you been?"

"Pretty good. You?" He wondered how in the world she covered the wide expanse from her hands to her feet in order to even reach her toenails.

"Having a little chest pain today. It's crazy, heart problems don't run in my family. At least it's better than yesterday."

"Ohhh, sorry to hear that." She waved off his mock concern. If she was unaware of how big she was Kelly wasn't going to tell her. He was certain he hadn't known this woman. There was only one girl who'd been more than six feet tall and he remembered Danielle. If he had known Sendra in high school she'd grown up and out since then.

"That your little girl upstairs?" Israel said.

"Yeah," Sendra said, eyeing him. "She's the reason why I vanished Senior year."

"Oh, sorry. Sendra this is—"

"Greg Israel. Kelly and I work together."

"Really? Where at?"

"I don't—" Kelly began.

"At the Network. You know that Stout Roost guy? He's *missing*."

"Oh, I watch that show all the time," Sendra said, holding her pudgy hands up to her mouth. All notions of suspicion had been erased by a hint of scandal. The extra flab pooled beneath her arms made her look like a giant baby. "That and ChíChé. I *love* ChíChé. Speaking of..." Sendra turned and reached for a small television hidden to the side of her. She set it on top of her belly and flicked it on. She brushed her hands together and let them fall to either side of her. She belched, patting her fingers against her chest. It smelled like burnt plastic.

"You know who I used to watch this with all the time?" Sendra said. "Your mother. Right up until her surgery last year I came over to see her every day. Is she doing better since the cancer?"

Cancer? Kelly didn't know anything about that.

"Yeah. Yeah."

"You know, I meant to offer my condolences about Martha—"

"No, that's all right," Kelly interrupted. "Thank you, though."

"I wish I could have been there for you, but Hugo and I were on a cruise. Last time I'll ever do that. You never met anyone in your life more sensitive about being on the water." She snorted.

"We need to get rolling," Israel said, checking an imaginary watch. Sendra surprisingly was able to lean up, the television falling into the cushions of her thighs and she grabbed Kelly's hand. Her hands were dry and cold.

"It was so good to see you again. Tell your mother I miss her, okay?"

"Of course. It's good to see you too."

"Could you tell Hugo I'm ready for my tea?"

"Yeah."

Sendra started patting her chest again with her fingers after she sat back and hefted the TV back onto her belly.

They stepped out and let the curtain drape back. As they climbed the stairs Kelly remembered that there was this one girl in school who knew all kinds of things about him. His friends would tell him about her, how she would talk about how close they were and vacations they had gone on together and how she ate at his house all the time and he slept over at hers. He'd never met this girl and if she'd been around him she'd never spoken to him. He wondered if that was Sendra.

Hugo was perched on a footstool in the living room, watching television.

"Hey, the missus is ready for that tea," Israel said.

"Power back on?" Hugo asked.

Israel gestured to the television.

"Yeah."

Hugo got up as they went out the door. His daughter was still plopped on the couch, dead to the world.

"Let's go see your mom," Israel said.

***

"Where is Mother?" it asked in Hugo's native language.

"She is... downstairs." Even though he still had his accent, Hugo hadn't spoken it in years. He set the tea down with shaky hands.

It looked at him and somewhere far away at the same time.

"No, she is not."

"She couldn't be gone. She cannot move."

"She is gone."

"She has not—oh." Hugo understood. His hand trembled slightly, rattling the tea cup on the saucer. He teared up at the sudden realization his wife was dead. He sat on the end of the couch. It was going to be soon, but he wasn't ready for this soon.

"What... what will you do?"

"The same as your people have for hundreds of years. Survive."

It was staring at Hugo's daughter.

"No. Please. She is just a child." He switched to English. Strange that it was more comfortable.

"Hugo, I cannot inhabit my own people. Your brother Bruno carried me here so that I may live. You have not nurtured me this long just to let me perish?"

"No, I..."

"Then with your permission."

"I did not want this for her. She is just a child." Tears streamed from his eyes.

"We all must sacrifice. I did not die those many years ago for my own sake." He took Hugo by the shoulders. "I will take her to bride and she will be by my side for eternity, to be adored by all. What would you have better for her?"

Hugo nodded after a moment, swiped his eyes with the heels of his hands. He stood next to the couch, looking down on his sleeping daughter for several breaths before taking her hand between his, rubbing her fingers against his grizzled cheek. She stirred.

"She will be yours for a time yet." It squeezed him between the neck and shoulder as if trying to comfort him. Hugo knew it was incapable of empathy, but he must obey. Fresh tears sprang from his eyes.

"I give... my *child* to you... of my own free will." He collapsed to his knees and began moaning, rocking back and forth with his daughter's hand pressed to his face. Its form shattered into thousands and thousands of miniscule insect-like things that floated, flew and skated across the carpet in her direction.

"Daddy, what's wrong?" He wished she hadn't wakened, but felt her hand on his head. He closed his eyes and clung to that hand as they swarmed her, crawled over her, sank into her. He'd seen this once and couldn't bear it again. She screamed, spat and grunted, thrashing about before it was over a few seconds later.

There was a giant whooshing sound and Hugo could feel it behind him again. His daughter spat out imaginary bits of insect.

"Hello, Mother," it said.

She screamed again.

***

"Just a minute!" Ma called from somewhere inside the house. Israel's hand dropped away from the doorbell. A moment later a withered old woman appeared in the doorway in a bathrobe and thick bifocals that stretched above her eyebrows. This couldn't be Kelly's mother. She was just so *tiny*. She still had the high cheekbones and the hawkish nose and smooth medium brown skin. Her long jet black hair was swept back from her face and piled on top of her head, neatly held in place with two antique-looking hairpins.

"Hey, Ma."

"Kelly!" She pulled the latch and threw open the door, grabbing her son with surprising speed and strength, grabbing him around the waist. He settled his arms over her little body, stooping into an awkward and uncomfortable hug, being careful not to squeeze. She tipped her head back and puckered her lips and Kelly leaned down so they could peck each other's cheeks.

She slapped him.

"Where have you been?"

"Martha... the kids—I—"

"Poo. You're not the only one who grieved. Why you punish your mother so only the Man Upstairs knows."

Kelly shot Israel a mock-dirty look that dissolved into a big grin.

Ma stepped away from Kelly and looked him up and down before turning to Israel.

"Well don't just stand there," she said. "Who's your friend?"

"Oh. Uh, Ma, this is Israel. Israel, this is my mother."

"You can call me Ma Perdy. Everyone does." She slid over and shook his hand. "He's a handsome one. I had a few white boys in my day, y'know." Israel's cheeks turned fire red and Kelly's stomach lurched. "You boys come on in. I just made a wheatberry fruit medley."

The three of them filed through the living room, walking over the thick brown shag carpet then the linoleum tiled floor of the kitchen. Israel and Kelly sat at the table while she fished around inside the refrigerator. All the smells were still here like Kelly remembered. A thick, earthy smell he gradually stopped noticing the longer he was here. He found himself smiling as he took in several deep breaths.

She set out two non-matching bowls with likewise spoons before them before scooping out two lumps of a scarlet-colored, thin-looking jelly substance with what looked like seeds in it. Israel began downing it and was more than halfway done before Kelly had eaten his first spoonful.

It was semi-sweet, the seed-looking things spongy against his tongue. Kelly found himself scanning for some of his standby hiding spots for things he didn't want to eat.

"How do you like it?" she said to them both. It wasn't really a question, merely a prompting for them to compliment her on yet another successful dish.

"Good." Kelly managed his best possible smile while he swallowed.

"Ma'am, this is very good. Could I have some more?"

"Anything for you, cutie." She winked at Israel and dropped a couple more spoonfuls of the goop into his bowl. She turned to Kelly. "You?"

"No, not for me yet."

She put the big bowl back in fridge and sat down with a glass of milk in her hands.

"So how have you been, Ma?"

"Oh, so-so. I had the cancer last year. I had to spend some time in the hospital after they cut it out of me."

"I'm so sorry to hear that." Israel squeezed her hand and she smiled at him.

"Oh, it's okay."

"So what else is going on? Perry still around?"

"Yeah, she comes around every so often. Everybody's asked about you."

"Oh. I've just been involving myself in work. As a matter of fact, that's why we're in the neighborhood. We were down the street at Albert's house."

"Oh, that's where the African girl lives now. Well, she's not African but her husband is."

"I don't know. His accent was Jamaican or something, it sounded like."

"You went to high school with her, didn't you?"

"Uh, yeah. I don't think I ever met her, though."

"She used to come down here for a while. I haven't seen her in—ohhhh, three months now? Why were you down there?"

"Well, the Board hired Israel to find this guy who's the host of one of the shows on our network. I guess they want me to tag along, keep him honest."

"It's much more involved in that," Israel interrupted. "Your son has a special skill set that will be of great use in finding the missing man."

"What show?"

"Sorry Ma'am?"

"Ma Perdy," she corrected. "What show does he host?"

"*The Ghost Toucher.*"

"Oh, I *love* that show! I record it so I can watch the ChíChé, but right after that I watch it." She lowered her voice to a conspiratorial whisper. "He's missing? Oh my, what do you think happened?"

"Well, I'm not really supposed to say, but considering you're my partner's mother and all, I'll tell you. We think it might have something to do with all the women he's been with. He's a real womanizer."

"Oooooooo. I bet it takes one to know one." She jabbed in Israel's direction with her elbow. Kelly rolled his eyes.

"Well... let's say I've had my share."

"Kelly, when are you going to get back on that horse?"

"Ma, I'm not ready for any of that."

"It's been three years. You know Martha'd want you to move on."

"*Ma!*" Kelly stood up.

"All right. All right. Calm down. I'm sorry, baby." He took his seat and she rubbed his knee. "It's just I want you to be happy."

"I'm fine how I am. Can we not talk about this?"

She smiled at him. "You know, your face right now reminds me of the first time I saw you. Your cheeks were so red, like you ran from the other side of the world." She turned back to Israel. "Did I tell you this story?"

"No," Israel leaned forward in his chair.

"Ma, you didn't know him before a few minutes ago."

"Oh hush, you. You don't want me to talk about your wife, fine. But you showing up on my doorstep *is* my business.

"Anyway, as you may have guessed, I'm a little too old to be Kelly's mother by birth. James and I adopted him when he was three."

"I'm sorry, Ma'am—Ma Perdy, but you're not in your fifties?"

"Heavens no! I'm eighty-three. Kelly will be thirty-two in December. James and I had had a son, but he passed on when he was five, God rest him. We tried, but we just couldn't have any more. One day I just got on my knees and prayed to God to send me another baby. I didn't care if he was healthy or not. I just wanted another little boy. Less than a month later this one rang my doorbell in nothing but his under drawers."

"Oh God," Kelly said.

"I just knew at that moment he was ours. Knew it in my heart. We called the police and they sent a squad car down and someone from protective services came too. Neither one of us had any kind of record so they decided to let him stay with us until his parents could be found. But nobody ever came forward."

"Did they ever figure out what happened?"

"No. Kelly could barely speak, didn't even know his name. So we gave him our first son's name. He had this little rock thing, shaped like a horse shoe. As a matter of fact—" She got up and scuttled from the kitchen into what had once been the dining room. It had been converted into a bedroom/TV room because she couldn't go upstairs anymore. Kelly heard her rummaging around, curious himself. As many times as he'd heard the story told, he didn't remember anything about a rock.

"It was just so pretty I kept it and put it away. For years it just stayed in my little jewelry box." She came back in the room with a little necklace with a thing at the end of it. "James put it on a chain, but he passed before we gave it to you." She put it around Kelly's neck.

"Thanks, Ma."

"It's yours—you should have it."

He held it in his palm and examined it. It was shiny like a tooth, but pockmarked and deep yellow-orange. It was curved into a horse shoe shape, both ends blunted with deep, fingerprint-looking grooves on their surfaces. It felt cold and wet against his palm, but his fingers came away dry after he touched it.

"What do you think that is?" Israel asked, looking at Kelly. He had a look on his face.

"Who knows? I would have said an animal's tooth, but how could it have been in its mouth? Besides, that's not a tooth like I've ever seen. Not good for grinding food or tearing anything."

"Almost like it would be decorative." Kelly wondered if Israel was trying to tell him something. He let it pass for the time being.

The subject changed to his mother's surgery and they all had a cup of coffee. She still had hers black with no sugar. Kelly never understood how or why she did that.

He finally made the move to leave.

"Well Ma, we really need to get going. Gotta check up on a few leads before the day's done."

"Okay," she said. "It's good seeing you. Make sure you come back. Don't forget about us."

"I won't."

They kissed and hugged and Kelly was grossed out when she gave Israel even a chaste kiss. She watched them as they climbed back in the Parke Car and waved as they drove away.

Kelly let his eyes wander over the for sale signs that stood in many of the lawns as they drove down the street.

"Hold it."

"What?" Israel said. The driver slowed in the middle of the street.

"Gayle Hills."

"Where's that?"

"Not where. Who." Kelly pointed to one of the signs. "Some snot-nosed jerk I went to school with. Ninety-eight pound weakling territory. Went out of his way to make everybody hate him." He said to the driver. "Hold it right here."

Kelly got out of the car and walked over to a white for sale sign with red lettering in the middle of a lawn. 'Gayle Hills Holdings,' it read.

"You said this is all connected somehow, right?" Kelly said after Israel joined him.

"Yeah."

"Then we need to go here." Kelly pointed at the sign. "I've wanted to punch this guy in the face for seventeen years."

"Wow. Never fancied you for the bully type."

"No. You wouldn't understand. He only looked like the kind of kid you felt sorry for. He wore the bad clothes, he was nerdy, he didn't fit in anywhere, but he was far worse than any bully I ever met."

"OK. I'm with you. We'll go see him. But why does he catch your eye?"

They walked back to the car.

"Hardly anybody is selling houses in this market. Especially in this city. Look around; no fewer than a half dozen boarded up houses on this street alone and this guy has the nuts to try to sell even one house here. These for sale signs are a red flag for something wrong."

"Good enough for me." Israel googled the phone number and came up with an address. "G.H.H. is a couple blocks away."

Back to school

He navigated the driver to Thompson Elementary; a school Kelly and Gayle had gone to when they were kids. It had been closed after they finished the fourth grade and they went on to Barber Middle School. Gayle had transferred midway through the fifth but they had both started at kindergarten here. The imprint of the letters was still visible and just beneath them was a black sign with gold lettering reading 'G.H. Holdings'.

"That's gotta be it." Kelly snorted.

They pulled in and the driver found a spot up front. Kelly and Israel walked past several bushes Kelly lining an expansive blue-green lawn. The wooden playground equipment was all but destroyed or missing; a few pieces of log stuck out of the bare earth like broken teeth. Kelly wondered why he'd left it standing. The house just outside of the fenced-in area had a brown-green, patchy lawn and a roof that looked ready to slide off. The building itself looked almost the same as he remembered as a child except the old metal and glass front doors had been replaced with two big copper doors.

"Looks like he's done well for himself," Israel said.

"Yeah, well, he's still in Highland Park."

Kelly pulled open the heavy door and they went inside. They walked through the vestibule before they entered the building proper. Even though the décor was drastically changed, Kelly remembered there was the cafnasitorium to the left, the principle's office and a hallway leading to classes to the right. They turned right, walking past four leather seats encircling a glass coffee table. The concrete walls had been covered with marble paneling and the hallway came to a T-intersection.

Kelly pointed to the door on the right. "That was Mrs. Buer's room. She was my kindergarten teacher. Mrs. Simion's room was somewhere upstairs. If I remember right Mrs. Malfroid, Mrs. Huddleston and Mrs. Villareal are all upstairs too."

"Are?" Israel asked.

Kelly looked sheepish. "Were. I never got why they closed this place. After the original Thompson burned down this was built and it was the newest school in the district."

"Ah. Fascinating." Kelly got the picture. Enough with the memory lane.

They walked past the classrooms, most of them still had tiny desks and chairs scattered around. Many of the rooms had been graffitied and it looked like a few of them were in the process of being painted over. For all intents and purposes, the place was empty.

"Were there any cars in the parking lot?" Kelly asked.

"Don't think so. Let's go upstairs."

Kelly followed Israel who outpaced him, taking the stairs two and three at a time.

"HOW MAY I HELP YOU?" a booming female voice called over the PA system. Israel and Kelly stopped, looking around for someone else. "ARE YOU IN NEED OF REAL ESTATE SERVICES? A MORTGAGE? ARE YOU BUYING OR SELLING A HOME?"

"Is she talking to us?" Kelly whispered.

"YES. I AM TALKING TO YOU." There had to be cameras all around.

"Um, we're looking for Gayle Hills?" Kelly said aloud.

"ONE MOMENT, PLEASE."

Down the hall a red light turned to green above glass double doors. They looked at each other.

"PLEASE PROCEED."

They walked down the hall. A lot more refurbishing had gone on up here; Kelly recognized none of it. He pulled a door open and followed in behind Israel.

"PLEASE ENJOY REFRESHMENTS IN OUR CAFETERIA. TO YOUR LEFT ARE REFRIGERATED FOODS. JUST AHEAD ARE FRESH FRUIT, POTATO CHIPS, POPCORN, PITA CHIPS. ON THE FAR RIGHT YOU WILL FIND CARBONATED BEVERAGES."

"Pita chips," Israel said.

"Hey wait—" but Israel left Kelly standing there. This could be some kind of trap, but he didn't know what to do about it. This was a large room. Hills had to have knocked down the walls to a couple classrooms.

"To hell with it." Kelly went over to the pop machine and poured himself a Sprite. "Ugh," he said. Too much carbonation. He poured it out and tried the Dr. Pepper. Same thing. Finally he tried the Hi-C. Much too much syrup. He put in a little Sprite and it was as close to perfect as it was going to get.

Israel came over, munching on a bag of pita chips. "So now what?" he shouted.

There was silence a moment.

A green light came on over the doors just to their left.

"PLEASE PROCEED."

They went through the doors and went into another large, empty room. There were a few empty cubicles against the wall next to two empty offices on the corner then a row of empty cubicles.

There was a meaty click in the door a few feet over.

"PLEASE TAKE THE STAIRS TO THE THIRD FLOOR."

"Wonder why we couldn't take the elevator?" Israel pushed the door open and they took a flight of stairs to the third floor. There was the same click in that door and they stood at the mouth of a long, narrow hallway. There were more empty offices and cubicles here. A few feet away from them was some kind of supply room with a desk with a faux wood top, cloth office chair and a multi-line phone. There were several empty metal wire shelves against the far wall.

The Ghost Toucher

Kelly had been staring into the room when Israel tapped him on the shoulder.

"Heads up, somebody's coming."

From the other end of the hall a tall man approached them. As he got closer what Kelly at first mistook for a bald head was actually the sheen of jet black hair pulled tightly against his scalp into a pony that swung freely back and forth. He had on pleated khakis with a belt that looked like it had been a seatbelt in a former life hanging loosely around his narrow waist. The patterned shirt he wore showed off his powerfully built upper frame, the muscles of his arms and chest flexing with each step. His face was serene, as if he either weren't worried about two strangers in here or hadn't noticed them.

"Are we gonna have to fight?" Kelly asked.

"You must be Israel," the man said with a rich tenor voice. They shook hands and Israel winced. He turned to Kelly. "Kelly Greene." He squeezed his shoulder then drew him in. "Man, it is so good to see you again."

"Gayle?" Kelly asked.

Gayle Hills was a skinny boy who was about three inches shorter than Kelly Greene. Every day the two boys walked to school together. Not because Kelly enjoyed the company, but no matter how fast he walked Gayle kept up with him. Because of their gender neutral names and the fact Gayle never left him alone, eventually the two of them earned the moniker "The Girls". Kelly had worked hard to get in good with the popular kids and Gayle had all but erased that in a week just by being around.

But instead of regular bullying that the two boys would have endured for just being dorks their torment was increased astronomically by Gayle's ability to say and do the wrong thing to the wrong people.

Like asking if Eddie Carrington how long it would take the worms to eat his dead mother.

Or peeing on Eddie Crisp's new Nike's.

Or spitting on Mel Veach. You didn't spit on Mel Veach.

Kelly never did anything, but he was one of the Girls and thus, guilty by association. The beatings didn't seem to bother Gayle and eventually Kelly was taking both their share with threats for him to get that asshole in line or else.

Sitting across from this specimen of a human being Kelly wondered if he were physically capable of beating Gayle up if he'd smile and take it.

"So what is that voice on the intercom?" Israel asked. "Some kind of interactive program?"

"No-no-no." Gayle chuckled a deeper version of that twelve year old's annoying laugh. "I got fiber-optic cameras all over the place, I saw you guys coming in." He took out a flip phone, thumbed about two dozen buttons in quick fashion and pointed up.

"KELLY GREENE IS A POWER BOTTOM," called the female voice.

"Gee, Kelly. I didn't know you take it," Israel said.

"I do not take it. Anyway, how did you know our names?"

Gayle took a deep breath and let it out. His smile faded. "I know what you guys are into. The dead tell me their secrets."

"How do they tell you?" Israel asked.

"Trade secret. I'm not psychic or anything, but I have my ways." Gayle reclined and laced his fingers behind his head. "But along the way to building my fortune and buying this cool ass building I got other info. I heard about you guys coming a few days ago." He sat back up and rested his elbows on the giant oak desk. "Dead dudes know all kinds of stuff."

"So I hear." Kelly noted that Israel's body language had changed. He leaned away from him, tilted his head back slightly so he had to look downward at him.

"So what did they tell you about us because honestly, we're kind of floundering in the dark here."

"You're looking for some guy on television. They don't have him. Or rather, he's not on the other side. They took him, scared him a little bit, but you can't take the living over there. They don't know where he is now."

"Do they know where they left him?"

"Physical location doesn't really mean anything to them. A spirit is pretty much either there or not there. That's why the ones that come back are confused as to where they are."

"What do you know about men with funny-looking retinas?" Israel pointed to his own eyes.

"Oh. *Those* guys." Gayle laughed. "They're some kind of new-age cult. Nothing you should be worried about. They pretty much run their glee club of doom and leave everybody alone. Bunch of wannabes. They only talk about destroying the world—they don't have the stones. They worship this Caribbean god who's supposed to bring Armageddon and make apple pie."

"Well, I'd be inclined to believe you if I didn't get into a fight with one earlier today." Kelly rubbed his sore neck. "Uh, the harmless part. Not the god thing. He had the address to a guy who was supposed to have heart surgery. Know why?"

"Man, did he do anything to the guy?"

"No. Lucky for him he didn't show up for his procedure."

"Oh. That's good. No, I have no idea why."

"You're lying," Israel said.

"What?"

"I called you a liar."

"Why would I lie? I don't know him."

"How do you know you don't know him? We haven't told you who he was."

"Well who is he?"

"I'm not telling you *now*. You're in real estate, he's in real estate. That's all you need to know."

"So I'm lying because we're both in real estate?"

"I'm surprised you'd admit it so freely."

Gayle shook his head.

"So what else do you need to know?"

"We're pretty much at a loss here. Could we speak to your contact? Perhaps ask him where we should look?"

"I don't think so."

"We could really use the help. C'mon, for old times sake."

"No. I pay a considerable amount of money for proprietary technology. I don't just lend that out on a whim."

"I didn't want to do this, but I gotta play the favor card here."

"Favor card? That's a lot for you to owe."

"No. I'm talking about you owing me. I pulled your fat out of the fire a whole lot when we were kids."

"You're talking about twenty years ago? The favor card has expired."

"The favor card doesn't expire. No, the favor card doesn't expire."

Gayle placed his palms on the desk and straightened in his chair. He closed his eyes and pulled the scrunchy from his hair, the ponytail falling loose around his shoulders.

"I think we're gonna have to fight him," Israel said.

His phone rang. Gayle opened his eyes. They'd changed from light brown to hazel.

"Go ahead, Linda," he said after fingering a button.

"Mr. Hills, I have a phone call for you."

"Mr. Beans?"

"Yes."

"Put him through."

The line disconnected and a moment later the phone rang again. Gayle picked it up this time and listened a moment.

"Fraaank. Yes. Right now." He motioned for them to hold with a finger. "And what should I do with that package? Oh you'll pick up? Not a problem. Where are they going? Cool then—corned beef on an onion roll. No-no, don't give me that thousand island crap; if I want salad dressing I'll have a salad. Mayo. It is not gross." He put the phone to his chest and turned to Israel and Kelly? "Want anything?"

Kelly shook his head. Israel just stared at him.

While Gayle was talking Kelly tapped Israel with his foot. When he looked over Kelly pointed to a picture on the desk of Gayle hunching down to pose with a short, squat-looking man with a mustache in mid-growth. Gayle was smiling while the man looked like he lacked the necessary musculature to facilitate such a thing. Kelly raised an eyebrow as if to say 'What's up with that?' and Israel made the OK sign with one hand and fingered it with his other index finger.

"Well, we gotta get going," Israel said, rising from his chair.

"No, you guys should stay a while. Uh, let me show you something. It's cool. My real business. I'll give you my contact."

"Thanks, but no."

The Ghost Toucher

"Hold on," Kelly interrupted. "We need any lead we can get." To Gayle, "Lead the way."

"Follow me." Gayle went out of his office and Israel and Kelly trailed behind. Israel mouthed something but Kelly couldn't read his lips.

"Shut up?" Kelly asked, shaking his head. Israel rolled his eyes as they followed Gayle through a small door he had to crouch to get through.

"I keep this room dark," he said as a light came on. It was another massive room, with all white walls and a wooden floor. In the center was a tree in a glass enclosure, suspended in the air by four wires anchored to the corners of the box. The roots were naked and long; the only part of the tree that actually touched the ground. There was a port on the far side connected to a small wide tank that appeared to be empty.

"It's a tree." Israel pointed. "What I win?"

"Not just any tree," Gayle said. "There's no reason that tree is even alive right now. I found it in the middle of a wood not far from here. All the other trees were dead."

"Well, a lot of trees were taken out by Dutch Elm disease," Kelly said.

"This wasn't Dutch Elm. Trees that had stood for hundreds of years just fell over with a light push. It was a good place for a fire to start. I bought the land on a hunch and found this tree and it eventually led to me developing *that*." He pointed to the tank connected at the side.

"The reason that tree isn't in soil or outside where it could get sunlight is because it doesn't respond to those things anymore. I'd actually found two trees—that one and an older one and I figured out it doesn't ingest what normal trees do."

"Don't tell me," Israel said. "It eats people and you brought us in here to feed us to it."

Gayle laughed. "No. It doesn't eat people. It also doesn't consume carbon dioxide or sunlight. The only thing keeping it alive is the chemical compound coming out of that tank. It's odorless, tasteless, colorless and eventually going to make me a lot of money."

"How?" Kelly asked.

"The phenomenon in that wood isn't unique. I've been able to identify a few other places where it's happening and while most appear stable for right now, mine is growing."

"Congratulations. You're in the tree food business." Israel folded his arms.

"Not exactly. There were dead animals in the wood too. So far we haven't been able to isolate a living specimen, but I suspect it affects all life."

"It? What it?" Kelly asked.

"Anti-life. Like I said, the one in my wood is spreading. And if it does affect vegetation and animal life alike then we're in for big trouble. So far I can only produce this chemical compound in small amounts. It's very expensive. That tank will last my tree for the next ten years or so but just imagine one hundred trees, one hundred people, a thousand, a *billion*."

"And you haven't taken this to the government because you want to be sure you bring the world to its knees enough to pay whatever you want."

"Not true, Israel. So far we don't even know anything for a fact. It could just affect trees. That would be catastrophic but nowhere near as bad as a pandemic affecting all life. Maybe these trees are dying from something else. I need to be sure."

"And that's the official position?"

"That's the official position."

"Oh, by the way, Kelly, I was saying 'set up'. He's setting us up. Somebody's coming and he's buying time long enough for them to get here."

"That's ridiculous. Set us up for what?"

"Who would he have been on the phone with?"

Kelly looked at Gayle.

"He's right." Gayle shrugged. "A new business partner wants to meet you. Linda," Gayle said into his collar. "Need you here now."

"You *dick*."

"Let's get out of here."

"I really didn't need to hold you up. Just killing time. I control all the locks."

"He's right," Israel said. "Let's kick the shit out of him and take the key."

Just then the door burst in and a mid-fortyish woman with humongous breasts with her hair pulled back came through. She had on a navy blue pants suit and pushed her glasses up on her nose as she stalked over to Israel. He hesitated a moment but she didn't. All Kelly saw was her hand clasp around the back of his neck and he flipped over and landed on his back. She looked up at Kelly and he took a step back, putting up his fists and glancing between her and Gayle. She was short but her feet were fast. She crossed over to him and double-punched him in the midsection, knocking the wind out of him and sending him crumpling to the floor.

Israel appeared behind her, throwing a punch at her head. She side-stepped the blow, karate-chopped him in the groin and suddenly had him in an arm bar. Kelly tried to get up but his legs wouldn't cooperate. There was a sickeningly thick popping sound and Linda hovered back into view.

"Good shot, Linda." Gayle gave her a fist bump. Kelly raised his head and Linda stepped on it.

***

Mel was hungry, but he couldn't eat. Not that he hadn't tried, but shit if he couldn't hold anything down. But she could. Ate enough for the two of them. If he didn't have his Discover card on him he wouldn't have been able to pay for her dinner. For the second time. She hadn't stopped eating since leaving the gas station and as soon as she had pounded back the last Snickers she'd wanted more. He didn't even get to have one of them.

The nice lady at the window handed over two bags of food. She was kinda cute. He smiled and nodded at her and she gave one of those customer friendly smiles back. If he wasn't sick and didn't have the girl with him he could get her digits. The fries smelled delicious as he passed them over to the little girl. He licked his lips and felt his gorge rise. He stomped on the gas and pulled into a parking spot, leaping out and barely making it to one of those shin-high bushes before letting everything go. Actually, there wasn't anything to let go. He'd only felt like he was full of something.

Mel opened his eyes and saw the little bush had turned white. His stomach grumbled again and he wondered not for the first time if there was something wrong with him. Mel looked up and saw her standing against the window, a mouthful of fries, laughing. He climbed back in the truck, favoring his stiffening knee and promised himself to stop by emergency as soon as he had her dropped off. He was exhausted.

Dropped off? Where was that supposed to be? He looked at the little girl, *his* little girl and smiled at her. Her mother had abandoned her and his was off slutting it up somewhere in Arizona.

"Let's go home, baby."

***

Gayle Hills was still a dick. Big surprise. Kelly opened his eyes but it was still dark. He was able to move, but his back was against a wall. So the enigmatic 'they' were coming. He had to figure a way out of here. But where was here?

Had to be Gayle's corporate headquarters. No reason to move him if they were already coming. But that begged another question. Why were they coming for him? He was in customer service and even if you threw in this investigation, Stout Roost had nothing to do with these guys. But even if he did, Kelly knew less than Roost's fans and he still had no idea where to find him. It had to be something else, but what?

Never mind that. First order of business was to get out of here. Kelly found a wall and began feeling around until he found a seam. Once he'd felt all the way around the door he found it had no lock on the inside. Great. Maybe there was something in here he could pry it open with. Kelly felt around the floor but there was nothing.

He sat with his legs crossed, facing the door. What to do? He tilted his head back in the dark and asked no one in particular for help. Just then there was a thick latch unlocking sound and the door swung open. Blinding white light surrounded the figure in front of him. Kelly shielded his eyes, wanting to leap up and grab the man in front of him; gouge his eyes, kick him in the balls, *something*.

"Ready to go?" Israel said.

"How'd you find me?"

"You made a fist."

They had an easy time getting out. Either Gayle had left or he wasn't paying attention to his cameras at all. The doors weren't locked. Kelly was surprised at how much he remembered of Thompson and weaved them through a few hallways until they exited the main entrance.

The driver had fallen asleep, but Israel knocked on the window as they passed to the back door.

"Get us out of here. Quick," Israel said.

The tires peeled as the driver stomped on the gas. After a series of hard lefts and rights they were back on Woodward, heading north.

"Where to?" the driver said.

"I don't know. Anywhere. It's getting dark—we need to hole up for the night. Back to the Marriott."

"How'd you get free?" Kelly said.

"Played dead."

"Did they ever come?"

"No. I don't think so." Israel kept looking out the windows. "I never saw them. I think I was wrong. I think Hills isn't the player he says he is. He's involved in something, but I think he's just a pawn."

"Why am I in pain and you seem fine?"

"I always stretch before I get beat up by middle-aged women."

Kelly knew there was something Israel wasn't telling, but he dropped it for now. He was grateful to be out of there. Gayle was still a dick except now he employed the bullies.

Jemen was late. The gestational process had been much quicker this time. He sat between his brothers, shivering and naked. They had found Kelly Greene's home and One had accidentally started a fire. Any indication of where he might have been went up in smoke until her contact called.

She'd had to call him back and use the pseudonym 'Frank Beans'. Two was hungry and they'd just stopped by a restaurant that made sandwiches. They were on their way to her contact when she went into labor. Three didn't want to cooperate. Twenty minutes had gone by before she had to pull him out herself. She had to coo him and rock him until he was consoled enough to sit by himself. Three was going to be a sensitive one.

"Where were you?" her contact said. He was tall for a human, with black hair like a curtain down his back. She shushed the boys and got out, looking down on him.

"Whoa," the man said. "You're a big 'un."

Jemen didn't know what a 'big 'un' was, but it did not sound appealing. She let it go.

"Where is he?" she asked.

"That's what I'm trying to tell you—he escaped."

"You assured me you had him in your custody. How could he have gotten away?"

"He had somebody with him." The man turned and looked at the short woman next to him. Her hair hung down the same way as his. Jemen sniffed—just as she thought—they smelled of sex.

"What were you doing at the time?" she asked.

"I was handling business. Look, I'm not a babysitter."

"You are a buffoon. Had this meeting occurred an hour ago and you had failed you would be dead."

The short woman stepped in front of him. Was she his protector? Jemen smirked.

"Your man lives this day. Do not worry, little one. But this situation must be salvaged."

"Salvaged how?" he said.

"Show me where you kept him."

The man seemed to think a moment.

"All right, yeah. Follow me."

She beckoned for Three to follow. He slipped out of the SUV, wearing tan khakis and a burgundy sweater over a button-up shirt. He eagerly joined her side. Jemen's belly had already swelled with the fetus of her next born. It made the idea of sacrificing her son not so difficult.

They entered the building and the man led them to the place where he'd kept Kelly Greene. It was a small space beneath the floor; he lifted a panel to reveal it. She'd scoured the area until she found four short hairs. Not that much, but they would do.

"Open your mouth," Jemen told Three. She placed the hairs on his tongue and the change began immediately.

His skin darkened and his features became more defined.

She regretted having to waste Three, but it was a calculated step. All of her children would have relatively short lives, but his would be even shorter.

She'd used the hair to change him. The effect was rapid and even the one who had failed was amazed.

"He kinda looks like that," he said. "The hairline and eyes are different, though."

"Speak, my son," Jemen said to Three. She didn't feel the necessity to explain that two brothers who shared the same blood hardly ever looked exactly alike, either.

Three had only been able to make rudimentary sounds at first, but after a few minutes he was able to make full sentences. He developed a cough soon after.

"Do you have the phone number?" she asked the man.

"Yeah, but why would you want to call the police? You're not going to try anything stupid, are you?"

Ah, he was worried for himself.

"No. Thankfully, my plans no longer involve you." She picked up the phone and wiped blood from the corner of Three's eye. "Do I need 9 to dial out?"

Ride

Kelly's phone buzzed. Funny, why hadn't they taken it?
"Hello?" he said into it after digging it out of his pocket.
"This is LaGina Densmore. I was calling about your progress."
"My progress?" Israel shook his head at him. "Everything's just fine. Why?"
"I'm showing a transaction at a gas station in the amount of three hundred dollars. You do have a receipt for this, right?"
"Uh, yeah." Kelly patted his pockets. At least he hoped he had it.
"I'm certain you don't need to be reminded of the credit card policy. That's a lot of gas."
"Yes, well this car only takes premium." Israel gave him a thumbs up and a smile. "Can't talk—going through a tunnel." He flipped his phone closed and asked, "What the hell was that?"
"Somebody's gunning for you."
"Anyway, let's assess where we are. Gayle Hills is the bad guy. He's working with *someone* who's the boss of these guys with the strange eyes."
"The Caribbean god guy. I'm calling those people diffoids. But there's another player in this too."
Israel took out his phone and typed in something.
"Maybe this god is Bondye. Apparently he's a voodoo monogod, supposed to be very aloof."
"Doesn't sound like this guy. If he's taken a business partner I would imagine he's pretty active. What else?"

"Maybe he's... Baron Cimitiere. This guy wears a black tailcoat, top hat and dark sunglasses and watches over the dead."

"What else?"

"Erzulie, goddess of love... Damballah... Maman-Brigitte... I don't think we're going to nail it down right now. Maybe it's that Baron guy. They all seem to stem from African gods."

"Or maybe he's something older. Something forgotten," Kelly wondered aloud.

"Well, remember what I told you. All of this could be a ruse for the real deal. If some deity was really walking around when the Europeans came around with men in shackles it may have posed as something else to keep its true identity secret."

"But why would a god do that?"

"Easy. If man can enslave his own it's only a matter of time before he figures out how to do it to a god. It would be better to keep us guessing rather than knowing a god's true nature. Man has an uncanny ability to break anything in his path. It's best to just... stay off the path."

"So why now? If this Baron guy truly exists, why expose himself even on the smallest level?"

"Who knows? Maybe he's always done this kind of stuff. Maybe he's really just some guy who's posing as a god. How sane is your friend anyway?"

"He's not my friend. And he's as ape shit nuts as he ever was. One thing I know for sure is that Gayle wants Bruce Strong dead. He probably owns half the houses up and down that street. Maybe Strong's a hold out."

"Doesn't sound good for your mom."

"No, it doesn't sound good for him."

Kelly's phone buzzed again.

"Hello?"

"Mr. Greene, this is Detective Matthews. We're going to need you to come in for a few more questions and get an official statement."

"Excuse me, detective? A few *more* questions?"

Israel raised his shoulders as if asking what was going on.

"Yes," Detective Matthews said.

"I'm sorry, what did I say in my original statement again?"

The Ghost Toucher

"Let's see." Kelly could hear the detective shuffling through some papers. "At six oh-five yesterday evening you decided to give your life over to the goddess Bhuul and as an act of your newly found faith decided to destroy all your worldly possessions."

"Oh, I see. Well that seems pretty clear to me, detective. What more do you need to know?"

"Mr. Greene, you need to understand. We did send an officer to your home and we have since verified your home *has* been burned to the ground."

"My *what*?"

"I have to advise you that you will be arrested and that it would be in your best interest to turn yourself in. If you'd like to contact an attorney and have him meet you here at headquarters—"

"Detective, I have to say I don't remember doing any of this. I didn't call you and I didn't burn down my house. How do you even know it was me and not someone saying he was me?"

"Good point. Why don't you come down so we can straighten this out?"

Israel was making the kill sign with his fingers to his neck.

"I'll tell you what, Detective—"

"Matthews."

"—Matthews. I've got a couple things I need to take care of, but as soon as I'm done I'll be there so we can get this taken care of. That work for you?"

"It would be best if you came here straightaway."

"Well, what I'm in the middle of may actually help to clarify the situation. Just give me a little while and I'll be there. *Promise*."

"I really wish you wouldn't talk down to me. I'm trying to help you here. If an officer finds you on the street he'll arrest you. You don't want that. Turn yourself in. I know you've been under stress since your family, but if this were an accident—"

Israel snatched the phone from his hand and disconnected the call.

"Sheesh, I thought you'd never shut up." He shook his head.

"Hey, someone is trying to set me up."

"Well that much is obvious, but considering you have no idea who and how far it goes you're not going to settle it with a phone call. They could have been tracing the call. Shit."

Israel rolled down the window and tossed the cell into the street.

"Hey!"

"Expense yourself a new one. In the meantime we gotta get to Ferndale. I was checking through the file and this friend of Stout's might be a good lead. What he does is interesting, at least."

"What's that?"

"He tortures ghosts."

"What?"

The Ghost Toucher

Cole slawse, Peabo & how to kill a ghost

Getting out of the city was actually a good idea. The police wouldn't be as likely to search for him here and neither would Gayle Hills' people, whoever they were. Israel had called him, a guy named Primer, and they were meeting at some old haunted hotel.

They pulled into a cramped parking lot that could have used a resurfacing. The hotel itself was actually an inn; an old mansion or something someone converted at some point. It was rundown-looking, painted burgundy with an off-white trim. Israel and Kelly went inside and crossed a dull, creaky hardwood floor to a reception desk. A chubby fifty-something with thick dark red hair turned away from her paperback to peer over her glasses at them.

"We're here to see one of your guests."

She didn't say anything.

"A man named Primer?"

"He's probably here. Do you know his room number?" She didn't seem to be asking because she wanted to be helpful. It was more like she meant they were dumb and she had no intention of looking it up.

"Uh, yeah," Israel said.

"Then go on up." She waggled her finger toward the hallway behind them. "The elevator's out so you have to take the stairs."

Before they turned to go she had already gone back to her book.

They walked down the hall and bounded up the stairs to the second floor. Primer was in room 209. Israel knocked when they reached it and found the door was already open. He looked back at Kelly.

"The homies got here with the quickness." A tall, skinny white man stood in a doorway with his back to them. He seemed to be examining something. The room they entered was actually the bedroom; a giant bed set in the center with large windows in the wall behind it. Everything was a shade of red.

"What are you up to?" Israel asked. "Can we help?"

"Nah, skillet. Almost done. Just gotta be sure this room ain't wired. A lot of these haunted inns be fake." He ran his fingers across the seams of the doorway and then turned to look at them. He must have had terrible acne as a teen because his cheeks and jawline were deeply pitted. His eyes were sea green, matching the deep red of his hair, a shade or two different from the woman's downstairs.

"Don't worry, we not kin," Primer said.

"Primer, I'm Kelly," Kelly offered his hand and Primer just looked at it.

"Skillet, Primer was the name of my old band. Calls me Taze."

"So you're a musician?" Kelly asked.

"Naw. I sucked."

"Well, like Israel was explaining on the phone—we're looking for Stout Roost. I'm sure you've already answered a bunch of questions but we're hoping to find something that's been overlooked."

"Aight. But I ain't spoke to no detectives prior to now."

"No one has contacted you?"

"Why you talk so *white*?"

"What?" Kelly asked.

"You talk like him," Taze said, nodding at Israel. "Like you white."

"It's English. It's just how I speak."

"Whatchoo wanna know?"

"Like what he was working on when he disappeared."

"Don't know. Played 'em close."

Taze walked over to a painting on a wall of a brunette in a long blue dress sitting in a rocking chair. He grabbed the frame by its sides and took it down, examining the corners. He turned his head up to the ceiling, looking no place in particular.

"You gon' come out now?"

Israel was smiling, but Kelly had no idea what was going on. Taze fished out a box cutter from his jacket pocket, balancing the frame on his hip. He held the blade at an angle and cut the painting from top to bottom, going through the head and body of the figure in the painting. The line he made was almost imperceptible, but the effect was immediate.

A scream came from the bed.

"Most people think you can't do nothin' to the dead," Taze said. "Wrong. You can hurt a ghost if you can find somethin' they cared about in life and tear it up."

Kelly looked at Israel who had a blank look on his face.

"But you gotta do it real slow, like torture, or you break the link." He took a pen from his pocket and poked one of the eyes out of the figure in the painting.

Invisible fists began pounding at the mattress.

"So what are you doing this for?" Kelly asked. "Did she bury a treasure somewhere?"

"Nah, man. Just for the giggles."

"For fun?" Israel asked. "You do this because you *enjoy* it?"

"Yeah."

"Not ideal, but what's the big deal?" Kelly noticed Israel's tone, like he had something at stake.

"Nothing. Nothing."

"Some guy built this place way back in the eighteen hundreds. A wealthy logger or somethin'. But he had this fine wife. After her kid was born she was sick all the time. A couple years later the husband died. The kid grew up and was just as fine as her moms, but she was a hoe. She even did it in moms' bed. And with everybody—the blacksmith, the undertaker, the pastor—*knowwudahmsain?*"

Taze inked in a Hitler mustache on the face and the bed squeaked just before something hit the ceiling above it.

"Now that—" he pointed to the bed and then back to the painting, "and this are the mother who died in the bed or the daughter that came back after her mother kicked. Stand back."

Kelly took a step away from Taze and he felt a breeze go past that didn't touch his clothes. Taze grunted and fell into the wall, holding the painting up as if to protect his face. Kelly watched as red lines appeared on his cheeks before Taze raised the painting even higher and brought it down on the corner of the gold table against the wall where the painting had been.

The ghost screamed again, this time much higher than before. Kelly clasped his hands over his ears and then it was gone. Taze climbed off his knees, a small smile on his face. Kelly took his hands down from his ears.

"What the hell was that?"

"That's how you kill a ghost."

"What?"

"Might need to do it a couple times, but that's the way. I'm hungry—dog, you buy me lunch and I'll answer your questions."

"Let's go," Israel said, pushing past.

They'd walked to a restaurant kitty-corner to the inn. Kelly felt bad about the driver just sitting in the car so he invited her to come too. It was rustic-looking, white with brown trim on the outside, faux wood paneling on the inside. They passed an old woman who was just opening the door of a brown Cadillac. An old man was already sitting in the passenger seat. The car had a personalized plate with the letters "J-U-S-P-R-A-Y".

"That stuff work?" Israel said to her.

"'Scuse me?" the little old woman said, clutching her keys.

"The spray. Does it keep them away?"

"Keep who away?" She looked confused.

"I gotcha." Israel gave her a conspiratorial wink and opened the door. She was shaking her head as the four of them passed inside.

The only waitress on duty had a head full of blonde hair like straw had been forked up and dumped on her head and pinned down. She had the stare of a former drug addict—eyes that had had all their life scooped out of them and backfilled with an unnamed zeal. She kept it to herself, though, and the coffee coming.

Kelly had to saw through his steak and the eggs were barely runny. Taze's fish and chips looked okay; he wished he'd ordered that. Israel seemed fine with his double order of pancakes and the driver had a cheeseburger and fries.

Turned out Taze didn't know much more than what was in the file. He and Stout had hooked up during the show's first season. Taze had taught him a couple things he knew and then they'd parted ways.

"Check it—I don't know where he's at," he said. "Only thing he tol' me was he found some kinda bus."

"And that doesn't mean anything to you?" Kelly asked, swirling a square of steak through his egg yolk.

"Buses be all over the place, man. Does that mean anything to *you*?"

Great. Two days and still nothing. Even if they could find the bus Stout was talking about it wouldn't bring this thing to a close. It would just be another step in a long procession of steps that led nowhere.

"I suppose not." Kelly took another bite of rubbery steak and munched on it.

"Hey, baby girl," Taze said to the driver, "What's your name?"

"Anna," she said. She smiled, but it was more of a hey-I-only-came-in-for-the-food-please-don't-hit-on-me kind of smile. Kelly hoped he picked up.

"Aight, aight," Taze nodded. "You from around here?"

"Excuse me. Excuse me." Anna flagged down their waitress. The woman stopped suddenly, the coffee almost sloshing out of the pot in her hand, her eyes looking ready to shoot out of her head. "Do you have any slawse?"

"On a *burger*?" Taze said. "Man, that's *ill*."

"I'll see if we have any," the waitress said and took off, the silverware on the plates in her other hand scraping around. She came back a few moments later with an unopened jar. Taze snatched it up and began twisting at it until the lid popped. He unscrewed it and set it in front of Anna.

"Thanks," she said.

"Ain't nothin'." He tried to play it off but Kelly saw him wince a moment and rub his palm.

She lifted the bun and used her butter knife to scrape everything off the patty. Then she dumped three spoonfuls of slawse on it and spread it until it was dripping off the sides. It didn't look very appetizing, but when she picked it up and took a bite Kelly might have thought she was in heaven.

"That good, huh?" Taze asked. Anna nodded. "Can I get some dibs?" She rolled her eyes at him.

"Look," she said, her mouth full. Taze reared back. "Whatever it is you're looking to have happen—mm-mm." She shook her head.

"Why you gotta be all like that? I mean, dang, can't we be friends or somethin'? What, I gotta be Peabo to get some play?"

"Peabo? You mean, like, Bryson?"

"Yeah. Peabo the pimp." He banged his fist on the table with the last word. "Who else can hit it and quit it in one song?"

"What are you talking about?" Kelly asked.

"Y'all don't know about that 'Feel the Fire'?" Taze looked at the three of them as if they'd just landed from Mars. "And if I should lose your love," he sang in a decent alto, "for any reason, any reason at all, then let my record show, I gave you all the love I know."

"That's a love song," Kelly said.

"Yeah, but it's a love song about doin' it. All the love I know? He's sayin' he gave her two feet a' dick. That's why it's called 'Feel the Fire'. He whipped it so good it burned. And then he dumped her. And 'I'm So Into You'—you know what he's talking about. Rick James ain't got nothin' on Peabo."

"Suddenly I have a different perspective on 'A Whole New World'," Israel said.

Taze waved a hand at him. "Don't give me that Disney mess. Baby can you stand the *rain*. Peabo like blastin' 'em in the chest. Or goin' number one on 'em, I'm not for sure."

"That is not what that song is about!" Anna laughed. "What is wrong with you? Yeah, a lot of his songs are about love or making love, but you make it sound so *gross*."

"It's not gross," Taze said. "I think it's lovely."

"Okay, then *you're* gross. My mother took me to see *Beauty and the Beast* when I was little and ever since I've been a Peabo fan. He is not like that."

"All the ladies give him irrumatio, I'm tellin' you." Taze sat back in his chair and laced his fingers behind his head.

Israel covered his face, choking down a laugh. Kelly didn't know what the word meant and neither did Anna from the look on her face.

"I'm done," she said, wiping her mouth and placing the napkin on the plate. "Thank you very much for lunch, Mr. Greene. I'll bring the car over." She got up and headed out.

"We'll be out soon," Kelly said. He turned to Israel. "'Irrumatio'?"

"Uh, y'know." Israel made an 'ok' sign with his index and thumb and moved it back and forth near his open mouth.

"Oral?"

"Nah, man," Taze said, sitting up. "Mouth *pounding*." He belched, stretched and stood up. "It's a lot more giving than receiving. All right, peeps, I gotta get back. There's some other rooms I wanna hit up. Thanks for the eats." He gave them both a black man handshake and sauntered out.

It was five minutes before the waitress came back with the check. Kelly gave it back to her with the company card and it took another five before she came back with a receipt for him to sign. The pile of straw-blonde hair on her head looked ready to fall over on her face.

Like she'd been tooting up.

Or letting the cook have irrumatio.

Kelly smirked.

Stop it, that wasn't funny.

But it was.

He looked out the window and saw their driver sitting in the car. Perfectly still as if she'd gone to sleep.

Well, they *had* just eaten.

He signed the receipt and gave her a better-than-she-deserved tip. They stood and walked out.

"So where do you think we should head next?" he asked as they passed the driver's side window.

"Not sure, but—" Israel seemed hesitant.

"But what?"

"I think the driver's dead."

"What are you talking about?"

Kelly stooped to peer in the window. Everything would have been normal if her mouth wasn't stretched open in a rictus of agony.

"What the hell?" He stood up to look back at Israel. "I think she's dead!"

Israel just shook his head and pointed to his ear.

"What? What are you—look this isn't the time for charades! Anna is dead!" Kelly reached for his phone and remembered Israel had dropped it out the window.

"Give me your phone." Israel shook his head. Kelly reached for it on his hip and Israel slapped it away. "Fine—I'll call from the payphone in the restaurant."

He walked past Israel who grabbed him by the shoulders and quickly wrestled him to the ground.

"Get off me, you psycho! We have to call the police!" Then he thought he realized why Israel didn't want him to call. They might make a call to DPD.

"Okay. Up. I understand. Ferndale police might call Detroit police. I get it."

"*Earrr*," Israel whispered roughly into Kelly's.

What?

Then he remembered what Israel had told him about the Listening Ear. Like some kind of cosmic police. Guess they were both wanted men.

"What, are they nearby?"

"*Yesss.*"

"Where?"

Israel dragged him up onto his knees and pointed skyward. It was already cloudy so Kelly didn't see anything when he pointed to a nondescript-looking one.

But then he blinked and saw a giant blob of shadow behind it.

"What do we do?"

Israel made a walking motion with his index and middle fingers and they both got up. He pointed to the driver in the car and then to the trunk. Kelly nodded. He popped the trunk and they took her out. She was little, but it was difficult with her frozen in a sitting position. Kelly carried her by the feet and Israel by the shoulders and on the silent count of three they hefted her into the trunk.

"Hey, can I get a ride? That place is bol', dog." Taze was suddenly standing in front of Kelly. He opened the door and shoved the taller man in.

Israel crawled across the driver's side and into the passenger seat and Kelly got behind the wheel. The engine was already running. He looked up to see the shadow had extended as far as the eye could see. There was a large oak across the street and Kelly looked again after catching the top of it from the corner of his eye. The tips of the branches were curlicued and winding down, like boneless fingers. They pointed in the direction of the car and with each passing second it appeared they were getting longer.

Israel punched him in the arm and Kelly put the car in drive, pulling out onto the street and heading south.

"Hey, wassup?" Taze asked as Kelly pressed on the gas. The dark shadow had reached the street, covering the outsides of most of the buildings they drove past. Up ahead a man standing on the corner stepped out onto the street directly in their path.

Kelly let up on the gas and Israel shouted, "Just drive. Drive-drive-drive!" Kelly swerved violently around the man and righted the car, straddling the dividing white line of the two lanes. He looked in the rearview mirror and saw the man whirl around. It was dark enough now that he could see the glow of the man's eyes and he knew that wasn't a human being just before a blur of wings appeared over both shoulders and he disappeared.

"What was that guy?" Kelly said. "He just disappeared."

"A lesser," Israel said. "And we haven't seen the last of him if you don't drive really fast."

Something rocked the side of the car and Kelly had to regrip the steering wheel to maintain control. A moment later an ashen face appeared in Kelly's window. Those same narrow, yellow glowing eyes as before, above a beak on a mouthless face. The creature reared back and punched the roof of the car, rocking it again and

Kelly had to correct his grip on the wheel again. Kelly hoped it didn't realize it could do the same to the glass and kill him.

"The road-the road-the road!" Israel screeched. Kelly veered away from the approaching curb as they rocketed down the street. They sideswiped something he didn't see and ran through a red light.

The lesser's face lowered to eye level with Kelly. Its eyes widened as if it recognized him and began punching the roof of the car again. Kelly jerked the wheel from side-to-side and said an almost silent "Yes!" when it lost its grip, but it flew back and latched on again.

It jabbed its beak through the glass. Kelly could hear it sniffing. But instead of attacking again it yanked its head back and looked ahead; eyes wider than before.

The lesser broke away, but it must have been too late. Its wings shredded from its body and it fell against the car, obviously in pain from the panicked look in its eyes. It fell out of view and Kelly felt the rear tire bump over it.

"Slow down," Israel said. "I think we're out of it."

"Out of what?"

"Homies, I don't know what that was, but it was dope! Let's go back."

"Shut up," Israel and Kelly said.

"I don't know what they call it," Israel began as Kelly slowed the car. "It's their version of a patrol. But instead of sending a unit or whatever they just change the surrounding area to suit their needs."

"And why do they want you?"

Israel said nothing.

"Right. So more you're not telling me."

"Make a right here."

Something pounded in the trunk. Israel and Kelly both screamed.

"Who dat?" Taze said.

"The driver, but she's dead," Israel said. Kelly slapped his shoulder. "What—we didn't kill her."

"She ain't dead," Taze said. "I can hear her screamin'."

They pulled over and the three of them carefully approached the trunk.

"You alive in there?" Israel knocked on the trunk.

"Please let me out," came Anna's muffled reply.

"Okay, Kelly's going to let you out, but be real cool. I got a tire iron."

"Skillet, wouldn't the tire iron be in the trunk?"

They stared at Taze until he backed off. Kelly inserted the key as quietly as he could. He turned it, jumping back as the trunk popped open and the driver sat up. Her eyes raced from man to man, fear and sweat on her face. Israel and Kelly took a big step back.

Her irises were all wrong.

Not welcome here

It was dying. There was no hope for this body, but it had to survive. It had seen the prophesied Hated One and it couldn't die being the only one knowing He was here. It had to find a new host. It had crawled as closely as it could to the Jexclp'ar and that had only allowed it to feel the pain of its life's blood leaking away even more exquisitely. There was one who was close, but it would have to do something to draw him closer.

A cat was just behind it, licking its blood from the ground. Hated creature, boon to all his kind. In normal life, touching one would be suicide, but that would hardly matter here. It reached out, grabbing the cat by the neck and immediately its flesh began to burn. The pain equaled leaving the protection of the Jexclp'ar, but it worked as the cat began screeching.

The arm rotted away and the cat ran off. A moment later a man in a brown uniform and hat hovered into view. He wore a silver star over his heart. A lawman. How fitting.

"What the hell is that?" the lawman said, leaning over. He wouldn't touch it, no, but it needed him closer. Its body ossifying, it summoned the strength for one last twitch.

"Still alive, whatever you are, you bastard," the lawman said. He nudged it with his toe and that was enough. The leap from the dying form into the lawman was instant.

"Still alive," it said through the lawman's mouth.

The Ghost Toucher

***

"I think it's time for someone to take a Paul-cation," Israel said, holding her by the shoulders.

"Who's Paul?" she whimpered.

"*Exactly.*"

"Israel, cut it out. She's a human being. Kinda." Kelly stopped pacing and stared at him.

"See y'all got some pure Peabo in you," Taze said. "You throw the ladies in *trunks!*"

"She's working for the other team. We have to do *something.*"

"What other team?" Taze said, looking back and forth between Israel and Anna and Kelly. "You a lezzie?"

"Israel, stop." He let her go, but pointed a warning finger. "Taze, never mind. It's a long story." Kelly paced the width of the narrow alley. They'd come back to Highland Park, having no real destination in mind. First the driver was dead, now she was alive but one of *them.* Whoever *they* were, Kelly still had no idea. If they could rely on anything Gayle Hills told them they were just a bunch of fanatics, worshipping some Caribbean god. But if that god did exist then Hills was in business with him and Kelly was back to square one, wondering what their true agenda was.

"I have a husband and daughter. I'm not part of anything."

"Yeah right," Israel said. "Do you want it between the eyes or in the heart?"

"That's what Peabo say."

"I don't want it anywhere. I just want to go home."

"Well that's not going to happen. You're with them. When did it happen?"

"When did what happen? All I've been doing is driving you around for the last two days, then you invite me in to have lunch with you and then I wake up in the trunk."

Kelly stepped over and offered a hand to help her out.

"Thank you."

"Look, Anna, I'm sorry about all this. You shouldn't be involved. These jerks want something with us and you happened to be in their way. That being said, we will be watching you if you're working with them."

"If I am, I swear I don't know it."

The Ghost Toucher

"So he's the bad cop now?" Israel said to Taze.

"Why do you think I'm working with whoever these people are?" Anna asked. "Do they own Parke Cars?"

"You really don't feel any different?" Kelly asked.

"No. Why should I?"

He thought a moment, put an arm around her shoulder and led her to the front passenger door. He opened it, sat her down and flipped down the sun visor.

"Go ahead," Kelly said, taking a step back, gesturing to the mirror.

Anna looked confused, but reached up.

"Is there something wrong with my face?"

Kelly just shook his head and pointed to the mirror again.

She took a deep breath and opened it. Anna screamed.

"What's wrong with my eyes? What did you do to me? What did you do?" Anna leapt from the seat, clawing at the air until she caught Kelly on the neck. He backed away until he came up against a dilapidated garage. Kelly caught her hand before she could scratch him again, but she doubled him over with a knee to the balls.

Israel grabbed her from behind, spinning her away in a bear hug and pinning her arms to her chest. She kicked at the air, screaming like an animal.

"I think we can trust her for now," he said. Kelly duck-walked over from his bent over stance until he could lean on the car door. Fingers of pain gripped from his groin to the underside of his stomach; nausea crept up the back of his brain. He sat in the passenger seat, waiting for the slow-drumming ache to subside.

"You all right?" Israel was still holding her, but she sagged in his arms, like her bones had turned to rubber.

"What did you do to me?" Kelly heard her mumble over and over.

"She has every right to be angry," Kelly said. "Hell, I'm pissed too. I didn't sign on for any of this, either."

"Why don't you skillets just quit and go home?" Kelly peaked around the side of the car and saw Taze. He'd forgotten about him. Kelly thought a moment. What was he doing? None of this was worth it. Risking his life wasn't part of the job description. Maybe he should just go back...

Where? Home? Home was gone. Somebody claiming to be him had seen to that. Kelly had a feeling this was all tied together, that if he didn't see it through something truly terrible would happen. What role he would play in preventing this disaster or whatever it was remained to be seen, but this all went far beyond Stout Roost.

"'lo?" Israel said. "You with us?"

"Yeah." Kelly stood. There was a distant ache still in the pit of his stomach. "It's late. We need to get back to the hotel."

***

The Old Man clenched the remote in his hand. He didn't understand this show. Not because of the language, he actually spoke fluent Spanish, but it was completely unintelligible.

The little Mexican (he was actually half Mexican and from Denver) rode a bike into a giant cake that just so happened to be setting out in the street. The whole thing toppled over with him half inside it. He fell on his butt in the street and swiped the cake out of his eyes and ran his tongue across his thick mustache as the camera pulled back to reveal two bronze-skinned models in bikinis and high heels, one of them holding a beach ball.

"Oh *ChiChé!*" they giggled in unison, bending over to kiss him on either cheek. He smiled and shrugged his shoulders.

The Old Man flicked off the television and slammed the remote down. How were they supposed to compete with that? It made absolutely no sense. He was Curly without Larry and Moe, Oliver Hardy without Stan Laurel. And most of all he was without talent. He had none of the charisma of the Three Stooges or Laurel and Hardy. It wasn't quantifiable why anyone would like such a show.

The same could be said about *The Ghost Toucher* but he could hold his tongue about shows on his own network.

"Sir, someone is here to see you? A Gunner?"

That stupid name never ceased to annoy the Old Man. He took a deep breath and cleared his throat, careful not to let any of his agitation creep into his voice. Abigail wasn't the intended target of his anger.

"Send him in." He dimmed the lights. It helped the impending migraine about to walk through the door.

A moment later a tall, mid thirtyish man in a tan suit with his hair unkempt in a bright yellow tie with the knot loose down to his chest strolled in. Same attitude as always, like he owned everything he set his eyes upon and hadn't needed to lift a finger to earn it. The Old Man was bothered mostly this man was his own son.

"Why are you here?" he said.

"Dad. Chill. Just here to give you a prog report." He pronounced 'report' without the 't', like it was French.

He looked into the same ice blue eyes he stared at in the mirror every morning. What was missing with this boy? How had he been able to become a captain of industry but his own son was a steaming pile of... of *this* whose greatest strength was sabotage?

"I told you to give me those on the secure line."

"Hey, sorry for wanting to see my old man." He smiled. "I miss you."

"Oh really? Is that why you never come by to see your mother? 'What's her name and how much do you need?' is a better question. But then again, we've asked and answered that one before." The old man put up a hand. "This time I don't want to know."

There was something different about the boy. He looked the same weight as he'd been, his hair was still stupid. Maybe he'd been working out more?

You wouldn't be able to tell it by looking, but the Old Man was sick. His son wasn't. At least not physically.

"It's not like that this time. By the way, that new chick in the accounting department is *hot*. What's her story?"

"You don't seriously believe I'd know who you're talking about. There's only one thing you can do for the Network and you're already doing it. Now what's the report?"

"Oh, so you do want it." The younger man tried giving his father the stare down. Loser as always as his eyes fell in his lap. "Um, my moles are saying they're starting to get close. They haven't found him yet, but they've gotten a couple clues."

"And what are you doing about it? Or are you here again with another problem?"

"Well I got a couple ideas. Plus I still have my guy in pursuit."

"For your sister's sake, pray your guy finds them. Need I remind you how important it is for Stout Roost to stay 'lost'."

"Pop-Pop-Pop, don't worry about that. Stout has no way to reach the only woman he ever cared about. Taken care of."

"Hm." The Old Man didn't know what 'taken care of' meant and didn't want to know. So long as she wasn't dead he would live with it.

"Now the other reason I came—" his son pulled something out of his jacket pocket. Post-it notes. "I've been studying this stuff and I know I got the goods. Gimme a shot at *The Ghost Toucher*. I can do it."

The Old Man laughed.

"Son, no. While it would give me so much pleasure to see you fall on your face again, unfortunately by virtue of having my name associated with it, my reputation would be the one you'd be ruining. Reality television is dead. The market is saturated and people are going to want real television again."

His son bristled, but made no complaint. He knew better. The Old Man sat back and waited for him to change the subject, while pondering what was different with him. It was his skin. It looked different. Not tan, but not the right shade. Like his DNA had been infused with something Mediterranean. Had to be make-up.

"How is Mom, by the way? Still have that goiter?"

"Bigger than ever. Did you send her a card?"

"Oh, her *birthday*. I forgot."

Typical. What the boy lacked in follow-through he compounded with lack of focus. Maybe the real difference between the two of them was that he had grown up with nothing and so appreciated everything. Maybe he had made a mistake by laying the world at his son's feet. But then why was his sister so different?

"I guess I better get going."

"Make a beeline out of here. Speak to no one. Understood?"

"Yeah."

His son shuffled out, filled with none of the plume he had come in with. Now was not the time for his son to be filled with a hope he was expecting his father to underwrite. And just to add a little insult to injury...

"Abigail, Mr. Gunner is on his way out. Could you see to it that security escorts him to the curb?"

"Absolutely, sir."

He laced his fingers and enjoyed a chuckle.

***

Dick! Gunner wanted to deck those security guards after they grabbed him. He was on his way out anyway; they didn't have to get rough. But one of them was huge. If he could have taken the small one out the other would have folded him up like a pretzel. And they set him down in a puddle by the curb, getting his Ninos all messed up.

Gunner quickly dismissed them as he headed down the street. They'd get theirs 'cause he was gonna run this place someday and he'd remember their names. Steckler and Oliver.

He had to get this makeup off and quick. Maybe he was allergic to it or something, but it *itched*. He had to have something on so the Old Man wouldn't see what he'd done. Or rather, what that witch bitch had done to him. He only wanted a quick and easy way to contact the dead. She'd slipped him a micky or something and he'd woke up with these weird tattoos all over his body. Lucky for her she hadn't taken anything from his apartment, but that wouldn't help when he caught up with her. If he could find a two hundred year old dead guy in the netherworld he could find her.

Stepped into a Starbucks and raced for the restroom. Some douchebag was playing with himself at the urinal. Had to keep it in check; guy was just taking a leak. Gunner ignored him and began examining his face in the mirror, looking for tell-tale marks of an allergic reaction or something. No swelling or redness.

Shit. Not the makeup—the fucking tattoos! The double lines streaking across his forehead and down either side of the bridge of his nose were bleeding through. How could that happen? They were only tats. Gunner's skin felt hot. He began scratching his wrists and looked down to see the ink beginning to show on the backs of his hands.

He had to get out of here. Hop into an ice cold bath and think this thing through. "You almost done?" the guy said behind him.

Gunner said something. He wasn't sure what because his head felt like it was about to explode, but he knew he'd just hit the guy. He pushed his way through the small lunch crowd and back outside, falling into a cab that happened to be passing by. Something was wrong. Other than tats that couldn't be covered up by makeup. Something was very wrong.

***

LaGina subconsciously twirled the invite in her hands. She'd meant to toss the thing on her way out of the office, but had forgotten about it. She was somewhat intrigued, but knew her judgment in men wasn't the greatest.

She wasn't sure what to make of Kelly Greene. She'd done a little background checking and found he was unmarried and had no kids. But who was the woman and the two girls in the picture? And why was that other guy in it, for that matter? Maybe he was the single brother and they were the married couple. But wouldn't he have been next to his wife instead of Greene?

Maybe that was Greene's family and they had died. She'd checked the newspapers' archives, but if she wanted to read anything over ninety days old she'd have to pay for it. Considering LaGina didn't know if it would help her even if he had murdered his family she just dropped it. There had to be another angle.

The woman in front of her had on a pair of black calfskin boots that easily cost more than two of LaGina's paychecks. Too bad the thigh length tan coat didn't match. She wouldn't make that mistake if she ever could afford boots like those.

But that couldn't happen if she couldn't find Stout. She had to find evidence they were hiding him. The class action suit was stunted until they could find him and the Network's lawyers had blocked their attempt to force his mother to give a DNA sample.

She looked at her invite again as the woman took her cup of whatever away. LaGina's mind drifted back to Gunner. She'd watched him go into the executive wing. He probably was someone important. A producer or something.

Just then some jerk pushed his way through the line, knocking someone up against her, pushing her into the counter. A lady screamed and a second later the bell rang as the person went outside. LaGina pushed back and tried to look through the window to see whoever it was. She just saw a bobbing head and a then the sign of a taxi cab.

"I am so sorry about that, Ma'am," the teenaged-looking barrister with the stud through her lower lip said. She laughed a little nervously and bent to pick up something. She stood and held up LaGina's invitation. "Do you need this?"

Eye contact

"Master, I can't see much."

"I know. She is weak and will not last long." The Master glided about the room as if pacing. "Just tell me if it is there."

"I don't know. You said it could look like anybody. How would I tell?"

"Its eyes. You will see it if it is there."

Lewis had to wait until she looked at each man in turn. He focused and the picture in his mind cleared some. He couldn't hear anything. The connection with her *was* weak. Shame. She probably would die several times before she died for good. Maybe he would see her on the other side someday. Except he'd be Naked and she wouldn't.

There was some sort of discussion going on. One of them seemed to have something about his eyes. If she would just keep her head still...

Yes! He could see it now. Lewis couldn't identify what it was, but there was definitely something there not in the others. The people were even in a hotel—Lewis saw the name just over the clerk behind a big, semi-circular counter.

"Master, it is him. I even know where they are. Would you like us to go there?"

"No." Lewis felt the master's warmth upon his back. "You are nearly Naked Before Me. All of you should aspire to be like your brother."

The Ghost Toucher

Lewis beamed from the master's praise. He wished he could open his eyes to see the faces of the others, especially Cindy because he wanted to impress her. But how awesome was it to be complimented by a *god*?

***

Gunner picked up the phone on the third buzz. He flipped it open and clicked on the text message he'd just gotten. It was a simple address and nothing else. Normally, he would have been annoyed and deleted the message, but the sender's phone number told him something he needed to know. Getting rid of the first detective had been easy. These clowns would be no sweat, either.

He strode back into his room, texting a phone number back and clapped the phone shut before tossing it onto the bed. Gunner knew a guy who knew a guy who would put his contact in touch with some fine imported goods. He was a rich kid so Gunner knew he had to deliver something above and beyond to get him going.

Gunner picked up the silver jewelry box on his dresser next to an onyx container. He probably shouldn't leave that container there, but what was the harm? The Old Man would have wanted him to put it in a safety deposit box or something gay, but even if somebody broke into his place they'd never know what it was.

He opened the jewelry box. There wasn't anything in it, but it was very important, nonetheless. He thought about the address and bowed his head, holding the jewelry box up and then set it down to go back to his robes. He had to finish getting ready for his party.

***

She'd cried all day. Mel couldn't console her, she just wouldn't stop. She wouldn't even eat. Now all of a sudden she perked up and began pointing like a maniac. She cradled the cheap little doll he'd bought her at the gas station.

Mel started the truck and put it in gear. A Burger King was coming up on the left and he looked at her. She licked her lips, looking nervously back and forth between the sign and him.

"You want something?" he asked with a smile. He couldn't stand BK, but she wasn't picky.

She looked like she was thinking, drool running down her chin and then nodded. Mel rubbed his side as he pulled in the lot. It felt like he'd broken a rib from a coughing fit and his knee was completely locked up.

That's my girl, he thought.

***

Anna just wanted to go home. But she was just so tired. Mr. Israel and Mr. Greene had apologized over and over until she thought they were probably okay. She had no idea what happened to her eyes if it wasn't them. The only thing she'd had to eat today was that burger and fries during lunch. Maybe it was food poisoning. Maybe she needed to go to a hospital. Her stomach felt fine—maybe she could just take a nap first.

They'd decided to split up into their rooms for the night. Mr. Israel had convinced her to stay. There did seem to be something dangerous going on. He'd taken her to the room and she'd called her roommate after he left.

"Oh yeah," Christy'd said when she asked her to take care of the dogs. "You got a mean one, huh?" meaning a date she wanted to go to bed with. Anna's first instinct was to say no, but it was a much simpler explanation than the truth. "Well make that protection connection!" Christy was good for corny sayings like disease awareness was just recently en vogue.

Anna got off the phone before she said too much. She didn't want to admit, but she did feel a little different. Bigger, somehow. Like she could look outside and see for miles or touch with someone else's hands.

She didn't want to think about it. Just get in bed as soon as possible and put today behind her. She made a quick stop in the bathroom, taking care to avoid looking in the mirror. Whatever was going on with her eyes she could wait until a doctor gave her a shot.

Anna went to the door and cracked it open. Mr. Israel had his back to her. He had something in his hand, it looked like a squeeze bottle maybe. He was spraying the contents on the floor in wide arcs. She pulled the door closed just before he turned in her direction and a moment later she could hear the spray hitting the door.

What was he doing?

She plopped down on the couch and folded her arms. Was it cold in here? Anna had felt like this when she woke up in the trunk. Maybe she should go to the hospital.

Israel knocked on the door before letting himself in.

"Everybody decent?"

Kelly had just watched Taze snort a rail of something white. He didn't know his drugs so it could have been anything. Taze had been so casual about it, even offered him some. Kelly had politely refused.

Now he was holding a joint loosely between his lips. By luck, this was a non-smoking room and Kelly had avoided the argument by pointing to the sign on the door. It struck him as ironic that there was no sign prohibiting illicit drug use.

"Yeah, I'm tight," Taze said, the joint flopping up and down. "Just about to break out for a spliff." He took the joint out of his mouth and pointed the butt-end to Israel. "Partake?"

"Pass." Israel stepped aside to let him out. Once the door was shut he asked Kelly, "So what's the plan?"

"Me?" Kelly said. "This whole thing's your boondoggle. You don't have a plan?"

"Nope. The police are going to arrest you on the spot—we're both wanted, there are people trying to kill or kidnap us and I'm pretty sure someone at your network had something to do with Stout Roost's disappearance."

"Really? What makes you say that?"

"Well the police already called—"

"No. I meant Stout."

"Oh. We're being followed. That little girl at the gas station and someone else."

"How do you know? I haven't seen anyone. And that girl was only, what, three? I doubt she's a danger."

"She is. Look, you're going to see people who aren't people at all. Tools, weapons sent from the other side. The living on the other side can't just walk over here—that's like an astronaut stepping out of the space shuttle without a suit."

"So we have to be on the lookout for tools that look like people?"

"I know some of them. And no, not all of them are people."

"So what kind of weapon is she?"

"Think of her more as a detonator. She attaches herself to someone and turns him into a kind of bomb."

"Do you think those diffoid guys are weapons?"

"No." Israel shook his head. "They're human with something else mixed in. I don't know what. I've never seen anything like them before."

"What kind of bomb? I mean, do they explode or something?"

"You don't wanna know."

Kelly thought a moment then let out a deep breath.

"I suppose we have to do the unexpected. I say we find Gayle Hills' house and wait for him. Go on the offensive."

"And then what?"

"We make him talk."

"How?"

"I don't know. Waterboard him or something."

"Yikes. You're pretty hardcore. You got the stomach for that?"

"I have to. We have to do something to figure our way out of this thing. I have to keep him away from my mother's house. He's probably the one who had mine burned down. We can make him confess at least."

"Why would he do that?"

"Because he hates me as much as I hate him."

"I'm not so sure about that. Sure he kidnapped us, but it seemed more like a business move to me."

"Yeah, but until we know his partner's angle I say we stay on this track."

Israel headed for the door.

The Ghost Toucher

"Well I'm tuckered." Taze was waiting outside the door when he opened it. They shouldered past one another and Kelly thought they gave each other the eye.

Taze promptly pulled out his hand mirror, laid it on the counter and poured out a little pile of white powder onto it from a baggie. He chopped it into three smaller piles and made them into neat lines with a black AMEX card.

Kelly felt like he should say something. In practice, he believed it was a person's own business what they did to their bodies, but to see it in person... And why was he doing so much?

And how did he get a black AMEX?

Kelly passed by as casually as he could, spying the name on it where it lay on the counter. William K. Goode III.

Nah, he couldn't be related. Not *the* Goode family, could he?

He was high as a kite and probably wouldn't remember if Kelly did ask. Why not?

"So where you from, Taze?"

The skinny, younger man looked up from his work. His eyes were red-rimmed and bloodshot.

"Oh, skillet, all over. I mean, I was born here, but I lived in Greece, Japan, Italy, Topeka, Dublin, y'know."

"What, was your father in the military or something?"

"Nah, not *my* pops." Taze rolled his eyes. "Junior was a company man."

"Oh, what company?"

"Don't act like you don't know, homie. My granddad's more famous than the one-dollar bill."

Kelly shook his head, maintaining his blank expression. Taze let out a long sigh, rolling his eyes again.

"Bill Goode from Goode's, y'know the supermarket chain? Inventor of the potato chip?

"Oh, *that* Bill Goode. Man, he'd be well over a hundred years old now. How's he your grandfather?"

"I never met him or nothin', but he had my da—Junior—late. Like in his sixties or seventies. He'd had a family already but they died or somethin'. Junior didn't get married until he was seventy."

Kelly had never seen Bill Goode, Junior, but if he was in his sixties when Taze was born he had to be in the neighborhood of ninety by now.

"Skillet, you okay? Where you at?"

"Sorry. I was thinking—lost in a thought."

"I get that sometimes. When I'm high, y'know?" He pointed to the last rail left on the mirror. "Sure you don't wanna get down?"

"Thanks man, but no. I'm going to turn in for an early start."

"No probs. I think I'll stay up tonight. Hey, you think we gon' get into somethin' tomorrow like in Ferndale?"

"I hope not." Kelly rubbed a hand over his face. "I never want to see anything like that ever again."

"Alright, dog. Sleep tight."

"You too. Well, y'know."

Kelly hated not having anything clean to wear. Tomorrow would be the third day straight he'd be wearing these clothes. Even if they had to go to a Target he had to get something else to put on.

He went into the bedroom and shut the door. The sudden quiet was unsettling. He had a looming feeling something was about to happen so he left the door open a peak so a sliver of light came in. Kelly checked under the bed and in the tiny closet but he knew the monsters were out now. They were out there somewhere, looking for him. He collapsed on the bed, suddenly exhausted and with barely enough strength left to not leave his feet hanging over the edge.

***

Jemen drove around aimlessly. She didn't know where to search to find him. Right now Two was stationed outside of police headquarters in Detroit. Burning down Kelly Greene's house was an accident, but may have been a blessing in disguise on the off chance he did turn himself in. She somehow doubted it, but anything was possible in this world. In no other place had she seen so many coincidences, things that had occurred that could never happen again. Chance encounters between long lost loved ones, accidents that took the lives of would-be murderers, a poor man's fortune being made in an instant.

Divine providence was commonplace here. Surely the same would happen for her if she were to indeed save the world.

She laughed at her own inside joke. Bhuul was no goddess. A whore amongst the Greaters, she was not one to be worshipped, except by her whorish followers.

Jemen heard the beep of the fuel gauge, indicating she needed gas soon. There was a Sunoco gas station up ahead and she flipped on her turn signal. She pulled in, passing by a sickly-looking sallow-faced man with a hideous child in the passenger seat of his pick-up truck before stopping at a pump. She shook her head. Even the coin of divinity had an ugly side.

Oodles hopped out of her lap and she left the boys in the backseat, cradling her belly as she walked inside the store to pay for gas. Jemen stood in a short line, eyeing the rows of cigarettes behind and above the attendant. Artie had some in the glove compartment. Their smell was lovely and she had chewed them up when she was beginning her gestation with Two. Had she known she could have purchased more of these she would have had them with Three as well. She looked away to her car outside and saw the boys were excited about something. Imperfect as they were, they had one definite benefit. They were like hounds in their ability to sense things she could not. She'd learned very quickly not to ignore them.

It appeared as if they were watching the truck she'd passed by. More specifically the little girl not in a child seat, but standing and looking out the window. She looked at the child and realized it was not providence that created her but rather the crooked hand of man.

Perhaps she would have her share of divinity tonight! If that child was what she thought it was it was probably searching for Kelly as well. The man climbed back in his truck and Jemen realized she would have to risk not filling her tank.

"Hey Buddy," the attendant behind the counter said. "You need a fill-up or what?"

"I am no man," Jemen replied as she headed out the door. "I am a Greater," she spoke to herself, cradling her belly as she headed to the car.

***

Martin Hoops' shipment was due to come in today. He didn't care whether they were going to eat them, turn them into cure-alls or make-up. It was two hundred K, easy. He strolled out of the coffee shop, his chubby hands shoved into his deep, empty pockets and hailed a taxi that blew past. But his herpes hadn't flared up today so he didn't mind.

He spotted a taxi on the other side of a red light up the street. Right in front of him a blue hair was trying to parallel park a giant powder blue Crown Vic. He waved a hand to the taxi as he stepped out on the curb, hoping the driver wouldn't ignore him. The blue hair alternated between stomping on the gas and the brake, her head bobbling as she lurched ever closer to the Mercury Cougar behind her.

How long was this light? Martin kept his arm up. Some tall fatso in a Member's Only jacket bumped him and continued up the street even though the sidewalk was wide enough for the both of them to walk with their arms stretched out and not touch. Some people. Martin just stepped a foot or two into the street. What was taking that light so long?

His calm demeanor was starting to slip. He waved his arm faster as if that would somehow hurry the cab. The blue hair across the street revved the car in park then lurched in reverse again.

Cross traffic stopped up the street and the taxi crawled down the two lane street. Martin's gut told him to stay put but he wanted to get out of here and down to the dock. The taxi slowed as the brown-skinned bearded driver came into view and Martin's smile of relief froze on his face as something large to his right filled his peripheral vision.

Martin turned to see the blue hair just as the bumper of the Crown Vic crushed his shin. He slapped his palms down on the hood as he thought he saw her large, fish-goggled eyes locked on him as she continued to run him over.

He fell to the ground and the tire ran diagonally across his midsection crushing everything inside him from his hip to the opposite shoulder. Blood erupted from his nose and mouth and in the few seconds before he died, in the midst of excruciating pain he heard her stomp and go action as she reversed again and the taxi continued past.

***

A myoklonic twitch woke Kelly up. He slid his palm across his chest and he was on the verge of falling back asleep when he saw the silhouette of a man sitting in a chair, facing him.

"Hello?"

"I couldn't tell you everything I knew at the time. The Board is trying to play this as close to the vest as possible."

"Mr. Brimmer?" Kelly could only see the top of his bald head in the moonlight coming through the window shade. He looked like he had something sticking through his head.

"The Board has already been contacted by the lead attorney for the mothers. They are suing us *in toto*." Brimmer sat back, putting his face in the light. He was dead. A ghost—a crowbar sticking out of his head behind either ear. "I'll be up front with you. This whole child support mess would be nothing under normal circumstances. When we first signed Stout to do *The Ghost Toucher* we got him for a pittance. The stock was in the toilet and that was practically all he asked for. I mean, we couldn't give it away at the time and he asked for twenty percent plus scale. We have every suspicion he bought an additional twenty percent over the last four years through various channels."

"So that would give him controlling interest?" Kelly asked, propping himself up on one elbow.

"Yes, the savvy bastard. And if he's dead his stock rolls over to his children. We tried to get him to sign a clause that would default his stock back to the Network in the event of his death and his beneficiaries would get a payout of the value, but he balked."

"Wouldn't that negate his controlling interest if forty percent of your stock gets divided over fourteen people?"

"Under normal circumstances, yes. And that wouldn't have been so bad. But in an effort to get this whole mess settled our attorneys approached the families and offered a settlement. They turned it down."

"Why would they do that?"

"Because they have a deal with someone else. Someone who is paying for those high-powered attorneys. Someone who'd have special interest in controlling at least forty percent of the Network. I think it's Unicero."

"The Spanish station?" Kelly asked. Brimmer nodded. "I *love* that *ChíChé* show."

"Me too. Everybody does. Unicero already has eleven percent. Combined with that forty they'd be the rulers of the roost."

"Mr. Brimmer, could I ask—what happened?"

"Oh, you mean this?" he gestured to his head. "Thought I could eat my cake and have it too. It's kind of funny; I was there at the start of it all and now that I've crossed—" he wiggled both index and middle fingers "—it's kind of disappointing."

Brimmer stood. Kelly couldn't see any legs, but he heard clacking on the floor as if he were stepping on hardwood. Kelly thought he should say more but didn't know what. An invisible goat bleated before he disappeared through the door.

Kelly wanted to think about what he'd just learned, but he found himself unable to keep his eyes open. He closed them and slumped back onto the bed in less than twenty seconds.

***

Vosloo had had a good life in Lebanon, he wished he'd never left. But hair treatment at home was at least twenty years behind what they were doing in America. As he sat at the light, poking at his tingling scalp, wondering when the treatments would begin showing results, he didn't see the giant approach.

He knocked on the window and Vosloo jumped. He had to have come from somewhere behind his cab. There was a Jeep or

The Ghost Toucher

something with its blinkers on in the middle lane behind him; his car must have stalled.

"Would you follow that truck for me?" the guy said. He had really long, thick dark hair. Vosloo had hair like that when he was a boy until his mother had cut it off. It hadn't been right since. Vosloo rolled down his window.

"What?" Vosloo wondered what he used on it.

"That truck." The guy pointed with a ratdog in his hand at a truck two vehicles up and one over. He was cradling a low hanging beer gut in the other. "Would you follow it?"

Vosloo had no interest in giving this freak a ride, no matter how nice his hair was. He'd had a pretty good night, anyway.

"It depends on what kind of dog that is, guy."

"I am not a guy," the guy said. "And what about my dog?"

"Is it the kind that shits?"

"What?"

The light had turned green and the cars in front of him had already pulled away. Vosloo stepped on the gas, but the idiot in front of him stopped, forcing Vosloo to stomp on his brakes to keep from rear-ending him.

This time he did see the big guy approach, but he was coming up very fast. Vosloo felt a surge of panic, throwing the cab in reverse but a vehicle settled in behind the cab, trapping him.

"Go around!" he turned around and shouted, but he could see that the old man behind the wheel hadn't seen or heard him. He started to roll up his window when the guy was suddenly there.

He reached through the glass, his mighty hand clasping around Vosloo's neck. Vosloo felt a brief, stinging pressure across his chest and lap as the seat belt snapped and he was terrifyingly weightless a moment before crashing into a wooden telephone pole.

Vosloo woke up. This was wonderful where ever he was. He felt better than he ever had before. The street was strange, though. No cars for one and it looked like it was paved with cobblestone. They didn't even use that back home anymore. His feet felt wrong so he looking down and saw he didn't have any—he was floating!

This was great! Vosloo passed by a building and saw someone with a thick head of long, wavy chestnut hair.

It was him.

This place was too good to be true. There were some people up ahead a ways. Vosloo *floated* in their direction. They were all gathered around this building, trying to force their way inside. The architecture here was very strange. As he got closer to the people he saw they had on strange clothes. It was like something out of one of those children's books with that cat that wore that hat.

He wanted to talk to someone to find out what was going on. No one looked at him, but every time he got close to one he or she would wave a hand at him like they were shooing a fly. Finally he settled just outside the crowd and waited to see what they were waiting for.

A moment later a man fell out the window.

***

"Ay yo, homie, wake up." Kelly felt a hand on his leg. He sat up in the dark and could barely make out Taze's silhouette.

"What do you want?"

"Somethin's goin' down next door."

"Go for a walk or something. You're high."

"No. I mean, yeah, I am. But for real doe, there is somethin' goin' on over there. On the rilla."

Kelly climbed out of bed. He didn't think anything had happened; nothing had happened to the two of them. Probably best to check. He could hop back in the bed in a few minutes.

Still groggy, he weaved his way from the bedroom, through the living room and out the front door. He turned and Taze bumped into him.

Israel's door was open. Suddenly awake, Kelly rushed in and ran into the bedroom. He threw the light on and didn't know whether to scream or throw up from the smell. He clapped a hand over his mouth and tried his best not to do either.

***

Four minutes, thirty-eight seconds earlier—

Mel was exhausted. He didn't want to take another step. His whole body hurt. But she smiled at him and he was moving again.

He should be in the hospital. This had to be some kind of flu or something. He was burning up. Was burping a symptom? They were almost there now. As soon as they were done, though he was heading to the ER.

Done with what?

Mel looked over at the fat little girl on his hip. Man, what an ugly kid. She was breathing out of her mouth and drooling, her eyes locked forward. She kept kicking her fat little legs, her heels digging into his stomach and back like she was spurring a horse.

Where was she taking him?

That was an odd thing to think. How could *she* be taking *him* anywhere? He was the one doing all the walking. They stopped in front of a door in the long hallway. The sharp ache in his knees and back sat up like a good doggy and begged.

He waited as she looked back and forth between this door and the next one over. Finally she bucked her hips, grunting for him to move over to the next door. He went over and raised a hand to knock.

"Hey, is this where your mommy lives?" It all made sense to him now. Of course the kid wanted to get back to her mother as soon as possible. All of a sudden Mel's aches and pains didn't seem so bad (though he did have a monster fart cramping up his stomach). She'd been scared all this time and he'd finally brought her to her mother. All that business before, he'd just been confused.

She was smiling again, but kind of like she did before she ate. Mel was glad he wouldn't have to feed her anything else. He knocked and waited.

After the fifth time knocking, they both were growing impatient. Mel tried the handle but it didn't budge. She even leaned in to pound on the door with a pudgy fist. Sick of waiting, Mel lowered his shoulder and rammed into the door. He was a big guy (though noticeably smaller to anyone who knew him) so it gave way pretty easily. His shoulder made a nasty crunching sound, but he could take it. Hell, it didn't even hurt. Matter of fact, nothing did. Mel only felt a growing warmth in the pit of his stomach. It felt good to be doing something good.

He walked through the living room. Her mother was gonna be so excited. He felt hot all of a sudden, feverish. He stumbled and caught himself on the couch, his shoulder making a sick, twisting sound.

The bedroom door was open. Mel passed a mirror and saw his reflection. His skin was pasty and saggy, his eyes bloodshot. What was worse than the flu?

Never mind. Mel went into the bedroom. Someone was beneath the covers and she rolled over. He hated the thought of waking her. To be honest, it was a little stalkery him breaking in like this, even if it was to bring her kid. But he was here now and there wasn't any point in turning back.

The little girl pushed away from him. He set her down and let out a deep belch. Man, that stunk. His esophagus felt like it was on fire.

"Ma'am?" he tried to say, but his voice was all wrong. He couldn't even hear himself. Mel wiped the free-flowing sweat from his face, his skin feeling thin as paper. He stepped closer, standing over her and tried calling out to her again, but his voice was just gone.

Mel felt something move in his stomach, felt it clench and turn and begin inching its way up. It was giving him a wicked case of heartburn and a bitter, acidy taste on the back of his tongue. The last thing he heard before his head exploded was the little girl laughing.

***

"Skillet, what *is* that?" Kelly wasn't able to keep his gorge down after all. The stink from the bed was awful.

Something—and someone—had melted through it. Part of a foot teetered on the edge of a man-sized dark green, frothy ringed ovular hole that ran diagonally across the bed. Kelly didn't think he could look inside, but he was reasonably certain it went all the way to the floor. Whatever it was had eaten away the thin carpet around the perimeter of the bed, exposing the concrete underneath.

There were other parts that weren't digested (he had no idea why *that* word seemed to fit)—or at least not completely. There were finger bones, a piece of scalp, something that may have been an elbow in the green froth.

"Whatchoo gon' do?" He'd forgotten Taze was there. Kelly looked at him as if he'd grown some body part a man shouldn't have. Taze peered into the hole with casual interest, like some teenager on a field trip to the DIA, looking at a painting just to pass the time. Kelly had heard prolonged oxy use could result in the inability to feel empathy; it wouldn't be a surprise to learn that was one of his drugs of choice.

"Who do you think it was—the phatty or the skinny?"

"The what?"

"The pha—oh, right. The phatty, y'know, the girl, or the dude—the skinny."

"Skinny? I've never heard that before."

"That's 'cause I made it up.

"And guys are skinnies?"

"Yeah, 'cause that's the opposite of phatty. 'Cept you spell it S-K-I-N-N-E-E. I mean I-E."

"I get it. I think... I think we'd better leave."

Who had been in the bed was a good question. Kelly could easily imagine either of them killing the other, though the thought hadn't seriously crossed his mind earlier. He thought they could trust Anna and he thought Israel hadn't seriously intended to kill her. But then he thought of another question.

What if someone else had done it and they were still here?

Kelly crouched and spun around. Taze must have thought along the same lines because he was holding a hand cannon and pointing it in the general direction of the doorway.

"Guess we don't need to check under the bed." Kelly nodded toward the closet and Taze leveled the gun in that direction as they approached together. Taze fired a shot and Kelly pushed his arm away as if that would redirect the bullet.

"What the hell?" he mouthed at Taze. The taller man looked as if he didn't understand what he'd done wrong. Kelly walked up to the closet and threw the door open, hoping a dead body wouldn't fall out.

Anna's petite, limp body was huddled into the corner of the closet, Taze's bullet hole a few inches above and to the left of her head. She had all her clothes on and Kelly pulled her collar down to feel for a pulse in her neck. Slow, but there.

"We're checking out." Kelly stood and scooped her up. She felt heavier than he thought she should as they hustled out of the room.

The Ghost Toucher

Reach for it

LaGina rang the doorbell. Her black strappy dress hugged her curves well, but she felt uncomfortable in it. Maybe it was guilt at leaving the boys home with their grandmother, but she hadn't been out in a long time. She deserved this.

There was something about him. He was obviously important to be able to walk right into the CEO's office like that. There was a cockiness and a danger in his smile and the way he walked over and dropped the invite on her desk. Maybe someone else would have dismissed it as arrogance, but she could tell there was something more. She had to see what this man was all about.

A tall blonde woman in a red strapless dress answered the door. LaGina was a little crestfallen to see another woman was here, but she hadn't really known what to expect. It was an invitation to a party. The woman was pretty and blue-eyed, though LaGina's natural olive tone was much better than her artificial tan. LaGina didn't have her smile lines either, though they seemed around the same age. She was thin-hipped and busty while LaGina was shapelier everywhere else.

"Hi," the woman said, extending a hand. LaGina matched her limp shake, not wanting to dominate. She stepped into the apartment and the woman closed the door behind her.

"I'm Gina," she said, but the blonde didn't introduce herself. Smooth jazz played in the background. There were only a half

The Ghost Toucher

dozen people in the great room. It had tall white walls and a slanted ceiling. What looked like African art decorated the walls except for the one to the left which was all glass, looking out over the city from fifty something stories up.

From the depressions in the mauve carpet it looked like furniture had been moved out of the room. Two couples were standing in front of sculptures on opposite walls, apparently discussing them. A grizzled-looking middle-aged man in an ill-fitted cheap suit slumped in a chair at the large, dark wood table in the center of the room. He looked lost. He stared into space and if it weren't for the slow up and down of his chest she might have thought he was dead.

The woman in the red dress disappeared into what looked like the kitchen. Maybe LaGina had gotten the wrong impression. She expected an actual party. This looked like it was going to be a séance.

A tall man walked into the room in an all white thing cinched at the waist with a black rope. The upper part had long slits up the sleeves, exposing well-muscled arms. He had weird tattoos on his body everywhere she could see skin, including his face. It took a moment in the candle light, but she realized this was Gunner. She had the sudden feeling of déjà vu, as if she had seen this face before but couldn't recall where she would have seen him outside the office.

"Hey!" He clapped his hands once and everyone but the man sitting down turned. "Everyone's supposed to be seated, Linda!"

"Sorry Gun!" Linda came out of the kitchen, holding a fondue dish.

"Linda, that's for later!" He waved a hand at her and she turned around and took it back.

He turned around and his eyes locked on LaGina.

"Ms. Densmore." He took a few long strides over to her and took her hands into his own. "It's so *good* to see you. I'm glad you could come. Please." He gestured to the table and followed her there. Linda had an almost predatory look on her face as she passed.

He seated her across from him and Linda scooted into the empty seat beside him and glared at LaGina. The young couple in the two seats next to her were giggling and whispering. The young man saw Gunner eyeing them and the smile dropped from his face.

"Can we do introductions?" an older woman on the other side of the table said.

"Yeah, Gun," Linda said. "This is supposed to be fun. Let's everyone trade names."

Gunner made a face, but quickly recovered.

"Yes, yes. Good idea. I'm Gunner as you all know. I communicate with the alternatively living. You all have been invited here as my special guests."

He nodded to the older man next to him who'd already been at the table.

"My name's Henry Quint. I'm looking for my daughter." He dug a laminated picture out of his jacket pocket of an eight-ish looking girl with short curly hair and large dark eyes. If that was his most recent picture from the looks of the style of her clothes and hair she'd been missing a long, long time. "Please, if any of you know anything that can help me find my Katie..." The women in the room collectively awed, LaGina included.

He teared up and the woman next to him put a comforting hand on his forearm. Gunner put a hand on the older man's shoulder and LaGina could see real sincerity in his eyes.

"Well my name is Rachel," the young woman holding Henry's forearm said. "I'm here with my husband, Bill—we've been married two weeks!" Bill shifted as a smattering of applause went around the table. "We're here visiting my in-laws."

Bill just shrugged and said, "I'm Bill," before turning to LaGina.

"I'm Gina. I work for the Network. I'm in the controller's office." She didn't know what else to do, so she waved and immediately felt stupid.

"Oh, you probably see stars all the time!" an older woman next to Linda said.

"Have you met Stout?" Bill asked. Rachel's happy mask expression slipped and she shot Bill a dirty look.

"Actually, I don't typically meet the actors, but I've seen Stout Roost a time or two," LaGina lied.

"I *love* that show," the older man on LaGina's other side said.

"*James*," the older woman said with a disapproving look on her face.

"Oh hush, Phyllis," James said. "It's about as good as any one of your soaps. And how many times can one woman be kidnapped by the same man anyway?"

Something about Gunner's expression suggested he was uncomfortable or annoyed with the conversation.

"Phyllis... James... why don't we go ahead and get started?"

Everyone shifted around in their chairs, but didn't complain. Gunner bowed his head as if concentrating.

"I'm Linda, by the way," Linda whispered and gave a little wave.

"Shouldn't we hold hands or something?" Phyllis asked.

"Yes." Gunner didn't look up. "That would be good."

After everyone was holding hands (Rachel eyed Bill's hand holding LaGina's), Gunner said, "Do not be afraid of anything you're about to see or hear. I am your guide and I will protect you. Anything that may wish to do you harm has to pass through me first and I will sever the connection immediately before that happens."

LaGina was nervous, but she thought Gunner looked a little worried as well.

Okay, it was officially his first time doing this, but Gunner was relatively sure he knew what he was doing. The witch had managed to avoid being located by the detective he had hired but she was just as tied into the dead as he was. It was ironic that he would use them to find her. Gunner just needed to borrow a little life energy from these suckers and finding her would be easy. They'd all be fine; maybe a couple hours shaved off the end of their lives, maybe they'd get sicker more often than they were used to, but no one would drop over. At least he hoped. That's why Gunner had specifically targeted out-of-towners, except for Linda and Gina. They were both hot and he wanted to hook up some three-way action.

He began to 'concentrate'. He'd take what he needed in a few short seconds, but he had to give everybody a show so they had something to tell their friends and families about. Gunner kind of wished he'd been around in the olden days before people knew ghouls and ghosts were real. Now all the mystery was spoiled. It took something nobody had ever seen before to get even a remote amount of interest. The psychic business had taken a huge tumble now that anyone could communicate with the dead. You had to hustle to get people through the door; it was no longer just a walk-in business. You had to *be* the act. It was no longer enough to say you were speaking with the dead, you had to show it. Stout Roost had seen to all that. Now ghosts were mundane, another victim of 'reality' TV.

Gunner snuck a peak at LaGina. God, she was hot. He'd gotten them all here on the false pretense of contacting some long lost family member or friend except her. He had a thing for exotic-looking chicks and he'd made a beeline for her yesterday before he'd seen the Old Man. He couldn't think up an excuse to talk to her and found himself blabbing about the party and before he realized it he was handing her one of the fresh invites he'd had made at FedEx Kinko's. He hoped the ceremony didn't scare her off, but he had to do this if he was going to have anything like a normal life again.

Truth be told it was virtually impossible to contact one particular spirit. Maybe a certain kind of spirit. Like someone who had been a lawyer in life, but if you were looking for Johnny Cochrane forget about it. The other side was a very big place. The trick was opening the door just a little bit. Let the suckers see just enough. They'd all see a spirit and think it was the one they were looking for and before they saw anymore he'd slam it shut. But while he'd be doing that they wouldn't have a clue that he was also sapping the precious life energy he needed from them.

They'd be a little tired after, lending to the credibility of what they'd witnessed and go home to sleep it off. But Gunner wouldn't be sleeping. He'd barely slept the last few days. That would come after he made the witch take it off. And after he killed her. Maybe he could convince Linda and LaGina to sleep it off here until he came back. Well, Linda would be easy, he was already banging her.

"Semper ubi sub ubi..." Gunner started with a few phrases in Latin, meaningless stuff, but it sounded impressive. "aut viam inveniam aut faciam... auribus teneo lupum... in articulo mortis... in manus meum commendo spiritum tuas..." The real process had already happened in his mind but people needed a show to buy in. Gunner pressed a button beneath the table with his knee and super-cooled air poured out of hidden vents in the ceiling.

"Oh, I think I feel something," the old woman said. Phyllis, he thought her name was. Good. Her reaction would feed the others' perceptions. Linda squeezed his hand a little tighter, the platinum ring on his ring finger digging into his pinky and middle. Henry Quint, on the other hand, just kept his fingers stuck straight out like a dry piece of cardboard. Gunner wondered if he peered into the guy if there was any soul inside of him at all.

He almost felt bad for Quint. He'd heard a little bit of his story before inviting him because the guy would talk to anyone who would listen. Kid had vanished fifteen years ago, marriage evaporated after his wife had given up and he couldn't hold onto a job for more than a few months at a time. But he'd never wavered. That was dedication. Gunner wondered how much time the Old Man would waste before he gave up on him or his sister. No doubt Quint's little girl was dead and if he could help anyone it would be him.

Focus. He couldn't afford to get distracted. Spirits couldn't kill, but that didn't mean they weren't dangerous if you didn't keep a reign on them. Gunner felt one like a cold block of ice almost touching the back of his neck. It was here. He concentrated, moving it toward the center of the table.

"He's sweating," the pussy-whipped one said.

The cool was just past his forehead and there were a couple 'oohs'. Now was the time to work some magic.

"Spirit, if there is one here you knew in last-life please touch them."

"Oh my God," the old guy said. "Craig, is that you?"

"Hampton? You with us?" someone else said.

"Shirley?"

Gunner snuck another peak to see they had all broken the circle to reach up and touch the cold space above them like people feeling around in the dark. It was a spirit, but they didn't feel Gunner's connection to it, couldn't know the cold was more than an absence of heat, but that it also leaked a miniscule amount of life out of all of them and filtered it into him. He didn't need to take much—just enough to suit his purposes.

LaGina was staring up at it like she could see. That wasn't possible, but she stood and he could see recognition dawning on her face. Maybe there was something she could see and no one else. Gunner had heard if two spirits recognized one another the one in a living body could see it but that had to be a one-in-a-million shot.

He thought it was worth the risk until she reached out and said, "Stout?" and collapsed on the table.

***

Sheriff Wilson had been acting strange since yesterday. Ever since that weird no-rain storm over by Garbutt Park he just didn't seem himself.

Deputy Collie Eaves watched the man over his cup of coffee, leaning back in his chair. For starters, it was four in the morning and Collie was certain the sheriff hadn't gone home. He had on the same uniform as yesterday or else this mustard-stained shirt had an identical twin at home.

But it was more than that. His body language and mannerisms had all changed. The bit of Bostonian accent he had was gone and his walk was different too.

Right now the sheriff was looking at a map of metro Detroit, but he had it laid out on the floor and was crawling over it like an animal. Maybe he'd had a stroke. Maybe his wife's death had finally gotten to him. Except for her funeral he hadn't even taken off any time.

Collie stood, setting his coffee down and stretching out his big frame. No one else was looking. Good. There were over fifty people who worked out of this building and it would spread like wildfire if anyone else saw him like this. Collie quickly walked over to the sheriff, leaning against the wall to block him from view by anyone down the hall.

"Sir, can I help you find something?"

The sheriff made some kind of grunting sound, his head jerking before he looked up at Collie.

"What do you... want?" Sheriff Wilson's eyes were red and rheumy.

"You're looking for something." Collie crouched, putting his fingers on the map. The sheriff slapped them away. "May I help?"

"No. I—" he looked Collie up and down as if seeing him for the very first time. Collie turned his wrists back and forth, flexing the muscles in his forearms where they rested across his thighs.

"Yes. Yes, you can...help." Sheriff Wilson's head was parallel to the floor as he got to his feet. He stood up straight. "You need to find... location. This car—" he scrawled a license number on a post-it with his left hand—funny, Collie didn't know Sheriff Wilson was ambidextrous—and gave it to him. "Do not disappoint me."

Collie logged into LEIN. In a moment he had the name and number of the limousine service that owned it. Parke Cars. He dialed it and after a few rings a young-voiced woman picked up. Collie hadn't thought to ask why the sheriff wanted it but he told her the car had been involved in a minor traffic accident and they needed to speak to the driver.

After a few transfers and re-explanations and identifying himself several times he had the cell number and last location of the vehicle. Collie thanked the elderly gentleman for his cooperation and hung up.

He plugged the GPS coordinates into his phone and it popped up an address in Detroit on Grand River. A McDonald's on the West side. Going to the city. He wondered if the sheriff would want to give a courtesy call before they crossed Eight Mile.

"I found your car," Collie said. The older man stepped over to him and clasped his arm. His grip hurt. Collie resisted the urge to pull away and he eventually let go. "So what do you want to do?"

Sheriff Wilson walked out of his office and Collie followed. They walked out of the building and into the parking lot.

"There's a man I need to arrest. A rapist. A murderer. He must be brought to justice."

"Should we get DPD involved?" This sounded personal to Collie. He wondered who.

"No police. This one is mine. They killed the Dolores."

Dolores—wasn't that his wife? Whoa, Collie had heard she'd died of cancer. What kind of bastard raped and killed somebody with cancer?

"Sir, I'd like to ride along."

"There will be danger. Do as I say and nothing more."

"Yes sir."

They walked across the lot to a cruiser and got in. Sheriff Wilson started it up then paused a moment before putting on his seat belt. He turned to Collie and patted him on his balding head.

"Good job."

It was weird, but considering what had happened to his wife Collie thought he probably was just a little bit off. This whole thing was outside of normal procedure, but if it paid off there could be something big at the end of it for him.

The lesser looked at the big one through the human's meat eyes. Yes, bringing this one along could prove helpful. If this body was damaged, it could skip into that one. No doubt the Jexclp'ar knew it was missing by now. But perhaps redemption would come if it possessed the Hated one and brought it to the Jexclp'ar. Then all would know the Hated one was real and not defunct prophecy.

The lesser smiled as it plotted everything out with its meat brain.

She woke up.

"Hey-hey, I think she's coming around."

Kelly spotted a McDonald's ahead and flipped on the turn signal. He had to find out what happened in that room.

He found an open spot near the back of the lot by a dumpster.

"Taze, can you go get us some coffee or something?"

"Y'know it."

Taze got out of the car and strolled inside and Kelly went around to the backseat.

"Anna? Anna, how are you?"

The Ghost Toucher

She looked at him and at first Kelly thought she was still unconscious. But then she blinked a couple times—something suddenly familiar in her eyes—and she said, "You know we have to get rid of him," in Israel's voice.

Kelly leapt away from her, hitting his head on the ceiling of the car. "Anna?" he said from as far on the opposite side of the car as he could get.

He heard an answer, but had to shake his head. He'd heard somewhere that auditory hallucinations could be a sign of brain cancer. Or serial killers. She'd spoken in two voices, male and female, one saying 'no', but the other saying 'yes', though he was unsure which had said what.

"Who... who are you?"

"That's a complicated answer," Anna said in her feminine voice. "But Israel can explain it better than I can. He's here... inside."

"What—did you... did you eat him?"

"No. He saved me. And if you want to save me we better leave before *he* gets in the car."

Kelly turned to see Taze with three coffees coming out of the McDonald's.

"Okay," he said, not sure what he was doing. He hopped out, ran around to the driver's side, hopped in and started the car.

Taze was in the middle of the parking lot as they peeled out. Kelly caught a brief glimpse of him in the rearview mirror before pulling out into the street.

"Okay, you wanna fill me in on why I just did that?"

"Yeah," she said in Israel's voice. "But I actually could use a cup of coffee. There's another Mickey D's in a few miles right before Schaefer. Why don't you pull in when we get there?"

"All right. But tell me who you are really. Do you work with them? The diffoids?"

"No. I'm not with them. I'm Israel. Well, that's not my real name, but the human mouth can't form the proper sound to pronounce it."

"What are you talking about? Aren't you... *weren't* you human?"

"No."

"What happened to Anna? She has a family—"

"She was lying. She has a roommate and a dog. And nothing has happened to her. She's here still. But whatever those diffoid guys infected her with keeps killing her. They have some kind of weird connection to the other side and I suspect her body can't handle it. When we put her in the trunk the other day she was literally dead. She died sometime in the night again. I should know because I can only possess a dead body."

"Possess? So what—you're a ghost?"

"Ooo, I wish you wouldn't use the 'g' word. That's kind of offensive. Well, not to me, I was born on the other side."

"So you're from over there? That doesn't mean you're dead?"

"Yes. From a place called Lampheter. No, I'm not dead. I'm not technically alive. The last detective the Network hired crapped out. So they decided to go with an inside man and channeled me."

"I don't get it."

"The 'other side' as you put it already has living people there. They can't cross so they make things like me."

"One of those ma-*whatsits*?"

"A *machín*."

"And you possessed a dead body. Whose?"

"His name was Arthur Miller, he was a salesman. I don't know much beyond that, he'd been dead a while. Memories tend to get corroded after a certain amount of time has passed."

"Why did we leave Taze?"

"He's been compromised. He gets drugs in exchange for information on us."

"How do you know?"

"I didn't like him from the start. At first I thought it was because of what he did to that ghost at the inn, but then I realized it was my premonitory sense."

"Hey, you just said the 'g' word. What's a premonitory sense?"

"Well, I can say it, you can't. My premonitory sense tells me if I can trust someone or not. Once I knew we had been followed to the hotel I knew it wasn't just dislike."

"What happened at the hotel?"

"I took a little bit of your blood. I knew that little girl was coming, remember her? The ugly one? You were her target. I had to throw her off so I took your blood and I used it to scent my room. By the time I'd gotten back to the room, Anna had died again and I figured I could use her. I put her in the closet and got in bed and in a couple hours it happened.

"I had to... stay in the body until then. I can't exactly leap from body to body at will. It was awful. If I felt pain I can't imagine what that would have been like. I awoke in Anna's body and knew something was different. Anna's dead, but she's not. I can't possess the living but she's somewhere in between. I guess it may be a condition all these diffoids experience but I can't be sure.

"Also, these guys have a sort of hive mind. A communal mind they can tap into and exchange information. They were watching us through Anna but they don't know anything about the little girl so far as I can tell. They don't know anything about their god except he's from the Caribbean somewhere. Either he doesn't have a name or they don't know it. They also don't know what his plan is but it does involve you."

"What about me?"

"I wish they knew."

Siblings make the best strangers

Bradley liked being a Sibling. He felt like he finally belonged to something. Sure, his eyes were all messed up, but he got to wear sunglasses at his security job, so so what?

The Master hadn't said to follow them but he hadn't said not to. Bradley took the initiative and tracked down the hotel where they were staying. He'd guarded his thoughts from the polycomb—what a dumb name for it—so the others didn't know what he was up to and ruin it. He knew this could endanger his ability to become Naked, but no way would the Master fault him if he walked in with the guy they were looking for. It had to be the taller one—the white guy. Bradley's gut was never wrong. Besides, the short one was just some plain-looking black guy and the pit-faced skinny one was a drug addict.

The Master didn't have any use for people who abused their bodies. That's why the Master had picked Bradley. He'd had a brief pro boxing career and even after an injury forced him to retire he'd kept himself up.

He'd found their floor just as they'd burst from their room. No need to hide, they didn't know who he was. The tall one wasn't with them, but they were carrying the girl.

She was still going through Firstbirth. It was a scary period for all of them but necessary to die and live again over and over to purify one's self to behold the Master. He had come from the other side. Dying was the first way along the path to become Naked.

Bradley strolled past as they raced down the hall and ducked in the room to see if the tall one was still inside. He checked all the rooms but only found a huge stinky hole in the bed that almost made him earl.

He must have been outside checking for the all-clear. Made sense if they thought they were hauling a corpse. Bradley rushed to the stairs, leaping down them until he got to the first floor. He dashed to the outside but took his time getting into his car, double-parked at the valet by the front and saw them drive by in a beat up Parke Car. The valet knocked on his window as he started the engine, but Bradley gave the kid the finger, pulling out of the lot and into the street.

Bradley hung back about two or three cars, trying to see how many people were in the car. It was impossible to make out with the tinted windows, and he briefly considered pulling along side of them, but it was dark out and that could be too risky. He couldn't risk a high speed chase that might get the police's attention. He would have to wait until they pulled over or got in an isolated area where he could run them off the road.

***

If she had missed them they had just left. Jemen didn't know exactly what *he* looked like but she knew the *machín*. They must have sneaked out. She didn't get a good look at them, but there were two men carrying a woman out in a hurry. That couldn't have been them. The *machín* would have taken the form of a man and the one carrying the woman was much too short, the tall one much too sickly. The *machín* would have taken the form of a man with a dominating presence.

The cab driver had been a mistake. She did not like to kill, but his insults... No, it had not been his insults. Jemen was almost due and she became highly sensitive during these times. But he still did not have to say that about Oodles.

The boys would be fine for the time being. They knew to stay out of sight. The vehicle was Artie's. The police were more than likely looking for him by now and an abandoned SUV would intensify the search. Too bad they would never find him.

The Ghost Toucher

Jemen hadn't wanted to go inside because she had no way of finding their room. Besides, a six-foot ten woman would be remembered. She scratched underneath Oodles' chin as a bulky man emerged who could have been the *machín*. He jumped into a car in the valet area, prominently displaying his middle finger to the nearby attendant before driving off. That must have been how they said 'hello' and 'goodbye' to each other here.

She had a feeling she should be following him. He drove off in such a hurry she doubted he would notice she was behind him. She got into his lane with a black Crown Victoria between them. There was a man on a bicycle keeping pace with them by the curbside but he fell behind as traffic picked up.

Jemen was unsure if this was the *machín*, but it was her only hope. Maybe they had split up because they suspected they were being followed. She wasn't experienced with these things. Maybe it was something else. Regardless, when she caught the *machín* he would deliver him. He would have no choice; she was his mother.

***

They pulled into a McDonald's. Bradley pulled into a spot a few cars farther down and watched. He placed his revolver in the glove box—no need for any wetwork—and took out his sap. Bradley craned his neck and saw one of them walk inside. Not the one—dammit, it would have made things simpler if he were alone.

At least they were split up. They all looked soft, but three against one was next to impossible. He slid out of his car, keeping the sap against his thigh. He looked around as the sun was still a few hours away, no one was around. The first would be out before he knew it, the second would try to fight, but Bradley was big and knew how to handle himself. He'd be gone with the one before the third one could sip his coffee.

Bradley could see two of them in the back talking, but couldn't tell who was who. Maybe she was in the front seat but that didn't make sense. Bradley had to move now. He looked around one last time but the passenger door opened on the side opposite him. He froze, thinking the short guy who got out was looking at him as he ran around to the driver's side.

The Ghost Toucher

The driver's side. They must have spotted him! Bradley started to run, but tripped, the sap flying from his hand into the lot of the gas station next over. He put his hands out to break his fall and cold wet asphalt greeted him, grating the heels of his palms and his nose smacked off the ground as the rear end of the Parke Car came within a foot of his head before peeling off.

Bradley climbed to his feet as they pulled away. He looked over and saw the pit-faced one watching the road, holding three cups of joe. Bradley was pissed. Maybe they were luring him here and stranded this one when he made his move. Or maybe it was something else entirely.

Bradley balled his fists, looking at the skinny pit-faced man. He would certainly find out.

Byrd had to stop him. He scooped up the man's—*thing's*—weapon and raced across the lot. It was punching a tall, skinny man who was managing to hold onto three cups of coffee at the same time.

Byrd ran atop a white Ford Tempo parked a few feet away, leaping off the roof of the small car and coming down with his knees into the thing's back.

The thing laid still, a knot growing on its forehead.

"Skillet, ap*pre*ciated," the pit-faced man said, spitting a glob of blood.

"No thanks needed. This vile beast will trouble you no longer. Are you in need of medical assistance?"

"Nah. I gots my own medication. Want a coffee?"

"No. I do not consume stimulants."

"What are you going to do with him?"

"Give him to my people. We will deal with him."

"This guy was probly gonna put a beat down on my homies too. Man, they might be in trouble."

"Do not worry. I've been tracking this creature for some time. I saw he was following you and your friends so I placed a tracking device on your vehicle."

"Cool. When'd you do that?"

"Before you left the hotel."

"Hey, somebody should tell those guys they might be in trouble. You gotta ride?"

"Yes." Byrd whipped out his walkie and rattled off their location. He knelt and tossed off the creature's sunglasses and lifted an eyelid. Disgusting.

"Aw man, he's one of those dudes?"

"You've seen one of them before?"

"Yeah, this shortie who was drivin' us around. She had eyes like that."

"What is a 'shortie'?"

"A phatty."

Byrd shook his head.

"Your friends are in danger. If she hasn't killed she may soon. My bike is just on the other lot. Follow me."

Byrd hated to leave the creature here, but he couldn't allow more human life to be endangered. He whacked it over the head one last time for good measure and ran across the strip of lawn to the other lot.

Byrd hopped on his Schwinn and turned to watch the other man. He'd stopped and was staring.

"What?" Byrd asked.

"My man, you have a bike. Like a *bike*-bike."

"Yes. I do not drive motorized vehicles." Byrd was embarrassed. He'd tried to learn once, but it was all too much to do at the same time. He put up the kickstand.

"Okay, so you want me to... get on that. But on the back?"

"If you want to save your friends, yes."

The man said nothing, but tossed the coffee, got on the banana seat and held on. Byrd turned on the tracking device and rode out onto the street. He pumped his legs, paddling until he got up to full speed, pedaling non-stop, swiftly outpacing the light traffic at this early hour. According to the tracker they had already stopped.

Byrd was somewhat disappointed the man was so quiet. He purposely weaved around cars to scare him, show him not only the big, air-polluting monstrosities were vehicles to be reckoned with. They passed a police vehicle with 'Ferndale Police' printed on the side. Byrd thought there was something strange there but decided it must be because it was from so far out of town. He outpaced the police car, beating a traffic light and leaving it behind.

***

Collie didn't have much time left. Nasal cancer. Chemo couldn't do anything for him. They'd given him a year at most, but he'd have that beat in half the time. Being a cop was the only thing he had left. He would do the job until he physically couldn't anymore, but he'd become sexually indiscrete, having as many partners as he could. It was funny how his life had split in two, like Jekyll and Hyde. Collie had contracted plenty of STDs; gonorrhea, syphilis, the clap. He'd avoided the HIV but not for lack of trying.

Right now had an awful crotch itch flaring up and he desperately needed to scratch his balls. It would have been tolerable had he had something to occupy his mind, but the sheriff had barely spoken the whole trip. Couldn't start a conversation with the man for the whole drive.

Two homos on a weird-looking green ten-speed zipped by. Collie wished he could have opened the door on them as they passed. He couldn't wait to slap the cuffs on whoever they were going to get. He'd make sure to put them on nice and tight. Maybe he'd even get to shoot somebody. At the very least his knee was going to grind into somebody's nuts.

***

Wendy and Dale found it stumbling around in the parking lot. Byrd shouldn't have left, but then again, Byrd shouldn't have done anything but follow, even if a life was in danger. Countless lives would be saved if they could find where all of them met and destroyed the entire nest at once.

Dale knew how to make pipe bombs using ordinary household materials. Wendy liked to be more up front when confronting the enemy, it seemed more fair—a contradiction, considering evil sought to overthrow through hidden means—but Dale's bombs had their place as well.

The Ghost Toucher

The sun was just beginning to rise. The parking lot was filled with cars so she would have to play this sly. Dale pulled up next to a brown Ford Probe and reached for the door. She stopped him.

"Stay here. Keep it running." Dale nodded. He was already sweating. If she hadn't known him she would have thought she couldn't count on him. He swiped his hand over the top of his balding head and rubbed his hand on his pant leg.

She'd left her bow-tang in the passenger seat, a weapon of her own design, wishing it had been dark out so she could have used it. She would have to use femininity and guile—*lies*—to get him in the car and found the prospect as disgusting as Dale's sweaty head.

"Mister, are you okay?" she said, pouring sugary-sweetness into her voice as she reached for the door to the McDonald's. She turned away from the door to face him, affixing concern into her expression.

"No, no. I'll be all right." The knot on his head was split open. Byrd had really worked him over.

"You should get that looked at. Do you need a ride to the hospital?" She impressed herself with how convincing she sounded. But she would have to be as good as this beast that acted and looked human. Anything that came off as disingenuous might alert it.

"My car's... over there." It seemed confused. Perhaps it had just regained consciousness if it could actually lose consciousness.

"You could even use my cell phone to call 911." It took a step and stumbled. Wendy was right there to catch it and they were eye level.

"The man who attacked me—he put something in my eyes." Anyone not a Morrisite might have believed this beast's lies. Its retinas looked like they had exploded, the inky black of them like a Rorschach spot atop the whites of its eyes.

"Then you definitely shouldn't be driving." Wendy thought she'd done a pretty good job of not recoiling from it. "Here, come to my car." She was as tall as the beast and threw its arm over her shoulder, practically dragging it across the lot. There still weren't a lot of people around so she opened the door and rammed its head into the door frame.

The Ghost Toucher

It grunted and flopped over on the back seat. She shoved it into a semi-sitting position and pulled out a knife from her boot as she got in.

"Anything moves on you and I cut it off. Understand?"

"Yeah."

"Let's hurry up. I gotta get back to the gas station," Dale said and started pulling out before she could shut the door. As the car started going forward it leaned over as if it were about to cradle its head.

"I told you to—*oof!*" It sprang its legs out and caught her in the middle, ejecting her from the car as Dale was picking up speed. Wendy hit the street, drumming her head on the ground and rolled to a stop. She tried to rise but her arms and legs were paralyzed. She looked up in time to see Dale's silver Cobalt pulling away.

***

Alas, capturing him was not her destiny today. Jemen had had to pull over into the lot of a post office once her water broke. She tried watching the car as it continued down the road but it was quickly lost to her.

Delivery had been quick. Two smooth legs came out first, a breech, followed by a torso and arms and finally the head. The pain was sharp and brief. Jemen hadn't grown accustomed to the sensation so much as developed an appreciation for it. She sat him in the passenger seat and cooed to him, stroking his back while he sucked his thumb and stared at her. Oodles licked his thigh. This one would be big; he was at least four feet tall from birth and he was growing even now. His head rounded and expanded, making his face more human despite the translucent white skin. His collar bone and shoulders became more pronounced and his knees bumped against the dashboard. The majority of her children's growth came within the first five minutes after birth and he was almost as tall as his mother. In two days he would dwarf her.

"You're too skinny," she said, looking at her child's prominent bones. She knew she should be trying to find the *machín*, but she always got euphoric after birthing. Jemen rubbed his bald head. He wouldn't have hair for at least a month.

He watched a homeless man walking down the sidewalk, pushing a cart.

"Ahhhh! Ahhhh!" he said, pointing. Sadly, none of her children were capable of speech. But this was interesting. Had her son found his one?

"Do you want him?" she said. "That man there?"

Her child nodded, his eyes even wider than before. He fumbled and pushed at the door until she reached over and pulled the handle. He fell out and popped up on his hands and knees. He was lumbering in his movement but anyone watching would have understood this was a hunter stalking its prey.

Oodles had his front paws up on the window, watching, and he barked as her child was only a few feet away. The homeless man didn't turn and her child leapt on his back. The man screamed and tried to shake him off but he held on.

The man's long salt and pepper hair rose as if static electricity were coursing through him. The ends of his hair attached to her child's head and began peeling away from the scalp of the homeless man. He fell to his knees and her child spun him over and pushed him onto his back. He nuzzled his face into the man's as his skin took the hairs, creating a scraggly beard and eyebrows. The homeless man screamed again and her child plucked a tooth out of his mouth and into his own.

The man closed his mouth and moaned through his nose, attempting to keep him from extracting any more teeth. Her child pulled at his lips and when he couldn't get his mouth open he smashed him in the jaw with his fist, breaking it. The homeless man lay on the ground and cried as he yanked out the other teeth, rooting them into his own gums.

When it was over the homeless man lay naked on the ground, shivering, pale and in shock. If someone didn't come along soon he would die from exposure. Maybe he would die even if someone found him in time. But her boy had found his one and that was all that mattered.

She hated that another one of her boys would die when they eventually found Kelly Greene. But it must be done. She had to save the world.

The Ghost Toucher

***

Two was easy.

If that Amazon hadn't been in such a hurry to rough him up they could have taken him where ever they wanted. She'd been sloppy, nervous, *new*. He couldn't be mad, it worked to his advantage. As Bradley strangled the wimp in the driver's seat he made a mental note to find out who they were working for before he killed him.

He had a clamp on his carotids from the back seat, but the little freak was doing his best to shake him off, weaving violently from side to side. Bradley wanted to put him down ASAP so he could get back on the other one's trail if it were still possible and bring back two finds.

It wouldn't be so difficult to believe the Master had enemies. Or that there were others seeking to be Naked. But they would find the Master was a formidable opponent. Formidable because he had attendees like Bradley.

Baldy sideswiped two cars on the left and took a hand off the wheel, reaching towards the cigarette lighter. He pushed it in and Bradley smashed the driver's side window open with his head, immediately regretting it because of the sharp in-rush of wind blinding him a moment. The lighter popped back out and baldy grabbed it, reaching back to burn him, but Bradley easily swatted it out of his grubby little hand and went back to a two-handed choke.

Baldy's hand slapped wildly at the dash and the radio came on. 'Candy Man' by the Mary Jane Girls wafted out of the speakers in the middle of a verse. He scratched at Bradley's hands then went back, reaching for something in the passenger seat.

"*And when I need a little sugar/You go straight down to my head,*" JoJo sang. Bradley saw what he was reaching for; some kind of sword that had a chain-looking thing instead of a blade. Maybe he'd kill him with that.

"*You're the sweetest man I know/And our love will surely grow.*"

Bradley saw the speedometer crest over sixty just before the wheel cut to the right, lifting onto two wheels as they split between two cars and jetted through a red light into cross traffic as the song went into a chorus.

The Ghost Toucher

***

"All right, I'm a little confused. There's just too much going on right now."

"I know," Israel/Anna said. "I'm a little over my head myself. I'd only possessed a body one other time before so I'm no expert at this. I still don't exactly know how I can be in a *living* body."

They walked back to the car, parked as far back from the street as possible, sipping their coffee.

"You, Israel, are from the other side. You aren't dead, but a machi—"

"—*Machín*."

"—Yeah and you have the ability to cross over here and possess dead bodies."

"Yes."

"All right, I understand at least. How long do you think we're safe here?" Kelly took a long sip of his coffee and tossed the cup.

"I don't. I have a feeling a lot of people on both sides are looking for us."

There were a lot of weeds growing in the empty lot next to the parking lot. Israel stared as if he/she saw something.

"What, is there somebody out there?"

"Not exactly. Hold this." Israel/Anna handed him their cup and walked to the edge of the lot, stepped over the metal rail and vanished into the weeds. A moment later she backed out, stepping back over and bending down.

She was cooing to something and in a moment Kelly saw a hand come out of the weeds. Whoever he was, he was dirty and he had a couple broken fingers.

The man crawled over the guard rail all while Israel made fussing noises to bring him out. He stood on uncertain legs and it was obvious he had been dead for some time. He still had his tie on, but most of the jacket and shirt had been gnawed through at the sides. Ribs and gray stuff hung out loosely by his hips.

"Hey, maybe you should leave him be." Kelly saw the bullet hole just below his hairline. Even odder was the lipstick that had managed to survive on his cheek all this time. He looked like he'd been a few days. At least it looked like lipstick.

"What? He's harmless." Anna's voice now. "He's only dead. Besides, there's a spirit in there."

"But he could bite you or something."

"Bite me—" She looked perplexed. "Why? The dead don't eat. They're *dead*. Don't believe what you see in movies."

Just then a police cruiser pulled into the lot. Kelly turned to see, panicked, then relaxed when he saw it wasn't DPD.

He panicked again when a big white guy got out and aimed a gun at them.

***

It was glad it had brought this one along. The human was eager to please and showed as much by scratching at his genitalia, no doubt ready to obey his master. The lesser wondered if all humans expressed their excitement in such a manner. It accessed the Wilson Sheriff's memory on this 'Collie' and knew he had been an adequate soldier on the battlefield. Numerous enemy acquisitions and at least three confirmed kills. A low number in the lesser's estimation.

Plus if the Wilson Sheriff became fatally injured the Collie would be a competent replacement. Its hold on the Wilson Sheriff was atrophying regardless. Wilson Sheriff had a condition called Alzheimer's in only its beginning stages and the lesser's presence made it more pronounced. Perhaps sooner would be better than later to make the switch.

The Collie closed his cellular phone and pointed to a building ahead with a giant yellow 'M' on it. It had seen many of these since it had possessed the Wilson Sheriff. They must have been temples of some sort, but it did not understand the bags the humans came out with. The Wilson Sheriff's memory told it these bags contained food, but the lesser had no conception of what that was. The Wilson Sheriff's stomach made an odd sound. It had been doing that since yesterday. It supposed worship was done with that particular body organ. Also, the Wilson Sheriff's mouth must have been malfunctioning as whenever the lesser neared these places it kept filling with saliva. If only there were some efficient means of disposing with this moisture build-up it wouldn't have to resort to squeezing it from the human's mouth and wiping it on his pant leg. Perhaps after capturing the Hated One it would go through the 'drive-thru' and request a number two; it contained something called a 'cheeseburger'. Considering he would die soon it would allow this as a sort of last rites, but on second consideration it would go inside. It struck the lesser as disrespectful to not properly enter a god's temple to worship but this was apparently common practice. No wonder this was an abandoned world. The lesser would be glad to be rid of it.

The lesser turned into the parking lot. The Collie pointed, reaching for his gun with his other hand.

"That them?" He had his gun in his hand. The lesser had a feeling this could go wrong. It needed the Hated One alive, to bring him back to the Jexclp'ar, but the Collie was already out of the car before it could stop him. Without the Hated One there was no hope of securing passage back for itself. It put the cruiser in park and before it could tell him to stand down he shot. Someone fired back as it stood and the lesser felt the Wilson Sheriff's meat head pop before everything went dark.

***

"There they are," Taze said from the other side of the dumpster. Byrd was pretty fly at sneaking up on people. So far Kelly and Anna hadn't seen them. She stepped back over the guardrail out of some really tall weeds (she was gonna have an ill skin rash) and looked like she was talking to an animal or something.

"Those are your friends," Byrd said. "Where is the other?"

"That's the thing," Taze began. "He—yo, who dat?"

Some other clown crawled out of the weeds in a dirty suit. They couldn't see him from the front from this angle but his jacket had been all chewed up. Was that his spine sticking out?

"The other," Byrd said and stood. "Stay here." He started walking.

Taze was no punk. He wasn't sure what was going on but Kelly and Israel had been cool individuals and he wasn't going to let

The Ghost Toucher

them go out like that. He hadn't exactly bussed a cap in somebody's ass before, but he was pretty sure he could do it.

He pulled his Desert Eagle out, tight on Byrd's heels and there was a shot. Byrd spun around as a bullet caught his shoulder. Taze came around the corner, the jammy turned to the side in his hand, blazing. He hit the Micky D's twice, brick chipping in his face before he saw who had shot.

One of them went down, then the other. Taze hit the windshield three times before the gun clicked on empty. Then he saw the cherries on top of the car.

Oh, snap. Those weren't just dudes. Those dudes were cops.

Taze saw the tall one hadn't fallen. He was clutching the side of his head. He could see the bottoms of the shoes of the other one. Had he killed him? Taze had barely started to consider the ramifications of what he'd done. He didn't want to go to the pen.

But something weird happened; a car racing down the street flipped through an intersection, smacking into a car and tumbling about fifty feet before skidding to a stop in the grassy median.

Everyone froze, even the big cop by the cruiser, but the girl grabbed Kelly by the arm and hustled him to the car. The dead guy followed on his own sat in with Kelly. Taze ran to the car.

"I just... I just killed a police officer," Taze said.

"I thought we were leaving him?" Kelly said from the back.

"Not in that hell storm," the girl said. "I don't care what he's done." They wound around the building and peeled out of the lot. The sun had crested over the horizon and the Eastern sky was a pinkish-burgundy.

"I'm going to be sick," Taze said. "I need to call my dad."

"Where are we going?" Kelly asked.

"He's going to be so mad."

"Israel knows a guy who can help. He doesn't want to go there but there's little choice for it now."

"I don't know... I don't know. Maybe I should go to jail. I mean, I took someone's life."

"Look, Taze," the girl said. "What you did was a good thing. That police officer just shot that guy for no reason. He was a maniac. He probably would have killed us all if you hadn't been there. Where did you come from, by the way?"

"We rode on the guy's bike. He pedals really fast."

"There was an accident back there," Kelly said.

***

At least Wendy had her handi-wipes. The bus had come along just at the right time, but she was almost unable to get on. But Dale needed her. She'd gone through half of them on the short ride until she'd seen Dale's car wrecked up on the island between the north and southbound lanes.

The driver kept telling her she'd have to wait until they got to the curb to let her off, but they weren't going anywhere soon in this traffic jam. Dale's car was about sixty yards ahead on the other side of the intersection. Wendy didn't hide the anger she felt until the middle-aged driver had had enough of the menacing look she was giving him and let her off.

She shouldn't have been so stupid. Of course the beast hadn't been as injured as it had looked. She should have just taken it down in the parking lot and thrown it in the trunk. Now she had probably cost Dale his life. Wendy only hoped the beast had gone with him.

The cops hadn't arrived yet. That was either good or bad. It was good if the beast were alive and too much for her to handle alone. They could just shoot it. But it was bad if she couldn't get her bow-tang. And worse still that they would have Dale's body. Ren-Jon had said they have the technology to divine information even from a corpse. If not for all these witnesses she would take him with her, dispose of him properly, but as it stood it was a risk with her even approaching the car. People would describe her to the cops. They would look for her and want to ask questions.

Wendy ran between the cars and saw the beast emerging from the shattered rear window of Dale's car. It ran across the street. She crossed the intersection, pushing past the smattering of witnesses who had exited their cars and were attempting to help the injured man Dale's car had smashed into.

Dale's engine roared impotently as the front wheel continued to spin. A man on the radio was singing, "Been down so long, getting up didn't cross my mind/I knew there was a better way of life that

I was just trying to find./You don't know what you'll do until you're put under pressure,/Across 110th Street is a hell of a tester."

Wendy didn't listen to music; she didn't know the song. A woman in a business skirt was on her knees in glass by his Cobalt. Wendy thought the woman might have been thrown from the other car by the way she just sat there mumbling. But then she realized the woman was praying. Wendy gave her a wide berth and went around to the driver's side.

What was left of Dale was smashed beyond recognition and smeared across everything in the front of the car. The car rested on its roof, tilted onto the hood. Wendy circled to the front passenger door, intent on getting her bow-tang so she could finish the beast. The doors had been bashed and wouldn't budge. She walked around to the back and took a peek inside. Her bow-tang was right there. She looked across the street and saw the beast resting on its knee by a police car.

She panicked until she saw it wasn't a Detroit police car. They might try to intervene, but they had to be here for something else. Plus it was parked facing away from her. Wendy stepped through the back window, careful to avoid the shards of glass in the window frame and reached for her bow-tang.

There were only drops of blood back here, but she could feel it crawling over her hand. It would take hours to wash the sensation away. Dale's pulpy arm slid off the passenger seat, the wrist-nub falling onto her hand. Wendy screamed, stopping herself before she cut herself on the glass. She took a deep breath and took a step farther inside and grabbed the weapon.

The beast would die. Wendy didn't care about the mission. It had cost her comrade his life and Dale deserved vengeance. She would be sure of it. Gas had pooled beneath the car. Wendy took a book of matches out of her pocket, struck one, and dropped it once she was on dry asphalt. Flame lapped up the gasoline and engulfed the car. The woman on her knees fell back and crab-walked away from the car as fire licked at the sky. The pipe bombs in his trunk would explode any minute. Let them try to steal from Dale's body after that.

She crossed the street and no one tried to stop her. Wendy could feel the eyes of the rubberneckers still in their cars looking at her across the street. An ambulance siren was going off somewhere in the distance. She gripped the bow-tang, intent on splitting the beast in two when it promptly rose from its knee and disappeared in a blur.

She began to run, hoping she could spot it and at least track it, but a big cop stood up on the opposite side of the police cruiser.

"Freeze!" he said, aiming a Sig Sauer at her. "Drop the... drop the thing... in your hand."

Wendy didn't. Byrd was approaching behind him. He was wounded. The cop seemed confused. The left side of his head was covered in blood. He kept dabbing at it with his hand and wiping his red fingertips on his shirt. The shoulder was already a deep-soaked crimson from his bleeding wound. Byrd got as far as the hood of cruiser when the cop whirled on him.

"Stop!" he said. He kept turning between Byrd and Wendy. Byrd, despite his dark skin, looked green. "I said stop moving!" The cop focused on Byrd. Wendy was the one with the weapon, but again, because she was a woman, the cop dismissed her. Byrd wasn't even in a position to do anything.

"You're both under arrest." The cop clapped his hand over the spewing mess coming out of the side of his head.

"Wendy," Byrd began, giant beads of sweat standing out on his forehead. "This is the officer who shot me."

They'd been trained to respect officers of the law, to even avoid them as often as possible because many times Morrisites would be operating outside of the law. But Wendy's rage boiled up inside of her. She had missed the beast because of this cop. And he had hurt another one of her people. She'd been squeezing the hilt of the bow-tang until her hand ached when she looked down at it. Then, without thinking, it was spinning out of her hand and penetrating the cop's skull.

He pitched backwards onto the sidewalk, lifeless. Wendy retrieved her weapon by stepping on his face and snatching it out. She felt no regret for killing him, only that she had lost her restraint.

Byrd stared at her.

"What—do you have a problem with this?"

"No, I—" Byrd's eyes rolled up in his head. He rocked back and forth and collapsed.

"Crap."

***

Jemen hoped he had stopped somewhere. The *machín* didn't need to eat or sleep so there was a slim chance he had, but it was all she had to go on. She'd made her son get in the back of the cab. It looked better for a cab driver to have a fare in the back as opposed to being in the front seat, but he also stunk. He'd taken on the scent of his one and would probably take on some of his habits as well which meant she would have a hard time giving him a bath later on.

There was a car in the lot of a McDonald's that looked a lot like the *machín's*. Jemen was too late to turn in and had to work her way over to the far left lane to make a Michigan left turn. She turned around and had to stop at a red light of an intersection before she could make another Michigan left. She ran through the yellow light of the intersection this time and pulled into the lot, finding a spot right next to the *machín's* car.

Her son got out with her and smiled that toothless smile. The more she saw him like this the less she liked it. But providence did not come on one's own terms. She would have to be patient to see the purpose of her son like... this. He was at least seven feet tall now and infinitely noticeable. Jemen tried the door and found it unlocked.

"Get in," she told him. She got behind the driver's seat and turned around to look out the back window. She'd automatically assumed he'd abandoned the car. But what if he had gone inside? The key was still in the ignition, but that didn't necessarily mean anything.

She thought a moment. They were pressed for time but it would be good to search the car. If he had abandoned the car she could take his. The police might be looking for the cab, but not this car. She turned to her boy. His breath stung her eyes.

"Son, listen to me." She grabbed him by the shoulders.

"No cry," he said. Oh, *this* one develops speech, she thought.

"I want you to go inside and find the *machín* if he is there. Do not approach him. Only come back here if he is."

Her son nodded vigorously and opened the door. She grabbed his arm.

"And do *not* eat. Anything. Do you understand?"

His smile faded and he nodded again before getting out. He loped across the lot and disappeared inside. Jemen turned to the glove compartment. She opened it and found an owner's manual, tire gauge a baggie filled with zip ties and a handgun.

She checked the sun visors and found an old, folded up sheet of paper tucked away in the one for the passenger. Jemen unfolded it and read what looked like a child had scrawled, 'MY GOD IS COOL' with a stick figure wearing sunglasses. There were squiggly lines all around him as if to denote he emitted some form of radiation. Several smaller figures surrounded the bespectacled stick figure except they didn't have circular heads. Their heads were isosceles triangles, the two sides of equal length, coming down to a point with a semi-circle inside for a frowning (or menacing?) mouth. The sides went above the flat of the head, fanning out like antennae or feathers, where he had gone over and over, thickening them with extra pen strokes.

As rudimentary as these smaller stick figures were, there was something about them. Jemen had seen figures like these before. But she only had a passing awareness of anything on her home world. Greaters were solely dedicated to destroying one another. Paying attention to the lives of those who attended them was never a consideration.

He was taking too long. Jemen got out of the car to go get him so they could leave. She was still distracted by those stick figures and didn't see the man approach her or the device in his hand. The first shock stunned her and as she turned to see who had attacked her another one stepped around the trunk of the Caprice Classic next over and hit her with a stick of some kind. Her kind didn't lose consciousness, but she was disoriented, in pain. She heard the trunk pop open and felt her legs being pushed up to her chest as she was shoved inside.

Then everything went dark.

***

Mother say look for brother-not-brother. Mother say not eat. Walk in door. See people. See *food*. Mother say not eat. Brother-not-brother not sit at table. Ugly people sit at table. Eat *food*. Mother say not eat. More ugly people by *food*. Ugly people smile nervous. Smile back. Ugly people smell like *food*, but not *food*. Mother say not eat. Brother-not-brother not by *food*-smelling ugly people.

Walk closer. *Food*-smelling ugly people smell afraid. *Food* smell good. Mother say not eat. Smell deep for brother-not-brother. No smell. *Food* smell. *Food*-smelling ugly people give food to more ugly people. Want *food*, take *food*. Mother say not eat. Ugly people smell more afraid. All ugly people yell. Give *food* back. Ugly people won't take. *Food* smell *good*. Mother say not—

Ugly people push. No understand. Eat *food*. *Food* good. Want more *food*. Climb over, push ugly people away. *Food* hot! Still eat. Eat more. Eat more. Ugly people run away. *Eat-eat-eat-eat-eat-eat—*

Insides hurt. Go outside, mother make all better. Car make loud noises with funny lights. Ugly people get out. Ugly people yell. Afraid now. Mean ugly people. Where mother?

***

This one had a considerable amount of head trauma. At first it was difficult to maintain control. But it had knowledge of both the Hated One and its quarry and a mental connection to others that seemed much like its connection to the Jexclp'ar.

This one called itself Bradley. The lesser did not understand these 'names'. It was much simpler being a part of a group. To be called Jexclp'ar. They all looked alike anyway and may as well have had just one name.

The Bradley had come over just as the Wilson Sheriff's life was fading away and it jumped into his body. It quickly scanned his mind and spotted the tall bald-headed black man who had assaulted the Bradley in another McDonald's parking lot. The Bradley thing felt hatred at the sight of this human, but resisted the urge to kill him. There was a woman across the street who had tried to capture the Bradley before and no doubt she would try again.

The Bradley thing did not believe in coincidences. It watched the man stumble around then circled around the McDonald's. Perhaps he had some sort of conveyance it could acquire. The Bradley thing saw a bicycle on a kickstand. Not as convenient as it required but it would do.

The Bradley was also in this world and the lesser's as well. It did not understand how that was possible, but it didn't want to be detected just yet. It needed to find the Hated One if it expected to survive the transition back into the Jexclp'ar.

The human was a competent tracker. He had found the Hated One before and using those tactics in a much more sophisticated manner it was certain to find them again. Perhaps then it could trigger the Jexclp'ar itself using the human's connection to the other side.

There was a device secured between the handlebars. The lesser flipped a switch on the side and a section of map came up on the display. The Bradley thing recognized the area and the red dot in the center indicated something was located there.

Could it be the human that had assaulted the Bradley had been following the Hated One too? It was logical if he were protecting the Hated One considering the Bradley had had the opposite in mind.

The lesser got on the bicycle and began a furious pedal south. This conveyance would do just fine.

***

"Master, I feel another intrusion on the polycomb," Lewis said. The Master said nothing, only stared. "Different from the first one, though. And Bradley... I think he's *gone*. Whatever it is just... *removed* him. I don't feel him at all."

Lewis prided himself on being the most sensitive of all the Master's attendees. He could touch any of the others' minds and even feel what they were experiencing. Sometimes it could be a burden as he wasn't able to always control these feelings. They tended to intrude on him when one of the others was in an excited state. Of the times it had happened it was usually someone having sex, usually alone, but Bill and Amanda had hooked up a few times. That was a double whammy because he felt what both of them were feeling. He usually took a Valium on those nights.

They probably thought they could hide themselves, but they were wrong. Just like Bradley thought he could hide his thoughts when he went after the one the Master was seeking. Lewis had reported what Bradley was up to, but the Master had only smiled. It was strange that He would smile at the man's disobedience when they had been told to not approach whoever this person was. And now Bradley had completely vanished and the Master was treating that and this intrusion as if it were no big deal.

Almost as if Bradley had never mattered to begin with.

The Master wouldn't have the same attitude if it were him or any of the others, would He?

The Master still said nothing. He did that at times. Lewis decided to keep an eye on this intrusion in case they did need to get involved. He could feel exactly where it was.

It doesn't work like it's supposed to

"I just think you're lucky, is all. I mean, we're not in a position to be choosy is all I'm saying."

Marv checked his watch again. He wanted this dead body out of his Nitro. And to not be having this conversation with Dell.

"Dude, I *so* don't want to be having this conversation with you," he said.

"Okay, that's cool," Dell said. "But you do realize she accepts the whole eye thing, right? And she's *fine*. Where else you gonna find that?"

"What time is it?" Marv huffed, drumming his fingers on the door.

"Almost eight."

"What's with this guy?" I'm tired of being on corpse corral duty for him. It takes all day and the next to get out the formaldehyde stink. What the hell does he even do with them in there?"

"I don't know. But the Master told us to bring 'em, so we bring 'em."

"Yeah. But I don't hafta like it."

"Hey, careful with that kinda talk if you wanna get Naked."

Marv wasn't so sure he wanted that anymore. Over the last few weeks it had begun to lose its appeal to him.

"It's eight. Let's go."

The two men exited the SUV and circled to the rear. Marv popped the hatch and there it was, wrapped in two garbage bags.

The Ghost Toucher

"We shouldn't be doing this in the daylight," Marv said, grabbing it by the shoulders. Dell grabbed the feet and they slid it out.

"Forget the hatch," Marv said. "Let's just get this done. I'm outta Febreeze so let it air out."

"I bet he's probably some kind of necro-freak," Dell said. "This guy's small," he said, referring to the body. "Why's he so heavy?"

"Formaldehyde. The body is saturated with the stuff and it makes it heavier. Either that or we're just tired."

They'd been out since a little after one o'clock this morning at Gethsemane Cemetery to get this body. Graveyards were creepy and not always because of the dearly departed. They'd tried to be nonchalant and walked around outside the gates but there was some dude in there. Eventually he disappeared, but they never saw him come out.

Even in Detroit, walking around with a dead body wrapped in garbage bags and shovels at three in the morning gets noticed. To add to the risk they always had to backfill the grave in case they were sent back to steal another body at another time.

"I'll tell you what," Marv said. "This better be the last time I have to do this. They stopped at the door to the building and Dell propped it open with his elbow, giving it a hard shove so they could hurry inside.

The two of them had done this enough times that they knew where to go. This place had been an elementary school or something but it was empty now except for this Hills guy and his big-titted secretary.

"Hey, maybe I could ask his assistant out on a date," Dell said. "She deals with us enough. Maybe the whole eye thing doesn't freak her out."

"She's like fifteen years older than you."

"So what? Sometimes older chicks are the best."

"Let me hear you say that when you turn fifty."

"Aww, c'mon. Hey, do you think we'll be like this forever?" Dell knocked on a big white door with his foot.

"Come in," Hills said from inside. Dell made a face, obviously annoyed with having to open the door himself. They wedged their way through into a long rectangular all white room complete with

The Ghost Toucher

a white desk, white chair, white flat screen television against a wall and Hills on the far end of the room in a white t-shirt fitted to his muscular frame and white pants with at least a dozen pockets.

His long black hair was swept back from his face into a big poofball at the back of his head. He was standing in front of an easel with a palette and brush in his hands. The only color other than white was on the palette and the painting he was working on. Marv couldn't make out the painting. It looked like a rainbow Rorschach splotch or something. Screaming tree was the first thing that came to mind.

"Why's he painting a vagina?" Dell asked.

"Morning, gentlemen," Hills said. They both grunted in return. "Put her over there." He waved his hand without turning around to look at them. There was a bench by the wall behind the desk. Dell nodded his head in its direction and they carried it over and set it down.

Marv's back ached. He stretched and it popped a couple times. Not only the shoveling but carrying a body, even a frail old one, was hard.

"So what are you gonna do with it?" Dell asked. Marv rolled his eyes. All he wanted to do was leave.

"What?" Hills said without looking. Marv semi-panicked. The Master didn't say to ask questions. Only deliver.

"This body. What are you gonna do with it?"

"Oh, you mean Mrs. Meyers? Just ask her a few questions."

"What?" Dell said. Marv slapped his arm.

"Let's *go* already," he whispered.

"You fine fellows look like you're boiling over with curiosity. Would you like to know exactly what I'm going to do with her?" Hills put the palette down.

Dell looked unsure. Everything in Marv's head said to turn around and walk out, but he was rooted to the spot.

"Yes," they both said.

Hills thumbed a button on a white remote and a giant portion of the wall next to them slid away, revealing a much larger adjacent room. There was a black, blocky *thing* against the far wall—no, a part of it. It looked like it had grown out of the wall, like some kind of tumor.

The Ghost Toucher

Marv took an instinctual step away from it but felt a gentling hand at his back ushering him closer. Hills towered beside him and Dell, like a black Adonis with a beatific smile on his face. All three men approached.

It was only a machine. It looked really old and had what looked like a lawn mower engine installed at its side. This thing definitely hadn't come off an assembly line. It had been born in somebody's garage. There was a seat on the left with two holes in an arm rest-looking thing in front of it. The machine was tall and thin, part of the low tiled ceiling had been removed, with antenna or spires shooting off in all different directions, including the wall, floor and ceiling. It was like it had grown into the wall.

To Marv they looked like deformed, handless arms reaching out for help.

"Go ahead. Sit." Dell looked sheepish now, but despite himself, Marv was intrigued. He stepped past Dell and into the seat. Hills turned a small wheel overhead, releasing a bulky headset that fell in front of him, hanging by a cord.

"Don't worry, everything's cleaned after each use and you attach these." Hill handed him a small plastic package. Marv opened it and dumped out two weird-looking earplugs, a thing he couldn't identify and a bit-looking thing. "Put those in your ears, put that on your nose and put that in your mouth."

Marv took the two small hollow tubes and put them in his hears and chomped down on the bit-looking thing. Hills had to help him with the nose attachment as he kept sneezing every time he tried to put it on then he attached cords from the helmet to all three pieces and put the helmet over his head. Marv thought it was on backwards as there was no opening for his face.

He felt detached at the sudden deprivation of sight and sound. Someone guided his arms into the arm holes and he felt vulnerable when they cinched up, pinning him in place.

Marv felt the machine hum to life. A steady huff of air went into his mouth, nose and eyes, making him cough once or twice and blink repeatedly. There was a distant clicking in his ears. He felt someone tickling the tips of his fingers, at least that was what it felt like and then he felt loose.

Marv's feet were beneath him. He blinked and the city came into view. Except it didn't look like any place in the metro area he had ever seen. Maybe it was Chicago or something—he'd never been there. But how could he have been in another state?

This must have been CGI. But it felt real. There were people walking around wearing funny clothes and some people who didn't look like people at all. They looked like they were made out of cigarette smoke. Marv turned to walk to one a dozen or so yards away and was suddenly standing in front of her.

"Uh, hi," he said, feeling off balance.

She scowled at him and evaporated. He turned and saw her reconstitute and float down the street. She passed through a man walking with a woman and they both waved and spat as if flies had landed in their mouths.

Marv went to cross the street to speak to the couple but when he zoomed in front of them the woman yelped and the man waved his funny-looking hat furiously. He wanted to laugh but he floated in the air, a tinny-sick feeling radiating from his lower teeth down to and winding around his shin bones.

A taste like saccharin burned at the back of his throat and tongue. He zipped around the man and woman who looked ready to strike again. Marv tried to catch up to the ghost he'd just seen but she was moving too fast. He passed by several more people and slowed when he saw other ghosts. He—

Hills yanked the helmet off, furious. Marv blinked at the light, disoriented. He hadn't heard.

"I said, what the hell do you think you're doing?" Dell peaked out from behind Hills, wide-eyed.

"Marv, you okay?"

"I was just doing the machine. What is that, CGI?"

Hills said something long and complex. Necro-something. Marv stared at him. "It's a machine that speaks to the dead. You should have been able to see his memories and navigate around his mind. You were doing something else. What the hell was it?"

Marv explained to him what he'd experienced. The sights, the smells, how real it all had appeared, how sick he'd gotten when the man had touched him.

"It's not supposed to be that way," Hills muttered to himself. "They're dead. The memories aren't interactive. Could he really have gone there?"

"Gone where?" Dell asked.

Hills looked at Dell as if for the first time and thumbed a button on his remote. A moment later a teenager, squat and muscular with a stern expression stalked into the room. Hills stood away from Dell and the boy spun him around and leapt on his back, folding around until his body was completely above Dell's shoulders. Dell staggered at the considerable weight combined with the boy's massive thighs wrapped around his neck. He collapsed to his knees and flopped over onto his back in less than twenty seconds.

The boy got up and looked at Marv.

"How's my time?"

"Oh, I dunno," Hills said. "Thirty seconds?"

The boy cursed himself.

"Him?" he said, looking at Marv.

Hills put a hand in front of the boy when he took a step. As built and tall as Hills was, Marv was sure the boy could take him. He realized, looking at the two with the set of their shoulders and posture that these two were closely related.

"No," Hills said. "Where's your mother?"

***

Gunner finally had her right where he wanted her. He strolled out of the bathroom with his hands in his pockets. His skin wasn't fiery hot because he hadn't put on the make-up for a change. There would be no need for that this morning and perhaps never again. Besides, she needed to see. The things she had done to him, both inside and out. He was a freak because of her.

"Hello, Sandra." He had dipped his voice into that low tone he used with the ladies, only he wasn't going to bed this one. Gunner gripped the revolver in his pocket, turned it up so the end of the barrel pressed against his pants pocket—a snub-nosed erection.

Her mouth fell open and she half stood, knocking over some of her crappy wood and bone chotzkis.

"Mm-mm." He shook his head and she sat back down and closed her mouth. She looked at the chotzkis on the floor but didn't make a move to pick them up. Good girl.

"Slide over." She moved over to the other end of the couch and stared at him.

"I heard you was lookin' fa me." He snorted at the phony accent, sitting on the other end of the couch with the gun in his lap.

"Any guess why?"

"Why else? You blamin' me fa sometin' you ask fa."

Gunner leaned forward, his arm snaking out and bouncing the butt of the gun off her forehead. She'd leaned into it, surprisingly, leaving a nice little split an inch above her eyebrow. She must have been trying to knock herself out. Must have guessed he wanted her conscious for whatever he wanted.

He had to keep his anger in check. She was a woman, but she was unpredictable. She probably had a knife or something she could hurt him with.

"First, drop the phony accent." Exotic-looking she may have been, she was anything but. He'd done a background check and she was from Cleveland. Cleveland. "The next time I hit you with this it'll be with the business end."

She blinked the fog out of her eyes. He hoped she had a concussion.

"Can it be undone?"

"What?" No accent. Better.

"Don't play with me. *This.*" He gestured to his face with his free hand.

"What do you think?"

He wanted to smack her again, but pointed the gun at her instead.

"If all you got is lip I may as well kill you now."

"Okay-okay. The marks? No—I didn't do that."

"The hell you didn't. You put that thing on me to-to let me call up the dead. The next day I woke up like this." He put his gun hand back on his lap.

"It wasn't me. I swear. I do—have done the ceremony a dozen times and nothing like that has ever happened. Look, I'm more of a courier—I don't actually talk to the dead."

"So you don't know what you're doing, you're saying. You mean you screwed up."

"Yes—*no*. What I'm saying is not everything can be predicted."

"Why didn't you tell me that then?"

"Look, I'm in the business of giving people what they want. If I told you every little detail of what might go wrong it would probably scare you off."

"This is a little detail to you? I can't go outside without putting on a keg of Max Factor."

He could tell by the wildness in her eyes she'd say anything. Too bad she didn't know he was going to kill her no matter what. The only difference was if he would do himself next.

"Am I that stupid looking to you? I don't know, I think I'm kind of a smart guy. Smart enough to catch you. Maybe *you're* the dumb one. Maybe you're too stupid to realize I'm onto you. Hold out your hand."

"What?"

He cocked the hammer back.

"I don't ask twice."

She slowly raised her hand, her eyes locked on the gun. Good. She hadn't seen him slide the blade out of his other sleeve. He lashed out, slicing her palm open.

"You're crazy!" She snatched her hand back, cradling it in the other.

"Probably." He stood up and retreated to the little desk against the wall. "But I'm also a fast learner." He set the knife on the counter and opened a drawer, taking out a clear glass flask, carefully unscrewing the top with one hand and keeping the gun trained on her.

Her eyes widened with realization. She leapt at him, her teeth bared and hands fixed to tear into him with those long black fingernails. She was fast but just too far away and made herself an even easier target when he fired two shots, one going into her gut, the other shattering the glass tabletop.

She landed in a heap, half cradling her knees to her chest, moaning.

"And I know the dead don't lie." He kicked her in the back of the head and her moaning stopped. He had to move quick. Even in this crappy neighborhood cops were bound to come snooping when there was gunfire.

Gunner put the gun on the table and picked up the knife. He dipped the skinny blade into the clear contents of the flask and shook the whole thing gently. The contents clouded up then turned black.

He hadn't understood until now why it was called a glowing black. The liquid itself cast a shadow in the same way light glowed. He was mesmerized by it until she started convulsing on the floor. He really had to hurry. He steeled himself, drew the knife out and downed it. He instantly regretted not having this stuff in a wider mouthed container as it glugged out of the flask. But he finished it, wiping his mouth on his sleeve which began to sizzle and smoke.

What's this stuff doing to my teeth? he wondered.

Gunner looked at her on the floor in full seizure. He wished he'd brought a camera.

"Sorry, babe, gotta go." He whacked her over the head with the mallet he'd hidden in the drawer and she lay still. He found a very weak pulse in her neck and smiled as it slowed to a stop. Gunner unfolded a sheet of paper that had her real name printed on it at the top and another name, made from rearranging the letters of the printed name in his sloppy scrawl beneath. He cleared his throat and spoke the name as if speaking above a roomful of semi-loud people.

"Y-yes," her body sighed in an otherworldly voice. That was the other thing he'd learned about all this. Night time wasn't a necessary ingredient. Just another falsity to make the whole magic thing scarier, sexier. It wasn't even magic. No such thing.

This was so cool. Now he really wished he had more time. He stepped back to give her room. She wasn't moving. Why wasn't she moving? He said the name again. Still she didn't move, but she said, "Yes," again.

The Ghost Toucher

"Hey, you're supposed to rise." He nudged her with his foot. Nothing. Had he done something wrong? "Rise, already."

His father's words to him the other day came back to him. He'd screwed up again somehow.

The knife was still on the table. He picked it up and examined it. If he was going to be a screw up he may as well be the best one possible. It would be a huge embarrassment for the Old Man when the cops found the dead tattooed body of his son alongside a murdered ex-prostitute of dubious employment.

Hell, it was better than his original plan of just hanging himself in his apartment.

Don't think about it, just do it, he thought to himself.

He grabbed the handle by both hands, turned the blade inward and began jabbing himself in the heart.

By the fifth time he realized it wasn't working. He plunged it in again and looked as he withdrew the knife. Gunner tore his shirt open and felt the skin there.

He wasn't cut.

Gunner hurled the knife and it smacked harmlessly off the wall. He dropped his head into his palms and wept. Let the cops come, he would confess everything. And he'd make sure to drop his father's name as often as possible. The Old Man had been hands-off enough with the whole thing that he probably wouldn't get busted but he would be shamed out of the boardroom at least.

There was something warm at his back. Gunner turned, thinking she had played some kind of trick on him. Her body was still on the floor; he put his hand out, trying to feel for *something* right in front of him.

Bright golden light exploded in the dark room. Gunner fell back, shielding his eyes.

"I'm... dead?" When his eyes finally adjusted he saw a glowing figure floating several inches off the floor, kneeling over the body. It turned and looked at him. From what Gunner could tell it was the witch he'd just killed.

"You killed me?" it asked.

Gunner pushed back up against the wall.

"Don't hurt me."

"There is no reason to be afraid, Joseph." She glided over to him and reached out a hand. He tried to push back even further. Nobody called him Joseph except his parents. "I forgive you."

"You do?"

"Yes. You freed me."

"I did."

"There is work yet to be done."

"What... what do you mean?" Gunner looked around for the knife. Her skin brightened and he saw markings that were similar to his tattoos. He summoned his bravery.

"Did you do this to me?"

"No. Those are markings of your destiny. The universe needs you."

"Me? Why me?"

Her hand touched his cheek and it burned. No, not his cheek, the marks on his face, then all over his body. It was unbearable, but he couldn't move away. Gunner screamed and just as suddenly it stopped.

"One who has endured much suffering was needed," she said. He opened his eyes and looked at the mark on his forearm. It slid beneath the skin, like a fish slipping beneath the surface of a lake. Gunner sat up and saw the same thing all over his body. He stood.

"I have forgiven you, but the world's ills are upon you. You can be the savior of all."

"I can?"

"Yes, but you must submit."

"How do I do that?"

"Fall to your knees."

Gunner dropped in front of her.

"Do you give yourself freely to the will of the Goa'agnol?"

"The what? What's that?"

"It's another word for the universe."

"Okay. Then yes. I submit myself to the will of... of that."

"And of your own free will you will stand in for the T'iant?"

"Tee-*what*?"

"It means... uhh, hero."

Gunner wanted to be a hero. *The* hero. His father would look like a fag compared to what he was about to do.

"Yes. Yes, I will stand in." He put his arms out, his chest swelling with pride as she placed a hand on his forehead. The marks burned again as she spoke rapidly in another language. He felt something from her come into him and his skin glowed until she let go.

"Is that it?" he asked.

"Yes." She floated back over her body and smiled.

"Thank you." He teared up and wiped his nose on his sleeve. "What do I do now?"

She giggled as she faded away. Gunner stood, his limbs jerking to life of their own accord.

"What the hell?" he said, spinning around to face the door. He took several unsteady steps forward, bent, grabbed the knob and yanked it off.

"Stop," he said to himself. "I'm a hero. Stop now!" But his arm raised and smashed through the door. "No!" he screamed over and over as he walked out, unsure where he was being led. He brushed past two bummy-looking people who paid him no mind. Gunner stepped into the street and a car swerved around him without slowing. Gunner's head turned to the sky, his eyes fixing on the gibbous moon, still present in the early morning sky. He howled with a voice not his own and leapt skyward.

Reset

The phone hadn't rung all night. He'd picked it up over and over again hoping she'd call. His beautiful little Seleste. How could he have allowed such a terrible thing? His only daughter cursed as her mother had been. His wife had been willing. She wanted to know his culture so when he had revealed the *douchou* to her she had taken it into herself. He hadn't asked—she had volunteered.

She'd gained thirty pounds within two weeks and had picked up steam from there. It had upset her as with any woman, particularly because she'd been very petite before. He'd taken good care of her, but he'd had to move her to the basement when it became obvious she'd be too big for the house to support.

He'd explained that in order to host the *douchou* it was necessary for the hostess to acquire mass from everything it touched. It didn't matter if she ate or not, it would still happen, but if she didn't eat she would starve.

Hugo had hoped it would leave and his wife could return to something like normal again. He had told her it could kill her, but she'd still accepted it.

His wife's body had dissolved, reduced to a loose pile of grains of sand. Seleste had seen her mother's remains and asked, "Will this happen to me?"

He broke down and wept, holding his taller, much bigger child. She'd been on the heavier side before and already it was a labor for her to move around since she'd become host to the *douchou*.

"Yes," he confessed. "I did not want this for you. I was obligated."

But she'd been more concerned with what the boy Marvin would think. It was a symptom of hosting the *douchou*—complete self-absorption. She'd come back to the house but he knew she was already gone. He went to her room just before bed to find she'd disappeared and had been waiting by the phone ever since. He knew it was hopeless, that he was the last thing on her mind, but he had to hope.

He picked up the phone again to check if it were working and was surprised to hear a voice on the other end saying his name.

It was the *douchou*.

"I need you to go home. Prepare a place for me. I am weakening."

Most who knew of it thought it was a god, but he knew better. It was a parasite. Not just of whoever was its host if it needed one, but of the world. It had come here at some point and had been feeding off the Earth ever since. At least that was what he believed.

Even he'd worshipped the *douchou* at one time but after it appeared to him years ago he thought it seemed lonely more than anything else. How could a god be lonely? But it had a constant lost child look as if it had been left behind.

"Weak?" he asked. He knew what the *douchou* meant. Not weak as in vulnerable, but weak as in losing its ability to control its own power. It had shown him a place two days outside his village where it had become weak and scorched away all life as far as the eye could see. The *douchou* claimed to have no interest in ending human life, but he had seen that once before too.

There was no choice. Whatever he felt for his daughter had to wait for him to complete the call ceremony. Actually, if the *douchou* wanted it done now, then that meant it would be leaving soon.

And leaving his daughter.

He stood, suddenly excited. Perhaps there was time enough to save her. The *douchou* needed a woman's womb to 'rest' when it was away from home for a significant amount of time. But even there it could only stay so long. Hugo ran out of the house and had to run back in for his keys and passport. He would spend every dime if he had to to get back home. His every prayer would be devout and he would perform every dance and sacrifice the largest animal he could steal even if he didn't believe.

***

Part of what makes Morrisites Morrisites is a mind bred to process information in unique ways. They go through years of vigorous training, both mental and physical, eliminating ninety-nine percent of all candidates until they locate that special one percent.

Unfortunately, these minds tend to be extremely prone to schizophrenia, bi-polar disorder or a host of other mental illnesses.

In reality, Wendy had only stood there after the cop pointed his gun at her. She hadn't moved a finger when Byrd told her the cop had shot him. Events had played out in her mind, but her body had done nothing. A doctor long ago had told her mother this 'physical shut-down' happened in times of extreme stress and could last anywhere from a few minutes to several days. She'd gone quietly as he cuffed her and shoved her in the backseat of the cruiser and threw Byrd in a heap on top of her.

The cop had gotten in the car and raced off, screaming about his ear, clutching a wad of formerly white napkins to the free-flowing wound. For some reason he wasn't waiting for the police that were slowly weaving through the clot of traffic trapped behind Dale's wrecked car.

Wendy came out of her fugue state several miles later. She looked out the back window to see sirens of other police cruisers just behind them. Their car picked up speed rather than slow down.

She spotted her bow-tang in the front passenger seat, but before she could begin to think of a way to get her hands on it there was a hard left and she fell over onto Byrd's legs. She tried to wiggle her way back up but her arms were trapped behind her and Byrd's legs were like lead weights against her. Wendy lay there listening to the screeching of the tires and the cop swore and confessed the vilest things as if seeking absolution. Sex with women, sometimes men, diseases he had contracted and the cancer he realized God had cursed him with for his sinful ways.

This went on for almost ten minutes, with an abbreviated version of the Lord's Prayer mixed in, until there was a tremendous swerve that sent Wendy onto the floor in a tangle with Byrd. The cop got out to be greeted by a chorus of screams of, "Drop the weapon!" and, "Get down!" Seconds later came a cluster of pops, a few of the bullets tinging off the doors of the cruiser. Wendy had managed to get on the seat on her back and saw the cop's face, ear stump and all, sliding down the window, the life draining from his eyes.

Someone yelled, "Clear!" and she heard the clatter of metal on concrete. She felt the door open behind her and wormed around to see a new cop staring at her in the morning sun.

"Thank God for you!" she cried in her best tear-choked voice.

"Okay, let her up. Easy."

LaGina blinked several times as they sat her up, her eyes slowly adjusting to the sunlight.

Sunlight? Damn, the babysitter.

She mumbled something unintelligible to her own ears and flopped back down in whatever chair she was sitting in. A middle-aged man in a wrinkly suit and a chesty blonde hovered over her, genuine concern in their eyes.

"Gina, you okay honey?" the woman said. Linda. That was her name. The man in the suit was Henry Quint. "Look, I don't care what Gun says, we need to take her to a hospital."

"Agreed," Henry said. His face looked different and it wasn't just the daylight. He looked less haggard, like a man in his early fifties rather than his late sixties. He almost looked happy.

"You're going to be all right." Linda disappeared into another room while he held LaGina's hand. "We all are. My Katie's at peace." He smiled. LaGina realized Mr. Quint was more than just 'at peace'. The way the two of them fumbled around each other like a couple of teenagers it was obvious they had slept together.

At peace. Could he be talking about last night? Everything inside LaGina's head felt like she was swimming through mud. She wasn't herself. Then she remembered the spirit floating above the table and seeing its face.

Stout!

It had been him. She tried sitting up again and everything colored with red polka dots. She loved him but wanted to kill him too.

"Think we should call an ambulance?" Linda said in the background somewhere.

"No. It'll take too long. We need to hurry."

Linda reappeared and they pulled her to her feet, both taking an arm. "Why?" As they stopped at the front door to open it she saw a slack face in the mirror on the wall by the door, like there was no muscle beneath it. She was horrified when she realized it was her own. LaGina moaned.

"I think she may have had a stroke."

***

Vittorio had gotten the call yesterday but hadn't had the time to go to the dock. Russian whiskey, a ton of it, 'misdirected' into a dock only he and Tony knew about. All he had to do was be a warm body for this meet and he could go see to it.

But then a cop jammed a revolver into his ribs, directing them all inside. They all filed in, obviously the cops working with the Torres. Vittorio stood on the end of the line praying they weren't about to do what they were about to do as the men, cops and robbers, raised their guns and began firing.

***

Kelly woke with a start. He was surprised he'd fallen asleep so easily, but he hadn't really slept much. Anna or Israel, whoever, had pulled into a convenience store parking lot. He didn't know where he was but it looked like the East side.

"What are we doing here?"

Anna turned around.

"I wanted to give you a little time to rest. When you were little the children had their own urban legend, didn't they? They called him the Green Man. He lived in the alleys and slept in dumpsters and sometimes he would snatch up a little girl or boy who was never seen again."

Kelly nodded.

"Your memory of him is both true and false. Very few children actually saw the Green Man and what he was snatching was not real children, but shadow children—*tools*—not the real thing. If we saw what they really looked like we'd call them demons. They posed as children and would lure them to secluded areas and kill them. The Green Man was sent, another tool, to protect as the other side doesn't want more spirits coming over. But he was blamed for the deaths of a few local children and parents who remembered him from their own childhoods found him and burned him alive.

"The Green Man was part human, the part from the other side had to bond with a living creature in order to work properly. But I'm sure you know that's how these tools work."

"Okay, I remember the Green Man, but how do you know about it? I'm guessing you didn't grow up in Highland Park. Besides, that legend died out by the time I was in fourth grade or so."

"I know because Israel knows. He knows a lot more than he's told you with good reason. He's afraid of what you'll think but you have to forgive him. It wasn't his fault."

"What wasn't his fault?" Kelly sat up.

"I'm sorry, I'm explaining this all wrong."

"What are you talking about? What wasn't his fault?"

"The Green Man was a general protector of children. Israel was your personal protector."

"What are you—"

"When you feel pain, Israel senses it beforehand. That way he can keep you from serious harm. His connection with you was severed three years ago in July."

Kelly didn't like what he was hearing. His eyes narrowed.

"Where are you going with this?"

"An event that was so painful... too heartbreaking."

"Say it."

"You need a minute. I do too. Hold on while I get something out the trunk. Taze, a little help?"

"Geeah (pronounced JEE-uh)."

They got out, leaving Kelly with the zombie. Ed, Anna had called him after shooting down Taze's suggestion 'Ice Z'. It was chilly in the car; she had the air cranked all the way up to keep the smell down. He was in an advanced state of decomposition and had a glass-eyed stare.

Kelly picked up the Febreeze and gave him a spritz. The cold could only do so much.

He thought about what Anna said. Had Israel been there?

From the moment he met him Kelly had had a feeling like he'd known him. But Kelly would never have guessed.

He felt violated. That Israel had been around him all this while and hadn't told him and worse still he'd felt what was about to happen to Kelly's family and did nothing...

They were dead. The obscene part was how he could be alive when he'd been in the car with them. Alive and completely unharmed.

Kelly mumbled as his mind raced. Ed had been staring straight ahead, but then his head rolled in Kelly's direction. His eyes were still foggy, but Ed was looking at him.

Tears streamed from Kelly's eyes, but suddenly he was afraid. Ed blinked and rested his rotting hand atop Kelly's.

"Fine," Ed rasped. "All fine."

Kelly sat there, unsure what to say or do. Ed made a face as if confused or frustrated.

"Martha," he said. "Lilah, Amanda. All together. All fine."

"Martha and the girls?" Fresh tears streamed from his eyes. Kelly was stunned when he heard laughter in his own voice. He didn't understand it, but somehow this dead man telling him his wife and children being all right in the afterlife was a tremendous relief. Even more amazing was that he believed him. Kelly put his arm around Ed's neck and gave him a squishy hug. He let go and a string of goo stretched between them and broke.

Kelly's nostrils stung from the smell and he spritzed him again. Ed lifted his hands, examining his flesh.

"Oh," he said.

"Who are you?"

Ed looked around and his eyes settled back on Kelly.

"Les... Lee."

"Your name is Les Lee?"

Ed—*Les*—nodded. It rang a distant bell, but Kelly was certain he'd never met anyone named Les. He knew a Lee in grade school but that was his first name.

"Okay, I think it's safe to leave the z-man here," Taze said, opening the door. He grabbed Ed by the tattered shirt collar and pulled him out. "C'mon, homie." Taze shut the door and double-tapped a sideways peace sign to his own stomach before hopping back into the passenger seat. Anna shut the trunk and got back in too.

"Should we really be leaving him here?" Kelly asked.

"He won't last much longer," Anna said. "We really didn't need to bring him to begin with. He just... got in and I wasn't going to stop the car at the time and put him out."

She passed over a pile of magazines to Taze.

"Look at the porn we got!" he said. "We got Japanese stuff, old lady stuff, big titty stuff. You wanna get down on any of this?"

"Uh, not right now."

"Sure? We got some gay stuff too."

"I so didn't need to know what a power bottom is," Anna said. She put the car in drive and they pulled out of the lot and away from Ed.

"Nah. I'm good."

"Skillet, you cryin'?"

"No. Ed was getting pretty putrid."

"Use the spray, man. I'll crack my window. You should too. The police ain't around." Taze started peeling an orange, putting the scraps of skin in a paper bag. He threw the orange out the window and put his nose in the bag, breathing deep a few times.

"So to whom are we taking the porn?"

Taze turned around and looked at Kelly.

"What was that, Yoda?"

"Remember what I told you about the Green Man?" Anna said. "The human part of him died, but the other part didn't. The... the *machín* part. It survived and found other tools like it and they made a kind of amalgam. Israel knows about them because all *machíns* are hunted on this side. Nothing is supposed to leave the other side.

The Ghost Toucher

"Hey, did you know spirits of the dead are a nuisance over there? We're like their version of flies. Generally harmless, but annoying. They haven't figured out a way to swat us, though."

"Okay, but why the *porn*? When Israel—you—made me buy it I didn't ask because it was just so far out of left field."

Kelly had a bad feeling about the direction they were heading. He was right, it was the East side. He spotted a street sign and saw they were on Jefferson. Why would she be driving down here? Nobody was supposed to come here.

"Are we going to Downeck?"

"Yeahhhh boyyyyyy!" Taze said.

"It's developed a taste for it. The porn, I mean. It can point us in the direction of Stout, but we have to pay it a kind of tithe first. It should be somewhere down this alley. I can feel it."

Anna turned on the radio. At first he thought it was Warren Zevon but then it started into a verse and it was Kid Rock. Kelly's stomach did flip-flops. Everyone knew this was a bad place to be. Once an affluent suburb nestled within the city but something had happened. Daring teenagers came here and never were seen again. Or came back wrong. Or came back dead.

But some residents had stayed, like they were immune to whatever was happening here. Kelly had learned through osmosis not to ever come here.

"Don't buy that urban legend crap, home-team. I used to come here all the time when I was a teenager. Besides, I got the click-clack in case anything jumps off."

A lone dumpster was halfway down the alley. The car bounced and jostled as they crawled to it.

"Israel saved my life," Anna said. "He could have left me in the bed to be devoured by that thing but he let it get him instead. Here we are. Gimme your stuff." She held her hands out to Taze. He handed the stack of dirty magazines over. "All of it." Kelly saw the title as he passed over a magazine titled "Tight Gilfs" with a barely covered blue hair in a choker on the cover. She looked thirsty.

Anna rolled down the window and dropped the magazines out next to the dumpster and pulled up a couple feet.

Something large slammed against the side.

"Whatever you do, don't open the door." A moment later the car began rocking. The pace quickly picked up.

"Aw, ill, man." Taze popped a pill in his mouth and dry-swallowed.

The car's shocks had gotten a thorough workout before the rocking abruptly stopped. After a minute, Anna opened the door.

"We should be good now." She got out. Taze and Kelly looked at each other and followed. Whatever it was was a formless mass that seemed a different color depending on the angle. It was half slumped against the rear tire and it looked like it had eaten the magazines.

"We want Stout Roost." Anna's voice was commanding. A little louder than necessary, Kelly thought, and with a tinge of nervousness. Kelly wondered if it was safe to be near this thing.

It moved. Faster than he could see and it was suddenly an exaggerated shape of a man, dark green with broad shoulders and a waist as thick as one of Kelly's thighs, but instead of legs it stood on a black triangular base. It had an iridescent pink 'arm' wrapped around Anna's neck, pinning her to the car.

Taze went for his gun, but Anna waved him off. It didn't speak but its headless torso leaned in and Kelly could hear it sniffing.

"We want him," Anna said. "*Now.*"

It held her a moment longer then its grip loosened. The appendage fell down to its side and reabsorbed into its torso. It seemed to have lost its ability to maintain form and began sliding back to the ground.

A giant, lidless ovular eye opened in the melting mass and looked at Kelly. He took a step back as the thing puddled into the ground and floated down a sewer grate peaking out beneath the car, the eye open and staring the whole time.

"So what's poppin' next?" Taze asked.

"Now we go," Anna said.

"That's it?" Kelly asked. "That thing almost kills you and now we just go driving around again? There should be something more to it than that."

"I don't know what to tell you. Maybe that's why Israel didn't want to come here. A great deal of what he believes is what you believe. Maybe you're right and this is just a waste of time. I figured it's better than nothing."

"Maybe we should check out that last house. The one where Stout went."

"You know where it is?" Anna asked.

"Yeah. I think I figured it out."

"Well then tell me on the way."

***

Someone took the hood off Jemen's head. She was tied to a chair in a small room with pale, cinder block walls. It was cold in here.

"You sure are a pretty *thing*, aren't you?"

She focused on the man in front of her. A bulky baldheaded man with a gap-toothed smile. Jemen cocked her head at him, pondering how she might kill him once she removed the binds.

"Do you understand English?" he said slowly and louder than he needed to. She wondered if she should tell him that because this universe was an offshoot of her own that she could understand and speak every language that had ever been spoken on this planet.

He traced his fingertips down her cheek and across her collarbone. If he dared to go lower she would rip his fingers out by the roots. As if sensing her agitation he pulled his hand away and slumped in a folding chair across from her.

"Relax. I wouldn't touch you with a flamethrower, *beast*." He took a trial size packet of wet wipes out of his shirt pocket, took one out and began vigorously cleaning his hands. His breathing became pronounced and he closed his eyes, rubbing his hands even faster until he seemed to reach a moment of ecstasy.

He sat still a moment, pressing the tattered wipe between his hands. His eyes were a bit foggy when he opened them. She could beguile him into letting her go, but she wondered what these people intended. Perhaps divinity would lead her to her quarry if she were to trust where it had led her so far.

But what of her son? The others were old enough to take care of themselves, but he was not even a day old. What had he done when he came outside and found her gone? While he was big he wouldn't be able to fend for himself. She was finally thankful he had taken the form of that homeless man. Most people would simply ignore him. And even if he'd been arrested he would be fine in the custody of the police until she'd accomplished her task. She could come for him then and not worry about being clandestine.

The man sitting across her neatly folded the remnants of the wet wipe and placed it in a small trash receptacle by the wall.

"What do you call yourself?" he said in a loud voice.

"I am called Jemen." She decided the silent treatment had gone on long enough. Time to find out what these humans wanted. He seemed taken aback.

"Oh, so you *do* speak. Good. What is your goal here?"

"I am tied to a chair. I would like to get out."

"I mean *here*. On this planet. Y'know, not in hell."

"You know me? That I am not of your world?"

"So you *admit* it! You are a demon."

"Demon. I am not familiar with the term. Explain."

"It's what you are. That's all you need to know."

The gray door behind the man creaked open. A petite man with iron black hair and square glasses stepped in. He wore a black suit that was too big for him with a red tie. He shut the door and walked up behind the man, his eyes fishing up and down between Jemen and the back of the first man's head.

"Charles, what are you doing?"

The man spun around in his chair.

"Jesus! Mr. R. you scared the crap outta me."

Mr. R. continued to stare down at him. Charles stood.

"I was... I was just *talking* to her. I mean *it*."

"You have no need to speak to such a divine creature."

"Divine? Mr. R. she ain't divine, she's a demon."

Mr. R. rolled his eyes.

"You have no concept of symmetry. I only meant the word in that she is something far beyond human."

True. Jemen was glad she had not broken the ropes. She may not have been able to get so close to this one. Capturing Charles' mind would have been a simple task and more than likely a wasted effort. This was the one she wanted. He appeared to be one who was in charge.

"Leave now, Charles. I will deal with this one."

"Yes *sir*." Charles stepped around the chair and left the room without another word. Mr. R. sat in the chair, but squirmed around until he appeared to have found a comfortable spot on it. He put his legs together, knees almost touching, but was so short he had to point his feet to touch the floor. He clasped his fingers together and rested them on his legs, almost as if he were trying to push down on his lap.

"Would you like water?" he asked.

Jemen shook her head. His eyes, a deep brown, appeared much larger than what they probably were behind the thick lenses of his glasses. But there was a power behind them. This man, despite his size, had commanded men all his life.

"What is the purpose of your visit?" His voice was gentle, above a whisper, but not by much.

"Visit?"

"Surely, you do not intend to stay. Do you?"

It occurred to Jemen that he had let Charles come in first as a means of testing what she would do. Clever, but she could still kill him if she wanted.

"No. Once my purpose is accomplished I will leave."

"And what is your purpose, may I ask?"

"To gather the tools to save the world."

"To save the world from what?"

"The end."

"What is the end?"

"You would not understand. What are your intentions with me?"

"It depends. If you assist us in stopping the agenda of your kind we will simply kill you."

"And something much worse if I don't?"

He didn't answer.

"Perhaps I can propose something different. Something that may be an ends to accomplish both our goals." She smiled. Let them try to kill her, they would find out how much of an impossibility that was.

"What is your proposal?"

"There is a man I seek. He has something I need. A great power. I do not want to kill him, but this power must be taken away." An incomplete truth, but enough to set wheels in his mind in motion.

"What is this man's name?"

"Kelly Greene. He is searching for the host of the television show *The Ghost Toucher*.

"Stout Roost?" Mr. R. leaned forward. "He is missing? I love that show."

Jemen thought less of the man. Humans had an obsession with this television she did not comprehend. Perhaps because they had nothing like it on her world. Why watch a reproduction of a thing when you could simply go and see it for yourself?

"It would be easy to verify what you've told me. Especially about Stout Roost. We will take what you told us under consideration." He rose.

"And until then?"

"I will arrange for more... comfortable accommodations. Just because we are adversaries does not mean dealings between us cannot be civilized."

"Thank you."

He nodded, turned and left as quietly as he came.

For some reason Jemen was unworried about finding Greene. She also wasn't worried about finding her son. Providence was at work here and she was truly curious how it would play out.

***

Ren-Jon shut the door, his legs barely beneath him. Despite his outward appearance he was rattled. Charles stepped up to him, a big grin on his face. Ren-Jon put up a hand and passed him, heading for the basement stairs. He would not lose his heir of leadership in front of the others.

"Did the beast at least tell you where Wendy, Dell and Byrd are?"

He ignored the younger man, going upstairs and cutting through the kitchen and heading for the bathroom. There would

The Ghost Toucher

be time to figure out where those three were later. He passed Mama by, stirring something in a pot over the stove.

"Renny, when you gonna take out the garbage?" she said in thick-accented English. "Three times I ask you and you still no do it."

"I'll take care of it later, Mama." He stepped out of the kitchen, across the thin hallway, into the tiny pink bathroom and shut the door. He rushed the toilet, threw the lid back and collapsed to his knees. He barely pulled the tie to the side before he hurled.

"Don't you make a mess on your father's suit," his Mama yelled at him through the door. "And why you got it on, anyway? You trying to impress your creepy friends? I don't want any of them taking out the garbage. They didn't put the lid back on right and the animals get into it."

"Are you almost ready to go? I've got an interview later today, Mama." Ren-Jon stood. His legs were still shaky, but a lot better than before. He was unsure if he could take being in the presence of an actual beast again. It was too much for him. He was more of an in-theory man. He'd gone through all the training and kept himself in peak physical and mental condition, but it just wasn't in him to do anything beyond planning.

He stared at himself in the mirror. Thirty-nine years old, but he already had deep bags under his eyes and gray at his temples. It was what happened to his people, *Morrisites*, because they were special. Able to do things common people could not. But in exchange they aged faster or worse were plagued with mental disorders. He took the bottle of Scope out of the medicine cabinet, swished some around in his mouth and spat it out in the sink before placing the bottle back.

Ren-Jon washed his hands and stepped out of the bathroom. Whatever Eastern European dish his Mama was cooking he wanted no part of it. He'd never liked any of it growing up and had promptly stopped eating it when he turned sixteen and got a job. He'd been embarrassed whenever she spoke her native language and even though he understood it, refused to speak it until she'd had to speak English or not talk to him at all. He'd been grateful the Morrisites had found him when he was twenty three. He'd been rescued.

But they were greater then, in number and influence. Now they were barely hanging on as an organization. Depleted of funds as most of them were incapable of holding down a job for any length of time. He'd used the meager trust fund his father had left for the cause, but had to take a part time job to keep the group fed. Most of them lived at home with parents or friends. Byrd lived in a state run home that allowed him to be furloughed into the care of friends for brief periods of time.

Their one hope was the newest recruit, Cindy LeCroix. She was a distant relative of the Morris family and was due to receive a lump sum payout upon her twenty first birthday. She wasn't truly one of them, but had investigated her family tree, finding Goode's bastard secret in the Morrisites and immediately sought them out. Ren-Jon had taken her under his personal tutelage, shielding her from the others as they would recognize she was a phony. Ren-Jon was going on an interview of sorts. He was going to see her, to make sure she wasn't 'neglected' before she got her hands on that precious trust fund.

"Do I look all right, Mama?" She stopped stirring what looked like a pot of boiling cabbage. She looked at both sides of his face, licked both her thumbs and smoothed out his eyebrows.

"You have a face like your papa." She slapped his cheek. Not because she was angry, but it was her way of telling him she was done looking him over. "Tell your friends they have to leave. I don't want them in the house while I'm gone. You wanna take some with you?" Ren-Jon shook his head. Blintzes were the one dish his mother made he could actually eat, but he already had a taste for some slawse. He grabbed the bottle from the refrigerator and unscrewed the top, dipping three fingers into it and spooning it into his mouth. Delicious. For some reason he and the others all had a taste for it. His mother made a face.

"I wash my hands and I'm ready. Go on." She waved him away.

He peaked down the basement stairs and told everyone they had to leave before he went out the back door. Mary, a tall thin black woman with her head in a scarf was there. She was smoking a home-rolled cigarette with Charles.

"So what do we do with the beast, Mr. R.?" Charles said.

"Let her stew for a while. I have to check on some things."

"You want me to come with?"

"Unnecessary." Ren-Jon took the house key off his keychain. "I'm taking my mother to the doctor's. You and Mary hang around, keep watch. I'll call when we're on the way back and you can leave then. I have a sensation she could cause a lot more trouble than she has, but do nothing until I return unless absolutely necessary." He opened the door to the black Caprice Classic and got in. "She has given us information that may be of use to us. If it is, you will need to get her out of the house to kill her. I don't want my mother disturbed."

Ren-Jon's mother came out after the rest of the Morrisites filed out in front of her. She got in on the passenger side and shut the door as he turned the key in the ignition. Mary waved with her cigarette hand as he pulled out the driveway. The others would probably go to a Dunkin Donuts a couple blocks over. Charles winked at him with an over exaggerated nod.

The survival of the Morrisites might depend on what they could glean from this beast. Ren-Jon was nervous to be leaving her in the care of someone like Charles. Hopefully Mary would keep him balanced.

FLIES ARE MUCH BIGGER IN THEIR DREAMS

Flies are much bigger in their dreams,
Some have feathers,
Some have iridescent wings,
They like to stand on hind legs
And walk in fly shoes,
They eat people food,
And they read Fly News,
Yes, when flies sleep
They're not such silly things,
Much like pants,
One at a time, they put on their wings

"What?" Anna asked.

"The White Pages," Kelly said. "I remembered at the first house where Israel and I went there was a White Pages there. It had a sheet torn out, but someone had drawn a circle on that page and left an impression on the next one. I tore out the sheet behind it and kept it. Once I realized Stout was the one who'd circled the name I put my sheet on top of the same one in another White Pages and saw the name he'd circled. It was for this address—Belinda Moore.

They were still in Downeck. It had clicked for Kelly that maybe they were here for something else and once he'd found the Moore address it was all the reason he needed.

A little elderly woman with wide eyes answered the door.

"I don't know any Stout Roost," she said.

"Ma'am, why do you think we're here about him?"

"I know things. Just know 'em. Don't waste my time."

"Well we don't want to keep you, Ma'am," Kelly began, "but do you have a spirit in your home?"

She narrowed her eyes. There was a groan somewhere inside. She turned her head.

"No," she said, her voice a whisper. "He came here and I sent him away. Now *you* go away." She slammed the door.

"A husband?" Kelly asked Anna.

"Nah, G," Taze said. "It's the love you can't talk about."

Anna and Kelly turned to him.

"What do you mean?" Anna asked.

"The ring on her right ring finger. It was a weddin' band." Kelly made a face as if he didn't understand. "The old tattoo on her arm. A labris?"

"Ohhhh," Anna nodded. Kelly looked at her.

"Get off my porch!" Ms. Moore shouted from inside. They walked down the creaky stairs and across the sidewalk.

"What?"

"Let's say short of the cable guy you two are probably the most beef she's ever had in her house," Anna said.

"You mean she's a..."

"A card-carrying member."

"Probly a founder, knaemean?"

Anna looked into the sky.

"I think we'd better get out of here. We've been Heard."

"What do you... oh."

"It's that thing again? From before?" Taze seemed excited.

They got in the car and Anna started it up. By the time they'd gotten to Jefferson the sky was dark. Anna turned and by the time she blew through the first light it had reached the taller buildings lining the street to either side.

"This one's going to be close. Close your eyes if you need to."

She stomped on the gas and raced around a green Taurus in front of them. Kelly looked out the back window. A single dark cloud had formed and was rapidly approaching.

"If you can go any faster, now's the time!"

She didn't say anything, but cut around a car crossing through the intersection. A piece of the cloud shot out like a missile and hit the street right in front of them. Anna swerved into the left turn lane to get around it.

"Are we fine? Are we fine?" she shouted.

Kelly patted himself down. He was.

"Taze, you all right? Taze?"

The taller man had slumped to the side in the front seat, his forehead against the window. He was making choking sounds and twitching as if he were in the throes of a seizure. Kelly grabbed his shoulder and Taze's hand latched onto his.

"*Machín*," he rasped. Kelly tried to pull his hand away but he was caught in an iron grip.

"Taze, what the hell is wrong with you?"

"Hey, stop that," Anna shouted. "Stop it!"

"*Machín!*" Taze leaned over to Anna and let out a ear-piercing screech.

And then he was gone.

The cloud was gone too.

Actually, all the traffic on the road was gone.

"Anna, what happened to Taze?"

Israel turned around and looked at Kelly. Israel-Israel; not Anna-Israel. He raised his eyebrows and shrugged his shoulders.

"How do I stop this thing?"

"The brake. The-the pedal on the floor in the middle."

Israel pressed down on it and the car spun to the side and bounced like a balloon in slow-motion. The car eventually rested upside down.

"Let's get out of here before that thing comes back."

"Yeah," Anna said.

"Anna? That you?"

"Yes."

"What happened to Israel?"

"What do you mean?"

Kelly kicked out the passenger side window and crawled out. The engine was still running and Anna rolled hers down first before getting out.

"I'm probably going to have to pay for that," she said, looking at the busted rear window.

"Hey, your eyes." Anna's eyes had returned to normal. "What the hell is going on here?" Kelly looked around. A fog had descended as far as he could see and there was nobody around, not even cars.

"I wish I KNEWWWW—"

The street folded ninety degrees and Anna fell over the edge. Kelly caught her arm and saw. The sky was bent at the same angle. The car was gone. She was perpendicular to him, but gravity had changed to vertical instead of horizontal where she was. He lost his grip and she caught onto the street at his feet.

Kelly peaked over the edge and saw debris falling, literally, *down* the street to be swallowed up in an approaching wall of fog. Wind whipped in all directions as he bent over and held his hand out to her.

"Take my hand!" he shouted.

"You're nuts!" she screamed.

"No! My hand!"

"Don't you see that?"

"What?" Kelly turned and saw a towering cylindrical mass that had not been there before, looming overhead. The street behind him had collapsed away, making a thinning bridge of asphalt where he stood. He couldn't see the top or bottom as it came out of the wall of fog about two hundred yards away. It bent in the middle as if made of rubber until it was about thirty feet from Kelly.

It was made of flesh. Arms and legs and torsos all pressed together. The tower was ragged in spots where the limbs that didn't bend had broken, jagged bone protruding from gray wounds. It had several rows of windows, each at least five feet wide and there was a giant white thing inside passing by the windows on the top floor.

No, that was its eye. The tower had an eye.

Several stories down a crack appeared across the face at least twenty feet in length. The tower opened its mouth and roared at them, a huge mattress-looking tongue slowly lapping across the strip of street and coming Kelly's way. He looked at it and saw it was made of torsos, but with thick, long quills sticking out of it.

"Come with me!" Anna grabbed him by the pant leg and yanked.

"No! Don't pull me—I'll fall!"

"That thing is going to eat you!"

Kelly looked over the edge again and saw the fog was a few feet beneath her. Where the hell had Israel gone? Anna's toes dipped into the fog.

"It doesn't really make a difference." Israel clapped Kelly on the shoulder. Kelly jumped and turned to see him smiling.

"Where did you come from? What happened to you?"

"I'm in and out. Picking out a good spot for us on the other side."

"Other side? What are you talking about?"

"We made it. I didn't think that thing in Downeck could do it, but it did. And just in the nick of time too. That patrol was onto us."

"So what? Are we dead?"

"No. We can't die."

"What do you mean we can't die?" The flesh tower's tongue was about twenty feet away.

"Do you know what a psychopomp is? Never mind—I'll explain more in a minute. In the meantime, someone's not coming with us." Israel peaked over the edge.

"How you doing down there, Anna?"

"I'm okay. Are you coming?"

"No. You go on ahead."

"I'm-I'm scared."

"Here, I'll help you." Israel walked over to where her hands were and stepped on her fingers.

"Ow! What are you doing?"

"You need to go back, Anna. You're not dead."

"What do you mean, she's not dead," Kelly said. "I'm not either."

"In. A. Minute." Israel stomped on her fingers with each word. Anna lost her grip and scrabbled to grab on. She fell a couple inches into the fog and bounced, rising into the air.

"You'll be fine," Israel said. "I moved you someplace safe."

"What about you? What's going to happen to you?"

"We have to figure another way back!"

"How will I find you?"

"Don't worry about it. We'll figure that out later!"

And then she was a dot in the sky, too far away for them to hear.

"I don't think I can jump down there. Will we bounce?"

"No, we won't bounce. We'll go aaaaaaall the way down."

"Down?"

The tongue was five feet away. Kelly moved over a few feet and stopped. The street had crumbled and fell away on that side.

"I don't want that thing eating me," Israel said. He didn't seem worried, though. "Hurry up, already. I want to get going."

"I don't know what to do. I just—"

Israel picked Kelly up by the arm. He floated into the air and then Israel threw him at the flesh tower's mattress-tongue. Kelly spun around and watched as Israel waved and stepped off the edge. Kelly screamed as he clawed and kicked at the air until he stuck onto the tongue and was sucked into the tower's mouth.

Everything went dark. And stinky.

***

It had not made it in time. The police had already arrived and so had two ambulances. There was a crowd of people the lesser blended into and no one was looking at its bloodied face and clothes.

The Hated One was loaded into the rear of one ambulance, a woman it had not seen before in the other. A policeman was talking to the tall, pit-faced one as he sat in the back of a cruiser with his feet out the open door. It recognized him as the same pit-faced man the Bradley had beaten outside the first McDonald's and the same man who had shot the Wilson Sheriff. It had no use for him.

The nearest hospital to here was DMC, but one of the EMTs had checked the Hated One's wallet and said something about going to Henry Ford on the Boulevard. It was tied into the

Bradley on every level and now felt what it understood to be hope. Hope that the Hated One still lived. Or else it would be the one the Jexclp'ar came for next.

It turned on its bicycle, weaving through the throng of people as the ambulances drove off in the opposite direction down the alley. It would wait for them to arrive.

***

They had taken her right away. She was stuck in a hallway in the Emergency Department with her purse stuffed under her arm and hooked up to an IV. Someone had taken blood a while ago, but she hadn't seen anyone for what felt like an hour at least.

Someone in the hall was moaning. Nobody had bothered explaining anything. There were beds on either side of the hallway, creating a narrow aisle doctors and nurses raced up and down at random. LaGina hated it here.

She kept trying to get out of the bed or pull the IV off and every time someone would come along and ease her back down until a couple nurses put her good arm in a restraint.

Her cell made a long, continuous buzz in her purse. The nurses must have forgotten to turn it off after they dug inside for her health care card and ID. She'd heard somewhere that cell phones disrupted hospital equipment. She was horrified at the idea of an MRI machine flinging out some little old man. LaGina flopped her limp arm over to reach for her purse, smacking her hand into the wall. She couldn't tell where her numb fingers were going so she shimmied her other arm beneath the purse and pushed it onto her chest.

It was still going. A nurse was standing a few feet away, looking at a chart or something. LaGina grunted, still unable to speak, then grunted even louder. The woman looked directly at her then walked away. LaGina sighed in frustration.

Another nurse came from the other end. She heard his squeaky shoes before she saw him. He had a buzz cut and sea green eyes. He checked on the person in the bed across from hers. Then he turned and looked at her.

"How we doin', honey?" He thumped her IV a couple times then put his fingertips on the underside of her wrist while he stared at his watch. "This strap too tight?" he said. LaGina nodded. "Brandon must have done this one. He always does them way too tight." He lowered his voice to a whisper. "I'll loosen them just a little, but you gotta be good for me, okay?" She nodded again.

"I'm Marty, by the way." He loosened the restraint. "Now look, you've got room enough to make a little fist and knock on the wall." He made her hand into a ball and rapped it twice against the wall. "See?" he said. "Anytime you need me, m'kay?"

LaGina nodded. He spoke to her like she was six, but if it got her closer to the phone she'd take it.

"Whatchoo doin' down here?" the nurse who'd been looking at the chart earlier said. "This ain't even your floor. Go on, Marty."

"What?" Marty said, turning toward the woman. He kissed her on the cheek without stopping as he left. "West Side, Friday night?"

"You know it." The nurse didn't bother introducing herself. LaGina remembered her from earlier. She went to retighten the restraint, not paying attention to LaGina's whimpering. Could she not hear the phone?

Then an announcement came over the loudspeaker for a code blue.

***

They couldn't have known but it was already too late for Collie. Even if the fifth bullet that pierced his body hadn't gone through his heart, even if he hadn't left half his total blood volume in the valet area, even if he wouldn't have drowned from the blood in his lungs he was a goner. Collie knew himself in those fatal remaining seconds and that there was no hereafter for him. He was empty—drunk clean of anything worthy of a heaven or a hell. It wasn't just the cancer that had left a cavity in him. He was as dead as one could possibly get.

He'd never met Velma, one of the nurses on duty, but she had just finished adjusting the restraint on a lady who had stroked out and was trying to hurt herself. But she squeezed the bag to give Collie a steady flow of oxygen as the EMT performed chest compressions. Every time she squeezed air gurgled out of a hole in him somewhere. She said a prayer for him and shook her head.

A doctor ran alongside the gurney. He flashed a pen light in Collie's eyes. Fixed and dilated. The last remnants of Collie reached for the light even as he was being drawn away into oblivion. The doctor called time as soon as they got into the operating room.

"Was this the one from outside?" he heard the doctor ask. Collie felt frothy, incorporeal, then nothing at all. "Well, he picked a good place to get himself dead."

***

"He should be up and walking around," Dr. Hayes said. "Couple bumps and scrapes, but he responds to stimulus. His CBC's fine… So far we don't know what's wrong with him." The students gathered in the already crowded hallway. Some took notes. "The woman he came in with was pronounced as soon as she came through the door. As you can see we've put these kind people in our best guest suite—" he gestured to the crowded hallway and the students laughed. "But we're hoping to move half of them into rooms by tonight and discharge as many of the rest as possible. Now moving on…"

***

The lesser had misjudged how long it would take to get here. Construction on the Boulevard had slowed it down, even blocking off the sidewalk, diverting traffic to a side street. By the time it got to the hospital it had been delayed at least ten minutes.

As it stepped into the lobby a man in a security uniform rushed over and asked, "Sir, do you need medical assistance?"

"No," the lesser tried to say, but its jaw was broken, sudden sparks of pain making it cry out. It had never experienced pain before inhabiting this body, but had quickly developed a deep appreciation for it.

The Ghost Toucher

The guard rattled off something in a walkie attached to his shirt. A man rushed over with a wheelchair and insisted for the Bradley thing to sit.

The man wheeled it into the Emergency Department waiting room filled with several other people and left. The Bradley thing looked around. There was something wrong with these humans. Many of them had injuries, but there were others that appeared physically intact yet seemed injured. One man leaned forward, opened his mouth and spewed out some sort of white-yellow fluid. The people near him groaned, some got up and moved. Even the Bradley thing recoiled.

It wondered if the man had some sort of internal injury. The Bradley thing waited a few minutes and when no one returned it went up to a woman behind a glass enclosure and tiny desk.

"Excuse me, madam, but I need emergency service." It was easier to speak if it held the side of its jaw in place.

"Sir, I am so sorry to hear that, but I am helping customers as quickly as I can. If you could just have a seat for me over there I'm sure one of our other representatives will be with you in just a moment."

"Thank you," it said, but something about the tone with which the female spoke was disingenuous, even patronizing. The Bradley thing realized this was sarcasm being used upon it.

The lesser felt offended. It had an urge to go back and put its fist through the glass and grab her by the throat, but was unsure if this was its own desire or the human it inhabited. It looked around the room and saw an electronic box mounted on one of the walls. There was a human dressed in all white with a large mustache on the 'screen' who had just fallen in a mud puddle. Two thin female humans in 'bikinis' and 'sombreros' stood by. "Oh, ChíChé," they said in unison and shook their heads. The Bradley thing felt a tightening in its middle that quickly loosened and tightened again. A sound escaped its mouth. It was 'laughing'. The lesser looked around and saw others were doing the same. Perhaps this was a previously unassessed injury, but it seemed to have taken a mild amount of relief as the tightness in its shoulders eased.

The Ghost Toucher

It had an idea. One that wouldn't call for it damaging the human woman. The lesser let itself swoon and collapsed to the floor.

***

The doctors finally left. LaGina couldn't risk them seeing the nurse hadn't tightened her strap. She tugged until the center metal thingy in the buckle popped open then concentrated on her middle and index fingers, willing the strength into them to grab the strap and slowly tug at it until it came loose. She pulled her hand free and grabbed her little purse, digging inside until her hand closed around her cell.

She looked at the number, a string of sevens. LaGina was just about to thumb the 'IGNORE' button, but hit 'SEND' instead.

"Hello? LaGina?" a man said on the other side. It sounded a lot like Kelly Greene. "We need your help."

***

An indeterminate amount of time earlier, elsewhere.

"What... was that?"

"That's why I didn't want to go see that thing in Downeck," Israel said. "It's too risky and you can't predict when or how you'll cross over." Kelly looked at him, not Anna, but Israel. He looked like his old self, mostly, except his face had been softened, more feminized. Kelly slugged him.

"You!" he shouted.

Israel picked himself up and stood back. Kelly drew back again.

"Wait-wait-wait!" He held up his hands. "I can explain."

"Explain? You mean how you let my family *die*? How exactly do you explain that?"

"I always knew where you were—anywhere in the world. I felt it. I'd been watching you since you were a little kid, feeling everything you felt, but when I felt that it broke me, literally. For the first time ever I was lost. I tried finding you, but at first I had no idea where to go. By the time I found you, I was... obsolete. It was all I could do to save you."

"You should have saved them first."

"As long as I've watched over you, watched you grow, fall in love, have those children—it was like they were my children too. I loved them. But I had to save you. I had no choice... you have to survive."

"I didn't. I didn't survive. Don't you know it killed me when they died? I didn't even get scratched and you're telling me you couldn't do *anything* to save them?"

"Look, we need to move. The patrols will be able to find me here a lot easier. Broken *machíns* are supposed to report immediately for destruction and they know by now I don't work right. And when they see you..."

Israel ushered Kelly down the street. A few people had noticed them. A child stared openly.

"The innocent can see us for what we really are. Children, the mentally infirm. We'd best try to fit in. Act like everybody else."

They stepped over a giant green mound that looked a lot like feces.

"When we first met, all that stuff I told you about a Listening Ear was B.S."

"Oh, really." There was a ton of sarcasm in Kelly's tone.

"Yeah. I mean, the Listening Ear is real, but it's only real here. It was a lot easier to explain than saying this world's version of the police were after me because I'm a criminal."

"So this is where you live? Where you're from? I'd destroy it if I could. I really would. Then you'd understand."

"You shouldn't say that," Israel said. They came up to an abandoned store with plate glass windows still intact. Israel stood him in front of one and Kelly could see a golden glow coming from beneath his clothes. He lifted his shirt but saw nothing there, but he did notice his navel was gone. "This is where you're from too."

"What?" Kelly said, touching his stomach where it was supposed to be.

"I told you—the living from this world can't go into the other one. Space without a suit, remember?"

"But you... a-a-and me?" Kelly pulled his collar down to see if he could find where the glow was coming from.

"That's why Anna couldn't come. She's not dead. She had to go back. Look around. See those misty-looking people? Spirits."

People were walking around, dressed warmly, but Kelly felt no cold despite wearing only a dress shirt and slacks.

"Remember the little girl? The ugly one? I told you she's a weapon. A tool. That's why she was able to come over. She's a *machín*. Like me. Like you."

"I'm not a *ma-whatchamacallit*."

"Look," Israel hustled Kelly into an alley. "The word doesn't exactly translate into a human language, but that's what we are. Someone made me to follow you, keep you safe in that world. Because if you die there, you come back here. If you come back here I cease to have a purpose."

"But I am here."

"I know. But they don't yet because you didn't technically die. We have some time to get you back. My programming's defunct, but now I can choose what I do and now I see the greater purpose. I want to protect you."

"Wait, you said nothing here is allowed over there. Then how could they send you to protect me?"

"Because you could destroy the world."

A group of men were kneeling around a tree stump, holding what looked like thick playing cards low enough for each man to see with weird symbols on them. Each man had a small stack of thin black sticks by his right hand.

"Dealbreak," one man said. The others groaned.

"Bull," Kelly said. The man peaked over his shoulder at Kelly and Israel.

"No. True."

"Then who built me?"

"No one. To my understanding, you sort of... built yourself. There's this war going on between any number of Greaters. There are hundreds if not thousands of them. But they're all equal. One kills another and takes his power or another steals power away from one. It's chaotic, but on the whole, balanced.

"They've been fighting forever. Until one day one of them realized they weren't quite as strong as they used to be. Somehow a little bit of that power, energy, kool-aid—whatever—had become sentient and removed itself from the conflict. It wasn't enough to pose a threat by itself but if any Greater were able to acquire it that Greater would have the Deciding Difference and be able to unify all dimensions. And that's bad—dimensions unified means all existence is done.

"At least, that's what the scientists say. And not even all of them. Nobody really knows, so most of us want to keep it exactly as it is."

"Wait a minute, wait a minute. If there's this great war that's been going on since forever, where is it?" Kelly looked around. "I mean, it looks pretty serene around here, if you ask me."

Israel pointed up.

"Up there." Kelly looked into the sky for the first time and it didn't look like anything he'd seen before. They sky was a pale brown, but it looked solid. Veiny-looking, blue and green squiggly lines. Kelly saw other faint circular lines. The more he stared at them, the more they looked like...

"Fingerprints?"

"Something like that. It's skin. The outer atmosphere developed it as a means of protecting the surface and everything on it from what they're doing out there. It has an umbilical thing that goes into the surface of the planet. It uses it to suck nutrition out to feed itself."

"That is... disgusting."

Israel shrugged.

"Okay, go on," Kelly said.

"So this Deciding Difference, with the aid of like minds, escaped to the only place the Greaters couldn't follow: your Earth. Time between the two dimensions doesn't pass in a consistent manner, so the past thirty-one years for you has been thousands of years over here. So long ago that except for the Greaters and a choice few others you're an urban legend. A religious myth. Lessers are known for being zealots so if the one that saw you had recognized you it would have pursued you to no end. If a Greater catches you—" Israel snapped his fingers—"just add hot water; instant entropy."

"Why don't I remember any of this?"

"I don't know. Maybe you and whoever thought that was for the best. Maybe it was before you had an actual mind."

"All right. I'll bite for the moment. But since we're on the other side I want to see my family."

Israel scratched his head.

"That's another problem. They didn't come here. When I found you, just before the accident, your wife was still alive. When she transitioned, I checked and couldn't find her over here. I would have felt her if she had come over, even if I didn't know where over here. Near as I can guess is you put them elsewhere."

"Elsewhere. But how could I? I don't know anything about this. I don't even believe half of it."

"Reflex. Subconscious. If you could remember you probably thought of some place just before the crash. I'd bet that's where they are. If Earth is in another dimension who's to say there aren't an infinite amount of others?"

A spirit passed by the alley on the opposite end.

"Hey, isn't that that woman from my office?" Kelly said. "The one from the controller's office?"

"I didn't see."

They went down the alley and saw the spirit of a woman floating away.

"*Is* that her?" Israel asked. "What's her name? Dolores?"

The shape of the hips was familiar. She'd made a deep impression on Kelly in the few seconds they'd spoken. She turned to the side and Kelly saw her in profile.

"That's her."

"She's not dead," Israel said. "She's half in, half out. I don't know how it happens but it does sometimes. Most people mistake them for stroke victims. Did she have a droopy face when you met her?"

"No."

"Then it must be recent. If we hurry we can use her to get back. Like a fishing line."

"How?"

The Ghost Toucher

"With that." Israel pointed at Kelly's hand which was suddenly holding a bulky cell phone. "All we have to do is talk to her here and have her over there find your body."

"My bod—*I'm not dead, am I?*"

"Not yet, hopefully. If you were found in enough time you should be in a hospital be—"

The man from the Dealbreak game in the alley stared at Kelly, towering behind Israel. He narrowed his hawkish eyes at him, twitching his nose over his mustache.

Israel turned and saw the man staring and then put his arm around Kelly's shoulders and pushed past him. The man raised his hand and pointed as his buddies pulled him back to their game.

"Another zealot," Israel said. He may see you for what you are or he may only suspect."

The man screeched.

"Okay, he knows. Let's pick it up." They walked in the direction of the woman's spirit.

"LaGina," Kelly said. "She said her name was LaGina." They got to within ten feet of her and Kelly waved. She didn't seem to notice, but didn't move away.

"I think you have to call her on that." Israel pointed to the phone. Kelly looked and saw eight full bars on the display. He hit 'SEND' twice and a string of sevens popped up as the phone began to call. It was one long ring. Kelly stopped by some abnormally sweet-smelling trash cans, LaGina hovering about five feet away.

After about two minutes someone finally picked up.

"We need your help," Kelly said.

Just then the man from the alley was standing a few feet away from Israel. He screeched again, jabbing his finger at them. LaGina's spirit reeled back from them and all the bars on the phone disappeared.

Kelly turned and looked at the man. He was wearing some kind of long jacket, buttoned down on one side with a built-in pair of pants.

"Hey, could you not do that?" Israel said, putting his hands up. Kelly looked around. People were starting to notice.

LaGina's spirit was all the way down the street. She seemed to be caught in a leafless tree and a little boy dressed in what looked like a peach-fuzz basketball from the neck down looked away from them and began swinging a stick at where LaGina's feet would have been if she had any.

"We have to call her back, but we have to get rid of this guy." Israel took a step closer as he tried to step around him to get closer to Kelly. "Why don't you run around the block and I'll hold him up here?"

"He can hear you. Why wouldn't he just follow me?"

Israel turned his head to Kelly and blinked.

"Why would he know what I'm saying? He wouldn't know English."

"Uhhh. Didn't he just speak it in the alley?"

"No. Many of the words are the same, but the syntax is completely different."

Kelly shrugged and took off down the alley. He'd seen a few spirits so far and none of them had feet. He did and he was quickly getting winded. Maybe he should exercise more if he got back. Maybe there was something to what Israel was saying, but it just couldn't be true. At least not all of it. Could he still be lying? Holding something back? Kelly wondered. Maybe holding back the whole story had been for the best. Who would have believed a place like this existed?

Kelly passed by more oddly dressed people as he wheezed and puffed his way around the corner and down the street. A little girl with pigtails all around her head like a chandelier smiled and waved as he went by. She wore a blue, ball-shaped coat. An older man and woman across the street in a coat apparently meant for two people held their free hands together, watching him. A little boy set some boxes next to what looked like a trash can, which also smelled unnaturally sweet. The boy fell back, kicking the can over in Kelly's path. He had the same style coat as the little girl but it was cherry red with vertical wavy stripes all around.

Kelly leapt over the trash, wondering why the place seemed so Seussian. It was more than the clothes that was wrong; everyone was either middle-aged or a child who was four feet tall or less. He didn't see any teenagers.

The Ghost Toucher

He rounded the corner, crossed the alley then turned onto the other street. He didn't see LaGina's spirit, but checked his phone, seeing four bars. He pressed 'SEND' twice.

Kelly heard the man's screech from up the street. Several people had gathered around and he couldn't see Israel at first. But then the man broke through the crowd and Israel was right behind him. A few people took a few steps in Kelly's direction. He looked at the phone and two bars had disappeared. Kelly scanned both sides of the street above him and saw LaGina's spirit floating away from a white billboard.

He wondered why Israel didn't just knock the man down or hit him in the throat or something. Kelly crossed the street, heading toward the spirit, remembering what Israel had said about zealots. This guy seemed like a probable candidate. Hurting him would only aid his cause.

Kelly followed LaGina's spirit as best he could but the man and Israel were gaining on him. He passed a little boy in a pants-coat a lot like the screeching man's and the boy tried to grab him.

A vehicle that was literally a black floating bubble swerved to miss him, but clipped his legs. The bubble rippled where he hit and suddenly Kelly found himself floating as he was enclosed in his own bubble, heading upward toward LaGina's spirit. She hovered around him as he slowly arced up and back down onto the street where it popped and he landed on his butt.

Kelly still had a bar on his phone and it was still ringing. He spotted LaGina's spirit floating high up on his right. The screeching man was about thirty yards away with Israel close behind like they were in a foot race. More people were out and a few of them jogged behind. The screeching man tumbled and was caught up a moment later by several hands pulling him to his feet.

Israel passed him, crossed the street and shouted to Kelly, "In the building!" pointing somewhere behind Kelly. He spun and spotted the abandoned structure. Kelly ran for it and spotted the spirit swirling in that direction.

The door was boarded up with what looked like black plastic, but when Kelly put his shoulder into it at full speed the stuff caught him up like a sticky web, stretching and stopping his momentum a few feet inside. He pulled free of it and it snapped back in place, leaving him in a dark room. Kelly blinked as his eyes adjusted.

"Run!" he heard Israel call from outside and then he smacked into the webbing. Kelly could make out stairs to his left and ran to them, hearing the material stretch as Israel broke through.

"Get on the phone. They're coming!"

Kelly ran up the staircase, spiraling up the outer walls of the cylindrical building. He'd lost the call and kept looking down for a bar to show. Israel raced past him and from below he could hear the netting tear as several people were coming through.

"Look upstairs!" someone shouted. It wasn't English but he understood it.

"I'll go out back."

"Surround the back! He can't escape!"

"Someone call the Jexclp'ar!"

Kelly yelped as a hand reached out and grabbed him, nearly dislocating his arm as he ran past.

"In here," Israel whispered, pulling him into a room with shuttered windows. "Maybe they'll go straight up to the roof instead of checking room by room and we can sneak back down."

"Check room by room!" someone shouted.

"Craaap."

It was even darker in here. Kelly thought they might be able to hide, but only for a moment. Dot-sized creatures with wings a half foot long flitted around in a rounded corner over a pile of something dead-looking.

"What's that?" Kelly said, pointing. One of them glided over, stroking its wings up and down.

"Flies. Dead ones from your world. Turns out they have spirits too. How about that call?"

Kelly looked at the phone. Eight full bars! He redialed, peaking through the boards over the window. LaGina's spirit was just outside. He listened to the phone ring and the thundering steps below getting closer.

"C'mon, pick up!" he said as two more flies came over. He peaked outside again and saw she was still there. There was a mini-swarm of flies around his head and Kelly tried to wave them away. One brushed his hand and stuck to him like a magnet. Kelly tried shaking it off but it wouldn't budge.

"Wow. I've never seen that before," Israel said. "The Deciding Difference is supposed to be able to make a weapon out of anything. Maybe you can turn the door into a bomb or something."

"Even if I were this weapon—"

"Energy."

"—Whatever. I'm not killing people just because they're following some lone nut. They're still innocent."

"It's us or them and they'll turn us both over. The Greaters will rip you apart and use you to consolidate the universes."

"Then we'll have to figure out another way if we can't reach LaGina."

By now Kelly was covered in flies all lying dormant on him. He heard the people outside and he pointed. The flies flew off him and through the door. Outside the room people started spitting and stomping.

Someone picked up on the line. Kelly could hear breathing.

"Hello? LaGina? We need your help."

The person on the other end moaned.

"She might not be able to speak," Israel said.

"Look, this is going to be hard to believe, but this is Kelly Greene. We met the other day.

"Uh?" she said.

"I'm kind of not where I'm supposed to be and I need your help. I know it's going to be a one-in-a-million shot, but are you anywhere near a hospital?"

"Unnh-uh-unnh unnh."

Her spirit swam through the wall.

"I would just go on to two-three-seven," her spirit said. "There is no other path. The wall is softer." LaGina's spirit looked at Kelly as if it recognized him and then it was sucked up into the phone.

LaGina screamed, "Ow! That hurt!"

"You can talk. Great!"

"Yeah, I can. Oh my face. My face. My face feels better too! What did you do?"

"I'll explain later. Do you see anyone around who looks like me?"

There was a pause.

"There is this guy on a gurney. I think he looks like you. But he kind of looks dead. Do you have a twin or something?"

"Sort of. Could you do me a favor and go over to him and put the phone to his ear?"

"I guess."

The door busted in and the screeching man stood there with a few people behind him. There was static over the line and Kelly resisted the urge to yell for her to hurry up.

"What's all that noise?" LaGina asked.

"Nothing. Just some construction."

"All right. Say hello."

Israel punched the first one, but the next two grabbed him. Kelly kicked one of them in the stomach and put his arm around Israel, clutching onto the phone as he pulled him back.

Then Israel disappeared.

A man in long red pants up to his chest with a drawstring tied around the back of his neck fell down after losing his grip around Israel's waist. They all paused a moment; even the screeching man was silent. But then they rushed Kelly, grabbing at him.

They couldn't keep a handle on him but they did manage to push him back into the only corner in the room. Somewhere in the struggle he lost the phone and heard it skitter across the floor.

They crowded him, grabbing at almost every part of him. Kelly couldn't see for all the hands in his face.

And then he was outside, floating slowly to the ground. The pale brown sky stretched and contracted in some spots. Then a dark brown spot appeared. It was the lessers. Kelly turned over and began pedaling his arms and legs, but it didn't make him fall any faster. They came down around him, the surrounding buildings had a descending, darkening hue to match the sky.

There was a screech far in the distance, but not from a human voice this time.

Kelly turned around and saw it, descending from a low, bulging cloud.

"Crap," he said.

***

He opened his eyes. LaGina stared at him; she'd never seen metallic blue eyes on a black man. She didn't remember them being blue when they'd met.

"Was that you who just called me?" she asked.

"No." He sat up, rubbing his eyes. "That was Kelly."

She made a face. By no means was her memory photographic, but this was the same man she had met the other day. The same one who was in the pictures with the woman and two children locked away in his desk drawer.

"What?" he said. The voice didn't match what she remembered, either. Deeper. More nasal. He swung his legs out.

"If you're not Kelly then who are you?" He looked at his hands.

"This is Kelly's body," is what it sounded like he said, but that didn't make sense. "He must not have made it out." He grabbed her by the arm. "Where's your phone?" She held it up, not sure why he was asking and he snatched it away. He pressed the 'SEND' button twice and listened.

Whatever he heard must not have been to his liking. He looked physically ill, almost.

"It's all over." He sounded defeated. "The only way I can get back is to kill this body. And if I kill this body I can't bring him back because this is *his* body."

"What?"

"I'm not Kelly. I'm the other one. Remember the tall white guy? That's me. Was me. Not really, but—"

He trailed off, mumbling something about putting him inside Anna but how even that was a long shot.

LaGina thought this was just as good a time as any to check herself out.

***

The one called Charles had a gun in her face. Jemen decided she would kill him. Perhaps she would put her finger into his heart. Something slow enough for him to know she was killing him.

The Ghost Toucher

"I know you know more than you told Mr. R.," Charles said. "And I want to know what it is."

She looked up at him.

"Do you know why I haven't killed your master, *dog*? Because he was a gentleman. He had manners. You are very rude."

Charles laughed, but she could hear the nervousness in his voice. He pushed the barrel of the gun harder into her forehead, forcing her head back. Had he checked before he came in with his gun out he would have seen she had already snapped his ropes.

"Chuck, back off," Mary said. "Mr. R. didn't tell us to come in here."

"Didn't tell us not to," Charles said. "The way I figure, if we multi-task we take these beasts down faster."

"Chuck, I just don't know about this."

"It's cool," he said. "I just want a little conversation. It's not even an interrogation."

"Chuck—"

"Hey Mary, I'm a big boy. Could we get a little quiet time? You're messing up my ambience."

The one called Mary left without a word.

"You should listen to her, Charles."

"Don't call me that. In fact, don't call me anything, *beast*."

"Charles, if you shoot me you will be making the last mistake of your life. Are you ready to do that?"

"You threatening me, *beast*? I don't take threats. I *make* 'em."

They stared eye-to-eye a moment and Charles leaned back. There was something about his face. Jemen realized it and knew she couldn't kill this man. He may have looked like an adult, but he was just a boy. He had never grown up, but rather had taken on the heirs of a man. She almost laughed at his stern face as it suddenly seemed comical to her. Like a baby that had learned some trick for the entertainment of adults.

He needed to be cared for. There was a fragile portion of him that needed to be nourished, not shattered. Jemen unclenched her fists and relaxed. She smiled, hoping that would disarm him.

There was a loud pop from the basement. Mary jumped, almost choking on a mouthful of blintz. What the hell was he doing down there? She set the half-eaten blintz down and raced back downstairs. The door was wide open and the beast was on the floor, a tiny hole in the middle of its forehead. Blood was pooling underneath it. Real blood. Chuck was hyperventilating, his arms shaking at his sides as he stepped left and right over and over again.

"Chuck, what did you *do*?"

"I don't know. The gun went off. It wasn't my fault." He knelt, bashing his open fists into his forehead and groaning.

There was so much blood. It pooled out into the basement proper. She couldn't let it touch her.

"I-I'll go get some towels."

She ran back upstairs and into the bathroom. She grabbed the towels off the racks and the roll of paper towel too. As she ran back downstairs she thought she'd seen the back door open a tad, but wasn't about to stop to check.

The beast was still down when she got to the room, but there was someone in there with Chuck. A skinny, tall, pale *thing*. Chuck was down, blood soaking into his pants. The beast's belly wasn't round like it had been before and there was goo on the creature, crouched over him.

It looked up at Mary, its wide round eyes seeming to plead.

"I didn't mean to," it said. "He's still alive. We can get him to a hospital."

Mary dropped the towels and drew her knife. She could deal with the blood long enough to kill this beast.

"Please," it said. "Your friend needs help."

It would be difficult to slit this thing's throat in such small quarters, but she wouldn't let it just get away with killing Chuck. Mary advanced, crouching and holding the knife in an overhand grip at chest level.

It watched her get closer, no doubt plotting what its next move would be. Mary got within five feet and went to lunge at the thing, hoping to catch it unexpectedly.

Someone grabbed her wrist and pulled her off balance and spun her onto the floor on her side. She looked up and saw more things like the skinny one, except these were bigger, more filled out.

They looked like bald mannequins that had escaped from an Eddie Bauer. They hissed at her. Snapped their teeth and scratched the air at her. They all were holding her down, including her hand with the knife in it.

"Don't hurt her," the skinny one said. Mary looked again and saw it had changed. It had thin gray hair down to its shoulders and breast buds. They didn't seem to like what the female one had said, but they didn't attack.

"Whenever I am fatally wounded there is a spontaneous physiological response that causes my body to immediately give birth." It began stripping the clothes off the body on the floor. "I can't wear this shirt. It's soaked through. Get me something more appropriate."

"You killed him. You beast! You beast!" Mary struggled on the floor and one of them held her head down as one of the others let go of her leg, presumably to go upstairs.

"No, he is not dead. But he is near. After the birthing, my body's first response is to feed from whatever I touch. I can take nourishment from my former body, but a living one is preferred. If I could have made a conscious choice I wouldn't have."

It was definitely female. It was taller, with fully formed breasts and hips. It stood with the pants and underwear taken from the body and Mary saw the pubic mound with wisps of white hair beginning to darken as was the hair on its head.

"Ren-Jon will destroy you. It doesn't matter what you do to me."

"Child. I will do nothing to you and neither will my sons unless you force us." One of the albinos came back and handed her a striped sweater with a mock turtleneck. The beast's skin tone darkened to an olive and her eyes darkened to a deep brown. She towered over the others. "I do not know what your Ren-Jon will do to you once he's realized you have failed him, but if you care for Charles you will take us to the hospital."

"I...I—what?"

"Carry him." The albinos let Mary go, two of them picking up Charles. The other two stood to either side of her. Mary could try to fight them, but if Chuck weren't dead now, he would be by the time she subdued the rest of them, if she could.

Mary looked at the knife in her hand. Her Omni was parked a couple houses down the street. She put the knife back in its holster.

"Let's go."

***

Hated One. The lesser had been placed in a wheelchair in this area and left again. Perfect. Now it wouldn't need to be so careful with this frail human shell. It could turn this body into the weapon it needed to take the Hated One and perhaps call the Jexclp'ar using the Bradley's connection to the other side.

He was mumbling to himself and didn't notice it approaching. The lesser squeezed past a short female human going the other way down the congested hall as it refashioned its fingers into an eight inch long bone blade. The pain was sharp, but relished.

It longed to be away from all this *illness*. It did not like being around things it did not comprehend and these 'sick' people was the most confusing of all.

The lesser felt for the Bradley's connection to the other side and found it, triggering its individual clarion call for the Jexclp'ar. There was no response. It should have been instant.

Unless...

Unless too much time had passed since it had been away from the Jexclp'ar. Or too much time spent in... *flesh*.

The man looked up. The eyes were not the same. They were more like its original quarry.

It spoke a quick series of clicks that would initiate a reflexive response.

The quarry answered, then covered his mouth, his eyes wide. Yes, this was him. It knew human physiology well and with its regular hand punched him in the solar plexus. He was stunned a moment, then doubled over in agony.

"Hey! Hey, you can't do that!" It looked over the Bradley's shoulder at the woman it had just passed, determined she was no threat and pulled the quarry upright while standing behind him.

It felt the meaty pulse where its fingers dug into his neck. This quarry had found a way to possess a living body. Only a superior being like a lesser was supposed to have that ability, not a lowly *machín*. More questions it would ask later.

"Move," it growled in the quarry's ear, pushing toward an emergency exit. The lesser bounced his head off the door before they went through to keep him off balance. It had to find a place to wait for the Jexclp'ar to respond to its call before hospital security or police intervened.

It sensed someone rapidly approach from behind. It threw an elbow, presumably at the person's head, and caught only air. Two sharp punches caught it in the kidneys followed by a clipping blow to its ear. Had the lesser been as weak as a human it may have succumbed to the pain but it lashed out with its blade hand, glancing the woman's cheek. She yelped in pain, giving the lesser time to refashion the blade into a shackle it attached to her wrist. It would bring them both along. She would make a convenient hostage should it be necessary.

It dragged them both across the street with a minimal amount of struggle. From the Bradley's memory the Made Goode factory was long abandoned. Perfect.

Everyone's waiting

Mayer was still a little tipsy. Last night had been a trip. She hadn't been that drunk since college. Except she bounced back from it a lot easier in those days.

The dead guy on the table had been cute. Probably even cuter when he'd had two ears. Ah well, another lost love to go along with the many others never meant to be.

It was probably for the best. From the swelling and discoloration of his penis it looked like he had an advanced case of the herps.

Her phone rang and Mayer looked at the ID and saw it was Lisa.

"Hey, Lise." She dropped the sheet and walked away from the gurney.

Lisa began telling her about the party last night and she listened, but was somewhat distracted. She'd probably seen somewhere around a thousand corpses in all different phases of gore, but there was something unsettling about this one.

It reminded her of her dead nana in her coffin and how staged the whole thing looked. Like nana would get up any moment.

She kept glancing over her shoulder at the body of the deceased, her ear half turned to whatever it was her friend was saying. Mayer sprinkled in an occasional, "Uh-huh," and, "yeah," at appropriate intervals.

Mayer heard her say something about Scott Parker, the guy she'd been talking to at the party.

"What? What? Did you say, Scott? Did he say anything about me?"

"I don't think so," Lisa said. "Why would he? You do know Scott's gay, right?"

"Oh. Yeah, of course." Mayer was crestfallen.

There was a pitter-pat on the floor. She turned to see Collie Eaves standing up and looking around the room. The phone slipped from her hand. Mayer heard it clatter to the floor but it was a thousand miles away.

He was dead. There were several bullet holes in his chest. But he was standing.

"H-hello?" she said, her phone forgotten.

He looked at her. Despite his livid skin his eyes were a vibrant, soulful brown. His mouth worked up and down, but no sound came out. Then he coughed up a glob of congealed blood.

"Oh my God," she whispered. "You're dead." He looked at the glob with a puzzled expression then seemed to notice his own body for the first time. He stared at the backs of his hands with a look Mayer would have described as horror.

And then some guy with sunglasses came in.

"Here," the man said, taking new clothes out of a plastic Macy's bag. "Put these on. We're running behind."

The new man pulled out a pair of black slacks, a black polo shirt, black Nikes and black sport jacket. The dead guy leaned on him for support while putting on the pants, letting him zip them up, then he slid the shoes on his feet. He put the shirt and jacket on him, then pulled a pair of sunglasses out of his own jacket pocket and put them on the corpse's face.

All black. Like for a funeral.

Mayer was frozen against the cabinets, pressed as far back as she could. There was a pain in her butt where it pressed onto the counter; probably a pen or something.

She was about to relax when the man with the sunglasses turned to her for the first time. He dipped the glasses below his eyes, showing irises that looked like they had exploded.

"You have a good afternoon, y'hear?" he said.

***

The Ghost Toucher

"So what's going on? And don't give me that 'in time' crap." Gayle looked at *him* while sipping his Zima, a luxury he still enjoyed thanks to a contact in Japan. He loved this place. His old elementary school now was his office. Loved it so much, in fact, he'd converted a few of the classrooms into a bedroom and lived here. It had all been because of *him* and that machine he'd showed Gayle how to build. It allowed him to learn things from the dead. Rich dead people and the fortunes they'd hidden away before they'd died. The information was still stored in their brains, their eyes, their skin—even in the fluids still inside their bodies. Gayle's machine 'listened' to the dead and in turn translated that info so that he could hear, see, touch, smell and feel as they had in life.

He had been doing this with the famous and infamous of the metro area. People whose families had begun hospitals, owned furniture stores, became moguls in the music industry, ran car companies. And it wasn't just the physical items they'd left behind. They also had secrets; deep, family-shaming secrets the wealthy paid handsomely to keep hidden. Gayle knew about the illegitimate children, homosexual trysts and occasional equine encounters.

But now *his* minion had done something with the machine Gayle had only imagined. Ever since *he'd* come around Gayle had become fascinated with seeing the other side. *He* had told him it couldn't be done. *He* had obviously lied.

"Well?" Gayle prompted.

He must have been contemplating Gayle's question, but seemed like he might not have heard him at all. Gayle had never trusted *him* fully, even with the fortune *he'd* pretty much handed Gayle there was so much left to mystery. Gayle didn't even know *his* name.

"So can I go now or what?" his minion said. Marv, his name was. They'd placed the other one in the same place Kelly was before he'd escaped. Gayle still didn't understand how that happened.

He rose from a seated position in mid-air and those gold-glow eyes were on Gayle. They didn't intimidate him anymore and he stood his ground.

The Ghost Toucher

"There are some things even I cannot anticipate," *he* began. "I did not foresee Marvin would be able to see the Earthrealm with the machine."

"Hold on. There you go again with that Earthrealm. Isn't that here?"

"No." He chuckled in a way that came off very patronizing. "This is not the Earthrealm. This is an offshoot of it. A mistake."

"What are you talking about?"

"I suppose there is enough time." He took a deep breath. "A billion of your years ago, but perhaps only a thousand or two of mine. I was a scientist. My experimentations had nothing to do with matter or energy, it was more on the level of mice negotiating a maze, but suddenly there it was—a ball of energy and matter out of nowhere in my laboratory.

"It grew quickly, overtaking the building where I worked, sapping both energy and mass to feed itself. It took the most brilliant minds just to figure out there was nothing we could do about it. Eventually it stopped, but not before it grew to be a fourth of the size of Earthrealm. In those first years we learned much from it. Huge leaps in technology. We thought we were almost as grand as the Greaters themselves. But then the deaths came. One in eight and anyone who came in contact with the ones who passed died themselves. But not me. Soon it was realized I was also the one who was there when 'it' happened. The fear turned into hate. Some wanted my conversion—my people still did not know death; we have always advanced to higher or lower states of being. But most agreed I should be thrown into the hell I had created.

It had already been several million years here, but only a decade or so there. I remember the angry mob at my door. My children, crying for their father. My wife afraid to speak for fear they would take her too.

"I went willingly solely so they wouldn't harm my family. They threw me into the Whitelands—that is what we called the dimensional rift to this place—and for a period of time I thought I had been destroyed. There was nothing but whiteness for long and long. And then I existed. As this."

He held up *his* glowing arms, deep shadows of bones beneath *his* translucent skin.

"In that moment they put me in here almost everything that would ever happen on this 'Earth' became etched in my mind. I knew a little boy would be hated by everyone he ever knew would grow into a man who would secretly wish to be loved by all. You want to save the world, Gayle, and I adore that about you."

"Wait," Marv chimed in. "You *adore* him? This douchebag has been holding me and Dell hostage. You have us stealing dead bodies for him and this is someone you *adore*?"

He looked at Marv.

"Oh my God," Marv said. "You have a crush on him."

"I do not."

"Yeah, you do. Look at you. You've got a mancrush on this guy. My *god* has a mancrush. I guess that's why we had to drop everything to make sure pretty boy had everything he needed. Who have we all been following?"

Then he floated over to where Marv was tied up on the floor. Gayle could only see his back, but he leaned over and whispered something in the other man's ear. Marv tried to pull away and froze. The shapeless mass of his irises shrunk until they were nothing more than tiny pinpricks in respective seas of white.

"What did you do to him?" Gayle asked.

"Where was I? Oh yes. So I roamed this planet for a brief time. Perhaps ten thousand years or so. But I found once I came to a certain island I could not leave without becoming severely weak. So I watched man from a distance until he eventually found me. Naturally, I was worshipped as a god, though I am not. I found a very small percentage of people over the years who were more prone to my influence than others. These became my followers as well and I believe they are sensitive to the energies shared by this world and mine, but make no mistake: they are not equal. If Earthrealm were a human body then your universe would be nothing more than its hemorrhoid.

"Marv could see my world because there was a part of me that was inside of him. You cannot because there is another mission for you to fulfill. You must save the Earth."

"Save it. So I am right and these holes—"

"I have not seen it to its end. I choose not to know."

"Choose not to know? How do you do that?"

"If there were time I would tell you. I have to be somewhere now. But when the time comes you will choose who shall be destroyed."

Then *he* vanished.

***

The cops had been distracted with the one they had killed and had been watching Byrd more closely than her anyway, even though he'd been the one who had gotten shot. Typical, underestimating the woman. It angered her but worked to her benefit. She'd seen the beast shortly after coming in and had to follow it. One of hers had been killed and another injured. They would be avenged.

It had feigned losing consciousness and had been rushed to the ER. She waited by another door and when two doctors eventually came out she went in before the doors closed.

Wendy didn't know her way around but knew the general direction where she needed to go. She avoided hospitals as much as possible because she'd spent a great deal of time trapped in one in her youth. She would never wind up in a place like that again even if death were the price to avoid it.

An alarm sounded. Patients began milling about, ranging from confused to panicked. At first she thought it might have been a patient but then she realized a calm-voiced person would have spoken over the intercom. They wouldn't want to stress people any more than was necessary.

No. This sounded more like a fire alarm. She spotted a sign on the ceiling down the hall indicating an exit and raced to it. She pushed the door open and stepped out, scanning around outside.

There. About fifty yards away the beast was crossing the street. It had a man and woman in tow. It looked like they may have been going unwillingly, but she couldn't be sure. She might just have to destroy all three.

Wendy let the door shut.

She followed.

***

They'd been stopped at this light much too long. Ren-Jon was already annoyed at having to reroute to get to the hospital. Ten minutes late for the doctor meant at least an extra half hour spent in a waiting room. He had to get Mama home and over to Cindy's before two. She had classes at Wayne Community and he would have to wait until after eight to see her if he didn't make it in time.

Cindy believed in the Morrisites, but she was a bit of a flake. He had to touch base with her frequently to keep her in line. He had to continue her 'training' which largely consisted of general exercise.

He would never admit it, but he enjoyed that part. Cindy had a fantastic body, but seemed to have no awareness of it. Many times she would walk around her apartment in t-shirts and boy shorts, every supple curve displayed as she stretched and kicked and punched. From her long legs, exposed midriff or fist-sized breasts beneath her shirt Ren-Jon found it a chore not to stare at her with anything but absolute lust, but there was something more important than temporary pleasure. But perhaps if he could convince her to relinquish her trust fund if he were more of a guiding force?

No. It would be too risky. If he were to convince her to marry him no doubt her family would suspect he was after her trust fund. He was technically old enough to be her father. It would be better if it appeared to be her own idea to donate her trust fund to the foundation he had set up that would fund the Morrisites' future endeavors.

The Caprice Classic idled at a red light. Henry Ford was just ahead on the right, a cluster of red and white buildings surrounded by a black iron fence. As the light turned green he spotted a woman stumbling out into the street. A tall blonde and from here it looked like Wendy. Wait, it was Wendy. What was she doing in the hospital? She was deathly afraid of them.

He couldn't worry Mama, but he had to get her out of the car. He had to find out where Wendy had been and, more importantly, where she was going.

"Mama, I'm going to drop you by the front door, in the valet area. Y'know, so you don't have to walk."

"I don't want to go in by myself."

"Mama, I have to find a parking spot. Your leg—you shouldn't be walking so much."

"You no care about my leg. You're a puss-hound. You always chase after the puss. Always puss-puss-puss."

It was disgusting to hear his Mama speak that way, but he'd rather her think that than tell her the long and unbelievable truth.

"No, Mama, you're the only girl for me. You know that." Ren-Jon patted her on the knee and winked.

"You not so smooth as you Papa." She smiled at him and slapped him on the cheek. "Just get her number and come inside."

"Yes, Mama."

He stopped in the valet area, hit the hazards and got out. A skinny teenager with red zits all over his face sauntered outside and Ren-Jon put up a hand. He opened his Mama's door and while she got out he spied Wendy across the street as she climbed through a broken window of the old Made-Goode factory.

Why would she be going in there?

He leaned forward so Mama could kiss him on the cheek. She etched up the walkway toward the sliding doors and he shut the car door, running back to the driver's side and hopping back in. He regarded Mama for a quick moment then pulled off.

Ren-Jon was glad he'd insisted Wendy construct two of her bow-tangs. He kept the other in the trunk of the car.

***

Seleste had figured out how to find him. If she concentrated really hard she could feel him. Her father had been a weepy mess, but so what? It was his fault she was like this. Momma was his fault too. She wouldn't turn into a thing like that, trapped in one room for the rest of her pathetic life. She would find *him* and make him stop doing whatever it was he was doing. This was *her* body.

Marvin had stopped calling and she just knew it was because of the weight. She was big. Real big. Seleste was at least six feet tall and she'd screamed when she stepped on the scale and she'd tipped at two hundred and fifty pounds. Diets couldn't help this kind of gain. She'd been a little thick before all this but now she was a nightmare.

Luckily Daddy's truck was roomy enough to drive. She cruised south on Woodward feeling him getting close. Seleste had been driving around in Highland Park but suddenly felt him elsewhere when she'd changed direction.

A red light stopped traffic at the Boulevard. Wait a minute. He was down there. She was in the middle lane at the light with a car stopped next to her. Cross traffic sailed east and west on the Boulevard as she drummed her meaty fingers on the steering wheel.

A passenger in a red, rusted, cloth top Cavalier pulled up in the turning lane next to her. He was looking up at her, waggling his tongue between his middle and index fingers. Disgusting.

Seleste stomped on the gas and pulled a hard right, injecting herself into the flow of the cross traffic. A blue Toyota fishtailed after she cut him off, smoke peeling off his tires. Several other cars behind him had to stop, choking off the whole lane of traffic.

She passed by one of Detroit's finest, stopped by the Hotel St. Regis and it pulled out behind her. Crap. Seleste couldn't afford the time it would take for a ticket; he might be gone again by the time she got to where ever he was now.

The cop car pulled in close like he was checking her license plate. She'd slowed way down and almost didn't see the light turn yellow at the Fisher Building, but if she hit the brakes he'd rear end her. Seleste let the truck cruise through and the cop's lights went on. She considered running for it, but then the cruiser swung out from behind her and raced ahead. She followed, practically riding his bumper through the next two lights. Construction barrels were all around and it looked like one lane had just opened. She was driving past the hospital in less than a minute.

There. The building across the street from Henry Ford. He was in there. Or about to be. She didn't have a clue how she knew, but she was certain. Whatever was about to happen would also take the lives of a lot of people. Maybe she should leave, but then again death would be better than this. Either this ended today or she would die trying.

The Ghost Toucher

***

Wendy had just followed them in. The beast was distracted with the two it had in tow. She was sure they weren't with him but wasn't certain if she could save them.

She'd thought she recognized the place and realized this was one of the Made-Goode factories. She'd been in here on a school field trip long ago. Everything looked shut down, boarded up and cobwebbed but a spattering of lights were on and the constant high-pitched hum of a machine somewhere in the distance.

Where did they go? Her instinct told her straight ahead. Beasts typically preferred open areas for their sacrifices and this hall was coming to a wide open room. She came through the door in a crouch, picking up a bar on the floor. It wouldn't do as well as her weapon but it would do to split a skull in a pinch. Wendy hefted it in her hand and heard rustling behind her. She turned a moment too late and caught the beast's shoe heel in her chest.

The wind exploded from Wendy's lungs as she reeled back, her arms pin-wheeling as she stumbled back. It was on her as soon as she hit the floor.

"Wait!" a woman screamed. "That's not it!"

It hesitated and Wendy saw it wasn't the beast but the man it was dragging across the street. He had his fist raised but relaxed, letting his hand rest on his thigh.

"Sorry."

Wendy wasn't. She punched him.

He was cradling his jaw on the seat of his pants when she stood. She offered her hand to help him up and he was a head shorter than her. The combination of radiant blue eyes with brown skin was odd, but she put it out of her mind.

"Hey, sorry, I thought you were that thing."

The woman she'd heard came out of her hiding spot behind some palettes. Her eyes were wide, darting to every dark corner.

"He isn't human," she said. "As soon as he brought us in here his body started changing. He... he used parts of his body to make new parts. Non-human parts."

"Yeah, like human Lego blocks." The man didn't seem surprised by that for some reason. He wasn't even looking around for the beast. He tied a strip of shirt sleeve around his head over a cut.

"Do you know what it wants? Why it brought us here?" the woman asked.

"Probably to eat us. Or sacrifice us to its god," Wendy said. "I've studied books on these kinds of things extensively."

The man laughed.

"You don't know anything. That *thing*, for lack of a better term, is a bounty hunter. It hijacked that poor sap's body and is twisting it all up to make more efficient use of it. The only thing I can't figure is why the rest of them aren't here."

Something fell on the floor a few feet away. The man walked over to it, bent over to look at it and stood back up.

"It's his tongue," he said. "The whole thing, I think."

"Aren't you scared?" the woman said. "We have to get out of here."

"No reason to be scared of him. He only wants to keep us here until the others come."

"They're coming for you, aren't they?" Wendy asked.

"Yeah. But they're not picky. They'll take you too." He sat down on a concrete block.

"Look, can't we just go back they way you came?" the woman asked Wendy.

"Nah. That's a trap."

"Not if I kill you first." She took a step closer and raised the pole. He smirked.

"Wouldn't work. You can kill this body, but not me. I'd be very disappointed if you did that, though. It belongs to a friend."

"Beast!" Wendy charged him and it dropped from somewhere above, knocking her down and drumming her head on the floor. Her eyes went back in her head, but she rolled, hearing its mouth chomp at the air where she had just been. She turned back, throwing an elbow into its head.

It roared and snapped at her again, but the man pulled at what looked like its legs. Wendy got back to her feet, but unsteady and the woman came over to help. It snapped at him too, but seemed reluctant to actually bite, instead trying to pull itself free from his grasp.

He struggled but held on. Wendy saw the bastardization it had made out of a man's body. It had the upper head of a man, but the lower jaw was gone, a loose loop of muscle with teeth in its place. The shoulder's almost touched in front of a concave chest. The arms were too long and the legs too short. There were twice as many fingers on the hands and she realized the extra ones were toes. There were ribs in a wreath pattern around its head, giving it a flower-like appearance.

"What this thing has done," the man said, still keeping a reign on the beast, "is cannibalize this man's body to make itself more recognizable when the rest come. It's not supposed to be away from the others and if they don't know it when they come they'll destroy it. They probably will anyway."

"So if I can't destroy you, beast, how do we escape?"

"Who says you can't destroy him?"

Wendy turned to see Ren-Jon step through the doorway.

And he had her bow-tang!

Wendy walked over to Ren-Jon, almost elated enough to give him a hug. He handed her the bow-tang, handle first. She had a dozen questions to ask him, but first she would deal with both of these beasts.

"Somebody's here!" the woman said.

"Yeah, we all see him," the man said.

"No, I mean somebody *else* is here."

It was true. Wendy heard a door swing open somewhere in the distance.

"Is that them?"

"No," the man looked confused. Even the beast he was holding had stopped moving. The steps were heavy. "I have no idea who that is."

***

Jemen followed the girl through the hole. The boys had spotted her and this time Jemen had not ignored providence. Mary took Charles across the street to the hospital and they had parted ways.

She'd had unfinished business in her eyes, but Jemen could see this young woman was affected in a similar way that Charles was. She would not let any of Ren-Jon's people hurt her or her children, but she had no intention of killing them either. But if all went well in the next few moments it would never come to that.

They hung back so as not to scare her, but at some point she would have to know she was being followed. Jemen went ahead of her sons, catching up to the younger woman.

"Excuse me," she said. The young woman yelped and spun around.

"What do you want?" She was clutching a rock like she was ready to throw it.

"I believe we may have a mutual interest. I'd like to help you."

"Did he do it to you too?"

"Did he do what?"

"Make you big and manly-looking. I was at least a foot shorter only yesterday before my father let him do this to me."

"Uh-yes." Jemen hated lying, but she figured it was the fastest way to earn her trust. "I never saw him, though. What does he look like?"

"He looks like..." her eyebrows went together. "He looks like a rainbow. I dunno what he is. My father says he thinks he's a god but he isn't. But he is really old."

Jemen had heard of such a creature. The First One was rumored to have survived being thrown into the Whitelands, but as far as she knew no one in Earthrealm knew with any certainty.

"So he's here?"

"Well, yeah. At least I think so. Don't you feel him?"

"No. I cannot." The girl nodded.

"I think he's just through here." She opened the door and stepped aside. "After you."

"Thank you, child." Jemen stepped through, but saw the young woman's face as she passed.

Jemen threw herself back against the door as the girl slammed it behind her. She wedged something against it so Jemen couldn't get it open.

"You're probably with him," the girl said through the door. "He probably sent you to stop me. No way. I'm going to make him take this off me. He draws energy off me. That means I have power over him. *I have the power.*"

"You don't know what you're dealing with. Please, let me help you. We can figure it out together."

"No thanks."

She could feel the boys coming, but the girl would have disappeared into the bowels of this place by the time they got Jemen out. A fist pounded on the other side.

"Hurry! We must catch her."

Something crashed into a wall and the door swung open. Jemen stepped out to see her four sons. She put a hand on her already swollen belly, wishing Three and Six were here as well. Perhaps afterwards there would be time to find Six. Oodles was more than likely gone unless the police had seized him along with that rude taxi drivers cab.

Five was agitated. He kept sniffing at the air as if he had sensed something. He kept trying to go ahead of the others before she realized he had found his one. Could it have been this girl?

"Find her," Jemen said. He ran. It was all the others could do to keep up.

***

It took a while for Kelly to acclimate. He'd been away so long.

Time over there was different or something because he had to have been gone several months at least but the man who had gotten him out of the hospital had told him he'd only been gone a few hours.

He'd ushered him into a limousine in the valet area where several other people were inside. When he sat down Kelly saw they were wearing sunglasses.

He was sure they were diffoids but what was he to do? Kelly didn't even know where his own body was.

Maybe they'd found out he was this 'Deciding Difference' thing Israel had told him about. Maybe they intended on harvesting it on Earth. Despite how long he'd been gone Kelly still didn't fully believe he was this thing.

One seat directly in front of him was left empty.

"Sorry I'm late," a disembodied voice said from the open space. A body faded into view of a nude man who was blue, orange and red. "You are all Naked before Me. Driver, we can go now."

The limo pulled out into the street after traffic was clear. The man smiled at Kelly.

"I can see you don't remember me."

Kelly shook his head.

"I'd know you no matter whose body you were in. You saved me a long time ago. I studied the portal I came through and concluded no living creature could survive the transition. It took me a long time to realize my purpose until thirty-one years ago I was able to return the favor.

"You came here but you needed to be hidden. I helped construct a body for you and delivered you to a family who would care for you."

Kelly looked at the others in the limo.

"There is more to this than they know. Until now they believed I wanted you captured, but it was necessary to manipulate others to push you in certain directions. For you to meet certain people, go certain places." No one moved in the limo. The driver made a left onto a side street. "They wouldn't have known what to do with you had they caught you."

"Bruce Strong?" Kelly rasped.

"A ruse. I didn't need that man and already knew he wouldn't be in the hospital. Just a name out of a hat." They made a right. "I had to put you onto the trail and he was but a bread crumb."

Kelly thought about the keylock Israel told him about.

"So Stout? We're not going to find him?"

"You'll find him after you find the bus." They made another right.

"Is Israel in on it?"

"I am unsure what you mean. Is Israel helping me? No. Has he been keeping you safe your whole life? Yes. It is what he was designed to do."

"My wife. My girls—"

"There was nothing he could have done. The Greaters have been trying to kill you for a long time. Their influence is weak

The Ghost Toucher

here, but still present. Odds were in their favor they would eventually get to you in some manner."

Kelly thought for a moment. The limo made another right.

He looked up and saw everyone was staring at him.

"What?"

"Now," the glowing man said, "I ask you for the favor."

"Favor?"

"You lend me something. It will cost you nothing personally and you'll have everything back as it should be once we're done."

"What is it?"

"You."

"Me? What do you mean? What do you need me to do?"

"You? Nothing."

It sounded nefarious, but Kelly had a feeling he wasn't lying. He nodded. The glowing man stood in a crouched position and turned around. Kelly got an eyeful of butt crack before he sat down.

Instead of sitting in his lap, the glowing man disappeared into it. He leaned back and pushed into Kelly. He felt saturated, full somehow, but otherwise normal. Well, as normal as could be expected considering he was inhabiting a corpse.

The limo stopped, double-parking next to a row of cars on the south side of the Boulevard. Cars honked behind and one angry driver swerved around, a drink of some kind in a foam cup smashed into the rear window as he passed.

They watched. Kelly was unsure what to do. A woman in a red dress opened the door and another woman next to him smiled. She leaned in for a hug and Kelly could feel goo being squeezed out of this body. She let go and turned her legs to let him pass. Kelly got up, bumping his head on the ceiling. This body was much too big. He hoped he didn't have to get used to it. He crouch-walked and carefully stepped out.

"Uh, goodbye everyone," he said after he'd gotten out. "It was nice, y'know, it was nice." The man who had brought him out of the hospital leaned over and shook his hand.

"We can't wait to see you on the other side, Master. We'll wait for your sign."

"Yeah. Okay. Well, see you then."

Kelly stood and saw the hospital across the street. He turned around and saw the faded 'Made-Goode' sign on the old building behind him.

"There?" he asked them. No one moved. Unsure, Kelly turned and made his way toward it.

***

"I know he's here. Where is he?" The big girl stomped around the room. She had to have been six-six at least, LaGina thought.

"Who?" the man who wasn't Kelly asked. The creature was still but he hadn't let go of its legs.

"You know." She leaned forward as if in conspiracy and whispered, "*Him*." She didn't seem to notice what Kelly was holding onto.

"Oh, *hiiiiim*. He's not here right now, but maybe if you'd like to come back later?"

"Yes, he is. Or he's going to be." She clapped her hands and shouted, "Come out! I know you're in here." The creature seemed aggravated and started struggling again. It swiped at her leg and she yelped, swatting it with one of her meaty hands. Something crunched and it lay still, whimpering.

LaGina checked on Wendy. When that little guy had handed her that funny-looking sword she'd frozen. Her eyes danced around in her head, but other than that she was still.

"What the hell is that?" the little man said. Everyone turned and saw an albino crawl into the room on all fours. He sniffed at the air like an animal and turned to look at the big girl who'd come in the same way. He leapt at her.

She screamed and swung at him, the blow catching him on the side of the face. He caught her arm to keep from going down and quickly got his feet underneath himself. He was almost as tall as her, but much skinnier. The girl grabbed him by the shoulders, shaking him left and right like a rag doll.

He didn't struggle and it quickly became obvious why. Her eyes bugged in her head and she tried to shake him off, but they were stuck together.

"No!" a giant screamed who came in the room with three more albinos just like the first one. They all stood and watched as her mass transferred into the albino. He grew several more inches while she shrunk; her dark brown skin faded while the albino's turned olive then light tan.

She fell to the ground and the new creature stood, looking down on her. It was no longer male, if it had been to begin with, with curves everywhere a woman would and a man would not. The giant walked over to it and stroked its cheek.

"Baby," the giant said. "You've finally found your One." She looked down at the girl. "I suppose you've gotten what you wanted. You shall live if you seek medical treatment promptly."

"H-h-help... me." The girl's voice was barely a whisper. LaGina rushed over to her. There was something wrong with her mouth. LaGina looked and saw she had no teeth.

"You're going to be okay. We'll get you to a hospital."

"Mr. R.," the giant woman said, turning to the little man. "Or should I call you Ren-Jon?" The little man took a huge step back. "Don't worry, I won't harm you. So long as you and yours stay well away."

"Beast!" he said through clenched teeth. "How did you escape?"

"Providence. You may want to accompany this young lady to the hospital across the street and check on Charles. Mary is there as well."

The little man's eyes bugged, but he said nothing. The giant woman looked at the man who was not Kelly.

"My child," she said. "I have been searching for you. You and Kelly." She took three big strides across the room and was standing in front of him. "If only I could have been your succor in your time of need."

"My time?" he said. "But it was Kelly—"

"No. It was you. He was the one who was given sympathy while you languished alone in agony. You were broken and left alone to suffer through it. You and your brother should have been there to comfort each other."

"My *brother*?"

"Yes. I am your mother. I gave birth to you both." She held her arms out to him. "Come, so I may heal the wound inside you."

He looked unsure, but dropped the creature's legs. It didn't attempt to move. He embraced her and after twenty seconds or so a bluish white light passed from him to her and he went limp. She sat him down on the floor and he didn't move except for the occasional blink. One of the albinos walked up behind her. She turned around and embraced him. His body seemed to swell as the same bluish white light passed into him and when she let go his face was different.

"Mmmother," he said. She smiled at him. He smiled back as his skin took on a pinkish hue. He looked exactly like the man she had seen Kelly with at the Network.

"I should slay you. I should." The little man was holding the sword-thing he'd given to the catatonic woman. He looked green. "I could kill you both. Kill you all. I know how."

"Then why haven't you, Ren-Jon?"

"I... I... *can't*."

The giant woman went back to her son.

"I love you, son. Everything's going to be all right."

Then the lights went out.

***

The Jexclp'ar tended to drain light whenever they appeared. Over the last few months (over there) he'd become very adept at avoiding them and couldn't believe he was walking into their hands.

"Trust," was the only word that came to his mind.

He'd learned a lot about the people over there. They had families, friends, fought for causes—there was even racism over there. They had no such thing as music and were amazed when Kelly whistled for the first time. Rather than trying to explain what little he knew of music he'd made a rudimentary instrument out of a jug and they'd rapidly begun making music with jugs they had made themselves.

The most significant thing was death. Or the lack of it. Either they had evolved beyond it or it had never been anything they'd ever experienced. Until the incident that had created the Earth. Well, some thought it was on purpose. A government conspiracy.

The Ghost Toucher

Anyone who even touched it was instantly vaporized. Prior to that, one whose body had grown old would simply transition to another state. Like a tree or an animal and after that lifespan they might become human again. All life was recycled. And there were those who transitioned into this big rainbow-wall thing Kelly still couldn't pronounce the name of.

Family would come and visit and sometimes their loved one would respond. Some people guessed that was why the dead from Earth came there. Earth humans were a kind of cousin life form and that it was only natural for them to return 'home'. But most thought the dead were just a nuisance they couldn't do anything about. They didn't join with the others and most wandered around like lost animals pestering the living.

***

Kelly went down a long hallway and bumped into a wall he hadn't seen. He felt along the wall until he came to an opening. There were people speaking but he couldn't make out what they were saying. He blinked a couple times and then could see several people standing around.

"Kelly?" the man said. He looked familiar, but Kelly didn't know anyone who dressed like they'd just come from the Gap.

"My child," a big guy said. Kelly looked twice then realized he was looking at a woman. She took a step in his direction and bumped into someone.

The Jexclp'ar descended from the ceiling. They were all black but somehow he could see them clearly in the darkness. It was impossible to tell what he was looking at. He'd seen them before but every time was like the first time. Creatures in what looked like a gaping mouth directly overhead crawled out and down the walls. This new darkness surrounded everyone and the creatures, *lessers*, fell and jumped off the walls, landing on the floor and circling them all.

Kelly saw someone sitting on the floor by the tall woman. It was his body! He took a step and the lesser nearest to him hissed and skittered over in front of him. The man who had spoken

The Ghost Toucher

stiffened, but didn't move. Two albino-looking men and a ghastly transvestite gathered around the tall woman. She looked serene.

A giant, dog-looking thing on the floor looked up. The lesser nearest it bent over and seemed to consider it a moment. It grabbed the dog creature by the scruff but what it picked up was something that must have been inside the creature. It was another lesser.

It threw the other lesser out of the shroud of dark. The lesser bounced off a wall, scrabbling to its hind legs and back to the shroud but it couldn't penetrate. It screeched in agony, pounding and scratching at the air as its body dissolved, eventually slumping to the floor.

More of them had surrounded everyone. At least three to a person. A fourth one came over to Kelly. A small one crawled over LaGina's back and she squealed, jumping away from it. An extremely long and skinny one reared back on its three hind legs into a crouching position until it was eye level with the blonde haired woman standing by LaGina. The giant woman still stood with her arms folded, seeming to be undisturbed while several lessers surrounded her and the two albinos behind her.

A short one grabbed the man standing by them and pulled him to his knees. Kelly couldn't see him for all the people standing in front of him, but he heard the creatures make a chittery sound. He saw other lessers scamper over to where the man was. The people parted some and Kelly could see one of the lesser poking his face around his eyes before letting out a small screech. It reached inside him and pulled a glowing, bluish-white translucent figure free. It was Israel.

The tall woman stepped through the line of lessers and grabbed the one holding Israel. She removed its grip and he went back inside the body. Kelly caught a glimpse of the man's face. It was Israel. But how could that be? His body had been destroyed.

"You will not touch him," she said. "I am your Greater." She threw her head back and the creature backed up a few steps. It looked around at the others, seeming unsure.

More came out of the mouth overhead. These were bigger and didn't go on all fours like the first ones. They had a more human shape, but with long, ovular, slanted tapered heads. They had no mouths and deeply recessed red eyes. They surrounded the woman, but didn't touch her. She made no attempt to move.

A lesser half Kelly's height stiff-armed him in the stomach. He took a step back and looked down at it. The blow didn't hurt. The others looked at him. They all left the other people, save for the man-shaped ones and began approaching him. The one that had touched him made a trilling sound, an antennae extending from its head. It snapped at his hand and he pulled away too late; his middle and ring fingers were gone. The lesser tossed its head back and gobbled them down.

It jumped on his leg and sank its beak into his thigh. There was no pain. Others joined it, latching onto his body—biting, tearing, devouring him. The single word, "Trust," kept ringing through his head until his body was gone.

***

LaGina couldn't stop crying. That poor man had just *dissolved* right in front of her by something in this room and the same thing was probably going to happen to the rest of them. Whatever else was in here she couldn't see, but something had crawled on her back. She held onto the girl in her arms, squeezing her for as much her own comfort as the girl's. She didn't want to die. Her sons didn't have a father; she needed to get back to them.

She saw something from the corners of her eyes that looked like shadows standing around in a cluster where the man had been. Gradually these figures came into focus until she could see them directly. Creatures of all different sizes and shapes, but they looked similar. They seemed to be confused. A big one by the tall woman stepped over to them. It prodded one, rolled it over onto its back and began sticking its fingers inside its torso.

One of the little ones' back turned bright red. The big one pulled its fingers out of the one on the floor and paused. Then it shuddered in a way LaGina could only have described as a sneeze, two stripes of red suddenly trailing down its back. It turned and shuddered again, a huge crack appearing in its torso. White goo the color and consistency of cottage cheese fell out of its body. It clutched at its wound, looking to the other upright creatures. They seemed unsure, taking a few steps back and looking at each other.

LaGina looked up and saw a thing like a mouth, quivering. Large chunks of black muck fell out of it. It had smelled in here before, but now the air wreaked of a sick stench. Something was going on as the creatures began screeching and making noises. All their backs had turned red in different patterns. The little ones had stopped moving save for the few that had fallen over. The big ones began climbing the walls, going into the mouth-thing above their heads. It looked like it was starting to close as muck rained from it. One of the creatures shed its legs, using its arms to drag itself to a wall. The creature that had touched the smaller one was on all fours, a pile of cottage cheese beneath it. Its body had turned dust white and it didn't move. A few of the creatures made it into the mouth before it disappeared. The bodies of the ones left behind dissolved in seconds.

"Now that that's done I can go home."

They all turned to see who had spoken. There were two men, but one glowed a fluctuating blue, orange and red and floated a few feet off the ground, dusting his hands.

"What did you do?" the other man asked. Was that Kelly? She couldn't see him that well; he was translucent.

"I introduced them to death. It won't take long."

"*What* won't take long?"

"*You*," the tall woman said. She ran over and wrapped her big hands around the floating one's neck and began choking him. He didn't seem to mind. "You killed them! All of them!"

"I'm sure some will survive. Perhaps a half percent?"

"Of everyone?" the one who looked like Kelly said. It was weird to see him and the man sitting on the floor with the same face. "You *used* me."

"Yes. Your mother was foolish enough to believe she could fool me by using one of those things to take your place. She would have killed you if she could have."

"I would have sacrificed one to save trillions," she said, breaking off the choke hold and falling to her knees. "It would have been just."

"No. It would not. You know what he is. How valuable a tool he is. Even a trillions of lives would not be a worthwhile exchange."

"I didn't give birth to him on purpose."

"Perhaps you didn't. But that is the nature of a Greater. To destroy other Greaters. How better to do that than to wipe out everything?"

"What?" Kelly said. "*She's* my mother?"

"Yes. You are the bastard son of an almost all powerful creature who gave birth to you as a more efficient means of killing. She couldn't help herself."

"No," she said weakly.

"So you loved him?" The multi-colored one laughed. "Is that why you abandoned him? Why he created an entirely new universe and escaped into it? *You* were the one I wanted to kill, but I'll settle for your whole world."

"It was your world too."

"In case you haven't noticed I've changed."

"I knew people there," Kelly said. "How could you?"

"Because *you* knew a handful of people, mass murder is so terrible a thing?" He laughed. "Twenty-four hours ago you wouldn't have cared about any of them. Try a billion years and you'll get that feeling back."

He floated over to the young woman LaGina was holding and looked at the creature that had attacked her.

"Yours, I presume." He looked at the tall woman, smirked and joined with it.

"Now I will go home." It walked to the opposite doorway from the one where LaGina had come in. "You shouldn't worry about Earthrealm. You should be more worried about your precious Earth and what your friend Gayle Hills is doing to it."

"What do you mean? What is he doing?" Kelly said.

"In time." It walked out.

"All of you are beasts. All of you will be destroyed." The little man grabbed Wendy by the arm and dragged her away in the same direction the other one had gone.

Kelly walked over to the tall woman.

The Ghost Toucher

"You abandoned me. I don't know how I feel about that. I never knew you. I have a mother and she loved me. Next time I see you I'll assume it's for the worst."

One of the albinos stepped up and touched him with his index. A spark jumped between them and it stepped away. The tall woman stood, her mouth open.

"What was that?" Kelly asked.

"*Providence*. Come, my children. There is hope yet." The two albinos gathered around her and she looked at Israel. He looked torn, looking between her and Kelly.

"There's so much I need to know. I'm sorry, Kelly, I have to—"

"Go. I think I would understand if I were in your shoes."

The four of them left, leaving LaGina alone with the girl and Kelly.

"So *you're* Kelly?"

"Yes." He looked at her. His eyes looked funny.

"Are you okay?"

"No." A tear streamed down his face.

She set the girl's head gently on the floor, stood up and tried to hug him. She passed through him, squeezing only air. He quivered—once, twice—then he began bawling.

"He killed everyone," he sobbed.

She stood, awkward, rubbing her arms and watching the floor until he was done. He wiped his eyes and she looked at him. He didn't have legs and she realized for the first time from the thighs up he was completely naked.

"I don't know what to do," he said.

She looked over at his body, sitting on the floor still.

"Maybe you should... y'know." She tipped her head.

"Oh man!" He dragged his palms down his cheeks. "It's been so long since I've even seen that." He glided over to his body. "I'm not sure how to do this. I don't even know if I want to."

"It might be a little on the odd side if you don't, don't you think?"

"Yeah."

He embraced his body and the entire room was bathed in golden light. When it faded, only Kelly was there, but LaGina had to catch him before he collapsed.

"What happened?"

"You fainted," she said, sitting him down. She wasn't certain if she would have believed the last ten minutes if she hadn't lived through it. So much had happened in so little time. But staying here any longer was out of the equation.

The girl stirred. Good. LaGina helped Kelly back on his feet and draped an arm over her shoulder. They walked together and she held a hand out to the girl.

"Can you stand?"

"I think so." She looked down at herself. "I'm back! I'm back to normal!" LaGina pulled the girl to her feet and the two of them leaned on LaGina to walk out. They weaved their way around the maze-like factory and made it to a door leading outside.

That's what your mother said

It turned easily and they were blinded by sunlight, though the sun was setting. LaGina wanted to cross to get back to the hospital, but there wasn't a break in traffic.

"I think I'm okay," the girl said, standing on her own. She seemed unsteady, but her eyes weren't foggy.

"You should get checked out by a doctor," LaGina said.

"And tell him what?" LaGina didn't have an answer for that. "I'll just see my own doctor later; right now I need to find Marv." She walked away, disappearing around the building.

"You're welcome," LaGina said, wondering what the girl would say when Marv asked what happened to her teeth. "How about you? Do you need to go to the hospital?"

"I want to go home," Kelly said.

A bus pulled up with a straw bend in the middle. She had seen a few of them in the nineties but thought they had been discontinued.

"You think you can make it up the steps?" He nodded. They climbed up together and he grabbed onto a rail while she reached for her purse.

Crap. She'd left it in the Made-Goode factory. LaGina looked back. There was no way she was going back in there. She'd cancel the credit cards and get a new phone.

"No fare today, honey," the cherub-faced, middle-aged driver said. Her curly black hair was barely contained by her hat and framed her freckled face.

"Thank you," LaGina said and the driver nodded, closing the door. She put her arm around Kelly's middle and guided him to the back. The bus was mostly full and filled with elderly people. They found two open seats behind an old woman with a big church hat and wide eyes.

"Where are you two going?" she turned around and asked.

"Taking him home."

"Mm-hm." She stared a moment without speaking.

"So... where are you going?" LaGina finally asked.

"Lampheter. I'm going home too."

"That's good." LaGina didn't have anything else to say and thankfully the old woman sat back down in her seat.

"Where do we need to get off?" she asked Kelly.

"This bus will go north on Woodward for a little while. We need to get off on Tennyson. We can borrow my mother's car and I'll drive you home."

"You look awful. Are you feeling okay?"

"No. I feel like something terrible happened and I don't know what."

LaGina was unsure how much she should say. The glowing man had said he'd done something that was supposed to have killed those shadow creatures and trillions of others. That didn't make sense—there were only a few billion on Earth. Maybe there were a trillion of those shadow things. So far as she saw killing those couldn't have been a bad thing, but she had a feeling she'd only seen part of a bigger picture. But the look in his eyes—he was haunted, that much she was certain of.

The past few hours had been a lot to take in. Seeing Stout's spirit at that party, the stroke that had come from nowhere and a complete recovery thanks to a phone call from Kelly and then seeing him detached from his own body—it was a lot to take in.

Maybe he was an angel. No. Angels didn't need to be rescued. By her count she'd saved him twice now. LaGina put it out of her mind. Whatever had happened she would probably never understand, but she'd probably have nightmares. Best not to think too much about it.

She looked at Kelly. Really looked at him. Not a bad-looking man, but not traditionally her type. He was taller than she recalled, but she liked that. Back at the office he'd appeared to be her height. She'd dated black men before, so that wasn't the problem. He just seemed to be so *nice*. Looking over her dating history she'd never really been into nice guys.

Stout was the epitome of bad, dropping her without so much as a goodbye after the twins had been born. She'd found out on one of those entertainment programs when they did a story on a special he was shooting in Europe somewhere and he was photographed with some Czech model dripping off his arm.

She couldn't believe she was thinking any of this. A couple days ago she was ready to blackmail him if that's what it took to find Stout.

LaGina looked out the window as they passed through an intersection. She couldn't recall the bus stopping at any red lights or any other bus stops. They had to have been doing fifty easily.

"Our stop is coming up," Kelly said and stood. She scooted over and got up as he rang the bell. The bus slowed, cutting off a car as it moved across two lanes to get to the curb. They went down the two steps to the rear door.

"Goodbye." The little old woman waved to them as the bus came to a stop. LaGina waved.

"Wait a minute." Kelly went back up the stairs. He knelt in front of the seat next to the old woman and reached down by her legs. She whooped and pressed her knees together as if he were about to sneak a peek. He got up and they walked out together.

"See you later, sweetie," the driver said, standing at the back door. She winked and it shut in front of her, the bus merging back into traffic.

"Who's driving?" LaGina said.

"Let's just get out of here. I don't want to know." Kelly pulled her away.

He put her himself between her and the street as they began walking down the block. A thin layer of sun was on the horizon behind them. She felt the chill on her bare shoulders and needed to get her mind off the cold. She looked over at what was in his hand.

"What do you have there?"

"It's a tape." He held it up. It was one of those little tapes that went in some older models of camcorders.

"What's on it?"

"I don't know, but I have the feeling it'll help us find Stout."

"There have to be I don't know how many dozen busses in the city. What are the odds we got on the same bus he got on? And how would you even know he ever made a tape?"

"Keylocks. Never mind, it's something Israel told me. I don't know the odds of finding a clue on a bus, but I imagine they're pretty slim."

"You know Stout did carry an old camcorder and those were the kinds of tapes he used."

"How do you know?" LaGina thought of some other tapes she wouldn't like found.

"How are you going to play it?"

"My mother. She has a camcorder in her basement. I bought it for her for Christmas when I was seventeen. She never could figure out how to use it, but she kept it. I'm pretty sure this is the same kind."

They passed several houses in various states of disrepair. About a third on the first block were boarded up, burned out or abandoned. This didn't look like a safe place to bring up a child, but there were several children running on the sidewalk across the street.

LaGina started shivering. Winter was a couple weeks away. Even though it had been warmer than average the last few days, she was cold.

"Hold me?" she said to Kelly, rubbing her arms. He looked down at her and wrapped a bare arm around her shoulders. She was sure of it now, he was taller than before.

"So you grew up here?" They crossed to the next block.

"Yup. I don't know if it's my sense of nostalgia or what, but it doesn't seem to have as much life as it used to."

"Well it says something when the state has to take over your city."

The Ghost Toucher

He cocked an eyebrow at her.

"What do you know about HP?"

"A little. I read the papers every now and then."

"Everything that happens in Detroit happens here. Except the effect's worse because we don't have even a tenth of the population. City council plundered twelve million and it sent the city into a tailspin. And we had our corrupt mayor before they had theirs. I was still in high school when Chrysler went to Auburn Hills. Their headquarters was right down from my street across Oakland."

"I had an uncle who used to work there."

They walked in silence for a while, crossing to the third block. An occasional streetlight came on in the dusk, bathing them in electric blue whenever they passed under a lit one. He stared at a light green house on the corner as they walked past it. The patio door was open as if someone had left in a hurry.

"We almost there?"

"Yeah, just a couple more houses."

They turned onto the walk of an emerald green and white house with an enclosed porch. He knocked on the door but there was no answer.

"She's probably in the back," he said pointing a thumb over his shoulder. "We have to go around back." They walked up the driveway past a broken down-looking light brown Plymouth Sundance parked behind a bright red Dodge Ram with running boards. He came to a chest high fence with a chain on it and began to climb.

"I'm so not doing that in this dress." LaGina shook her head.

"It's okay," he said, holding out his hands and wiggling his fingers. "C'mon."

He had to be kidding. He'd been passed out not more than an hour ago and if he thought he was about to lift her he was—

LaGina's heart raced as he scooped her up by the armpits. She tried pinching his hands between her ribs and arms, embarrassed he might be getting her sweat on him. Kelly lifted her up like she was weightless, even tossing her up to catch her by the hips to take her cleanly over. She clenched his shoulders until he'd eased her to the ground, his grip gentle and steady.

The Ghost Toucher

LaGina was a little self-conscious of her area being in his face when she hadn't had a bath in almost twenty-four hours. She looked him up and down, wondering where this muscle had come from. He might have been taller, but strength was not something that body exuded.

"Can we go?" she asked, turning away and hoping he hadn't seen her flushed cheeks. They rounded the house and came to a dull red deck, climbing the stairs and passing some white deck furniture. Kelly stepped in front of her and walked to the patio door barricaded with potted plants on the inside.

He cupped the sides of his head and looked in, pausing for several seconds. Then he knocked and peaked in again.

"Okay," he said and turned to the security door to the right.

She looked around. She didn't know anything about Kelly, but she wouldn't have guessed he grew up here. She'd grown up in a poor neighborhood, but nothing like this. He hadn't left, he escaped.

He put his arm around her again and pulled her close. After a few moments in the chill air a flood light overhead came on. The windowless white door behind the security door swung in. A frail old woman with big eyes behind bifocals parked on her nose and salt-and-pepper hair swept into a bun parked on the back of her head looked out at them.

"Hey there, Kelly," she said, sliding the latch to the security door. "Come in, come in."

"Hey Ma," he said, ushering LaGina in ahead of him. She took the step up and saw how little the old woman really was. LaGina towered over her and she was only five-foot three.

She looked LaGina up and down, making no secret of it and taking both her hands in her own.

"You are gorgeous," she said. "Kelly, where are you manners. Introduce your girlfriend."

"She's not my girlfriend, Ma. This is LaGina. LaGina... I'm sorry, I don't think I've ever heard your last name."

"Densmore. LaGina Densmore."

"LaGina, this is my mother."

"Oh you know what I mean," his mother said. "Call me Ma Perdy by the way. It's just nice to see my son with a woman again after so long."

"Ma..."

"Oh! Oh! I didn't mean it like that." She grabbed LaGina's hand again. "I didn't mean it like that at all. My son is very capable of—I didn't mess things up, did I?"

"Can we just come in and sit down with you?"

"Oh yeah." Kelly's mother stepped back and ushered them through the small kitchen after he'd shut and locked the door. The dinner table was cluttered with board games and large plastic bowls and a large television. They passed the refrigerator decorated with torn-out crayon-colored sheets, some with messages like "Love you, Grandma!" and a stove with pots and pans covering the eyes.

They went into a backroom that had a large entertainment center in the corner. The large TV had a movie on. Ma Perdy walked over to a dark green recliner next to a circular table piled with various knick-knacks and prescriptions and sat down.

Kelly sat on the futon against the far wall and LaGina sat next to him. The house had an old, earthy scent spicing the air. She rubbed an index beneath her nose, hoping she wouldn't sneeze.

"So what's new?" Ma Perdy said. "You didn't give me a chance to miss you this time, you were just here the other day."

"Yeah, it's about this case. We had a little trouble."

"Is it your friend? He was a cutie—is he okay?"

"Yeah, well he... I think it's best I don't talk about it. Y'know, confidentiality issues and all."

"Ooo. Sounds *sexy*. So what's your story, Miss?"

"LaGina. I work at the Network with your son."

"Oh, you work together. Kelly, you should've told me about her."

"Well we just met the other day." LaGina could tell he was getting uncomfortable. She was a little uncomfortable herself.

"Mrs. Greene could I use your phone? I need to call home."

"Call me Ma Perdy. Everyone does." She handed over a cordless phone. LaGina dialed as she walked into the kitchen. She could hear them talking behind her. Kelly sounded like he was semi-exasperated with his mother.

"Hello?" a voice said after a few rings.

"Hey Mommy."

"Gina—thank goodness! *She's okay*," her mother said away from the phone. "Where *are* you?"

"Highland Park."

"What in the world are you doing there? Are you there with some man?"

"No, Ma. I'm here with a co-worker. I just want to know if the boys are okay."

"They're fine. We're all just so worried about you."

"I know, I know. Sorry, I'll be there soon. I actually had to go to the hospital."

"Hospital? What happened?"

"I, uh, I hit my head. Doctor thought I had a concussion. I'm okay, though."

"*Ugh*, Gina, you're such a *klutz*."

"Thanks, Ma."

"When will you be home?"

"As soon as I can get back. We're at his mother's house now to borrow her car and then I should be home."

"A co-worker. Gina, I don't understand. It's Saturday. You've had sex with him, haven't you?"

"Ma! No!"

"I'm just saying. You do have a history."

"Okay, Ma. Give the boys a kiss for me. I'll be home as soon as I can."

"Love you. Be careful."

"You too, Mommy. I will."

She hung up and came back into the living room. Kelly was gone but she could hear water running.

"Kelly's taking a shower. Sit down, let's talk."

"Okay. About what?"

"About you and Kelly. You'd make a good couple."

"What?" LaGina didn't mean to laugh.

"He's a really good catch. He was married for six years."

"Married?" She hoped her tone came off as sincere.

"His wife... passed. Car accident, bless her soul. You look a lot like her except you're shorter and a little fuller in the hip. But face-wise, you could be sisters."

"Okay."

"See up there? That's her picture." Ma Perdy pointed high up on the wall. Amongst several other pictures of children was a family photo of Kelly with a woman with a short haircut and two little girls. They did look alike except her face was a little thinner than LaGina's. If you gave his girls short haircuts they'd look like younger, darker-skinned versions of her sons.

"Beautiful family."

"They were in the car too. It was a few years ago and I know it's been hard for him, but I wish he'd move on. He deserves it. He's such a good boy."

LaGina looked at the much older woman and saw tears in her eyes. This was more than just a mother trying to hook up a date for her son.

"I'm dying and my son is going to be all alone."

"I'm so sorry."

"He needs someone to take care of him. To have someone at least to think about him. He doesn't do anything for himself anymore. He does things because he knows I would want him to. I only want to see him happy again."

"He never got over her."

"No. It's more like everything inside him was scooped out and splattered all over that highway. Y'know he was in the car when it happened? He was thrown clear and didn't have a scratch on him. It almost would have been better if he'd died."

LaGina was uncomfortable with all this sharing. She didn't have anything of this caliber to share back. It was like he was being stripped naked right in front of her.

"One time when Kelly was little, maybe eleven or twelve, I came into his room. He was just sitting on his bed, staring out the window. I must have called his name a half dozen times before he turned his head. It was like his brain was on Mars. He was so lost. He still didn't answer, just stared at me like he didn't know me. I've raised him since he was three years old and he looked at me like I was less than a stranger. It scared me for some reason. But then he blinked his eyes and smiled at me and there was my boy again."

"That's awful. I don't know what I'd do if one of my boys looked at me like that."

"He doesn't smile anymore."

LaGina's heart went out to her. But she didn't date guys because their mothers begged. The whole thing was weird.

The shower turned off. Ma Perdy wiped her face and smiled at her.

"Have you told him?"

"No." Ma Perdy showed a flash of anger. "And I'm sure you won't either. I don't want him to know."

She wondered how Ma Perdy expected that to work. As hurt as Kelly had been to have his wife and children die unexpectedly, wouldn't his mother passing unexpectedly be even more pain? LaGina nodded, not knowing what more to say.

Kelly came in a moment later with an old Pistons t-shirt indicating the 1989 and 1990 championships and a pair of black shorts.

"Oh Kelly, it's too chilly out to be wearing shorts."

"The jogging pants had a hole in the crotch and none of the underwear in there fit."

"So you're pretty much running around free in there," LaGina said.

"Sorry. Over share." He shook a leg and shifted his high-top sneakered feet. "Ma, I also needed to ask to borrow your car. We kinda lost the Parke Car."

"Sure. It's in the driveway. Let me get the keys."

Ma Perdy shifted out of her chair and shuffled back into the kitchen. She brought back the keys and handed them to him.

"The truck doesn't run, but the Sundance does. You know your cousin. He'll get to it someday."

He looked at LaGina, holding up some kind of odd-looking cassette.

"Look what I found."

"Aren't you going to thank your mother?" LaGina was mildly furious.

"Oh. Uh, thanks Ma." He bent and kissed her. "Thank you."

"You're welcome, baby."

"What is it?" LaGina said.

"Well, I couldn't find the camera, but I found something even better." He thumbed something on the top and a tiny window popped open then he inserted the camcorder cassette and closed it back.

"You might need to change the battery," Ma Perdy said.

Kelly looked confused, turning the cassette over in his hands. LaGina yanked it away and popped off the battery cover. She took out the old AA battery and took a remote off the entertainment center. She took a battery out of it and put it in the cassette converter. It hummed, stretching out the ribbon in the tiny cassette to be played in the VCR.

"Do you mind if we watch this, Ma Perdy?" LaGina asked.

"Go right ahead."

LaGina turned off the movie and popped in the tape. She rewound it until it stopped and pressed play.

After a few pops and clicks and static lines across the screen went from black to white. An out of focus hand reached across the lens and made an adjustment and the view changed to a blue sky.

He stood by the curb, waiting for the bus as traffic passed. The camera was only getting a look of the street and the calves of whoever passed.

Stout turned left and right. There were three people to either side of him. A man in a trench coat and black slacks, a guy with blond hair down to his shoulders in jeans and a barefoot woman with black toe nails. Stout tipped the camera slightly to get a view of her feet.

The bus roared into view and stopped in front of them. It was really *the* bus. Stout filed in behind the woman with no shoes. The bus driver was humming.

"How much is the fare?" Stout asked.

"Just have a seat, sweetie." The driver said. She was a sweet-looking, middle-aged black woman with freckles and curly hair. He would've done her twenty years ago.

He passed by several seated people, making his way to the back. If it were any other bus he might have thought it was the light in here, but their skin looked off. But considering they were all dead he kind of figured that was normal.

Lampheter. He would go as far as he could before they kicked him off. The living couldn't go there and Stout wasn't willing to die to cross over. Someone brushed by going the other way and the bag holding the camera spun wildly around.

He steadied it, sitting in one of the side-facing seats across from a man in a black suit.

"You see that?" Stout whispered, hoping the camera was picking up his voice. "You see that? That guy's *dead*." The man in the suit didn't move, but he had on a pair of sunglasses. He'd always been into ghosts, not corpses, but how could anyone not be excited by this? Ghosts were yesterday, now he was on to *zombies*.

"There's something going on here nobody knows anything about. The dead are up to something." Stout tried to sound as official as he could, but he knew he sounded more like Steve Irwin than Huel Perkins. That was okay, people would still watch.

He didn't know how long he could just play it cool before he was noticed. A dark, feminine figure appeared to his right and he realized it was speaking to him.

"Excuse me? What?" Stout said.

"You don't belong," it said in a deep voice.

"I'm just going downtown. Isn't this the downtown bus?"

"No. This bus is headed to the Fairgrounds."

Yeah, right. Stout knew this bus wasn't going anywhere near Eight Mile, but he'd better not press his luck. He'd found it once, he could always find it again later.

"I-I'm sorry. I can get off at the next stop."

"...late."

"What did you say? Sorry, I didn't hear you."

"*TOO LATE.*"

Something on the left side of him flipped his camera out of the seat, sending it to the floor.

"Wait a minute." Kelly rewound the tape and played it back in slow-mo. The figure was blurry because the camera had turned so suddenly but it looked like the shadow of a woman. Daylight came through the windows of the bus and through the two misshapen holes where her eyes should have been.

"What the hell is that?" Kelly said. LaGina hit play.

The camera hit the floor, the view upside down and facing the rear door. Stout was saying something in the background. He sounded nervous, afraid. Feet walked past the camera, some of them bare. There was a brief struggle and then he screamed.

The bus whined as it came to a stop and the camera slid a couple inches over, giving it a full shot of the rear door. It opened and a man stood there. His face was covered in weird tattoos.

"Gunner," LaGina said.

"You know that guy?"

"Sh—let's hear this."

He stepped onto the bus and stood right in front of the camera.

"I've given you what you asked for. Now give me what I want."

There was a slick, sucking sound following by a loud pop. Gunner turned around, screwing the lid back onto a black container. He turned toward the bus once he'd stepped off, his face in the camera again.

There was a sliding sound then Stout's head fell in front of the camera. The camera adjusted, bringing him in focus. Who or whatever must have dropped him. Only one eye could be seen, contracting in the red light of the camera. A hand pointed at his head.

"I don't care what you do with him," Gunner said, turning and walking away. The door closed and there were several hisses. Someone picked up the camera and flung it, then it cut out.

"Oh my God, how horrible." LaGina covered her mouth with her hands. She had to fight back the tears.

"So there's part of the mystery solved," Kelly said. "That is, if you actually know who that last guy was."

"Yeah." She wiped a tear from her eye. "His name is Gunner. I met him the other day at the Network. He came in to meet one of the executives. He just walked in like he was a big-wig or something. He even invited me to a party at his apartment."

"And you went?" Kelly raised an eyebrow. LaGina felt defensive and she was about to say something.

"So you know where he lives?" Ma Perdy said.

"Well, yeah. He's right in the city."

"Then you'll find Stout's spirit in that black container, like as not."

"Ma, how do you know that?" Kelly turned away to his mother.

"I know a thing or two. That container he had should be onyx. Keeps the soul locked in. I wouldn't be surprised if it was some kind of carbonate. If it is, that soul is either leaking out or gone."

"Ma!"

Ma Perdy shrugged, but didn't go into any more detail how she knew what she knew.

"So what, we go to Gunner's place and find this container," Kelly said. "Then what?"

"I'm sure we can figure that out after I get a shower."

***

Israel rode in the back with his 'brothers'. The golden albino was up front and the regular one sat next to him, staring. 'Mother' drove. He had no idea where they were going, but she turned whenever the one up front gave her direction.

He still couldn't believe what he'd learned at the factory, but he supposed it made sense. He knew Kelly was the Deciding Difference, but to be related to such a grand being. Maybe it was his programming that put him in awe of such a thing.

The golden albino made some sort of barking sound.

"Right here, baby?"

It nodded.

Mother pulled over next to a cornfield. They hadn't seen a house for a good mile or two. Everyone got out.

"Mother, what is this place?" Israel asked.

"This, my child, is where we make our stand. I foresaw the force that would try to destroy our world and I had hoped to stop it. I was too late to stop him, but only in this universe. This is a thin point."

"What's a thin point?"

"You probably have thought time is random between the two worlds. It isn't. Depending on where you are in both worlds it is faster or slower. Sometimes it can even move backwards. At this thin point we can cross over to before he sent death to Earthrealm."

"But the living from our world can't cross over. How can you get there? How did you even get here to begin with?"

"A bridge. Your brother Kelly is one. He will bring down the walls between the universes."

"But isn't that bad? Wouldn't life in every universe compacted into one destroy all life?"

She laughed. "No. If there were time I would explain it to you. There will be harmony once the universe is born."

"Why isn't he here? How can you get back without him?"

The golden albino walked into the cornfield. Mother and the other albino followed. She beckoned Israel to come too. By the time Israel got to where they were the golden one had pushed the cornstalks down in a circle big enough for about a dozen people to stand in.

Mother had a big knife.

"Sacrifice."

The albino got down on its knees in front of the golden one. He looked up at him like a dog would its master. Mother stood behind it, tilted its head to the side and jabbed the knife into its neck. She yanked it out and a jet of bright pink blood sprayed the golden one. All three raised their hands, the golden one's body elongating until he appeared as a beam of golden light stretching up into the sky.

The albino fell over, dead. Mother put her arms down and turned to Israel.

"We will ferry as many as we can." She walked over to Israel and looked down at him as she put her hands, one bloody, on either side of his face. "Stay. Wait for us, my child." She stepped into the golden beam and vanished.

Israel wasn't sure what he was supposed to do. But he knew one thing for certain.

His mother was lying.

Overt ops

They took Woodward downtown. What little traffic there was raced north and south, sometimes through red lights. LaGina wasn't exactly sure how to get there, so they felt their way around until she saw a building that looked familiar. Even then it was hit-or-miss until they found the right one.

They had to park a couple blocks away and walk. Ma Perdy's clothes were a little snug on her, but she wasn't about to wear a pair of Kelly's old jogging pants. They were at least thirty years old, but the pants were definitely in-fashion again. LaGina would love to have more time to raid her closet someday. At least the gym shoes fit. On the way they discussed how to get in the building considering neither of them had a key.

"I say we just push buttons at random and see if someone lets us in," Kelly suggested.

"That'll only get us in the lobby if it works. How do we get in his apartment?"

"I don't care. I'll just kick the door in."

They got lucky. A man was just leaving as they got there and he held the door open for them, staring at LaGina the whole time. They crossed the lobby to the set of elevators and Kelly pressed the up button.

"Do you really think we'll find that container up there?" she asked.

"I'm hoping. Otherwise it's back to square one."

The elevator opened and they got on. LaGina hit the button for Gunner's floor. They rode up without anyone else getting on and he followed her out. Gunner's apartment was three doors down from the elevators.

She stopped next to it and nodded to him. Kelly tried the handle and jumped back when the knob turned and the door popped open. The lights were out.

"What do we do?" LaGina asked.

"I don't know. We gotta get in there."

"What if somebody's in there?" She felt dumb even saying it. He peaked in and stepped back. "You stay right here."

"Being chivalrous?"

"Hell no. If I scream, you better come save me."

She nodded. He ducked and disappeared inside. He bumped into something and was quiet for a few minutes.

"Hey." LaGina yelped as he tugged on her dress. Kelly was on his hands and knees. "You gotta see this."

"What?"

"No—no. You have to see this for yourself."

She got on her hands and knees and followed him. It took her eyes a moment to adjust to the dark and she realized the giant table that was in the center of the room had been moved against a wall. There were three doors down a narrow hall and one of them was open with a light on. Someone was moving around in there and making a lot of noise.

LaGina grabbed Kelly's ankle. He stopped and turned around.

"It's the Old Man," Kelly said. "He's in there."

"But why?"

"I'm not entirely sure, but the guy from the video—"

"Gunner?"

"Yeah, him. The tattoos threw me, but when I saw him in there I made the connection. Father and son."

LaGina thought a moment. They had that same high, square brow, the same deep blue eyes and chin. If only she had realized before she might not have thought he was an exec. Who was she kidding—if she had known he was the son of the president of the Network she would have still been here last night.

They crawled up to the doorway and peered in. The Old Man had on a pair of baggy jeans, gym shoes and a bomber jacket. Maybe it was the clothes, but he seemed withered somehow. In suits he'd always appeared robust, larger than life, even though he was only a few inches taller than her. He'd made a pile on the floor of papers, clothes and other items. There was a dresser against the far wall with all its drawers pulled out and amongst the few knickknacks on top of it was the black container.

He reached behind the dresser and yanked until it came crashing over. The container rolled and bounced off the wall by LaGina and Kelly just out of arm's reach. The Old Man started into a coughing fit, bending over and putting a hand on his thigh.

Kelly reached inside, catching the black container with the tip of his finger. It skittered a couple inches away and he froze as the Old Man took a deep breath and went back into his coughing fit. Kelly stretched and snatched it, pulling out of the doorway.

"Who's there?" the Old Man said. Kelly's lips moved, but LaGina didn't hear him. "Dammit, I saw you. Come out. I have a gun." Kelly signaled for her to stay put, but she didn't think that was a good idea. If he came out alone and the Old Man saw her he might shoot out of panic. Plus he'd be less willing to shoot two people than one if he were up to something. Especially if one of them was a woman.

"It's not time, is it? It's not time?"

"I'm coming in," Kelly said. He stood and stepped into the doorway, his hands raised to his shoulders.

"I'm coming too," LaGina said, following him.

"Wha—" Kelly closed his mouth.

"Get in here," she heard the Old Man say. Kelly stepped in and LaGina followed, putting her hands up. He waved the little gun for them to come closer and they both had to step over the pile he'd made in the room.

"Y-you," he said to them. "Mr. Greene, I shouldn't be surprised, but Ms. Densmore, why are you here?"

"Why do you think?" she said. "You have to know by now I have a paternity case against Stout. We're tied together by mutual interest. We both want him found."

"But why are you *here*?"

"We know," Kelly said. LaGina could see Kelly nodding from the corner of her eye. He paused as if waiting for it to sink in. The Old Man's eyes went wide for a moment, but then he narrowed them.

"What do you *think* you know?"

"Oh, you mean about your son kidnapping Stout?" LaGina's stomach fluttered. She didn't know as much as him, but it sure felt like he was winging it. If the Old man was involved he probably didn't know details. She hoped he wasn't about to get them shot. "I studied that file Artie gave us. Stout had gotten three tips for haunted places he was visiting. One of them was a bus. Guess who else got on?"

The Old Man made a face like he was biting his cheeks. LaGina took her eyes off the gun long enough to see he looked off, like he was ill or something. His eyes were bloodshot, his skin was pale and he was hunched over. He raised the gun.

"We have a tape," LaGina said. Kelly looked at her and the Old Man paused. "That's right. Stout carried a camera everywhere, remember? Apparently, your son co-starred in his latest feature."

"And what are you going to do with that tape? Take it to the police?"

"Of course not, they'd never believe us. That's why if anything happens to us it gets downloaded onto the internet. Stout rules the sixteen to thirty-four demographic and they'll eat it up. Imagine what a coup it'll be for the Network to miss out on the commercial revenue of its signature show's final episode."

"You *wouldn't*."

"As much as the Network's lawyers have stalled the paternity cases against Stout, I think it would only be fair. And when the Board sees your son at the end of that tape they'll make their own connection. I bet there's a clause in your contract that comes with a hefty fine if you do anything detrimental to the Network."

"But they can't prove I had anything to do with—" The Old Man bit his lip. "You..." he pointed the gun at her. LaGina gasped and took a step back. His face turned white as a sheet and he lowered the gun. The Old Man brushed past them and into the bathroom. A moment later she could hear him throwing up. They both put their hands down.

"We have the container, let's get out of here." LaGina tapped Kelly on the shoulder and turned to go, but Kelly was looking at something on the floor.

"What are you doing? Let's go!"

"This was Martha's." Kelly picked something up off the floor. She grabbed him, yanking him out of the room by his arm. He reluctantly followed her out the front door.

The toilet flushed.

"Stop!" the Old Man shouted, his voice a pool of jagged rocks. They made it out the door, heading for the stairs. "Wait!" he screamed as they opened the door to the stairwell. Kelly picked up his feet and followed. They were about two flights down when she heard the door above, but there was no gunfire.

By the time they made it out of the stairwell LaGina was covered in sweat and panting. She swiped her hand over her forehead and looked at Kelly. He was clenching whatever he'd picked up.

"You still with me?"

He didn't answer.

"Hey, are you with me?"

"Yeah." Kelly blinked a couple times and looked at her. "Yeah."

"I don't know what's out there. He could be waiting for us in the lobby or he could be on his way down. I want to make a run for it. Can you do that?"

"Yeah. I can do that."

"Look, I'm sorry for whatever you're feeling right now. I'm sure it was hard enough the first time around. But we need to hustle as fast as we can and get to the car. Can you do that for me?"

"Yes." He nodded, focusing on her for the first time. He took the keys out of his pocket.

LaGina peaked through the little window and didn't see the Old Man out there.

"Ready?"

Kelly nodded.

She threw the door open and paused a second. She ran out and at first thought Kelly hadn't moved, but then she heard his footsteps fall out of synch with hers and saw him through her peripheral vision catching up. They both went through the same time through the revolving door and jumped out when it turned outside. They ran the two blocks until they reached the car. Kelly got there at least thirty feet ahead of her.

He had just gotten the driver's side unlocked when she reached him. LaGina nudged him aside, took the keys and got in.

"Go around!" she said. "I'll drive!" Kelly ran around to the passenger side and got in as she was starting the car. She pulled out into the street and turned right at the first corner.

"So where do we go now?" LaGina asked.

Kelly held up the black container.

"I'm not sure," he said.

The Old Man had tried to give chase. He'd only been able to open the stairwell door when he collapsed into another coughing fit. The chemo had taken all the fight out of him and he barely had strength to keep himself upright. He didn't want them to think he was really going to shoot them. Or maybe he did, but he wouldn't have shot. But he couldn't let them leak that tape. It was just the kind of screw-up Gunner would have made.

Gunner.

That son of his. Of all the times he should need something of his son. He wasn't going to find him on his own. And this needed a lot more discretion than an ordinary private detective.

He pulled the card out of his pants pocket. It was wrinkled and dog-eared. It had the letters 'S.K.' with an 800 number below it in raised crimson lettering.

It would be expensive. But he had to. They would be able to find that tape.

Plus he wanted to know where the young man had gotten the tooth on that necklace. He'd given it to someone almost more than fifty years ago.

The Ghost Toucher

No such thing

Finding Stout had been simple when they really thought about it. Gunner hadn't taken him off that bus, he'd left him there. At some point they had to have dumped him. They'd made a few calls to psych wards and hospitals around the city, looking for a 'lost brother' who may have hit his head or be in a coma.

By chance, LaGina found an unnamed person who'd been found, roaming down Eight Mile and barking like a dog.

"I think it might be him," she told Kelly.

"Where to?"

"Herman Kiefer."

They'd called from a couple payphones outside of a Starbuck's in Ferndale. Kelly took Nine Mile to 75, cut across the Davison and took the Lodge south. He got off on Chicago and weaved around until they got to Taylor Street.

Herman Kiefer. She'd driven by this place so many times without really seeing it. An H-shaped building studded with windows all the way around. She'd had a cousin who came here when she was little. Poor Jay had been picked on by her older sisters until something in her snapped. Uncle Marty had said she'd needed 'rest'.

The lobby was big and old. It had a sickly sweet mediciny smell. LaGina looked at Kelly to gauge if he were as uncomfortable as she was. Nothing. God, his mother was right. He was a blank slate at times.

"We called earlier," he said to the tired-looking, heavy-set white woman behind the desk. "You have a patient here we need to claim."

"Name?"

"Leslie Messler. You have him under John Doe."

Kelly pulled the paperwork out that had been stuffed into his pockets. He smoothed it out on the desk and handed it over. The woman whipped up the receiver and plunged her chubby index onto a few buttons then pressed the receiver between her shoulder and ear. She turned away from them and mumbled something into the phone, never even glancing at the paperwork.

"Where'd you get those papers?" LaGina asked.

"They were in my pants pockets. I don't know how they got there—Israel must have put them in after the accident."

"What accident?"

"We were being chased by these... things. We didn't exactly get away."

"He'll be right up," the woman behind the desk said.

"Thank you," they both said at the same time.

"You look nervous," Kelly said to LaGina.

"Just need to get back home. Miss my kids."

"I didn't know you had kids." His face softened. Something more human crept into his eyes. "I could have dropped you off."

"No-no. I don't mind. You shouldn't be alone."

"What do you mean?"

"Do this alone, I meant. There should be two people. At least."

"Oh. Okay."

Her brief conversation with Ma Perdy floated back into her mind. He wasn't lost-looking just now, but there was a loneliness to him. Maybe they could be friends or something. That would certainly be a different speed than what she'd normally had with a man.

"So what? Did you go to a party or something last night? What was with the dress?"

"Something like that. Kind of a blind date thing that didn't work out." She didn't want to say it was at Gunner's apartment. He was still hanging on to that locket and touching this tooth-looking thing on a little chain around his neck.

"Oh."

"What about you? How'd you wind up in the hospital?"

He looked confused a moment.

"Well, it had to have been the accident. I hope I'm fine—who knows if I hit my head? I was gone so long, I really don't even remember."

"Gone where?"

"Long story," Kelly said. He looked closed off again. "Why were you in the hospital?"

"Believe it or not, I thought I'd had a stroke. I couldn't talk and my right side was completely numb. But then... some guy who sounded like *you* called me. He told me to put the phone up to your ear and then you got up. Except you didn't seem the same as you are now. Do you even know what happened at the Made-Goode factory?"

"Yes and no." Kelly made a face like he was struggling to remember the details. It was this morning, how could he have forgotten? "Pictures of some of it. Something bad happened to someone, but I don't know who. Man, it's like I have this big hole in my memory."

"You said something about something bad happening earlier. You were crying."

"Me?" Kelly rubbed a hand over his head. She could tell he didn't remember.

As lost as he seemed LaGina felt right there with him. Maybe it was best to forget about what happened at the Made-Goode factory.

A man in a tuxedo stepped off the elevator. An orderly pushing a man in a wheelchair followed. The man had on a blue thin jacket with baseball logos all over it. Was that...

"Stout!" LaGina ran over to him. His face was slack and his eyes slitted and dull. The orderly didn't stop until he was behind the doctor at the receptionist desk.

Stout looked different. He'd put on weight in his face and his hair was more of a sandy brown instead of jet black. She hated him for all he'd put her through, but she couldn't help but kiss his cheeks over and over.

He looked at her, but she could tell he didn't recognize her.

"He's just been given a heavy sedative to keep him calm, but he's been violent since coming here, so be careful," he said to Kelly. "Oh, and he also likes to drink out of the toilet."

The Ghost Toucher

LaGina hoped the fresh minty smell on his cheek was aftershave. She thanked the orderly and took the handles of the wheelchair.

"Keep him in a quiet environment, preferably indoors and away from traffic. An orderly broke his leg chasing him across the Lodge."

"Thanks," Kelly said. "We're going to take him to his mother."

The doctor nodded and they shook hands. LaGina was a little offended he didn't shake hers.

"So how do we get his spirit back in?" she asked as they walked outside. "And who's in there now?"

"I have no idea and I think a dog's in there."

"A dog? How would a dog's spirit have gotten in there? I thought dogs don't even have spirits." Kelly opened the rear passenger door and they half lifted Stout and put him inside.

"You'd be surprised."

An orderly came and took the chair as they got in the car. LaGina turned around and looked at Stout.

"I keep having this feeling I'm forgetting something," Kelly said. "Or someone."

Stout whimpered.

"Don't change the subject. How would a dog have gotten in there? If Gunner took his out then someone had to have put that one in."

"Not necessarily, but I do appreciate the irony." LaGina made a face. "I may not watch the show, but I've heard about the guy. I know his reputation." It wouldn't have been a spectacular leap for Kelly to make the assumption Stout was the father of her children and she was glad he didn't ask. "A roaming spirit can take possession of a body under the right circumstances."

LaGina waited for him to continue.

"Like?" she said when he didn't.

"I don't know," Kelly said. "It's not exactly in a book. I just saw it happen." LaGina doubted that had happened to Stout. A lot of people hated him, both living and dead. With as many women as he had screwed over and as many of them who must have had husbands it was obvious somebody had gotten him back. A dog had gotten a dog's soul. LaGina's only question was why Gunner and the Old Man had done what they did. Stout's show was second only to *Chí-Ché* in its time slot and number one for the Network. They should have been able to settle the lawsuit easily. She'd heard a rumor that the Old Man's daughter had had a baby by Stout, but she couldn't be certain.

Kelly's face changed in the glow of dashboard lights.

"Speaking of Gunner—how much do you know about him?"

LaGina was hoping to avoid this. Kelly was holding that locket in his hand again. She didn't want to involve herself with whatever he was thinking. She'd seen the end results of men and their vengeance.

"I don't know anything about him. He invited me to a party and I came." Maybe a little more of the truth would help. "It was some kind of séance and he called up a spirit. I thought it was Stout. Please don't do anything. Think of your mother."

They stopped at a red light. He looked at her.

"You thought it was or you know it was?"

"Well I must have been mistaken. I mean, you have the container right there. Can't get out of onyx, right?" She'd remembered what Ma Perdy had said.

"Unless it's not real onyx." The light turned. He kept looking at her.

"Yes. Yes, it was Stout. I know it in my heart, it was." He pulled off. "You're not going to do anything, right? I mean about Gunner. You'll call the police?"

"I don't know. I'll think about it later."

"Where are we going?"

"Got to make a stop before we go to Stout's mother's. I just realized there's no such thing as coincidence."

"What does that mean?" LaGina asked.

"Hopefully a lot."

***

"Here you go, buddy, he's all yours," the deputy said. Israel looked up at the giant in the cell, his semi-wild eyes darting around.

"You gonna be a good boy for me so I can let you out?" the deputy said to him. Israel wasn't entirely sure he wanted to let him out. But it was what Mother wanted.

"He uhh, doesn't talk much, officer," Israel offered.

"Oh, I can see that. He's gonna behave, right? I'd hate for Chris and Jerry to have to hit him with the tazer again."

"He'll be good." Israel wished he knew that for a fact.

The deputy unlocked the cell and slid the bars back. At first the giant just let his hands fall to his sides. But then he walked out without looking at the officer who had opened the cage. He stood in front of Israel, his eyes blazing behind bushy hair hanging down all around his face then grabbed him in a bear hug.

"Hey-hey-hey-hey!" Chris and Jerry shouted, running over to them. Israel held up a hand.

This was his brother. He hugged him back.

Bum wisdom

"You *what*?" LaGina asked.

"I left it."

"So you had it all this time?"

"No. And I don't technically have it. It was in a dead body, but I didn't know it was him at the time. He told me his real name; I just didn't make a connection."

"How did you screw that up? Everybody knows what his real name is."

"Not someone who wasn't into the show. At the time we didn't know Stout had been separated from his body. We didn't have any reason to assume we wouldn't find him 'whole' for lack of a better term."

"You don't even know if he's there."

"No, but we can cross our fingers and hope."

They took the service drive to Jefferson and headed east until they passed through Downeck. LaGina felt a chill going constantly up and down her spine until they reached Grosse Pointe.

"There's that feeling again," Kelly said, shaking his head. "Like there's something I'm supposed to be doing. I wish I knew what."

After another ten minutes or so they were driving through St. Clair Shores. They crawled around a shopping plaza as he looked around. She still didn't understand how he could do something so dumb.

"I think it's somewhere around here." It wasn't. They drove around until they found another plaza that looked exactly the same.

"Okay, I don't see him. I want to look around some. Just keep him company." Kelly gestured to Stout, sleeping in the backseat.

He left the engine running and the heat on, got out and raced off. It looked like it had begun raining outside just when he disappeared around a corner. LaGina turned to look at Stout.

"What happened to you?"

She'd been in love with him and thought he felt the same. She should have known better; her taste in men was always bad and Stout was the poster child for bad boys. He'd wined and dined her, taken her to places she'd never been, shown her things she'd never seen. His rude behavior was shocking and made everyone uncomfortable but she'd loved it.

He was everything a Catholic girl from Lapeer wasn't. And then he dumped her.

She had every reason to hate him, but she didn't. Not anymore. She laid a hand on his arm and smiled. Maybe this was the closure she needed.

She got on her knees in the seat, facing the back and reached toward him. LaGina grabbed a little lock of hair with a hard tug ripped it out by the roots.

Stout's eyes yanked open and he looked at her. Those eyes were completely guileless. He looked at her hand and lifted it with his arm. LaGina let him guide her until her fingers rested against his cheek. He nuzzled at her hand, whimpering, until she began scratching behind his ear. She was careful to keep the hair pinched between her index and thumb while she used her other three fingers on his head. He closed his eyes and leaned into the scratch. Then he fell over on his side and shifted so he was belly up.

"You want me to scratch your tum-tum?" She tucked the hair into a napkin and put it in her pocket.

His mouth hung open. He was panting. She obliged and he shifted around on the backseat. He kept pushing her hand lower and lower until it reached his belt line.

Oh no.

"You dog," she snatched her hand away. "Never again. You are bad." She shook her finger at him. "Very bad. Very, very, *very* bad." LaGina turned around and sat. Stout whined.

The Ghost Toucher

***

'Ed' was nowhere around. Only a couple homeless guys. Kelly didn't know how helpful they would be but maybe the ten spot in his pocket might help.

"Hey there was a guy here earlier," he began, waving the sawbuck left and right in his hand. "Tall, white, looked kinda sick. Seen him?"

The homeless guy in the cardboard Samsung television box with his legs hanging out and folded looked at the money, then up at him. He took a swig from the bottle and handed it over to the one sitting in a Zenith box.

"You know, they 'on't let me in there n'more," Samsung slurred, swiping his mouth. "They don' like t'let m'drink 'n I don't agree." He tapped his soaked chest. "'M a grown men."

"What my esteemed friend means to say is we made acquaintance with a gentleman in dire straits fitting your general description a mere few hours ago," Zenith said. "He appeared lost, confused, out of sorts with a wound on his side so I gave him my jacket and sent him across the street to the soup kitchen."

"The soup kitchen? Why'd you send him there if he was wounded?"

"Good sir, I am sitting in the freezing rain and inadequately dressed. It should be more than apparent: I am drunk."

"Plussy got shot in th' head sree days ago," Samsung added, holding up four fingers.

Zenith tilted his head forward and pointed to a pencil-sized hole in his head.

"I can feel the rain water going in there."

Kelly looked then shook his head. One set of weird circumstances at a time. He dropped the ten spot in the Samsung's open lap and the man snatched it up.

"You should take your buddy to the hospital," Kelly said to Samsung.

"You try tellin' 'im. *Hisassisstucktoth'floor!*"

Kelly raced across the street. He saw LaGina leaning over the seat doing something with Stout. She was cute, but he thought she might be damaged goods. He supposed he was too, maybe more so, but there was an obvious history between those two. But he didn't want to pry. From Stout's file there were several paternity suits against him and she'd mentioned kids. He'd put money on them being his, but proving the point would be useless.

But when he looked at her it made him uncomfortable. She seemed so familiar to him, like they'd known each other for a long time, but the feeling was just wrong. Like he was stealing something. Or cheating someone.

Cheating.

Thoughts of her came to him and he barely stopped in enough time to avoid the car racing by. He dared not think her name. It was all he could do to look at their pictures every now and then and when he did he was still reduced to tears. Knowing that this Gunner may have played a part in her death was getting to him. The middle of Gratiot was no place for a breakdown.

Kelly stepped into the soup kitchen and looked around. There were about two dozen people in here, sitting in clusters. He walked over to the counter where a slender older woman stood behind a big silver pot with a scoop and a hairnet on her head.

"Some'n for the rain, honey," she said, hammering away at a piece of gum. She handed him a big foam cup.

"Uh, thanks." He took it. It actually smelled pretty good. He took a sip and it was delicious. Beef stock, celery, onions. Kelly's stomach grumbled. He gulped it down.

"How long's it been since you had a home-cooked meal?"

"Maybe two years?" It was the truth. Kelly had reduced himself to frozen dinners and eating out over the last few years.

"You clean?" She looked him up and down. He guessed she meant drugs, but she had a look.

"Yeah. I'm actually looking for a friend of mine."

"I'm lookin' for a friend too." She flashed a smile with a little too much teeth. This was headed in a bad direction. He began a coughing fit.

"You okay, honey?"

"Yeah-yeah, the doctor said it's all in my head, but you know they work for *them*. It was in that stuff we breathed in Iraq. They said Saddam didn't have nerve gas, but they said that to protect their precious *oil*."

The Ghost Toucher

"You look a little young for Desert Storm," she said. "Wasn't that when soldiers said they got exposed to something?"

"That's the weird thing. My buddy was the one in Desert Storm. I think he *gave* it to me."

"What?" She scrunched her face.

"Look," Kelly leaned in and he could see her withdrawing even though she didn't move, "what's your name?"

"Leticia."

"Leticia, I could always use a new friend, don't get me wrong, but my buddy is on borrowed time, y'know?"

"Yeah, that's sad." The glint was gone from her eye. "What's yer friend look like?"

"Tall. White." Kelly put his arms around himself and began scratching his sides. "Really bad complexion. Looks like he's dead."

Leticia was scratching her forearm. She noticed what she was doing and stopped.

"You must mean John." She wrapped her arms around herself. "He's over there against the wall."

"Thank you." Kelly smiled and stooped over like he was going into a dry heave. He stood and turned, scanning the far wall. There were only three people there and this was a small place. How had he missed him?

His back was to Kelly, sitting at a short white cafeteria table. Kelly walked over and sat in front of him, taking out the black container. Ed looked up, a Red Wings cap on his head.

He smelled. Kelly breathed through his mouth, glad it was still relatively cold in here.

"You ready to go home, Stout?"

"Hnnnh," Ed/Stout said, nodding.

He wasn't sure how this was supposed to work. The container was slippery in his hands, falling through his fingers a couple times before he got the lid off. Ed/Stout watched the container with his remaining eye. Kelly sat the container down between them.

They waited.

"Okay, aren't you supposed to... get in or something?"

Ed/Stout looked at him.

"I don't know how this works. Do you know how it happened the last time?" He shook his head. Kelly drummed his fingers on the table, unsure of what to do and frustrated.

Ed/Stout was staring at his hand.

"What?" Kelly said, turning his hand over and examining his fingers. He put his palm back on the table. Ed/Stout tried mimicking his action, but the two middle fingers on his hand didn't move at all. He growled and swatted Kelly's hand.

Something electric passed between them. Kelly rubbed his thumb over his fingertips and Ed/Stout stared at his hand. Kelly thought he had an idea, but wasn't sure of what he was about to do.

He took Ed/Stout's hand in his and stared at him. The dead man was transfixed; he sat still as Kelly half stood, leaning forward until their mouths were an inch apart. Kelly took a deep breath and felt a pinch of electricity on his lip as Stout's spirit leapt into his body.

Ed's head drooped. Kelly caught the body before it could fall and gently laid the head on the table. He felt full in a way that had nothing to do with the soup. He picked up the black container and got up, seeing Leticia was gone and turned for the door. When the police started asking questions they'd want to know how a corpse had been rotting in here for days. Leticia might have been able to describe him from head to toe but the problem with Kelly being a suspect was he'd been here a long time after Ed had died and people had seen him walking around before that anyway.

Kelly dashed back out into the cold rain. He crossed the street back to the Sundance and got in.

"You smell like soup. What took so long?" LaGina asked.

"I'll explain on the way. I got him."

"Give it to me. I'll hold it." Kelly gave her the black container.

"It's not in there, though." Kelly burped. "It's inside me."

"How did you—never mind."

Kelly put the car in drive and they were off.

Crazy old lady, pt ii

Stout had growled at Kelly the whole way there. LaGina kept shushing him, but each time that only worked until she faced forward in her seat again. They'd had to go back down to 696 and head west and it was sometime after eleven o'clock when they got there. No decent senior citizen would be up at this hour so it struck LaGina as strange when Mrs. Roost—*Messler*—answered the door, bright-eyed and in her Sunday best.

Like she'd been expecting to see them.

She looked like she'd put her make-up on in the dark with a paintbrush. Streaks of lipstick cut from one jowly cheek and across her thin mouth to the other. She had black rings around her eyes from where she had over-applied eyeliner several times over and her thick foundation was much darker than the pale waddle of her neck.

Mrs. Messler's thin hair was like a white-blue halo around her head. LaGina could see the light from within the house reflecting off her scalp. She looked emaciated, her skin hanging off her like an ill-fitted suit.

Stout didn't make any noise, but it was obvious he didn't want to go inside. LaGina had held his hand (he seemed fascinated by this) to lead him to the concrete porch.

Kelly hadn't done anything to assure her he knew what he was doing. He'd gotten Stout's spirit inside himself, but didn't know how to get it out. And he was insistent that they needed to go to Stout's mother's right then, but didn't have a reason why.

"Good evening, Mrs. Messler," he said. "Remember me?"

"You," she began after her eyes had rolled over to Kelly, "are that cock*sucker*."

"I'm sorry we must have gotten off on the wrong foot, earlier. May we come in and sit down with you a moment?"

"Dog-raper!" Stout put his nose behind LaGina's ear and whined.

"We'd like to come in." Kelly put his hand on the door handle and it creaked as it turned. A bird tweeted inside somewhere. Mrs. Messler stepped back, a big grin on her face. Her dentures clacked in her mouth, the four front teeth missing. She shifted from side to side, like an athlete trying to stay warmed up.

"Is she okay?" LaGina said to Kelly before he went in.

"It's going to be all right." He had a weird look in his eyes, like he had just learned something and was keeping it secret. She pulled Stout in behind her and as they walked over to the couch Mrs. Messler stepped closer to her son.

LaGina's hand suddenly stung from Stout's fingers snatching away from hers. Stout and his mother were rolling around on the floor, biting and snapping at each other. She tossed him, bouncing him off the wall and onto the couch. Mrs. Messler hopped onto the balls of her feet and turned to LaGina. Kelly got behind her and wrapped an arm around the old woman's neck. She half wriggled out of his grip and sank her remaining teeth into the crook of his arm.

Kelly screamed and she spun around, punching him in the side of the head and grabbed him by the throat, shaking him like a rag doll. His eyes bugged as he slapped and scratched at her iron grip, gulping fruitlessly for air.

LaGina grabbed a big book off the coffee table, hefting it once before she bashed Mrs. Messler in the back of the head. She let go and Kelly slumped to the floor like a sack of meat. He didn't move.

The bird was chirping non-stop. There was something going on outside the house—it sounded like bird wings. LaGina backed away from Mrs. Messler, the book held shoulder high as the much older woman crept closer, her arms held up like a praying mantis.

The Ghost Toucher

Stout pulled himself off the floor, growling at his mother. She looked at her son and LaGina could see there was no recognition in her eyes.

"Oh dear," she said in her shaky little old lady's voice. "More cock*suckers*."

***

Kelly woke up. He was back here again. Except it was all different. A light coat of dust was on everything—even the air tasted chalky. The sky had lost much of its translucency, turning a dark brown, the veins thin curlicued shadows he almost couldn't make out.

"I'm so sorry for everything I done. I been a great big *dick*." Kelly looked down at the spirit floating next to him. It was Stout, trails and wisps swirling around him. Kelly stood up, the memories of his time here flooding back. He remembered the *douchou*, or, Grand Jerk, as it translated into English. Even though it was thousands of years ago, he was hated still. They'd erected a monument to him they threw sweet-smelling trash at so they wouldn't forget and even made a holiday out of the day they threw him into the Whitelands.

Now everything was dead. If there were any survivors they wouldn't last long. The ground crunched underfoot when he took a step. That couldn't be good for growing crops. There was a giant groaning in the distance. Kelly turned and saw a building in the distance slowly falling over.

The douchou had done it. He'd killed everyone.

Perhaps some had escaped somehow. There was supposedly a way for it to be done and other dimensions to where they could have fled. Hopefully the Resistance had found a way out. But over six trillion people had been murdered.

The fact Kelly had played a part in it no matter how unwittingly made him feel like he'd been gut-punched. He should have grieved for all the lost lives, but he felt like he already had.

"I hurt everybody I ever touched." Kelly had forgotten about Stout. Other spirits roamed the streets. They seemed fine apart from being dead, that was. The hereafter belonged to them now.

The Ghost Toucher

If everything he'd been told were true nothing could kill him in this world or any other.

"I should be here. Yeah, I deserve it. In fact, I deserve someplace worse."

"Stout, would you like to start redeeming yourself?"

"What? Oh man, you can see me?"

"Of course I can. I see all of you." Spirits had begun floating their way. Kelly pointed to a few floating around this world's version of a fire hydrant, a silver box-shaped thing with a spout like a duck's beak built into the top. "Would you like to go back? Start making up for what you've done?"

"Yeah, man, yeah. Are you an angel or something? If I could go back I'd be so much different. And not just with all those chicks I banged. Dead people didn't deserve what I done. I swear man, I'd go back to every place, every house and I would make it right or die trying."

"Nobody needs you dead, Stout. There are a lot of children who need a father. Make sure they get one. I'll take you back. You're not going to be in your body at first so you'll have to remember to do one thing for me and it's extremely important you remember: kill the bird. No matter what you see or what you think is happening, kill the bird and it'll make it all better.

"Can you do that for me, Stout? It's the most important thing you can do in the next few minutes."

"Yeah, man."

"No. This is really important. If you mess this up you're dead for good. So is one of the mothers of your children. Got it?"

"Yeah, yeah. I got it. Thank you."

The way back was obvious for Kelly. Over here he had realized he was a bridge. He could go back anytime he liked.

"Then take my hand."

Stout reached out and grabbed it. He had that gross feeling like an overly wet sponge. Kelly's body buzzed and threw off the red glow like before. Hundreds of spirits had gathered when they crossed and the vacuum in his wake sucked all of the ones into it that were close enough.

***

That guy had done it. Stout was back. The first thing he could tell this time was he wasn't in some dead guy or locked in a container. But this felt like a bird.

Maybe it was some kind of pigeon, he couldn't tell but when he flapped a wing several more responded. He wasn't just one bird—he was a thousand.

Stout was in a tree. Several trees all looking at one window. He knew this window. It was to his mother's kitchen. There was something going on inside. Made a couple of him take wing and fly up to a higher branch. He didn't have control of the birds completely, like trying to hold onto a fistful of marbles, some would drop out of his control. It would be difficult. He felt thread thin, stretching into so many small creatures. And they all had a mind of their own, however miniscule, even if they did have a hive-like way of thinking. He knew if one took off they all would and he'd be spread so thin as to not exist.

At first they wouldn't move at his urging. But he began exerting his will on the flock rather than the individual birds themselves. He had to break that window and get in there. The first one took off and from there it was like nudging pebbles off a cliff. The effect snowballed until they were moving en masse on the window. The glass began cracking after the first few beaks hit, but many more were bouncing off the side of the house because it was too focused of a point for so many. The glass shattered and they were in, swarming everything.

A birdcage on the kitchen table was knocked over, a little canary inside. Many of the birds continued and wound up in the living room. A man was on the back of a little old woman who had just punched another woman in the face. Some other guy was on the ground, clutching his forearm.

Stout thought he should help. No, he needed to do something else.

Kill the bird.

His mind shifted back to the kitchen. The pigeons swarmed the bird, still in the cage and there were more flying in from outside. Surprisingly, the more that flew into the aluminum siding or the walls inside the house and died, the greater his control was over the rest.

Stout refocused on the cage and they began tearing at it. The canary flittered about in its cage and all those beaks quickly made several entrances inside. It was over in seconds.

***

The bird thing was weird. Weirder than Kelly leaping off the floor like a madman after Mrs. Messler had snapped Stout's arm, weirder than a seventy-something year old woman with a mean left cross.

The weirdest thing of all was how frightened Mrs. Messler looked when the birds went silent. She looked around, wringing her hands as unseen wings fluttered around the room. LaGina looked, but didn't see any bird. All the pigeons in here were dead or walking around. There was a fair amount of bird poop on the floor too.

Kelly picked himself up off the floor and used the distraction as an opportunity to punch the old woman in the stomach. She doubled over and LaGina grabbed his arm before he could hit her again. She shook her head at him.

Mrs. Messler leapt back and howled before pitching back, landing on her palms with her back arched up. She walked like that on her hands and feet until she bumped up against the wall. She turned over and crawled diagonally up the wall to the ceiling, grunting with her eyes closed and her mouth working silently up and down.

Then she fell.

They walked over to Mrs. Messler and stared at her, lying face down with her arms and legs spread.

"Is she?" Kelly rasped.

"No." LaGina slid an arm around his waist. He looked at her but didn't move away. She was surprised too. "Look, you can see her back moving."

Kelly put his arm over her shoulders and gave a squeeze as if wanting to be sure she was really there.

I thought *you* were, though. The way you just fell there. You were so still, but then you got up so fast."

"Were you scared?"

"No." LaGina couldn't meet his eyes. She tried to pull away but he squeezed again.

"Well I was scared when she choked me out. I haven't had a woman do that to me since third grade. My whole neck hurts. I was scared when she punched you in the face, but you have a pretty good beard."

"Gee, thanks." She looked at him. He was smiling. "That's a terrible joke. She could have killed us." Maybe it was everything that had happened today, but it was funny. LaGina laughed and Kelly joined in. They laughed harder with each passing second; LaGina could feel her sides aching as tears streamed from her eyes.

"I don't even know if it's over," Kelly managed to say. "What's up with all these birds?" They broke out in fresh laughter, but quickly sobered up when Stout crawled over to them.

"What do we do about him?" LaGina asked.

"I don't know." He made a face as he stared at Stout, looking moon-eyed back at them.

"Somebody... somebody help me." Mrs. Messler got to her knees and LaGina helped her to the couch and looked her over. The old woman was tough. Other than a bruised cheek she seemed fine.

Kelly had gone completely still. Almost like before except he was standing up. A pigeon had landed on his shoulder and he seemed to be having a staring contest with it.

The bird fell off his shoulder and didn't move again. Kelly's head slowly rotated to Stout, still kneeling on the floor. Kelly formed his mouth into an 'O' and blew.

"Stout can't come back on his own, Mrs. Messler," he began. "He needs to be rooted to someone who cares for him."

"Wha-what?" she said. She looked around and spotted her son. "Oh, my baby. My *baby*." She jumped off the couch and threw her arms around him. Mrs. Messler peppered his cheeks with kisses.

"Guess that answers your question," LaGina said.

"Y'know, two might be better than one."

"I think I drank my fill from that well." LaGina put her hands up. "I'm good."

The Ghost Toucher

Kelly shrugged, put his hand on top of Stout's head and said, "It's time to go, boy." Stout looked up at him. LaGina couldn't see his face from her angle so she couldn't see what translated between them, but Stout's posture changed. His shoulders relaxed, his head cocked to the side in that way LaGina had seen so many times before. She thought she heard a dog whimper but the sound was brief.

"Ma?" Stout said.

***

Kelly stayed the night. Not that anything was about to happen between them, but he was too wasted to drive home. LaGina had winked out shortly after giving him directions to her house. They'd left Stout and his mother when the ambulance arrived to take him to the hospital.

"Come in. Seriously," she'd said to him when they pulled into her driveway. "You can crash on the couch." She'd put her hand on his and he could tell she meant it, the invite too. He could see it in her eyes even though he could barely keep his open.

"Thanks, but I don't think I can make it out of this car. Every part of me hurts. Could I come in for breakfast and a shower, though?"

"All I have is PB and J in the house, but you're welcome to it." She smiled. Despite himself he smiled back.

LaGina climbed out the car and he felt like some kind of traitor watching her go. He closed his eyes and put his head back, kicking himself for what just went through his mind. He let himself slide down into sleep and got that nagging feeling again that there was something... someone he'd forgotten all about.

He hoped it wasn't too late. But for what?

Sometime later, maybe a few minutes or a few hours, Kelly felt someone slide a blanket over him. He mumbled something as a hand stroked the side of his face.

"They're waiting for you," an old woman's voice said.

Kelly opened his eyes. Or thought he did. He felt asleep still and could feel the warmth of the blanket. He was back on the other side except it was different. It was like he was standing inside of a picture. Nothing moved. Well, there wasn't anything that could have moved. Everything was gone.

Except for a hooded figure sitting about ten feet in front of him. He blinked and then it was five feet.

"When you're ready," the old woman said.

"Ready for what?" Kelly asked.

"To go to them."

"Who's waiting?"

"Everyone. I stayed behind to tell you."

"Martha and the girls?"

She said nothing.

"I need to know—are they okay?"

But the old woman said nothing else. Going back to being a part of the stillness all around. Kelly tried reaching for her. He wanted to shake her, make her answer him. But he hit his hand on something, the pain dissolving the dream into blackness.

I forgot about that

Taze had made the ultimate score. A ton of H was waiting for him courtesy of his trust fund account. This giant storage container would keep him and his closest hundred homies sky high for the rest of their lives if he wanted.

He wanted. After yesterday afternoon he needed a break from reality. That thing with all the porn had knocked out the skinny and the phatty. Taze giggled. He didn't care. Skinny for guys made total sense.

He unlocked the door after looking around and went in. Sunrise was still a long time coming. Taze wondered how he was going to get all this home. Maybe it was better if he didn't; if he got busted with this much he'd go to prison *forever*. And no H meant no more fun.

Taze flicked on his flashlight and saw several dozen crates as he swept it back and forth. He guessed that made sense. How else are you supposed to ship tons and tons of drugs? He giggled at the thought of a gigantic baggie. It was hot and stale in here. Had a farm stank too.

There was a crowbar on the floor. He picked it up and walked down the makeshift aisle to the back. They were stacked up almost to the ceiling. He got an ill feeling down his spine, like a chester was watching him. He spun around. Nothing there but an open door.

Maybe he would have to sell some. There had to be tons up in this piece. Even he felt full at the thought of doing all this stuff.

There was a sound. Taze spun back around and saw one of the crates, standing halfway out in the aisle.

Had it been there before?

"Chill," he told himself. He'd just crack that one open and do a li'l bit. He jammed the crowbar in between the planks of wood and wedged it partially open. They really had this thing nailed tight. He wondered why all the crates were so little as he peaked inside of this one when he saw something that looked like two green eyes.

"Nah, those *emeralds*." What were emeralds doing in there? He wrenched off the side of the crate and saw the side of a cage. It was plastic or plexiglass with air holes in the side, but there was a big-eared, green-eyed blue thing in there.

And no drugs.

"Snaaaaap." He hoped this was a fluke but all the crates were the same size. If he'd paid for somebody's Tasmanian bunny that was bol'. He wasn't about to go pushing these in West Bloomie.

He'd gone to exactly where he was supposed to and the number on the side of the container had been the one dude had given him. The guy had just screwed up.

Taze knew what he would do. He'd sue. Put Dad's money to good use and make skillet get his H.

As he was thinking over the logistics and all that the bunny thing sniffed at the little crack in its cage where he must have whacked it with the crowbar. Maybe he shouldn't have ignored that 'Open With Care' sign. It leapt at the crack as if fresh air was some kind of drug. Taze held a finger out over the crack and it leapt again, the skin on its back and belly turning bright red. It scratched at the crack with tiny fingers ending with jet black hooked claws. It sliced through the tip of his finger and he snatched it back.

"Ouch!" Taze felt it, but it really hadn't hurt. He looked at his finger and a thin line of red appeared all the way back to the first knuckle. He tried to wiggle the end of his finger but it wouldn't move.

Cute or no, Taze was outtie. He stood and the thing's belly and back turned bright pink as it pushed and clawed at the opening. He stubbed his foot on another crate. He *knew* it hadn't been in the aisle and narrowly avoided bussing his head open on one poking out right in front of his face.

They all were moving. Like more of those creatures were inside.

The Ghost Toucher

Taze ran for the door. He heard something break as he put his hand on the heavy door to push his way out. Something yanked him back and he pulled the door closed with him. He smacked onto the floor and the flashlight, where ever it was, lit up the little creature from the cage from behind a few feet away. Its chest was a glowing white as its little hand blurred past Taze's face.

It gobbled something down and he was suddenly coughing up blood the washing into his throat. Taze put his hand to his face and his nose was gone. There was no pain. His nose had brought him here and it was the first thing to go.

He turned onto his elbows and began to push himself up. It leapt on his face, tearing and eating. Taze screamed, dying shortly after finally understanding what irony was.

***

LaGina knocked on the window. Kelly popped up and looked around, confused. He stared at her as if he didn't recognize her, then he gave a weak smile. He got out of the car and stretched.

"You smell like dog." She squinched her nose. "Shower. Now."

"Good morning to you too."

"Oooo. No talking. I have an extra toothbrush you can use. *Have*. You can have it."

She led him into the house and knew he was watching. She always knew when men watched her. She'd even put on her light yellow sun dress even though it couldn't have been more than forty.

"I heard from Stout this morning." LaGina handed him a kid's toothbrush on top of a wash cloth and towel and an old shirt and jogging pants. "I've never been apologized to more in my life. He says he's going to make it up to all of us. I guess we'll see."

"You believe him?"

She shrugged. "I've hated and loved him at the same time for so long... I'm just grateful I have my boys."

Kelly smiled again. She liked that. Something about it made her warm inside.

The Ghost Toucher

"He also has some great new idea for the show. Said he's going to the network with it this morning. He's going back to all the places where he did shows and is going to make amends. He wants to call it 'The Ghost Healer' and he'll give all his profits to all the women he... y'know."

LaGina looked away. She felt foolish for being one of those women.

"Seeing your boys makes me miss my girls."

It was the first time she'd heard him mention his family. It caught her by surprise.

"Toothpaste in there?" He held up the toothbrush, washcloth and towel, gesturing to the bathroom. She nodded. "Thanks." He closed the door and LaGina stood there a moment. After the shower went on she just couldn't stand there any longer.

She went in.

"Kelly I didn't want you to think that wasn't something big for you. Talking about your family to me, I mean, it's just that your mother told me what you went through after they died. She told me how you don't smile anymore. She misses that. You smiled yesterday. Today too. I thought you were a lot more responsibility than I could handle. You're cute and all and the complete opposite of everything wrong I ever looked for in a guy. But then you say that to me and I know it's not a responsibility; it's an honor that she asked me. I think I'd like for us to take care of each other. You're lost and I would love for you to be able to find yourself in me. I mean *with* me. I don't know how to do the relationship thing the right way, it's never been something... I've been good at, but maybe... this could be... a fresh start for both of us... kinda. Y'know?"

Kelly peaked out from behind the Mickey Mouse shower curtain, his head covered in foam.

"I didn't see you there. Did you say something?"

"Oh. It's nothing. It's just before noon, but if you want breakfast still I can make you something. My mother stocks up when she's stressed. I can get a head start if you want something."

"Oh. Could I have bacon and eggs? Sunny side up?"

"All right. See you downstairs. Sunny side up."

"Yeah. Thanks."

She smiled and nodded, then stepped out and shut the door. He liked his eggs sunny side up.

After breakfast she walked him back to the car.
"You should go see your mother."
"Why?"
"I promised I wouldn't say." She shook her head, putting her arms around his neck, wanting him to know she wanted him to stay. He meshed his body against hers.
"Okay. I guess I'm going to see my mother. But I'll be back."
"Can you... hurry? She wasn't sure she should have said that.
His eyes went wide. He nodded.
"You know, as strange as the last couple days have been, it's been nice being there with you."
It was her turn to nod. She felt like it would have been far worse had there been anyone else with her. She put a finger to his lips.
"Don't say anything else. No promises except you'll be back."
"Deal."
They touched foreheads. She couldn't believe what she was about to do. A distant part of her was saying this was all too soon but it felt right. She could tell he felt the same, that he wanted her as much as she wanted him.
She closed her eyes and waited for him to kiss her and felt him pull away. She looked and saw he was staring down the street at a police car.
"Something wrong?"
"I think I'm about to get arrested." He straightened and sure enough, two police officers got out of the cruiser that stopped in front of her house.
"Kelly Greene, we need you to put your hands on your head and get on your knees, facing away from us." The officer was as casual as ordering a number five from McDonald's. "Ma'am, I'm gonna need you to get back on your porch."
"Kelly, what happened?" LaGina asked.
He shook his head, looking embarrassed.
"Somebody burned my house down and called the police to confess. Apparently, they think it was me. I wouldn't burn down

my house. Other than some pictures at work, it was all I had left of my family."

Guilt bubbled up through her shock. She'd seen those.

"Ma'am, could you step back please?"

If it had been anyone else, if she hadn't experienced what she had over the last two days, she wouldn't have believed him. But she knew there was more to this than how it appeared.

"I'll come bail you out." LaGina hugged him and dug the keys out of his pocket before going back up on the porch. "Where are you taking him?"

"Thirteen hundred Beaubien." The officer put handcuffs on Kelly, stood him up and walked him back to the cruiser. He got in and watched her as they drove away.

***

Gayle Hills was standing in the middle of the wood. He raised his hand and flame shot out, burning the strangled tree a few yards away from him. Ms. Fleming stood next to him, but their son had wrestling practice. He wished he knew how to stop the advancing deadening. That was what he called it.

He slid his hand out of the skin glove and handed it over to Ms. Fleming. She put it back on the plastic model of his hand and in the case. Amazing how he couldn't see on the other side but he could use items that had crossed over. Many 'people' or whatever they were had tried and died but a few of their body parts had survived. These remnants could do things. Like the skin glove shooting fire. He had a pair of contacts he could use to stare tumors into someone and another skin that made the back of him invulnerable.

Gayle heard leaves crunching in the distance. Ms. Fleming reached for her gun, but he stopped her. She killed too easily. A moment later he saw them. *His* followers. He didn't know what they called themselves, but they all had a weird, lost puppy dog look. And they were nude for some reason. Gayle hadn't heard from him in the last couple days. He'd left, evaporated, *whatever*, and Gayle took that to mean their partnership was over. To tell the truth he was glad to be done with the whole mess. For an otherworldly being *he* could be pretty high maintenance.

What could they want?

They didn't say anything. Only stood and watched as he and Ms. Fleming watched them. He thought he understood after a moment. With *him* gone, the mantle had been passed. Gayle had inherited *his* leavings by default.

"So who wants to get my coffee?" he said.

EPILOGUE
Down boy, down

The black container rolled to a stop next to the dead dog. The animal's legs scissored back and forth and it rolled onto its feet. Cars raced by in the dark. It didn't know where it was. It tried to cross to the grass a few yards away but kept darting back when another car came. Finally it ran for it and a truck clipped its hind legs, throwing it back onto the shoulder.

It hurt but it wasn't dead. The dog climbed back to its feet, but its hind legs didn't move like they should. Before it could try to cross again a car pulled onto the shoulder and ran it over again.

The dog got back up. This time in the middle lane. Another car ran it over. Then another. Then another. Then another.

It twitched where it lay. In all three places. Everything hurt.

The dog whined as it heard another car coming.

END

Dead Bait

"If you don't already suffer from bathophobia and/or ichthyophobia, you probably will after reading this amazingly wonderful horrific collection of short stories about what lurks beneath the waters of the world" – *DREAD CENTRAL*

A husband hell-bent on revenge hunts a Wereshark...A Russian mail order bride with a fishy secret...Crabs with a collective consciousness...A vampire who transforms into a Candiru...Zombie piranha...Bait that will have you crawling out of your skin and more. Drawing on horror, humor with a helping of dark fantasy and a touch of deviance, these 19 contemporary stories pay homage to the monsters that lurk in the murky waters of our imaginations. *If you thought it was safe to go back in the water...Think Again!*

"Severed Press has the cojones to publish THE most outrageous, nasty and downright wonderfully disgusting horror that I've seen in quite a while." – *DREAD CENTRAL*

Available at www.severedpress.com, Amazon and most online bookstores

RESURRECTION
By Tim Curran
www.corpseking.com

The rain is falling and the dead are rising. It began at an ultra-secret government laboratory. Experiments in limb regeneration-an unspeakable union of Medieval alchemy and cutting edge genetics result in the very germ of horror itself: a gene trigger that will reanimate dead tissue...any dead tissue. Now it's loose. It's gone viral. It's in the rain. And the rain has not stopped falling for weeks. As the country floods and corpses float in the streets, as cities are submerged, the evil dead are rising. And they are hungry.

"I REALLY love this book...Curran is a wonderful storyteller who really should be unleashed upon the general horror reading public sooner rather than leter." – DREAD CENTRAL

Available at www.severedpress.com, Amazon and most online bookstores

THE COLLECTOR OF NAMES
By Miha Mazzini

Available in English for the first time by bestselling Slovenian Author Miha Mazzini comes and unforgettable tale of terror, comradeship and survival. On an isolated island "The Name Collector" waits to fulfill his destiny to bring death and destruction upon the world. Standing in his way-Aco and his band of brothers- a geriatric fighting force that have been training and waiting for this day since childhood. As the Name Collector asks each his name he takes it. But what's in a name and can anyone survive without a name-even for one horrific night? **"The Name Collector is a monster like no other"**

Available at www.severedpress.com, Amazon and most online bookstores

SKIN MEDICINE

Drawn against the rough and tumble tapestry of the American Old West circa 1882, Tim Curran (Street Rats, Toxic Shadows) hauntingly paints a sprawling tale of terror pitting man against monstrosity in an untamed, superstitious land. Tracking a merciless murderer, haunted Civil War veteran turned bounty hunter Tyler Cabe must overcome the demons of his own tortured past to battle something beyond the imagination of living man

"...Skin Medicine...Its one of MY all time favorite horror novels" – DREAD CENTRAL

Available at www.severedpress.com, Amazon and most online bookstores